Maggy Whitehouse is a journalist who began studying the mystical roots of religion after the death of her young husband in 1990. She is a qualified healer in two separate disciplines, a former radio and television producer and also a writer on relationships for women's magazines including *Bella, Living* and *Woman*.

Maggy's youthful ambition, to produce a network television show by the time she was 30, was achieved with 11 hours to spare. It is believed to be a coincidence that the programme, *Pebble Mill at One,* was de-commissioned almost immediately...

She has studied the Toledano Tradition of Kabbalah since 1992 and is currently the producer of the BBC's holistic health community website, *360, Changing the World by Degrees.* Maggy lives in London but hopes to escape soon.

Her website is www.treeofsapphires.com

INTO THE
KINGDOM

Maggy Whitehouse

A *Tethered Camel* Book

A CIP catalogue record for this book
is available from the British Library

ISBN 1-904612--00-8

Printed and Bound by Anthony Rowe, Ltd.,
Eastbourne, E. Sussex.

Tethered Camel Publishing
PO Box 42329
London N12 7XD

With acknowledgment and thanks to
Z'ev ben Shimon Halevi

In loving memory of
Louis Randall
who so loved the story of Esther

Prologue

In the eighteenth year of the reign of Tiberius Caesar Augustus, a Judaean holy man was crucified just outside Jerusalem. His name was Yeshua of Nazara and he was my brother.

Some days later another Judaean man died; though how he died is a mystery. Some say that he killed himself in a fit of remorse for betraying a friend; others that he was murdered. A third story tells that he died from an internal rupture. His name was Judah of Kerith and he was my husband.

I sat by the fire at our little home in Cana as these two men planned the whole event together. It was vital, Yeshua told us, that his death should happen on a high holy day in Jerusalem where so many people would be gathered. Only a public death would draw people's attention to his resurrection of the ancient Jewish teachings which had been forgotten for so long.

We knew that Yeshua was the Anointed of our time. The Teaching makes it clear that there is one Messiah for every generation; Moses, David, Esther and many other nameless ones all came before him. But now, so many years after his death, many believe that Yeshua was the only Anointed and that the man who helped him to die was a traitor.

As the stories of my husband's betrayal circulate and grow throughout the Roman world, even I sometimes wonder if I imagined that whole conversation in Cana. But all I have to do is close my eyes and I can see that fireside with Yeshua reasoning with my husband and Judah walking up and down, protesting.

'If not you, then your wife must do it,' said Yeshua, at last.

Who am I in all this?

Somebody's daughter; Somebody's sister; Somebody's wife.

I am the blood-daughter of a long-forgotten fisherman and his red-headed Petran wife who lived in Bethsaida, North of Galilee. When our parents died my brother, James, my sister, Salome and I were adopted by our father's brother Joseph and his wife Miriam. We became their children, growing devout in their care and learning to love their blood-son, the elfin child Yeshua.

James and Salome took the path to family life; I, crippled by an accident and unmarriageable, followed my new brother like a devoted puppy to the Essenes at Emmaus where I was healed. When Yeshua's friend Judah took me to wife, I followed them both all around Galilee and Judaea listening, learning and teaching the ancient truths of the Jewish oral tradition as they did.

I learned to read and write; to heal with herbs and prayer; to live life for the day and to understand the secrets of life.

This scroll, the second of two, will be hidden in the caves above Qumran, next to where my bones will lie. The first scroll tells the story of my life with Yeshua. This second one, written in two separate parts, tells of how I had to learn to stop being Somebody's daughter, Somebody's sister, Somebody's wife.

If I were to survive the anger and the backlash, the misunderstandings and the stealing of power that followed Yeshua's death, I had to become nothing to anyone but to God and myself.

My name is Deborah and this is my story.

'Maybe thou art come into the kingdom for such a time as this'
The Book of Esther 5:14.

One

Messiahs were ten-a-penny in those days. They came; they went. Nobody took much notice.

Holy men proclaimed themselves to be that generation's Anointed of God, attracted followings, performed miracles, annoyed the authorities and were either killed or faded away.

Most of the stories were apocryphal and those which were not stood up to very little examination. They were wishful thinking on the part of people who felt oppressed by the Romans and who romanticised stories about robbers and brigands who had been 'sent by God' to release us from the heathen rule.

I remember as a child going to see a crucifixion of a robber-rebel who had been hailed as a Messiah. The other children wanted to see the show but I was frightened and sickened when I saw the man's suffering. I did not know how he could stand the pain or how he could knowingly have put himself into a situation where the punishment was so severe.

Just because you happened to know about a 'real' Messiah did not mean you were going to be believed, which was why Rizpah, Magdalene, Joseph Barsabbas and I kept our mouths shut on that 13th day of the Omer while we travelled South from Jerusalem towards the shores of the Dead Sea.

The road was no more and no less crowded than usual and several times each day groups of people passed us by, stopping to talk about the weather, the heat, the dust and whatever news there might be from Jerusalem or Jericho.

We assumed that news of my brother's execution and rumours of a miracle would have spread before us and we were right about that but what little gossip there was put it down as just another of the fakes.

'Aren't we denying him by holding our tongues?' asked Magdalene anxiously as we passed on from another group who cheerfully discounted what they had heard on the road as just another story of an over-ambitious Zealot who did not have the sense to avoid walking into a Roman trap and whose followers made up a cock-and-bull story to make it look as if he were some-one important.

'We are not denying him,' said Joseph stoutly. 'If we are asked directly if we know anything we will speak but for now it is best to be discreet. Our time will come. Remember, it's just a waste of time to tell people things that they don't want to know.'

'But we're doing what Cephas did!' Magdalene said. 'He denied that he even knew the Master after the soldiers came to the Garden of Gethsemane and took Yeshua away. And we are no bet-ter. Just now when that group of shepherds asked if we'd heard the story of the latest fake Messiah we didn't say we knew him or that what they had heard was rubbish. We should be speaking out, shouting from the rooftops that this story is real!'

'We spoke the truth,' said Joseph. 'We said that we had heard and that there would surely be more to be told when more was known – and that you can't believe everything you hear on the road. It was enough. They wouldn't have heard any more than that. You have to balance revelation with caution. We'll be shown a time when it is right to speak. It is not now.'

'Humph!' said Magdalene, trying not to sulk. Normally she would have fired up and argued until sundown but the last weeks had hit her harder than any of us. She had loved him more deeply than any of us. Despite listening to our friend Joseph's wisdom, amassed from his youth in Aramethea and later Alexandria and his years of disciplined Essene life, it was not, in the end, the older man's advice which stopped her speaking out. It was her own good sense in realising that she could not bear to have her sacred belief tarnished and trampled underfoot by those who would, quite understandably, deride it. Her silence came from the grief of a woman who has lost the love of her life as well as her teacher and friend.

'I know he is alive in the Heavens,' she said over and over again as we continued South towards Qumran where we hoped for refuge nearby the Essenes. 'I know all is well in the scheme of things. I know we are never given more to bear than we can handle. But I hate our being the only ones who know it. I hate the idea that everyone else will think we are crazy. I hate it because they can only see physical reality – and I'm just as bad as they are because I want to see him again with my physical eyes and to touch him with my hand. I miss him so much, so very much and all the knowledge in the world can't take that away.'

Great tears would fall from her beautiful almond-shaped brown eyes and she would bury her head in her cloak. At those times I, too, would weep for my beloved brother and husband and Rizpah would join in out of sympathy for both of us. Poor Joseph had his work cut out with three emotional women and at times he hardly knew where to turn. Years of ascetic, celibate life as the leader of the Essene group at Emmaus had been tempered by his travels with Yeshua and the other disciples but, even so, girls were still rather a mystery to him.

Also, I was far weaker than I had believed and only too grateful for the sturdy back of the little donkey which was almost my only possession. In the chaos and violence that followed Yeshua's arrest I, too, had been taken to Pilate's jail and my mind was still scarred with images of rats and soil and degradation.

That night I found it hard to sleep and, when I saw that Magdalene too was wakeful, we curled up together under one cloak and talked as the stars wove their patterns above us. As the darkness of night deepened my friend told me, stumbling over her words, of the hours of agony waiting to hear of Yeshua's fate and the fear and grief as she watched him approach Golgotha with the wooden burden on his shoulders.

She had fainted as they raised him on the cross. Then my mother and she had stood together, apart even from Salome, Susannah, Joanna and the other wives and friends who huddled a little way away. Of the men only John had been present, his eyes riveted on his holy teacher and his breath matching every one of his Master's.

'Throughout all of it, despite the tears, we knew it was part of a plan,' she said. 'It was like a kind of detachment from the pain and the degradation. Oh curse this language of ours! There are so many things I want to tell you but the words don't exist. It is like knowing the truth through unbearable but totally bearable – even blissful – agony. Like giving birth and making love and dying all together but more – much more!

'Yes, he was in pain, dreadful pain – and sometimes he felt it as you or I would do. But there was a greatness about it. I could see angels, Deborah! Bright lights of strange colour all around him but they were – not people – oh – things! Images or ideas even – no shape or form or – oh I don't know! I can't explain! But even if I did not have the slightest idea what any of it was or what it meant – and I still don't know – it wasn't just another event that didn't really matter.

'And, thank the Lord, I was there with the right words at the one moment he did nearly fail. Whatever happens to me now I will never cease to be grateful that there was a moment when I said the right thing.

'He looked down, you see, not up and I could see that suddenly he saw and felt what most people see every day, the dirt and humiliation and the pain and the misunderstanding without the knowledge of the Lord. He saw and felt our unbelief; the unbelief of every human being who has ever lived and who ever will live and their hopelessness and despair. Can you imagine that? Do you know what I mean?'

'Yes,' I said.

'I told him to look up,' said Magdalene. Then she took in a sharp breath and lifted her head to the sky. 'I love you,' she said – but not to me.

We were silent for a while.

'Did Miriam see what you saw?' I asked.

'Yes.'

'Did John?'

'Oh yes.'

'What about the others?'

'They weren't there. None of them was there.'

'Neither was I. I wasn't there to see him die.'

'I didn't see your brother die,' said Magdalene. 'I saw the Anointed.'

We were planning to go to the communty surrounding the Essenes in Qumran to recoup while the rest of the disciples returned to Galilee; staying in Jerusalem would not have been a good idea with the anger of the Sanhedrin hanging over us like a sword. But that next morning I awoke with a fever so we rested in a corner of some farm land with our donkey carefully tethered so she would not damage the crop. Both Rizpah and Magdalene scared birds for the farmer and weeded his pasture in return for our food and space to rest. Joseph read to me from a little bound volume of the Torah he had brought from his home in Alexandria many years before. He had a deep and beautiful voice and it was both restful and comforting to listen.

The story, of the Exodus from Egypt, I knew almost by heart and my mind drifted back to the days when Joseph used to read to all of us, men and women alike, at the Essene community at Emmaus. He would read in both Greek and Hebrew and, even before my knowledge of either language was good enough to understand what he was saying, I still heard the melody within the stories. Even so, a book was a rarity, for nearly all we had at Emmaus had been written on sheets of papyrus or scrolls. The Sadducees and many of the Essenes would not touch books, their leaves being made from animal skins that might be impure. Many, from the sects that ate no meat, would not touch any animal product at all. Luckily, the group at Emmaus had been slightly more liberal for, as Joseph said, it was most unlikely that any book that originated in such a cosmopolitan city as Alexandria could be considered ritually pure!

This resting time also gave me the opportunity to hear the full story of Rizpah's journey from Tiberias to join us.

Rizpah was the adopted daughter of a Rabbi in Tiberias – a town built on ancient graves and so avoided by the most orthodox of Jews. Her uncle-father, Jairus, summoned Yeshua to help when his birth-daughter Chloe was sick unto death. By that time not even death had dominion over the powers Yeshua brought from God and, when he arrived, the spirit had returned into Chloe's body and she lived again.

Judah and I had stayed in Tiberius to help the family get used to this miracle and its effects but, although they were grateful, none of them was interested in learning about the teaching we brought. No one, that is, but Rizpah. It was hard for this little changeling for no one in her family understood her and it was soon made very clear that we were no longer welcome in that home for tempting her with our foreign ways. Chloe herself wished to forget that anything had happened. She refused to speak of the experience and only wanted life to go on as it had before.

'It was as though she turned her back on everything deliberately,' said Rizpah. 'I thought she was just shocked from what had happened and that she would want to learn later – after all, how often does something like that happen to anyone? I wanted to know if she had seen anything or felt anything before Yeshua came. Was it like sleep or did she go to the higher levels? What was it like? But she simply refused to think about it and when I questioned her she would get upset and I would be in disgrace.'

'Chloe was not the only one who did not want to know more,' I reassured her. 'Many, if not most, of those Yeshua healed went on with their ordinary lives. Some of them became ill again later on, possibly because they were still living the same life which had made them ill before.

'It would not have been the same for Chloe for she was too young to have made so many mistakes. Her story would be a very different one. Is she still well?'

'No ... not really.' Rizpah hesitated. 'She always was sickly. After that time she was very well for a year or so. She got married and had a baby and lost all her strength again. She doesn't do very much at all now and Mother takes care of her son for her. She was always spoilt, you know. Always the favourite.'

'And you?' I prompted her.

'Oh, I got married too,' said Rizpah, staring at the ground and drawing patterns in the dust.

I tried not to react but it was a huge effort. After all, Rizpah must be all of fourteen by now, well over marriageable age. 'Oh?' I said, eventually.

Rizpah sighed. 'He was a relative; the son of a cousin. He had been promised to Chloe from birth but she chose another and our parents allowed her to have her way. They said it was better she married a local man for she could stay with them. Instead, I offered myself...' she tailed off in embarrassment. I waited.

'I was so in love with him, you see,' she said in a rush of words, twisting her skirt in her hands and staring at the ground. 'I had tried to study and to think but I never had any help and he was so wise and encouraging whenever he came to stay; he made me think he would help me. I don't think he ever loved me but he thought I would press his case with Chloe. He was angry when she married Daniel – he never came to the wedding – and, although he accepted me instead because our families wanted the link, when it came for the time for our betrothal he sent someone else to stand in as his proxy. I was so upset... I thought of him night and day and I really believed he would help me learn. I had heard he was studying with a very important Pharisee called Gamaliel in Jerusalem and that he was a forward thinker. I really believed that he would let me learn.'

'And did he?' I asked. Rizpah shook her head. 'He did not even come to see me once in the year of our betrothal and I asked that it should be broken for he obviously had no need for a wife. No one listened to me and when the wedding day came I felt so confused that I could hardly look at him.'

'He did come for the wedding at least?'

'Oh yes, and he stayed with us for three months. But we did not suit.'

'Rizpah, it's hard to tell at first whether you will suit,' I said as gently as I could.

Rizpah began to cry. 'I loved him so,' she said. 'Just for a while. It didn't last but, you see, he was so lovely when he was there. And he had such a gentle way with people that he made me feel that I was special.'

I was confused by this. Had this marriage gone wrong or not? All I could do was wait and listen. Once she had dried her eyes Rizpah went on.

'He didn't really care,' she said. 'He was like that with everyone. It was a kind of act to make you feel special. In reality he didn't care at all. And he didn't want a wife who asked questions or who wanted to learn. Before we were married it was all right but afterwards I had to obey him.

'I did try, honestly I did. I did everything I could to please him but I asked him all the questions I wanted to have answered and he hated it. He still loved Chloe, I think. It was as much my fault as anyone's.'

'What was?'

'I was too ardent for him. It embarrassed him. He told me I should be more chaste. I couldn't do anything right – and I didn't get pregnant. Perhaps if I'd got pregnant he would have stayed. But he went away after three months, back to Jerusalem and he didn't write to me. I got a scribe to write to him – I can write a little as you know but not well enough for that. I thought it would be better from a scribe. But that angered him. He wrote back to my parents saying that I had to change to become a suitable wife to him, to be womanly and quiet and to accept my lot in life. That I was to stop writing because it was unseemly...' she broke off again, in tears and then gave a great sigh. 'I sent another letter,' she said. 'I said I deserved a husband who would be with me or, at least, have me near him. I reminded him of his duty as a husband to be with me each Sabbath Eve.' She stopped again. I put my arm around her gently, to give her the choice whether she wanted to nestle into me or to stay alone. She reached out for my hand, gratefully, but stayed kneeling.

'He wrote again,' she said. 'Telling my parents that he divorced me. That they had brought me up so badly that I was a totally unsuitable wife for any man of faith.'

'When was this?'

'A few weeks before Yeshua died. I was in disgrace. They wanted to turn me out. A woman who is divorced is a disgrace to a family. Instead they arranged for me to be sent to other relatives near Bethsaida, for a time at least. There was a caravan going that way and I could join it. I was so upset I didn't resist. And then I had the dream. Except it wasn't really a dream.' She stopped and raised her head. Now her eyes were brighter and she set her shoulders back. 'It was while I was awake, not asleep. I had just gone to fetch water and, as I looked into the well, a man looked back from out of the water. I knew it was Yeshua, your brother. He

said "Talitha cumi," just like he had to Chloe and then he told me
to go to you. That was all. Then he vanished.

'I left the next day but I didn't go all the way to Bethsaida. I
went to Cana, to where you used to live. There were people in the
caravan going very near there so I only had half a day's walk on my
own.

'Judah's family said you had been long gone but that you had
not taken a little wooden chest that Yeshua had made for you. I
suggested I brought it with me and they were glad to let me do so.
They let me stay until I could find a group going to Jerusalem –
although they didn't approve of me at all! – and then I came
South.'

I hugged her and we spoke more about her incredible story. I
could not judge her for acting as she had done but I knew most
others would condemn her – and her husband would have been
seen as absolutely right in casting her off. Rizpah could see that
too but she had a strength and stubbornness beyond her age.

'What would you have done if you hadn't found me?' I asked.

'There was no possibility that I would not find you,' she
replied.

That evening the four of us discussed the situation. I had slept
through the early evening, still needing time for my own recovery
and, in my half-waking state while the others prepared supper,
Yeshua's words about marriage came back to me – that divorce was
only necessary because of the hardening of men's hearts. Now, in
any case, there was little we could do. We would not send her
back.

Joseph, as I might have suspected, had thought long and hard
about the situation. 'We all know that the most important thing
is to serve the Lord,' he said. 'We also know that Yeshua is His
messenger. If Yeshua told Rizpah to come to us then it is for her
highest good to be with us. She can serve the Lord best in this
way.'

'But the marriage,' I said, feeling worried. 'He was so firm
about marriage.'

'Yes,' said Joseph. 'But he also said, "Those whom God has
joined together let no man put asunder." It would appear that

God had very little hand in Rizpah's marriage; it was her family's idea and, on her part, a marriage of physical desire. That's not a marriage made by God.'

We sat and thought on this for some moments. 'Aren't those just excuses?' I asked, causing Magdalene to speak out with her accustomed frankness. 'No!' she said. 'If so, I should have gone back to my own husband,' she said. 'He wouldn't have me. That was not a choice which was open to me. My only choice when my family would not take me was to earn my own living and you know how few ways there are to do that for a woman. That's the way it is, Deborah; that's the way it is.'

'Deborah, you are not well. You are not thinking clearly,' said Joseph sternly. 'The Lord makes things perfectly clear if you listen to him. Yeshua's purpose was not to block your way to God; it was to open it. If Yeshua spoke to Rizpah and told her to come to us, then that is enough. In any case, for all we know Rizpah and her husband may be reunited one day. Gamaliel is a good man and if this student of his is worth his salt he may change his mind.'

'I don't want him back,' said Rizpah stubbornly.

'You will do what the Lord God wishes you to do!' said Joseph. 'And the reason for that is that it will be the path which will bring you self-realisation and peace. Are there any more questions?'

We sat silently, surprised at Joseph's vehemence. He had always carried authority but rarely spoken so firmly as this. 'Thank you,' I said. 'You are right, I was not thinking clearly.'

By the third day, I felt much recovered and we set off again slowly towards the South. The Sun was gaining strength as it moved towards the summer but it was not blinding or debilitating and I was able to ride in comfort as the others walked. At midday we rested and, after picking and eating the vegetables and fruit left so readily for travellers in the time-honoured Jewish custom, we heard the sound of horses' hooves coming from the road from the North.

Rizpah stood up, brushing corn husks from her lap and shading her eyes to see better. 'It looks like Roman soldiers – one on horseback and another in one of their cart things – chariots,' she said.

At once we scrambled off the road and led the donkey behind a clump of olive trees in the nearby field. There should have been no need to hide but it was always wiser to be out of the way when soldiers came by in case of trouble and most Jews preferred to melt into the background.

The horses and the chariot swept past, choking the air with clouds of yellow dust which hid them from view long before the sounds of the hooves faded away.

We made wry faces at each other and wiped what dirt we could from our faces and clothes.

The next village was only a short walk away and, to our surprise and unease, the soldiers were waiting there, the three horses tethered to the innkeeper's drinking trough and the men looking bored and disdainful as only Roman soldiers could.

We hesitated but they had seen us as soon as we saw them and making a detour around the cluster of houses would have made it seem as though we felt guilty about something. Magdalene and I exchanged glances. Joseph offered me his arm as a courtesy.

One of the soldiers, a tall, intelligent-looking man dressed in the uniform of a Centurion, came forward and hailed us.

'We are looking for a red-haired woman, Deborah bat Joseph, sister of Yeshua of Nazara,' he said in halting Aramaic. 'She has nothing to fear but the Prefect needs to speak with her.'

We froze. Loyally, none of the others was going to give me away but there was nothing to do but to speak up for myself.

'I am Deborah,' I said.

The man walked up to me and looked down. His face was strong, his eyes dark grey and what hair I could see, silvered. 'We have orders to take you back to Jerusalem,' he said. 'You need not be afraid' – he saw that I was beginning to shake – 'You will come to no harm and I will deliver you back to your friends afterwards.'

'She cannot go alone.' Joseph stepped forward and spoke in the colloquial Greek of the residents of Jerusalem. 'It is not fitting.'

The man looked at him with a mixture of relief that he might speak in a comfortable language and a separate, weary kind of amusement. 'Perhaps not' he said, in Greek, with more kindness than he needed to show to one of a conquered race. 'But there is room for only one passenger in the chariot so there is really no alternative unless there are extra horses here and you can all ride.'

Neither Rizpah nor Magdalene could fathom his quick speech but they could understand the implication.

'I'm not leaving Deborah,' said Rizpah with the fire we were beginning to recognise in her. 'And neither am I!' said the magnificent Magdalene with a toss of her head which immediately attracted the admiring eye of the charioteer.

Despite myself I laughed. This Roman was behaving as though we were his equals when all he had to do was pick me up and carry me off and there would be no redress.

'I thank you for your courtesy, Sir,' I said in Greek. 'If you are not in too much of a hurry and if it is well with you, we will find transport and all come.'

'We are in a hurry,' he said. 'Your brother and sisters may follow but you must come now.'

I laughed even more (within a core of deep and icy fear) but the others were outraged.

'It is disgraceful!' said Joseph. 'A woman could be outcast for riding with a Roman soldier.'

'I already am,' I said, feeling hysteria threatening and controlling it with all my strength. I must have grimaced for the soldier looked at me curiously. I turned to the others; any more resistance and we might find ourselves in trouble.

'Please follow behind as fast as you can and wait for me outside the Prefect's rooms,' I said as though the matter were decided.

I hardly heard Joseph's protests as the horses were untied and I climbed into the back of the strange wooden conveyance, helped up by the young charioteer. There were no seats and I would have to hold on tightly if we were going to travel at any great pace.

Had I had room for any coherent thoughts other than fear and how to hide it I would have asked them to go slowly to start with but, instead, the Centurion drove his own horse to a gallop as soon as the village was behind us. The charioteer too whipped up his horses and followed at the same breakneck speed with me clinging on behind him for my life. What energy I had left was wholly taken up by the need to hold on, to survive. A fall at this speed would surely kill me. In moments my friends were left far behind us.

We could not keep up that pace for long, however, and once the horses had slowed to a trot I had time to gather my thoughts together. I did not like what they said to me – what reason could Pilate have for wishing to see me? I threw up a fervent prayer for protection. At that moment, the chariot lurched dramatically and the charioteer cursed loudly.

He called out to the Centurion as we came to a lumbering halt. He, too, swore and turned his red-golden-coloured beast to look at what was wrong. Not knowing the technical words they used I could only assume that something had broken. I jumped down from the chariot and stood to one side, waiting until they should address me again.

To my inexperienced eyes, the wheel looked quite badly damaged. Both men were now kneeling on the ground, looking closely at it. I noticed, almost without thinking, that the Centurion had a limp. 'Is this your work, Lord?' I asked silently. 'Is this to stop them taking me back to Jerusalem?'

The answer to that prayer, too, came swiftly and it seemed that the reply, to the second question at least, was, 'No.'

The Centurion got up and walked over to where I stood. His face was angry but he had his irritation under control and he was still treating me with unusual respect. However, what he had to say came as a complete surprise.

'Can you ride a horse?' he asked simply. I looked up at him in horror and, to my surprise, he smiled back at the fierce little face before him.

'I don't know,' I said. 'I can ride a donkey but that is hardly the same thing.'

'Have you ever sat astride?'

'Oh yes, when I was a child.'

'Then you can ride. You have a choice. You can either come up behind me and hold on to me or you can take my horse and I will ride one of the chariot horses. The charioteer must stay here with his charge.'

Memory from then on becomes a little blurred. I suppose I must have said I preferred to ride alone for, before I knew what was happening, I found myself being lifted up on to the saddle of what seemed a great, golden beast. I do recall that the feeling of the Roman soldier's hands made me dizzy with nausea and I had to grip the horse's mane to stop myself from falling before we even started off. Then there was nothing to think of but an even greater effort to hold tightly and to keep my balance as the two of us set off again for Jerusalem. The Centurion said (but I did not believe him) that it would be easiest for me if we went swiftly. 'The slower paces are harder to sit,' he said. I did not reply; I could not. I looked at him doubtfully and caught my breath as he spurred his horse on and mine followed with what seemed like a great leap. With a prayer I clamped my legs around its body as hard as I could and held on for dear life.

To my surprise, the Centurion was right.

At first the dust and the speed and the lurching and the un-reality of it all dazed me so much that I began to think that I was hallucinating. But, after a while, a strange feeling of exhilaration began to creep in, together with wonder that it was actually quite easy to sit astride an animal going so fast and excitement at the speed itself. I had never had any idea how it would feel to travel so swiftly.

At one point, despite myself, I laughed out loud and the Centurion heard me. He turned his head and we shared a moment of understanding. He, too, loved this speed and excitement and, for one tiny moment, we were friends. Whatever was ahead of me this, for all its terror, carried a crazy delight. Everything around was blurred, unbelievable, streaking past us, but I was secure in the centre of the storm. I felt as though I were riding on the back of an angel. During the slower paces, to rest the horses, I found it far more difficult and unpleasant and then I did have to hold on tightly. But the faster we went the safer I felt, like sitting closer to God.

Apart from checking that I was still behind him and still safe, the Centurion said nothing more to me for the entire journey. The horses were strong and carried us sturdily into evening and then into the darkness of the night. To the Jews, the gates of Jerusalem were closed at dusk; to a Centurion, they were opened in a matter of minutes.

We clattered up the stone streets to the Roman headquarters and, at the gate to the barracks, I tumbled down from my golden steed, tired, hungry, dirty and aching all over. The Centurion looked down at me and inclined his head slightly as a parting gesture and I felt touched by disappointment that he gave me no word of praise or of farewell. Other men appeared instead and I was shown to a kind of guest room in the barracks behind the Prefect's dwelling place. There I was given a plate of bread and cheese together with a mug of ale, the end of a candle already guttering and a bowl of hot water for washing. Little was said; no clue to why Pilate wanted to see me was given. There was a bolt on the inside of my door and, as they left, I pushed it home gratefully.

I was left to rest with the injunction to be ready and waiting by the time the horns blew for the opening of the gates when Pilate would see me. In the meantime, I had the darkness to wait through and the swirling pit of terror to face again.

Deep in the heart of that night I finally understood that no one is truly alone when they pray. It was not the same as in the desert, that sacred place where to be alone was impossible for God was in every rock and every breath of air. But, even in the tiny Roman cell, some essence was there with me, calming and soothing and helping me through. After I had shivered and wept and looked my fears full in the face, a kind of peace descended on me and I was able to sleep, curled up on a lumpy, flea-ridden mattress, secure inside myself if nothing else.

I was washed and tidy with my hair plaited as neatly as it would allow when they came to fetch me. Two soldiers led me through first stone and then marble corridors until we came to an open space which seemed, to me, filled with men.

Pilate, small, hook-nosed and irritable, was pacing around his marble court room like a caged lion. My head swam with the knowledge that this was where Yeshua had been condemned and in front of me was the man who sentenced him.

This time however there was no sign of the Temple priests who had accused him and could accuse me. I was not on trial.

'Ah,' said Pilate as he saw me, his eyes sweeping me like a hawk's. 'Yes. Deborah bat Joseph. Yes.' He walked up to me and looked me directly in the eyes before swinging away with another of his bird-like, sudden movements.

'These men,' he said, gesticulating at a group of four soldiers looking acutely uncomfortable in the corner. 'Do you recognise them?'

I looked, rather warily. I did not want to recognise anyone. The four men looked back at me and my heart pounded and then sank. I did not recognise them but I knew exactly who they were.

'Well?' said Pilate, still walking around the room.

'Why do you ask?' I said bravely. He swung around again and came closer until I could taste his stale breath as he stared me in the eye.

'I ask,' he said, 'because my soldiers are under strict orders not to touch Jewish women – in that way. Strict instructions. On penalty of death, you understand.' He swung away and began to pace again.

He knew what had happened to me in that jail as Yeshua was crucified. I had sworn to myself that no one would ever know; I had tried to block it from my own mind. But even if he knew – and how would he know? – why would Pilate care?

I looked at the men again. This time they avoided my gaze and I could see fear in the face of every one of them. Suddenly, I knew that I did recognise one; the youngest. He had felt guilty afterwards and, as I left, had given me ale and a cloak when I left the prison without charge, the day Yeshua died. He had told me to find his father, a Centurion, and given me his name – Vintillius – should I need any help. But he had been one of the ones who had lain with me too.

'I'm waiting,' said Pilate.

'Who accuses them?' I asked, to gain time. Who knew what would happen to a woman who accused Roman soldiers without proof?

The little man moved toward me again and this time I felt the force of his anger.

'Don't mess with me girl,' he roared. 'You should be grateful I have brought you here to mete out justice. It is your turn now, Jewess. On your word four of my men will die... and rightly,' he added, throwing a look of utter contempt at the men.

'I will not have disobedience,' he said to no one in particular, his attention seeming to be drawn by the ceiling. 'That is the worst crime. Not the other. That is... understandable.'

Then I felt angry. Rage welled up inside me. How dare he say that! I felt a great urge to accuse; to blame; to have revenge. For once I had great power and right was on my side. They had abused me and I was to be given the chance to condemn.

My eyes must have flashed with the anger I felt. The youngest soldier began to weep.

In one swift movement, Pilate crossed the floor and slapped him on the face. The boy's shock and fear woke me from my anger.

'Help me!' I prayed.

I was named for Deborah the Judge of Israel, who foretold the death of Sisera by the hand of a woman and they named me well.

I had my first vision when I was twelve, on the Sabbath Eve after my uncle-father Joseph died. By the time I was 20, with the Essenes, I was known as a prophetess. Without warning, the veil between my everyday world and the heavens would lift and light pour through. I didn't like it; I even feared it but, when it happened, I knew to obey the voice that I heard.

For everyone else in that room it would only have been a second or two before I spoke but, for me, time had expanded and angels spoke to me inside my head.

I heard and saw both justice and mercy and the balance of life and death. I understood that to act for revenge was to deny everything I had ever learnt from Yeshua. I realised that to condemn the men – three of whom I could not even recognise and the fourth who was young and thoughtless and who had tried to say he was sorry – would be to attack Pilate for his ignorant words. I would be hitting out at him to ease my pain; I would not be acting with discernment or reason; I would be destroying lives in order to demonstrate my power instead of allowing the Lord to show them the consequences of their actions dispassionately and fairly in His own time.

But I wanted to hurt them. I wanted revenge. I did not want them to get away with it. How could I not speak? What human woman could forgive such things?

The veil quivered. 'Vengeance is mine sayeth the Lord,' said the voice in my head. 'It is not yours.'

'Well?' said Pilate. 'Are you dumb?'

'I don't accuse them,' I said. 'I stand here whole and unhurt.' It was the best I could do.

Time stopped. I saw the range of emotions on each man's face; from incomprehension though amazement to relief. Then in three of them I saw the beginnings of disdain as they despised me for an act of mercy they would never understand. I was so tempted then to withdraw my words and to point the finger that would send them to their death. Their sneering was like a knife in a wound and I wanted to hurt them so much that it was a taste of bitterness in my mouth. Then the youngest looked me straight in the eyes and it was not he, but Yeshua who was standing there, waiting for his sentence of death.

When I looked again at Pilate's face, it made me want to laugh. Several different moods were battling for supremacy. Disbelief and fascination were the strongest with outrage close behind. He was, for once, intrigued enough to drop his mask of boredom and anger for a few vital seconds. This was new. This was different. This was almost interesting.

He walked around me three times looking at me from head to toe while he rubbed his nose with a claw-like hand and furrowed his brow in thought. I often wonder what he would have said to me but, at that moment, one of the accused men belched as he relaxed his stance, showing both relief and arrogance. At once, Pilate recovered his mask and roared at him. The man jumped to attention, his face snapping shut. Then Pilate roared at me too and with a sinking heart I realised that he had decided that my action had humiliated him and put his authority in jeopardy.

He brought in a guard from the jail who swore he had seen the men enter my cell and heard them boast afterwards. He threatened to jail me and even to give me the lash. I almost broke, the fear of imprisonment and what might happen to me there was so great. For whole minutes I stood with my head bowed and my eyes closed, fighting with my fear. When I looked up again, the young soldier was still looking at me. Yeshua looked though his eyes, supporting me and giving me strength. I knew Pilate was bluffing. I repeated my earlier words and said nothing else.

In the end, he dismissed me. I was escorted to the front entrance by two tall and unbending soldiers and, as I stepped into the street, the door slammed shut behind me, the vibration making me jump and bringing tears smarting into my eyes.

My friends were not there and I did not know whether I was in the wrong place or if they had not arrived, been moved on, or worse. A part of me wanted to panic and to run through the streets of the city to search for them but I knew the most sensible thing to do would be to wait until I was calmer and then try to find someone to help me or advise me on where they might be.

As I stood there, a patrol of Roman soldiers came around the corner and headed towards me. To my shattered vision it seemed as though the men from the court room, multiplied and armed with spears, were coming for me again. There, in the street, I would be helpless before them. It was just too much and I fled down the cobbled road towards the crowded market streets of Jerusalem.

Two

When I came to my senses I found myself at the foot of the cool marble walls of the great Jewish Temple.

The Essenes never came here if they could help it for they did not believe in the principle of animal sacrifice. They were fierce in their condemnation of corrupt practice by the priests and I had been happy to accept their beliefs as my law, pleased to be able to avoid the sight and smell of death which had revolted me as a child.

Most of Yeshua's disciples, however, went regularly to the Temple as it was their heritage as well as their holy place. When some of the others who had knowledge of the Essene teaching protested, Yeshua told them it was an important exercise in rising above prejudice and seeing the spirit within. The Temple was a house of God, he said, whether or not it was run with spirit, and it was important for us to be able to see beyond its form and its faults. 'The Temple is still a meeting place for those searching for the truth,' he said. 'It is just as easy to become arrogant if you work with the soul as it is if you are blind to all that is within you. The spirit of the Lord is in the Temple as much as it is in the fields, the synagogues and in the hearts of men and women.'

Thinking of Yeshua comforted me then. I had not been inside the Temple for a long time but going there now would feel safe – as if he would be there to meet me. I could go into the women's rooms to wash this day of fear from my body and, if I were lucky, there might even be space in the bathing area where I could lie in

warm water and soak in oils to alleviate my aches and pains. I had
a little money, maybe just about enough to buy that luxury.
Afterwards I could cleanse my soul in the Mikvah and walk in the
Temple grounds to relax and clear my mind before I tried again to
find the others.

There was a bath free; I did have enough money and I relished
the pleasure of that hot, aromatic soaking for my body and my
wounded, worried feelings! Then there was the joy of that leap of
faith, cascading down into the ritual bath, being immersed in liquid light. So many times I had seen the Mikvah used for duty's
sake but I had an irregular cycle which meant that it never became
routine for me – and both Miriam's and Yeshua's teaching had
helped me make it special. This time, as always, it was like breaking through to another state of being. Just for one moment but
that was enough.

The day was beautifully warm. It was too early for the searing
heat of summer but the sky above was a clear deep blue. The scent
of late spring flowers planted in pockets across the Court of the
Women drew me with their fragrance but I had no Temple tithe
and no money left to buy one. In the old days that would have
sparked guilt that I had taken care of myself rather than done what
was 'right' but I knew that taking care of my body was just as valid
a way of doing my part as any. I sat for a while in a quiet corner
of the outer court, basking in the warmth and singing psalms
inside my head, allowing myself to recover from the day's ordeal.

As time passed, I became drowsy and it was easy to slip into a
daydream. I could almost see Yeshua sitting, teaching, just ahead
of where I myself was resting. I saw the light in the eyes of those
who truly heard him as well as the enthusiasm of those who listened avidly but who, like most of us, would forget it all moments
after returning home. I saw, and heard, the mutterings of those
who disagreed with him and felt the irritation of the disciples at
their un-thought-out or deliberately provocative questions. I could
see Judah, his dark, greying hair falling into his eyes, to be brushed
away impatiently as he leaned forward listening with all his
strength. Cephas, Thomas, James and the others were there, too,
but it was my husband's face and figure on which I feasted with
hungry eyes until, it seemed, he caught my longing gaze and

looked directly back at me. The beloved deep brown eyes widened slightly and with a slight shake of his head he warned me not to concentrate on him but to listen to Yeshua's words. I knew he was right but it was too late and another onslaught of grief overtook me, causing me to wake and to burst into racking tears.

Almost at once two women stopped by me and bent down, concerned at a sister experiencing grief. 'Why are you alone?' one of them said. 'Is there no one here to grieve with you?'

I shook my head. As far as I knew there had been no one to mourn for Judah of Kerith as tradition demanded it. I had not seen him since before Pesach began – before Yeshua died – and no one had been able to tell me what happened to his body. His family, so far away, would have done their part but the distance between him and them in mind was greater than that of the body.

'Are your men within the Temple? Why are you not in the Court of the Women? Come with us and we will grieve with you,' said the other woman, crouching down to look into my face. It was done with kindness and so hard to answer with truth.

Before I could find a suitable answer, a voice familiar as my own called my name and I saw Cephas, not a dream figure, but real – as real as the rock he was named after – walking swiftly towards me, his arm raised as he hailed me. My heart both leaped and recoiled for I did not know how he would respond to me. Even so, the presence of a man reassured the women who had stopped to help me and they smiled and moved away.

I staggered up and Cephas held his arms out to embrace me. I hesitated, knowing how reserved he normally was with women in general and me in particular. He heartily disliked Yeshua's idea of overcoming the purity laws and that meant that he would try to touch no woman in case she might be impure. This time, however, his arms stayed open and his dear, craggy face was alight with pleasure. It felt as though nothing had ever gone wrong between us. I curled into his embrace like a child and he enfolded me to him so that I was lost in the rough, warm wool of his robe. For those moments my Father held me, both my father on Earth and my father in Heaven. I wept anew, burying my head in his chest and holding on to the folds of cloth as I had done as a child.

Once my outburst was over, we walked together for a while,

saying nothing, just appreciating each other. A part of my mind wondered why we felt so close for there had been so many reasons why we should not. Perhaps the one great thing we had in common was enough.

'So,' said my large, grizzled friend, at last. 'What brings you here, Deborah? And alone too. We thought you, Joseph and Magdalene had gone to the Essenes at the Sea of Death.'

'We tried,' I said. 'But the Romans brought me back to see the Prefect again. It was nothing,' I added hastily for I did not want to go into the subject with Cephas. 'I think the others are following me.'

'Well, I am glad you are here,' said Cephas. 'We were unfair to you when we were all so upset when the Master died and I, for one, would be grateful to be allowed to make amends for that.'

I looked into his dark, deep-set eyes with the ingrained laughter lines and the great, shaggy eyebrows which made him look so fierce. Sometimes, when we had all been with Yeshua, it had seemed as though some of us could talk to each other without using words. One would think of something and the other answer it without the question having been asked. Now I wanted to see if I could ask whether Cephas knew what Yeshua and Judah and I had known before my brother went to his death.

Cephas smiled at me in response. 'No,' he said. 'No, Deborah, I don't know what happened. But I should not lay blame because of that – and I have been guilty of doing so.

'Like the others I was unable to see through my illusions when the soldiers came into the Garden of Gethsemane. It was as though I slept. Maybe it was temptation and we succumbed. But, in our defence – in my defence – it was the greatest and most difficult temptation you could imagine. It was so much easier to have someone to blame. If we were to believe that it was all planned, each one of us would have had to have realised that we were not trustworthy enough to be chosen to carry out the task. In that case, the fact that we slept through the greatest of tests was enough to show that the Master was right. We weren't.'

I said nothing. My heart was so full to know that he was willing to listen to the truth as I knew it.

A pedlar came by, offering oranges for sale. 'Are you thirsty?'

said Cephas. I nodded but managed to indicate that I did not want an orange. 'Water?' he asked and I nodded again.

I sat on a stone bench as he walked over to one of the drinking fountains to fetch me a drink. As always the spring was surrounded by people but Cephas seemed to melt through them as though he were the only real person there. I was not surprised that he was able to bring me back water in a cup. Usually all the cups were chained to the fountain and you had to hold what water you could in your hands.

The drink was cool and refreshing. I offered the cup to Cephas when I had taken my fill and he took it, drinking to the dregs. Despite myself, I laughed.

'You would never have shared my cup before,' I said.

'No,' he said. 'And another day, again, I may not. I am not made of the same stuff as Yeshua was and the laws mean a great deal to me. But I can, and I will, make exceptions and I will not blame myself for not being what I cannot be.'

I don't know how long we sat in silence together with the sunshine glancing off our shoulders and the merchants around us going about their business. Then Cephas began to talk. He had been there for the last precious days with Yeshua and now he told me about them. It was like drinking from the fountain of life. As I listened, I watched the money changers and soon Cephas began to talk of them too.

He said that Yeshua had caused a huge outrage in the Temple by throwing over some of their tables a few days before he was arrested. The temple tithes had to be paid in a special coin and the only place to buy them was in the Temple itself. That left the way wide open for unscrupulous money changers who could charge whatever they wished.

Cephas, whose temper was legendary, had asked Yeshua afterwards why he had been so angry that day when he had ignored the men so many times before. 'Most of the others were horrified,' he said. 'You know that to many of them the Master was never to be questioned. But you know, as well as I do, that he loved questions. He said every time a question was asked, he learned more.

'You should have seen their faces, Deborah, when I asked him if he'd lost his temper! He said he had, as well. He'd just felt something snap inside. That was incredible to them. But he said too that it was a point that needed to be made. The Temple is a holy site but it is being used to cheat people. Then, of course, everyone wanted to go back and kick over a few more tables but he persuaded us that while it might be fair to try and make a point once, it was foolhardy to press it!

'Miriam, your mother, said she was surprised he had not been arrested then and there. He very nearly was, of course, and he told her she was right and perhaps it was not the wisest of things to have done but that he had a reason for giving into his temper that one time. He said he wanted to spare one of us the pain of a difficult task.

'Then, of course, I didn't know what he meant but now I think I do. If he had been arrested in the Temple, then, it would have been public enough and Judah would not have had to lead them to him later.'

We sat in silence for a while and I thought of my brother's generosity in trying to make the way easier for Judah and myself. That the Lord did not allow him to be taken at that point showed that the great plan did have to have taken place as it did. Had I had half the strength Yeshua had, I would have needed no help to keep faith, continuing to know that all was well. However, to hear this story from Cephas was so heartening.

'Why are you here?' I asked eventually. 'I thought I heard you all agreeing to split up and leave – to go home to Galilee or to safe places so you would not be arrested as he was.'

'We did. We went North,' said Cephas. 'John and your mother intended to set out for Ephesus and the rest of them were planning to stay in Galilee. But I...' he hesitated. 'Well, what would I care if I were arrested and killed? I was the one who betrayed him after all. I was the one who denied him three times. He told me I would and I did. I could have been with him. I should have died with him. I know he forgave me – he told me so – but after he had left us, I thought I would come back here. I thought perhaps I would be of more use here.'

'Everything works together for good in the end,' I said. 'I know it does. Perhaps what you see as your weakness then will make you stronger now. After all, someone has to continue the work.'

'It's not easy, though,' said Cephas. 'You can't know how it feels. You didn't deny him. You, a woman, supposedly weaker – the Lord knows I've accused you of weakness often enough, of holding us back, of being an inadequate vessel. But when he was taken you faced up to the truth and owned that you were his sister when I ran away.'

At that moment, something made me aware that someone was listening to us. Hastily I nudged Cephas to stop. A young man, short but handsome in an intense kind of way, was hanging around us trying so hard to look as though he was doing nothing in particular that it was obvious that he must have been trying to overhear.

'Temple police,' snorted Cephas quite loud enough for the young man to hear. He had a low opinion of those who enforced the laws of the Temple, thinking them officious and corrupt.

The man obviously felt the cut. He lifted his aquiline nose proudly, staring at us and I looked back at him rather nervously. I had had more than enough of officials and the thought of any more trouble made me feel weak. There was something about this man too; an attitude and a strange strength. He could either be a prophet or a demon, I thought, then mentally shook my head, thinking that I must be imagining things.

'Come on, Deborah,' said Cephas, getting up and trying to lead me away. I felt a flash of irritation. With his usual lack of tact, he had just told this strange man my name, and I suspected that the man would remember it.

'No,' I said, on impulse. 'I want to talk to him. I don't know why. Sir! Is there anything we can help you with?'

Cephas gave another of his distinctive snorts – confusion, irritation and resignation in one explosive sound. 'You're just like your wretched brother!' he said. 'Well, I don't want to talk to him. I'll wait over here.'

The proud young man and I stood looking at each other as Cephas moved away. The stranger was still youthful and he was uncertain as to how to address me or what to do. An odd shiver ran through my body as I observed him carefully.

I waited in silence until he gathered his courage together and greeted me formally. His voice was deep and soft and powerful and hypnotic and, when he spoke, it was in the accented Aramaic of a fluent Greek speaker.

'I was listening and I beg your pardon for it,' he said and the warmth of the voice was strangely mesmerising. 'I was listening because I liked what you said, about everything working together for good.'

I inclined my head politely.

'I would add a little to the phrase myself,' he said, and smiled. 'I would say, 'The Lord God works all things together for good to those who love Him.''

The spell he cast became stronger at that point for the smile, like the voice, was hypnotic and had a scent of its own. How can I explain that? It was a scent – not a sense, nor a sound, nor a look – of great power. I could not tell if it came from an angel or a devil but it was not only of this World. I tried to concentrate, feeling as though I were swimming in silk. I knew that if I had any doubt at all, about anything, I should back away. Here I had many doubts. Someone who could hold people so easily could just as easily misuse his power.

It occurred to me, as I fought the hypnotic charm, that this man would always want to improve on things; to annexe an idea and alter and enhance it so that it bore his seal and could carry his credit.

'How interesting,' I said politely, in pure Greek, rather than my natural Aramaic or the colloquial Koine that was generally spoken in Jerusalem. I intended to put this arrogant creature in his place. 'That would improve it indeed.'

He started at my change of language but it seemed to confirm something for him.

'Your name is Deborah?' he asked and, speaking in his natural tongue, his voice became like melted honey. 'Would that be Deborah of Nazara, sister of Yeshua?'

Two things happened simultaneously. Cephas arrived back at my side, furious at what he perceived as the man's over-familiarity, and other voices called my name. I gave an involuntary sigh. The spell was broken.

As Cephas put his hand on my shoulder in paternal protection I swung around, only to see Magdalene, Rizpah and Joseph Barsabbas hastening towards us, their faces wreathed in smiles. But even in that brief moment the picture changed again. Rizpah stopped and put her hand to her mouth in dismay. She looked childlike, as though she had been caught out in some great mis-adventure, called to book by an adult.

The man before me was transfixed and my whole being felt a rush of fear as I understood that he must be some family member – or worse.

Initially, the young man's dignity earned my admiration. He bowed to us all and to Rizpah in particular.

'Madam,' he said formally in Aramaic. 'I give you the greetings of this morning. Perhaps you would be so kind as to introduce me to your friends.'

Rizpah looked like Lot's wife must have done and the air screamed with silence until she spoke.

'D-D-Deborah, J-Joseph, M-M-Magdalene, this is Saul. My... my former husband,' she said, scarlet with shame.

A small wind of fear played its way across my heart.

Saul bowed to us all, disdainfully.

'So these are the friends you have been staying with for these past weeks?' he said to Rizpah.

'Y...yes,' stammered Rizpah. 'Th...these are the people... some of the people... who helped my sister Chloe.'

'Yes,' said the man. 'I had realised that.' Then he turned to Joseph and resumed speaking in pure Greek, a pointed discourtesy that Rizpah and Cephas could not but notice. I winced because it was my pride which had given him the opportunity to behave so.

We were all frozen for a moment, testing the air for danger. All this man had to do was call for the other Temple police or the Sanhedrin and accuse us of some trivial crime and we were trapped.

'It was not,' replied dear Joseph Barsabbas in fluent, melodi-ous Greek, smoothing the waters with his calm good sense. 'That man has been taken from us as you may have heard. He is now in Heaven with our Father, the Lord. But we are glad to have met you, Sir,' he continued before anyone else could speak. 'This young woman is, indeed, under our protection for the moment. We have taken care of her at her own wish and messages have been sent to her relations to confirm that she is safe and well. They have accepted that she has chosen, for some months, to live in the care of these two good women here.' He indicated to Magdalene and myself. I felt a huge rush of gratitude. Of course Joseph would have done all that he could that was right when Rizpah first came to them. I should never have doubted it.

The two men bowed to each other coolly. Rizpah fidgeted, not understanding but knowing she was under discussion. The man looked from her to me and back. Joseph continued calmly.

'We were not aware that you would be in Jerusalem,' he said. 'But, if you are planning to travel to the North, perhaps you would be kind enough to send your former wife's regards to her parents and maybe even carry a letter? Rizpah!' He changed languages fluently and smoothly. 'Perhaps it is time we wrote again to your family.'

'Oh,' she said, not understanding what had lead to this pronouncement. 'Yes, of course.' She stepped back into Magdalene's protective shadow and the older woman put her arm around her. The three of us exchanged glances. There was so much to say, so much to ask and to tell but, for now, we must wait.

It was obviously a surprise to the man that more than one of Rizpah's friends were learned enough both to speak his language so well and to be able to write. He bowed again. 'If I were going North I would be pleased to help but now I live and work here in Jerusalem,' he replied. 'As Rizpah has not introduced me to you fully, I will do so myself. I am Saul of Tarsus, pupil of the esteemed Gamaliel and loyal servant of this Temple and its priests. Perhaps you, Sir, and you' – here he turned to Cephas – 'would care to dine with me if you are staying in the city?'

Joseph ignored that additional discourtesy to Rizpah, Magdalene and me and explained peaceably that we were all on our way South to visit the Essene community in Qumran.

'Had our sister Deborah not been required to speak with the Prefect this morning, we should have already been there,' he said.

Saul hesitated, though words of disparagement of the Essenes were obviously forming on his tongue. He could not know why I had spoken to Pilate nor whether relations between us were friendly and it might not be wise to antagonise us completely. He looked sideways at me and I sensed that he viewed me as the

source of all this trouble. However, he was interested too and, had
we been alone, I know he would have questioned me closely. For
the moment, though, there was nothing more to be said and he
made his farewells silkily, bowing to each and every one of us
before he turned and walked away.

"I don't think we've seen the last of him,' said Joseph thoughtfully.

In the confusion of words and greetings and relief and questions,
we were all so jumbled and so eager to speak and to listen that for
some moments there was no sense to be made from any of us.
Cephas's presence was accepted gladly by all; any previous antag-
onism on either side was lost in the recognition of fellows of the
same belief. He did not recognise Rizpah, of course, but that story
could wait. She herself was very quiet, understandably so, and we
were careful to include her in our gladness. If she had any more
to say on the subject of her marriage, she would tell us when it was
appropriate.

At one point during the glad and noisy exchange of views and
hugs and delight, I saw Saul of Tarsus still watching from a distance. There was a kind of hunger in his face, though what it was
for I could not tell. I felt slightly sorry for him but, looking back
on that moment later, I realised that was a feeling I could not
afford to have. There was a ruthlessness about this man which
made me hope, fervently, that Joseph was wrong. I had no desire
ever to come across him again.

Cephas was staying in a boarding house just inside the city walls
and there was room for all of us to join him. He had sacrificed a
lamb at the Temple and offered now to share a meal of nourishing
stew and bread which fortified us all. Joseph bought a skin of
wine and, if I am honest, I must admit that we all drank a little
too much. It was good to let go of all the grief and tension and
just to have fun with friends.

With his usual logic, Cephas said it was obvious that the four
of us were not meant to go South to the Essenes after all – we
must have been brought back for a reason other than for me to
speak to Pilate. I had been careful not to make much of that
story; I told them that he had wanted to ask me about where

Yeshua's companions had gone but I agreed with the others that it seemed that going South was not the path that we were meant to take.

That night I woke, sweating and terrified, from a dream where I had been trapped in the cells again. But this time it was Saul of Tarsus who was attacking me. I lay, wide awake and breathing fast, staring up at the roof of the dormitory and trying not to disturb the others. Magdalene slept on with Rizpah curled up against her back. I shook my head to try and lose the images and sent a plea above for balm to help me clear my mind and sleep again.

A cool breeze seemed to brush my forehead and I sensed the comfort of angelic, silvery softness around me. It felt just as I would have expected a baby bird to feel under its mother's wing and, having experienced some of this gentleness before, I listened for the message it contained. 'It's all part of the plan,' my mind and heart understood. 'All things do work together for good to those who love God. All is well. You have only human fears and they are as nothing in the higher Worlds. Be at peace. Be trustful. All is very well.' And I slept again, this time to dream – was it a dream? – that I floated in the blue sky of the Heavens, surrounded by unrecognisable beings and people whom I loved.

In the morning, however, I felt weak and unwell and could eat no breakfast. The others were excited for Cephas had received word that his brother, Andrew, and my brother, James, were on their way back to Jerusalem, together with Nathaniel and the other James. The rest of the disciples were scattered around but intending to return within a matter of days. There had been no witch-hunt pursuing them and they believed it would be safe to come to Jerusalem to prepare for Shavuot, the Festival of the Giving of the Law to Moses on Mount Sinai. James sent word that he was anticipating some great event that day and they all needed to be gathered together in time.

I was content to spend my days resting and trying to recover my lost strength while the others planned to meet and talk with the disciples on the Mount of Olives. Although Cephas assured me I would be welcome if we all went together, I did not want to be there even if I had felt well enough. Maybe I misjudged them but I did not want to hear the same old arguments and squabbles without Yeshua's calming presence to make the men see sense. From what Cephas had said to Joseph on the first night we were reunited, there were plans to continue teaching as Yeshua had done and to found their own synagogue. I could see that it would be wonderful to go on teaching but, if I had understood Cephas correctly, they intended only to teach what they had already learnt. I wanted to learn more. I felt as though there would be a whole world more for me to take in as I grew older. I couldn't explain it to the others and did not try very hard. They were so enthusiastic at the thought of continuing Yeshua's work.

Rizpah was torn between being thrilled with the excitement of it all and nervousness. She was eager to go with the others and hear all the stories she could about Yeshua and the teaching but she knew she was an outsider and one with very little knowledge at that. Cephas was stern with her, but fair, and said she might come as long as she stayed with Magdalene and did not interrupt.

'Though what we are to do with you in the long run, I don't know,' he said. 'You should be back at home with your family, young lady. Not that I approve of their choice of a husband for you but Yeshua's teaching was that marriage is for life.'

'Deborah said that was for marriages made by God,' said Rizpah with spirit. 'Ours was made for social reasons only. And my husband would not let me study or understand. He divorced me, not I him, though I am glad that he did it.'

'Even so,' said Cephas. 'You have no place with us. You have no knowledge of the Teaching and you are not one of Yeshua's chosen.'

'Yeshua himself told me to come to Deborah and to learn the Teaching so that's what I'm doing,' Rizpah fired back. 'He told me in a dream. I'm staying with Deborah for as long as she will have me and even if she won't, I'm not going home.'

This was not the way to speak to such a traditional man as Cephas! I made a gesture to Rizpah to be quiet but it was too late.

'Enough!' he said, angrily. 'Such behaviour is not appropriate for a woman and you will act as appropriate if you are to stay with us.'

Rizpah bit her tongue and looked at me imploringly. 'We'll talk

later,' I said gently. 'Yeshua gave you into my care and I will not
desert you. But have a little tact, child! Yeshua loved women and
believed in them but it is sometimes difficult for others to adapt
and open defiance will get you nowhere. You have to be a little
more subtle, especially as your marriage has made some difficulties for us.'

'I'm sorry,' said Rizpah at once. Her temper was always as swift
to go as it was to come and she realised that she had been speaking without due thought.

'Harrumph!' said Cephas. 'Well, are you going to behave if you
are allowed to come?'

'Yes,' said Rizpah. 'I will watch and learn and be silent.'

Cephas looked at her long and hard. 'Harrumph,' he said again
and then his face creased into a smile. 'I don't believe a word of
it,' he said. 'Be silent? None of the women he has chosen has ever
been silent! Still, it might be wise to try, child. It would spare you
a lot of unnecessary trouble.'

I felt better that day from whatever this strange tiredness that had
overtaken me might be so I spent some time walking around the
city of Jerusalem. It had always been my delight to wander up and
down the traders' avenues, to look at the beautiful homes and
buildings and even to admire – secretly – the Roman baths and
theatres. Someone once told me that Jerusalem was the third
largest city in the whole world, after Rome and Alexandria, and I
felt proud and privileged to know it so well.

On this day it was certainly busy. I was sure that there were far
more people in Jerusalem than there had been when I was a child
– and even then the bustle had seemed incredible to my country-
born eyes. As I wandered around now, I was amused to see how
my tastes had changed over the years. In my youth it was the
bright colours of the cloth merchants which I loved the best but, as
I grew older, my preference changed and my eyes were drawn to
more subtle hues. I was always excited by the range of exotic food-
stuffs sold by the merchants from across the sea but now I was just
as interested in those who sold eating vessels and household luxuries. Neither stone nor glassware needed ritual cleansing, unlike
the wooden ones most people used, so there was a big market for

such expensive items in Jerusalem. Some of the glassware sold in those years was so beautiful it was hard to believe it could be real. Colours and exotic designs were woven into the fabric of the glass and, sometimes, a merchant would even display glass with images on it which the Jews would argue over fiercely as to whether they broke the second commandment. Those were the kinds of squabbles which were always going on in Jerusalem where the Roman rulers thought idols were an important part of their worship and the Jewish people thought them sacrilegious. Every year there would be some kind of revolt or fight over the arrival in the city of something which broke our religious code and that would lead to recriminations and even massacres. It was an unfashionable view to think that the Romans were really very tolerant of these fierce, conquered people's beliefs but Yeshua had taught me to see that most of the centurions and city officials did do their best to shield us from our own bigotry and discrimination.

Boys seeking rebellion and adventure sometimes sneaked into a Roman temple to look at the idols but superstition about the wrath of the Lord falling on you and your family if you did kept most of us away. There were plenty of other things to look at which were disapproved of, if not forbidden, so we could all rebel a little in the great city, if we wanted to.

That afternoon, I bought some bread with money Cephas had given me and went down to the pool of Siloam to eat. My stomach began to feel much stronger as the Sun began to dip in the sky and I was very hungry. As was the custom, I shared some of my bread with others who were gathered there in return for olives and cheese.

My heart still jumped whenever I saw a Roman soldier and there were too many around for me to be able to relax completely. I kept my shawl drawn close around my face in case there might be anyone around who would recognise me. I felt watchful for other reasons as well as for my own worries. I was sure that something else was yet to happen; something momentous. Perhaps it was the meeting of all the others which was happening nearby and I could feel the grace of God streaming down upon them. What they were doing was good, I had no doubt about that. It just did not feel right for me.

That evening James, Nathaniel, Andrew and Philip all came to eat with us. About twenty people poured into the lodging house and there was much excitement in the air. Some of the wives had come, too, including James's wife Rachel who was still nursing her youngest son, David. She seemed more at peace with her husband than she had been for some time and greeted me cordially. When Yeshua had been with us it had been hard for the wives of the disciples to understand why their husbands wanted to leave for months on end, neglecting their family duties and relationships. It was believed to be the marital right of a woman to have her husband lie with her on Shabbat eve and many of the husbands had turned their backs on that law. I could sympathise with the women for many were simply abandoned for half the year. I remembered asking Yeshua about the unfairness of it and he answered me kindly but firmly. 'You are here, Deborah,' he said. 'Do you think I would turn away the wives of my disciples?'

'But the children,' I said. 'They couldn't leave the children.'

Yeshua looked at me intently. 'You mean they don't want to change their lives in any way or even look at how to solve that problem,' he said. 'We could travel with children. Or we could set up camps where the women could take it in turns to take care of all the children, so giving each other a chance to travel with us for some of the time. Have you seen any sign of anyone suggesting that?'

'No,' I said. 'But you are being hard on them all the same.'

'Oh yes,' said Yeshua. 'I am hard on you all. But no one ever said that following the Holy One – or one of his servants – was easy. It is simple but it is rarely easy.'

Everyone who came to our lodging house greeted me in a friendly manner. Thomas, who could be the bane of anyone's life, he was so inquisitive and sceptical, particularly gave me an affectionate hug. However, I felt strangely distanced from these familiar faces. James seemed to have changed the most. He had a new air of authority. The reason for this emerged as we ate. He was now the leader of the group. Cephas, as before, was the organiser and the one who dealt with everyday matters but James was in Yeshua's place. Magdalene explained that James was Yeshua's heir

– the nearest blood relative – and therefore the natural choice to succeed him. Like the right of Kings, Yeshua's blood should rule.

'Do you see nothing strange in that?' I asked her, perplexed.

'No,' she replied. 'That is the way it is. Without Yeshua we are a shadow of what we were but it is good to have a leader.'

I felt disloyal but I continued. 'But James came late to our group. He does not have all the knowledge that Cephas – or Joseph – has or even that you and I have. There's… there's no light in him, like there is in Joseph or in my mother or in you.'

Magdalene laughed. 'You aren't suggesting a woman should lead, are you? It's a nice idea but I would like to go on living! We wouldn't last a week, even if the others agreed.'

'No, I'm not suggesting anyone leads. I'm not sure anyone needs to at the moment. But if they do, it is God who will decide who it should be. After all, the place of the Anointed One is never left empty and someone must be holding that mantle. I'm not at all sure it is James. Anyway, following the blood line is working only in the physical World. Yeshua taught us to work in the World of spirit where blood does not matter. You know he did not acknowledge blood relationships – not even with his own mother.'

Magdalene was not impressed by my reasoning. 'There has to be a structure. A teacher. Someone to make rulings on issues we debate. I'm sure James is the best choice. We can't expect such another as Yeshua. The next Anointed may not even live near us. You must realise that.'

Clearly Joseph and Rizpah shared Magdalene's feelings and there was such an air of expectancy and enthusiasm about the disciples that I did not argue any further. In any case, the disciples' happiness was a joy to watch. Logically, electing James as the leader made sense in the short term. I wondered whether I was jealous or blinded by my love for Yeshua. I had been far closer to him than James had. Perhaps James was the best choice – if we were meant to be choosing.

For the few days leading up to Shavuot, a group of us met regularly and, despite my earlier doubts, it was comforting and peaceful to listen to the others debating and going over old times. We were in the last few days of the Omer – the period between Pesach and Pentecost where each of the days has a special meaning according to the Tradition – and it was as fascinating as it always had been to watch the quality of the days fit perfectly into the allotted aspect for that time. Rizpah had learnt her lesson about speaking out of turn so she too watched and listened and learned and did not get in anyone's way. Three young men, who had arrived with Nathaniel, were enjoying the teaching too and they obviously found a pretty young girl an asset to the group.

There was talk of everyone's going North again and of teaching – and hopefully healing – around Galilee. We had pooled resources and there was enough money to live on but soon we would either have to return to making our living or begin to live the life of travellers, depending on the donations of those who heard us or whom we could help.

I did not join in the discussions for, despite the civility expressed towards me, I still felt I was there only on sufferance. Nobody mentioned Judah at all and although James made it clear to me, privately, that he now shared Cephas's view, he warned me that nobody else was fully convinced. Thomas and Matthias were just as friendly as they had always been but it seemed as though it was only the pressure of their leaders which encouraged the others to talk to me – or to Magdalene for that matter. Without Yeshua's presence the place of women was in danger of sliding back to what it always had been before.

On top of all this, I was still feeling unwell each morning. It worried me for I knew I was not eating enough and yet I was not losing weight. Thoughts of the people I had met with strange swellings in their stomachs and who died swiftly and in great pain began to tug at the edges of my mind. I had been childless through seven years of marriage and deemed infertile even before that so symptoms similar to those that any other woman might have greeted with delight were of no joy to me.

On the day before Shavuot, the men decided to hold a ballot to elect a successor to Judah. Maintaining the number 12 was important to them because it represented each of the tribes of Israel who, in turn, represented each of the signs of the Zodiac. Everyone agreed that the contest was between Joseph Barsabbas, the former Essene who had taken Yeshua's body from the cross and placed it in a grave of his own purchasing, and Matthias, one of the men who had begun to follow Yeshua a year or two ago and who had won hearts all round for his generosity. Of course I was keen for Joseph to take Judah's place for he, at least, would support the beliefs that my husband had held and would allow women their fair place in Yeshua's teachings.

To be fair, I could not be detached about the situation for, as my grief for Judah began to become bearable, it was replaced by the desire to know how he had met his death. Some of these men must know the truth but I could not ask them and now they were holding an election to replace him without mourning him or his strengths.

I'm sure Cephas, Thomas and Matthias voted for Joseph but he was not elected. That in itself told me everything I needed to know. I knew I could be blind but this I had seen clearly. A young and almost untried man had been chosen over one who had led a group of the Essenes and risen above their ascetic laws; one who had been loved and appreciated by Yeshua himself even before he began to teach – and the man who had laid his body to rest. I had nothing in common with these men any more.

Joseph accepted the decision with his rare strength of character. It seemed to my biased eye that he shrank a little, physically but, for all that, he did not lose strength. It was as though it flowed deeper inside him instead.

The next day brought Shavuot. As with all our festivals, it began at dusk and I was glad to feel both well and rested by the time we gathered together, in the upper room of the house that Cephas had rented, to begin the age-old ritual. Rachel, as the wife of the leader of our group, prepared to light the candles to bring the Shekhinah down into the house so that James could then bless the wine, water and bread before the men left for prayers in the Temple. It was the first major festival without Yeshua and hard for me because he had always asked me to be the one to light the candles. To be relegated to the back row after being a leader is always a difficult test and harder still when you know that the woman taking on the role does not understand the significance of what she does. Rachel always lit the candles in her usual, practical way, in silence, following the ritual with the shortest of blessings. When I lit them, I would sing the Hebrew meditations of grace which Miriam had taught me as preparation for the holy moment of bringing Azilut, the World of Light, into the home. Believing I was right was always one of my weaknesses and it took a great act of discipline, that night, to swallow my feelings. As usual, once I could do so, I could see good coming from the changeover. For once I would be able to appreciate the ceremony as an observer, receiving a blessing brought down by another woman instead of always having to lead and pass the light on to others.

For the rest of my life I have been eternally grateful for that one action of disciplining my resentment and irritation. Had I not then nothing might have come from that moment and my life would have been immeasurably the poorer. Rachel's simple striking of the flint was enough, this time, to bring the light in the form of a blinding, silver lightning flash which seared its way through me, causing me to lose my balance and fall back in shock.

I assume someone caught me for when I came to my senses I was lying at the back of the room with Magdalene's arm around me and Rizpah's anxious face before me. Behind them James was continuing the age-old ritual.

'It's all right,' I said. 'Go and join the others. I am perfectly well. I just need a few moments to myself.'

Magdalene smiled and nodded and drew the younger woman away firmly for Rizpah was not so easily reassured and would have stayed, questioning me. Their figures merged with the family group and I, alone within the crowd, was allowed precious time to wonder and consider the miracle which had struck me from above.

Time had stood still in that moment as I received my message. It could have been a full day before I returned into the physical World though, of course, it was no time at all. With God there is no time; all is in the present moment and when the messengers of the Holy One speak there is no limit to any dimension.

The angel's words of prophecy to me had been of exile from the only land I had ever known but I hardly heard that part. What I had heard was the voices of unborn souls, echoing like the chimes of tiny bells and bubbling like a clear mountain stream, flooding into the air around me. In their centre was Gabriel, silver and shimmering and, deep within him, was the tiniest, brightest glow of light yet, whiter than silver, bluer than the sky, richer than the deepest purple. I held out my arms and the light engulfed me, striking with terrifying clarity into my physical body. I saw within myself, created and formed but incredibly fragile, the beginnings of a temple already created for this soul and I felt the soul within the light hesitate as it touched the living flesh. This soul too had its choice – whether to commit to staying or whether to go back to the higher realms.

For an age – which could have been a second or a thousand years for all I knew – it wavered and then I felt the life-force surge into me, tying a cord of light between the two of us so that the soul could dance between the Worlds as it waited for its physical vehicle to be completed in mine.

Gabriel bowed and dissolved back into the cosmos and I was alone.

Not much of a miracle you might say and, if a miracle at all, one which thousands of women experience every day. But the knowledge of it – being able to see how it happens to each and every one of us and that choice is involved on both sides – was an even greater miracle than the coming of pregnancy for a woman who had believed herself infertile.

It was not until the next morning that the others received their own, perhaps greater, miracle but it was not only I who felt that there was a sacred presence in that room from that moment on. The service and the discussion which followed it were alight with a strange, quiet joy as though great news was on its way. Later, as usual, the women left the men to talk and debate and went about their business, taking care of the children and clearing up after the dinner. Perhaps my eyes were biased but I saw a new dignity in them as they completed their normal routine – tasks hardly thought about or appreciated by those for whom they were done – but tonight it seemed each action was done for the glory of the Lord and that transformed everything.

Magdalene watched me carefully to see if I wanted to talk but I felt exhausted and turned in upon myself, wishing to rest, pray and be quiet. I could not tell anyone yet.

She smiled at me lovingly and I smiled back, appreciating the strength in her which was willing to wait until I wished to talk. I slept like a child, curled up between Magdalene and Rizpah and feeling as though their bodies nurtured me as my own nurtured the spark now within it.

In the morning I was weak and nauseous again but this time I understood and could bear it more easily. In fact I laughed at myself for being so foolish. How many times had I seen other women going through exactly what I now felt myself? It was only my belief – and that of all my family – that I could never conceive which had blinded me to the truth. And yet, without that visit from the Higher Realms, would this child truly have been conceived? I had never realised that the temple within could grow in preparation before the soul arrived. Had I not received the link with the soul, perhaps my body would have released the temple as an empty vessel. Maybe a miscarriage was caused when a soul could not or would not connect with its Earthly mother? So many thoughts were going around in my head that I could hardly notice what was happening around me.

Much was, for it was that morning that the Holy Spirit came upon the disciples and those who were studying with them. As everyone gathered together to leave for the morning's services in the Temple each of the men began to cry out in different languages: in Koine, in pure Greek, in Aramaic, Hebrew and Latin. As it happened we women stood as though stunned, listening – not to the men but to the voice of the highest of angels, running like lightning into us and out though the men, creating a full circle of fire.

I don't know exactly what happened to the others, apart from the shouting and singing, for I was lost inside myself. It seemed that I had been separated from this gift though not denied it, just protected for the sake of the miracle I had already received. I could see the joy on everyone's faces but it was as though a play was being acted out in front of me. Vaguely I became aware of crowds gathering in the streets and that they had come to hear the apostles teaching and praising God. Apparently it was only a

short time before there was pandemonium – more and more people arriving, attracted by the noise and the crowds. The only way
to deal with the throng was either to go out of the city and teach
on the Mount of Olives, as Yeshua had done before, or to take
them into the Temple. That day Jerusalem was taken by its heels
and shaken by the new teaching of resurrection. The men proclaimed Yeshua as Messiah at the tops of their voices – and people
listened. Nothing – for any of us – could ever be the same again.

We all went to the Temple to listen and wonder. Cephas, in
particular, suddenly developed an extraordinary gift for oratory
and people flooded into the courtyard to hear him, ignoring the
normal rituals and prayers in the Court of Israel. Even I, sceptical, grumpy Deborah, listened to this gruff old fisherman with
amazement, though perhaps the secret knowledge, held within
like a treasured jewel, may have helped me to be a little more charitable than usual!

Magdalene, Rizpah, Joanna and the other women who had
been present did not speak publicly but they continued the
women's mission, waiting on the edges, talking gently to those
who wanted particular information and explaining and clarifying
the men's eloquence. My sister Salome was there in the crowd,
having travelled down from Galilee with her husband and family,
and stayed overnight in another guest house. I searched the
crowds for a sign of Miriam who would have come with her. I was
not certain, now that Yeshua was gone, whether she would want
to remain known by her given name of Miriam. At this time I
wanted her to be Imma, my mother, so I could talk again to her
of Gabriel and what was happening to me.

She was not there but she was, at least, in Jerusalem. Salome
told me that had stayed behind with her grandchildren at the
lodging house, so I would have to wait to hear her news and to tell
her mine.

Instead I sat in the courtyard, a little apart from the crowd,
watching and listening and enjoying the sunshine. After a while I
became aware of a presence beside me. Sometimes the sight from
the sides of our eyes will reveal things that we cannot see if we look
at them directly. As I stared straight ahead I could half-see Yeshua
sitting to my left; if I turned to look, there was nothing there.

This was no great visitation of an angel, just a brother and companion resting for a while and watching. I waited for a moment until I was sure it was not just wishful thinking.

'I thought you had gone on through to God' I said softly. He laughed.

'I'm on my way,' he said. 'This is my last moment here. I just wanted to talk to you before I left. I can't talk to my brothers and sisters at the moment. They are so excited!'

'Yes. It's wonderful.'

'Yes it is. Now they can move on instead of looking backwards. Deborah, I have four messages. Will you take them?'

'Of course.'

'Tell Cephas that he has enough courage. Tell Magdalene that she will soon be with me. And tell Paul... ' he stopped, hearing my unspoken question. 'Yes, Paul – you will come to know him – that I am not God. I am a part of Him as we all are but I am not God. I am a pathway not a goal.'

'I will. But Magdalene...?'

'You will know the right time to tell each of them. Deborah, listen.'

'Yes?'

'Take the untrodden path. Always the untrodden one. Nobody else's path but your own. That's the one where you will find joy. Don't need to be understood. Don't need to be loved.'

'I'll do my best.'

I kept staring straight ahead. As long as I did not look at him I could see him; just the same as always, if not younger. So handsome and oh, so dear to me.

It seemed as though he moved round in front of me. I closed my eyes and lifted my mouth to be kissed – and then he was gone.

Three

They said afterwards that three thousand people were baptised that extraordinary week, each acknowledging the Messiah of our time. They flooded into the Mikvahs and to the Pool of Siloam and used ritual baths in private houses as well.

Of course, it was festival time and Jerusalem was crowded. There were no Jewish market stores open but even the foreign merchants sent messengers to find out what was going on for they had fewer customers than usual. Romans, Syrians and Samaritans followed the crowds around outside the Temple, trying to see what was going on. Amazingly it was all good humoured, for riots could easily have broken out. It was as though a veil of something gentle were suspended over the entire city, smoothing away all the rough corners and making those who would normally be enemies smile at each other and talk as though there were no divisions. 'Angels are watching over us!' said Joseph Barsabbas with a smile as we passed in the street one day and I stopped and looked up to see if there was anything I could see. I did think I caught a flash of silver light but it was probably just a reflection or my eyes seeing what I wanted them to see.

Then I hurried on for I was on a particular quest. Weaving my way past the crowds in the street I made my way to the Temple, my nose twitching as I went. I could smell nothing – and that was the whole point.

The outer court, where gentiles were allowed, was full to bursting with people of all persuasions and normally I would have stopped to enjoy the sight of so much colour and variety. Instead, I pushed my way through to the Court of the Women even though I had not been to the ritual bath and had no tithe. I was not here for worship but on a mission for I was certain that this would be the day that Yeshua had spoken to me about, all those years ago. It would be the day the sacrifices ended! Filled with hope, I danced and dodged around until I found a place where I could see into the Court of Israel. There, I knew, I would see a hoard of animals and birds wandering or fluttering around, alive and unharmed. My dream had been that all those who had brought animals for slaughter would set them free when they saw the truth. I was ready to dance and sing in praise that the world had changed and people had seen sense.

The dream was shattered like the illusion it was; the great altar was just as much a charnel house as it had always been with the priests receiving the sacrificial animals and draining their blood over the stone. My elation turned instantly to anger, then dismay and bitter self-recrimination. How had I managed to deceive myself so? There, in the Temple grounds, I could easily have smelt the burning flesh if I had stopped and allowed myself to do so, even if it was not discernible outside. The wind had been blowing away from our lodging house that morning and I had scented no stink of burning meat when I awoke. At first I had not noticed anything, until Rizpah commented on it. Then the hope in my heart had been so great that I had convinced myself that my wishes would be true. But animals and birds were still dying, their blood mingling in that holy place, just as it always had done. In a blinding temper I pushed my way out again, through the courtyard and out into the street. I was bitterly angry with God and with my own gullibility. And yet, was I so wrong? Why could it not have happened?

I knew that I had to spend some time composing myself before I could face the disappointment rationally and join in with the others. The power of the anger was immense and I so wanted to blame someone else, not to see that I had built my hopes on my own personal wishes. I was even angry with Yeshua. Why had he made that promise if he had not meant it? At the back of my mind I knew that it had just been the passing remark of one child to another. But everything else he had told me was true; why not this?

It was some time later that I made my way back to where the disciples were teaching. Magdalene noticed that I was subdued and, like the good friend she was, she coaxed the problem out of me. When I told her, I could see that she was having trouble in keeping a straight face. It says much for our friendship that I did not hit her!

'Give it time!' she said. 'You are such an idealist. God can do miracles but men usually take a little time to change their habits. If Yeshua said that the sacrifices will stop, then they will stop. Maybe just not yet. Don't forget that God doesn't worry about time the way we do. It could take another thirty years before the sacrifices stop. It may be the work of the next Anointed One. We might never see it in our lifetime. You know as well as I do that everything will be taken care of in God's good time and not when we want it to be done.'

Her sturdy good sense cheered me a little so I could even smile at her. 'You're a goose, Deborah!' she said. 'It's meant to be me who's impatient and cross about things. You usually have to lecture me!'

'It just seems so unfair,' I said. 'I was hoping so much…'

'Quite!' said Magdalene. 'Where is the place where we are meant to be in the World of Yetzirah.'

Yetzirah was the name that our tradition, the Merkabah teaching, gave to the World of the human psyche – the place where we fight the battle between the ego and the self before contacting our soul and our free will.

'Tiferet,' I said in a small voice.

'And what is Tiferet all about?'

'Detachment from the ego's desires,' we said in a chorus and, despite myself, I felt the first twitches of laughter pulling at my mouth.

'Stop it!' I said. 'I want to sulk! I've got a right to sulk if I want to!'

Magdalene made a face at me. We put our arms around each other and, laughing, went back towards the Temple.

All the disciples, Joseph and the other followers, were so busy

that week that they hardly had time to eat. We women ran around
sharing out bread and fruit and listening to those who had witnessed miracles. Once I had got over my sulks and my morning
sickness, I joined in too and the work did as much as Magdalene's
good humour to revive me. It was almost like the old days, when
Yeshua walked the paths of Galilee talking and teaching to all who
would listen. People's eyes were shining and their backs straighter
as they realised that it would now be easier to face the world.

The cynic in me wondered just how long that feeling would
last. It was fairly easy to inspire people and show them the Way
to God but maintaining that knowledge and acting on it was
another matter. Sitting with us and sharing the mood was one
thing but going home and trying to explain to people who had not
been there and who were only concerned with their supper or
where the next day's money was coming from would be very different.

I remembered Yeshua's parable of the sower; how the seed
sprang up fastest on shallow soil but withered later for lack of sus-
tenance; how some was strangled by temptation and other people's
disbelief and how only a little took root and grew well.

'Wait and see; wait and see,' I said to myself as I got on with my
work. 'There's a greater impulse behind this and it's our job to
help them hold on to the dream.'

I sat down with a young woman who was sitting with her eyes
closed, swaying backwards and forwards in ecstasy. She was calling out to Yeshua to save her and lift her to the highest Heaven
and she was so enraptured that she was in danger of leaving her
body. I took her hand gently but firmly and began to talk her
down. Too many visions too soon could lead to madness and that
would never do. Around us, people bustled and chattered and
sang and the woman resisted my efforts to bring her back to the
mundane World.

'But you can bring this beauty with you,' I said gently, as she
tried to snatch her hand away. I knew how she felt but she was
alive in the World and the task before her was to combine her new
knowledge with her everyday life.

Each night we worked on way past dusk. Some of the eupho-
ria had died down as the week progressed and a few members of

the Sanhedrin had been very bad tempered with those of us who were repeatedly in the Temple. We did not care, and showed it, but Cephas and James were careful to warn everyone each night, as we ate, that we must not provoke those who might oppose us.

Day followed day and the interest hardly abated. All the time the Sanhedrin watched and grew more and more fearful, their priestly tasks threatened by this new revolution but, so far, the Romans did not seem to mind. They thought we were mad most of the time in any case and those in charge of policing the streets kept a wary eye open but I actually overheard two soldiers saying that they'd have to find out a bit more about this particular Jewish festival as it had made everyone so friendly and helpful.

'If only they could always be like this it would be a pleasure being here,' said one. 'Well they won't,' said the other. 'Give them a week and someone will be throwing stones at some poor unfortunate who's put a foot wrong somewhere. Load of savages, that's what they are!'

I thought that was rich, from a nation which set men against animals and who worshipped more gods than there were stars in the sky, but one of the men smiled at me as I walked past and I found myself smiling back.

Generally the Romans had no concept of why we Jews behaved as we did. Sometimes it seemed as though we did not know either and it was entirely true to say that the term 'Jew' covered a multitude of different aspects of the same religion. But, despite our divisions, my race would fight to the death for their right to be Jewish and to oppose Roman beliefs. We were lucky that nothing went wrong that first day, nor on the ones that followed. No, I am being cynical. We were blessed and protected so that nothing could go wrong. After a miracle there is usually a period of Grace. Even when the Sadducees, who were responsible for the running of the Temple, had Peter and John arrested at the end of that week they could find no charge against them and, after warning them fiercely not to continue teaching, they had to let them go.

Could it last? As we were carried along on the wave, more and more people seemed to come and listen to the men and they grew bolder in what they taught. John and Peter carried out healing, just as Yeshua had, and their delight in their gifts was as great as the joy of those who found that they could walk again or whose skin and eye diseases vanished overnight.

At the start I was as enthusiastic as the rest but then some instinct began to tell me to withdraw. Not because I was not delighted with what was happening – it was like watching light flood down into Jerusalem and it made my heart sing with gratitude and belief that the World was coming closer to God – but because I had matters of my own to consider. Magdalene and I could hardly find time to talk of my pregnancy and I desperately wanted to talk to someone. I did not want to discuss it in front of the other women because, although I was fond of them all, there was no greater link between us than that. They had not followed the inner teaching with the fervour and interest that we two had. It had been enough for them that Yeshua was the Anointed One and that they might travel with him and serve. In that respect, they were a lesson to us all but those of us with a hungrier heart sometimes found it hard to see how much more a traditional woman was valued than a female disciple. It was only natural; who would not want someone to take care of them and feed them? And somebody had to do it, after all. We had more than enough to do just to take care of the everyday matters, using the communal money to buy food for everyone who needed it, to cook and to clear up. As it was, we were lucky in having enough money. Much of it had always come from wealthy women like Susannah and Joanna and it had long been one of my irritations that their financial support for the men was so very taken for granted. Having said that, it was almost as much the women's choice as the men's that our role outside the home was slowly vanishing as the days went past and we were back in our 'proper' place. Yeshua had once said to me that women found it harder to be contradicted and more difficult to argue their point than men did, so they often gave up their spiritual life and went back to what they knew they could do well. I knew what he meant though I did not like to admit it and I had argued fiercely that it was men's attitudes which had led to that – if it were true at all!

'Hmm,' Yeshua had fixed me with his searching look. 'Some of the time, yes. Some of the time, no. How often have you seen a woman holding back her daughter in case she should shine,

Deborah? Or pushing her in a direction which reflects glory on her mother and family rather than on herself? It's not just men. Often it's the women too.

'Just think how blessed we were with the amount of times our mother could have made us obey or keep quiet or held us back. She never once did but I'm afraid other women are not always so strong.'

Oh, if only he could have been here and I could have talked to him! I missed our arguments more than anything else. He could make me so angry but then he would show me the way out so that I could change my mind or argue my point with greater accuracy. Sometimes I even out-argued him but, by the time I did that, both of us would be in fits of laughter so the outcome never mattered anyway. Oh, how I missed him.

As it was, it was only Magdalene who understood how I felt and who would be willing to try and change things. Only Magdalene would be able to discuss my pregnancy with reference to the Teaching. Only Magdalene was the friend of my soul.

We snatched a few moments here and there and she started saving some bread from her breakfast so that I should have extra to eat after the morning nausea had passed. She took on some extra work and bullied Rizpah into doing more too so that I should have no heavy carrying but she did it with such subtlety that nobody noticed. Now I knew myself that I was with child, I thought it must be obvious to everybody but that was just my ego trying to make me the centre of the universe as usual.

There was one other person I knew I had to tell. Somehow I had to find Imma. She of all people had a right to know. I was perplexed as to why she had not come into the city at all for no one had seen her or my female cousins, all of whom had come South for Shavuot.

On another level, I needed to begin to teach Rizpah the root of our beliefs. She was overwhelmed by what was happening but beginning to feel very left-out by her lack of knowledge. It was fine for her to help the other women but that was not what she had left home and family for. Everyone else was far too busy to sit and teach her; the women either did not want to or could not answer her queries and they did not want me to do so either.

Whenever we tried to find a little time for ourselves, someone found us an extra job to do and I'm afraid I was not strong enough to start a fight. It was a far cry from the time when my opinion was sought after and I was considered an important part of the whole. Then, I could choose when to teach, when to rest and when to work. I was doing my best with Rizpah but it was not enough. She was not encouraged to ask questions of the men when they came in to eat either. They were tired and they did not wish to talk to one particular, troublesome woman when there was so much more to do in the open. They did not even see why she was there and more than once she was accused of being a trouble-maker for not being with a brother or husband.

'Leave her be; she is Deborah's business,' growled Cephas once or twice and, as I swept Rizpah away protectively, I was grateful to him for speaking out, little as it was.

Susannah, Magdalene, Joanna and the other women were also looking after the wives and children of the men who were joining the crusade and spending all their time at the Temple rather than setting off back home to their everyday lives once the festival had ended. Instead of showing the radiance of the men, we women started looking tired and drawn and squabbling amongst ourselves.

All this made me think how sensible Yeshua had been in mak-ing sure that we always had time for teaching and time for learn-ing and time just to sit and be quiet, so everyone could have their turn. Shabbat kept us in one piece as there was no cooking for a whole day but, as we had prepared twice as much the day before, the resting time was only just enough to refresh us before we began again! There was little other respite that day, however, for there were even more people going in and out of the houses and lodging places; more queries to deal with and more advice to give.

Eventually I did find the courage to leave the other women to it, just for one afternoon, and I took Rizpah out with me. I felt almost as guilty as she did in doing so and that itself was enough to warn me that no matter how wonderful it seemed that so many people were coming and listening to the teaching, it was making slaves out of some of us just as it was making masters of the others.

I knew Imma was staying just outside the city, together with the rest of the family from Nazara, but it took us some time to find

the house.   When we arrived she was busy coping with two
screaming babies and four toddlers while their mothers, my
nieces, tried to cook and weave. The sight of such normal domes-
tic chaos made my heart sink as I realised that I too would soon
have to deal with the everyday business of babies. The revelation
was one thing, the work another. I was going to lose a lot of my
freedom and that would hurt.

Imma's dear face lit up at the sight of me but there was no possibility of our talking privately at all that day. I introduced Rizpah
to her and and then, of course, everyone else wanted to know all
about the stranger too and we were surrounded. Not one of the
women mentioned Judah and that concerned me deeply. Usually
women were warm in their condolences. What had they been
told? I tried to hide my feelings but Imma was not fooled and
caught my eye thoughtfully several times. I was shocked at how
much older she looked but so much had happened these last few
months that it was hardly surprising that any of us should have
changed. Rizpah and I spent a short while talking to Dinah, Ruth
and Mary and playing with their six children but then we made
our escape. I would have to come again to find Imma and tell her
in private.

Instead of going straight back, I led Rizpah down into the
Kidron valley and we found a shady corner where I could begin to
tell her properly about the Merkabah tradition.

I began by telling her the story of how God wished to give birth
to Itself through the creation of Adam Kadmon, the primordial
man, and how every human soul was one cell in that being. How
each of us would grow to perfection over millennia and how the
Tree of Life from the Garden of Eden represented the pathway
back to God.

I told her of the significance of the menorah in the Holy of
Holies of the Temple; how Moses had cast it from gold, to the
Lord's instructions, to represent this Tree of Life and how the ten
Sephirot on the seven branched candlestick each represented an
aspect of God – and an aspect of man.

I made her recite their names with me until she was word perfect: "Malkhut, Yesod, Hod, Nezach, Tiferet, Gevurah, Hesed,
Binah, Hokhmah, Keter."   Each of the Sephirot represented

aspects of our selves; in each of us some would be well balanced and work for good and some would not. Looking at each attribute, we could see what our characters had in abundance and what we lacked and the Work could begin by trying to redress the balance.

We translated the Sephirot into Aramaic so that Rizpah could understand them better. There are many different words that can be used for each one but, that day, I taught her that the first five represented her physical body, her everyday reactions, her thought processes, her wish for action and her perfect, beautiful self. Then I showed her the higher Sephirot of Discernment, Mercy, Understanding, Wisdom and the Crown of all Knowledge – the Kingdom of God. Between Mercy and Understanding I placed Da'at, the non-Sephira of eternal mystery and the pathway between Worlds but when this confused her (as it had confused me so many years before) I put it aside for another lesson.

To make it a little easier I showed her that there were three pillars within the Tree. The left one of passivity and the right one of action. Each of these on its own was destructive and they needed to be balanced by the central column of consciousness.

'You see, we humans chose the way of knowledge,' I said. 'Before Eve was tempted by the serpent in the Garden of Eden, mankind knew nothing but beauty. We made our choice and now increasing our knowledge of ourselves and the higher Worlds is the only way back to the Garden.

'When Adam and Eve left Paradise, the Archangel Raziel gave them a Book of Knowledge to help them on their search. As the years went by it was lost and forgotten, so Melchisedek came down from Heaven and taught Abraham again.

'Since then, this knowledge has been kept by those closest to the Kingdom of God and passed down from generation to generation. It is in the Torah but it is hidden. It is in the Ten Commandments and it is in the Tabernacle of the Exodus. But those who wish to look just at the written Torah – or inside the Ark of the Covenant – are looking only at the physical World. The real gem of the knowledge is held in between the wings of the angels on the lid of the Ark and it is in the spaces between the words of the Torah. That means that it is never written down – at least, not completely – but it is passed on from one generation to another. Until Yeshua and I were born I think it went only to men – but I don't know that for sure. My greatest wish would be to find another woman in the world who has the knowledge that I, and Magdalene, have and which I am now teaching you.'

It was the first time I had taught another person from the very beginning just as Yeshua had taught me. Rizpah was a keen pupil and asked intelligent questions which were a delight to answer. The best of all was 'What's the point?' and I leant back against a tree, whooping with laughter for, to me, life itself was the point. Everything on the Tree of Life was relevant to everything I thought or did.

However, I made an effort to be less scholarly and more realistic and told her how she could apply the rules of the Tree to everyday life, so that God could work through her.

'I'd like to be like Rebekkah, Jacob's wife,' said Rizpah. 'She didn't put up with unfairness; she helped Jacob get his birthright because he was a better man than Esau.'

'Yes, but the point is not to be another Rebekkah, no matter how powerful you might be,' I said. 'Rebekkah represents the ninth commandment, 'Thou shalt not bear false witness.' She lied to Isaac so that he would bless Jacob and not Esau – and she ended up lonely because of it.

'The point is to be the best possible Rizpah. That's what God sent you to be, not an imitation of someone else.'

The temptation to teach too much in one day was great but I just about resisted it and warned Rizpah not to tell the others what she was learning yet. The disciples were so happy teaching the coming of a Messiah and the general principles that Yeshua had given to us that they had not had time to consider how much of the inner teaching should be revealed. I had every intention of teaching Rizpah every ounce of knowledge I had but I knew it had to be done tactfully. My own place in the group was precarious enough.

Just how precarious became frighteningly obvious that very afternoon as we approached the city again. Philip was preaching to a crowd just outside the walls, assisted by Stephen, a charismatic and delightful young man who had followed Yeshua whenever he could in the last year. They were telling the story of the Christos, as they called him, including the tale of the first night of Pesach and the vigil in the Garden of Gethsemane. This was the first time, in public, that I heard Judah's name vilified. To do Philip justice he, himself, was not handing out blame and was trying to explain what he had been given to understand by Cephas but mob rule is a fearsome thing and people, when given a story, want heroes and villains.

Stephen did not help; he had not been in the Garden that evening so he did not know that Yeshua had greeted his friend with a kiss and a smile and the rest of the truth itself sounded quite feeble – even to me, listening on the edge of the crowd. What was worse, it sounded condemnatory of those who were enthralling the audiences now. As I stood there I saw the truth falter and fall for it was not what the people wanted to hear. Far better a story of triumph over evil than a simple pathway to grace, showing the shortcomings of the teachers. The disciples might have coped with the latter, but the listeners could not.

Angry tears fell from my eyes as I stood and heard their roar of hatred for my husband, the traitor, and all connected with him. I knew that if I were one of them I too would be roaring for blood. How could you possibly explain that Yeshua had planned for his own death? That he knew of a World after death and it did not frighten him? That he knew he must leave, and soon, otherwise the impulse of his teaching could not go on.

For myself it was bad enough but now my stomach began to churn with fear for my child. His life might be at risk once people knew who I was.

As I stood there, stunned, with Rizpah holding onto my arm in confusion and horror I also heard, for the very first time, the story of Judah's death. Stephen told how he had used the thirty pieces of silver, which tradition decreed were always given in exchange for information, to buy a piece of land and how he had fallen dead upon that land.

Judah was not young when I married him. For all of us forty to fifty years of life was a blessing and for women, with the perils of childbirth, death was a common visitor far earlier than that. Judah could simply have had a seizure as Abba had done. In that

case he would not have suffered and knowing that was some comfort. But what of the land? What had happened to that? Judah
had known that he would not live longer than his friend and master and he would have put the money to good use. I had never
thought of that! My mind raced, trying to assuage the pain by
sensible thought. Around us the people continued to murmur
against the good and honest man I had married, some even calling for vengeance against his family. Those who had never had
dealings with the Sanhedrin, and did not know that the exchange
of silver for information was a matter of honour, were calling the
payment 'blood-money.' They did not know the basic law that
information would not be accepted as true if the informer were
not willing to be paid. Suddenly I saw an image of the future, of
Judah's name unfairly reviled by those who had never heard the
truth. It was that, and the knowledge that somewhere there was
land that belonged, honestly, to me that stopped me falling apart.
If I could do nothing else in my life, I could raise Judah's son to
know that his father was a good man.

If this child were Judah's son.

With the strength of long practice, I enclosed all the pain in a
place where it could be dealt with later and motioned to Rizpah
to follow me. I kept my face covered as we made our way along
the edge of the crowd and, without a word – for I could not yet
trust myself to speak – I took Rizpah back to the house. Ignoring
the irritation of the women who were working hard to provide for
their men and who had resented our absence, I went directly to
the corner where I slept and where my few possessions were
stored. There, in the precious olive-wood chest that Yeshua carved
for me, I found the roll of supple leather which contained Judah's
and my marriage document. I hid it within my tunic. Then I
walked out, leaving Rizpah to face the others alone and made my
way to the office of records at the base of the Temple wall, to find
out where my property was.

I was lucky; there were still scribes at work there even by the
time I arrived. They did not want to deal with me, a woman, for
I should have had a husband, son or brother to do business for me
but I had learned enough from Magdalene to know how to overcome such resistance. From the day she was divorced she had had

to deal with everything herself and it could be done, if you knew how. If you were stubborn enough and peaceful enough and did not mind waiting they would help you eventually, even if only to get you out of the building. The scribe who finally assisted me would have done virtually anything to get me out as swiftly as possible. Even so, he was surprised to find that not only did he have the required copy of the deeds I wanted but the original itself, which Judah should have taken with him once the deal was made. That very little miracle saved me the problem of how I could pay to have my own copy made.

Judah knew what he had been doing and had anticipated my arrival. As the scribe unrolled the deeds, a small pouch fell out of the scroll of material. A note in Hebrew was pinned to it and, seeing my name, I snatched at it like a starving dog. It contained money and a note. I put them both hastily away in a pocket, daring the scribe to question me, but he only cared about getting rid of me as quickly as possible. He did not want to risk having to deal with the hysterical emotions of a widowed and friendless woman.

Holding the deeds, I ran all the way from the office to the pool of Siloam and collapsed into the shade of an old olive tree. With shaking fingers I pulled out the note and read, in Hebrew, my husband's last words to me.

'My beloved Deborah. This land is yours to do with as you wish. It is my gift and Yeshua's. We agreed it would be the best legacy for you. It has a house and crops. You will be safe there. Trust in the Lord always and let Him guide you. Your loving husband, Judah.'

So little! I was still young enough to want an outpouring of love, not something short and practical. But even as I felt disappointment seep into me, I heard Yeshua's voice again, saying, 'Deborah, don't need to be loved.' Choking back the tears, I managed to count the money – twelve silver pieces – and turn my attention to the deeds themselves. They themselves were proof that I was loved, in the Heavens as on Earth.

They included directions to this good, fertile land at a place called En Gedi, three and a half days to the South of Jerusalem, and a map of the property itself. If only it had not been taken over

by Amretzin, the wandering, often Godless people who did itin-
erant work in the fields, I could stay there with Rizpah and
Magdalene, too – if she wanted to come – and wait the coming of
my child in prosperity and peace. I was being taken care of; I
would not have to rely on the communal money of the disciples
and the new adherents of the Messianic Judaism being preached
in the city. I could be free and I could be safe.

I told Cephas of my plans that very evening, making him swear
that he would tell no one else of Judah's legacy or where I was
going. He understood, for he knew already that the legend about
Judah was unstoppable and that those connected with him would
be in danger of their lives. 'We cannot protect you,' he said. 'You
will be safer away from here. It is not only the men who find it
hard to have you here; the women too have been complaining.' I
knew that, for poor Rizpah had faced a barrage of irritation while
I was claiming my inheritance and I had found her in tears on my
return. My news that we had somewhere to go together, where we
could study and do as we wished, cheered her greatly but she was
still upset by the hostility surrounding us. I did point out to
Cephas that slavery was not meant to be Yeshua's inheritance and
that those who resented others who were seeking the truth for
themselves were not the best judges of other people's behaviour
but I could have said it more tactfully. He had the grace to see my
point of view and to say he was sorry I was going but I knew he
was relieved all the same. It would be far easier without me.

   I told James that Rizpah and I were leaving for, as the leader, he
had the right to know and he accepted my decision without comment. Blood ties were not important to me now and, for James,
it was not so much the loss of a sister but of a dangerous factor in
a well-run organisation.

   Somewhat to my surprise, Magdalene was all enthusiasm for
my plan. I had thought she would prefer to stay where all the
excitement was but, as soon as I had whispered to her that I was
leaving Jerusalem she said, immediately, that she wanted to come
with me. It was she who insisted on telling Joseph. He came over
to me immediately, obviously delighted to hear of my prosperity
but it was only when I told him the location of the land that I

realised how very well we were being taken care of. Joseph took the map and began to chuckle gently as he looked at it. To my amazement the chuckle developed into a deep belly-laugh, so much so that everyone else in the room turned and looked, wanting to know the joke.

'It's nothing,' he said. 'Just a memory I share with our sister, Deborah.' Then, as I looked bewildered, he bundled me out of the room into the street.

'You don't know where En Gedi is, do you, Deborah?' he said, once we were alone.

'No. No I don't. Just that it's to the South.'

'More South-East,' he said. 'It's by Qumran. It's at an oasis less than a day from where the Essenes live. If we had gone to them without knowing this you would have had to beg a place with them and faced possible rejection. Now you have your own land, within reasonable distance of them and not desert land either but good, fertile soil. No wonder the Holy One had to bring you back to Jerusalem!'

Like delighted children, the two of us did a little dance together, outside in the street, praising the Lord and feeling that wonderful knowledge that all is working according to a greater plan than we could possibly know.

Joseph offered to escort the three of us to our new home and to stay with us at least until we were settled, tilling the land and liaising for us, if necessary, with the Essene group nearby. I was so happy that the others obviously shared my dream but I couldn't help wondering why they did not want to stay in Jerusalem. They were adamant that they did not. 'It's not that it is too good to be true,' said Joseph. 'It is true. But it is getting unbalanced. The crowds are loving it but at some point the pendulum will swing back. It always does. Everything we have learned from the Tree of Life says that we have to walk the centre path, the balanced path. If we continue as we are, the natural forces will make sure there is a reaction – and probably a hostile one – to balance all the excitement. If people really are interested, now is the time to back away and let them follow.'

Magdalene agreed. 'Also,' she said, 'it is very obvious that we women are not required as teachers or healers and I would rather

be where what I have to offer is valued. It is one thing to serve –
that is our joy and our duty – but another to be a slave.'

Later, as I watched Joseph and Magdalene discussing our plans
quietly together, I wondered if there was a possibility that love
would grow between them as the months went by. Then I shook
my head. I was being stupid; Joseph was a vowed celibate and
Magdalene divorced. And yet, was I so foolish? Did not Rizpah's
experience prove that all was not necessarily what it seemed? Now
that I felt better I could see, again, that the purpose of Yeshua's
teaching was always to show us that it was Heavenly principles we
were following not laws graven in stone.

Before we left for En Gedi I managed to see Imma alone and
we walked together to fetch water. There was so much I needed
to tell her that I did not know where to start. In the end, all I said
was that I was with child and going to live on land Judah had
bought for me and that I wished with all my heart that she would
visit so we could have time to talk of other things that only she
could understand.

The wonderfulness of Imma was that she never fussed or said anything inappropriate. She accepted that I was happy to be pregnant
and that I was aware of the responsibilities of having no husband as
well as the risks of bearing a first child so late. She held me very
tightly and said she would come to me as soon as I needed her but
she, too, wanted to hide away and she felt that Galilee was the best
place for her at that time. She and Salome and the others were planning to go home in a few days, whether or not their menfolk followed. As Yeshua's mother she too was in danger of becoming someone the people knew about and she did not want that.

'I think what is happening at the moment will stop quite soon,'
she said, echoing Joseph's thoughts. 'Already the Sanhedrin are
angry and they will stir up the Romans if they can. Riots may
break out for although the disciples are teaching to the best of
their ability, they cannot control what others teach nor make those
who hear them understand.

'I will try to come to you for Hanukkah so that I can be with
you when the baby is born. If Joseph is still with you, would you
send him for me?'

I understood. We were all to back away from Jerusalem before the fervour grew so great that it caused its own automatic reaction. The very next day Magdalene, Joseph, Rizpah and I rose early and set off to the South.

Four

Judah's choice was a piece of land completely isolated from any other settlement and so well hidden behind a vale of trees that we would never have found it without the map. As it was we wandered in the area for more than half a day, doubtful about whether we should push our way through what seemed to be an impenetrable screen of trees and bushes or whether we were in the wrong place completely. At last we found the way and, although Joseph said the first task would be to cut back the creepers which blocked the route, I wondered whether the privacy it gave us might come in useful some day. The land itself was astonishingly lush and fertile for that area and the reason soon became apparent. It had not one, but two springs of water which bubbled cheerfully out of the tall rocks at its Western edge. One was even a tiny waterfall with a clear pool at its base containing what looked like freshwater shrimps. 'Shame we can't eat them!' said Magdalene. 'Maybe there are fish too,' offered Joseph, hopefully.

The land had an old but sturdy two-roomed house placed solidly below the small cliffs. It must have been unoccupied for a year or more since its last owners left and we all wondered who they could have been. Those who had left must have prospered elsewhere and they had not wanted to return to the rural life when the last resident died. Whoever they were, they had been quite self-sufficient with even a couple of goats which were still there, although now nearly wild. If we could catch them they would be good milkers still, for they both had kids at foot. What was more, there were signs of both wheat and barley crops on the small but fertile southern pasture. When we had first pushed our way through the undergrowth we had been tired and apprehensive, particularly after the barrenness of the surrounding area. As one, we had sent up a prayer of gratitude to see such a perfect place with so much provided.

The goats were easier to catch than we anticipated. As soon as we had finished looking round the house and went out to explore the boundaries of this secret paradise, they bolted in through the open door of the house. They were obviously used to living comfortably inside and protested violently at being cornered and tethered outside instead.

That night we built a fire and made some flat-bread from grain we had brought from Jerusalem and ate it with green olives and cheese. Sitting around those flames and watching the sky above us darkening, I thought that was one of the best meals of my life. There was a new sense of freedom and a feeling of connection with Judah again. Perhaps women would be allowed to study at Qumran; perhaps not. Whatever happened, we were together and of one accord.

In the first days we explored our new surroundings and decided what we would have to buy or exchange in order to live comfortably. We had brought pots and pans, dried foods and material with us, all purchased hastily in Jerusalem with the money Judah had left me. There was little more we would need once we made the land work for us but, to familiarise ourselves with our new home, we all walked to the nearest settlement as soon as we were fully rested. It was a small farming community, about a third of a day's walk and obviously linked to the Essene village itself which came into sight if you walked for the same distance again, nearer to the shore of the great salt sea. I felt uneasy in the village for the people were curious, as was to be expected, and as time passed I was content to let the others visit and chat to the neighbours while I stayed at home thinking about my baby and painstakingly weaving cloth by hand. Joseph, Magdalene and Rizpah visited quite often and we came to be thought of as a small group of proselytes to the Essenes, so any strangeness of our ways was tolerated if not understood.

The main Essene settlement nestled in the harsh desert land on the edge of the sea. Its land was fertile, for channels had been cut to divert streams from the mountains to provide water both for drinking and for the Mikvahs. These man-made streams were covered over with openings here and there so that people could draw water for their everyday lives. As in Emmaus, there were no women at the settlement itself though there were families in surrounding places, learning what they could without being fully accepted. They lived all around – though none so far away as we did – but the one visit I made there did give me the comfort of knowing that there were like-minded people should we need them.

The four of us went together on our first visit and we women waited outside the settlement itself as Joseph went in to enquire about who was now its leader, whether anyone we knew resided there and what the rules and regulations were. He, like Yeshua and Judah, had visited it several times before but, as he said, times changed with each different leader.

He returned to us with a half-serious and half-wry expression and suggested that we started making our way back towards home. Once we were safely out of earshot of any of the little hamlets he gave a sudden snort of laughter.

'I don't think we'll be going there much,' he said, as we pressed him to know what was so funny. 'It isn't really that amusing but, of course, they don't know the full story.

'I told them I was from Emmaus and had left some years before to follow Yeshua. They didn't have any problem with him but they did know of some terrible story about a female she-devil who passed herself off as his wife and who destroyed the whole community once he had left.'

'Oh dear,' said Magdalene heavily, looking at me. My face must have been a picture for I was both outraged and exasperated. 'It's not worth it, Deborah,' said Joseph gently and I gave a great sigh. Then, like him, I began to grin.

'Take care! Take care!' I said to Rizpah who was perplexed at whatever was going on. I waved my hands in the air and made as if to chase her. 'Beware, beware! The devil-woman is here and she will eat you up for breakfast!'

'You?' said Rizpah, aghast. 'They're talking about you?'

'Oh, yes!' I said. 'That was me. The woman who destroyed a whole community. Great Heavens above! How can they be so stupid?'

We walked on with both Joseph and I recounting the story of how I had once taught women and children (and some men too) of those on the outskirts of the Emmaus community. Just like those at Qumran, we had had our own community and the men had gone into the settlement itself to learn. They could not become full members because they were not celibate but their learning was often shared with the women who wanted to know. Joseph Barsabbas, as leader of the whole community, had looked after us all, celibate or not.

'Perhaps I went too far. Perhaps I trod on a few too many feet,' I said. 'When Yeshua was there it was tolerated but when he left a few – just a few – of the celibates decided to stop me.'

'And that's when we met,' said Magdalene, slipping her arm through mine. 'This she-devil was delivered to my home in Jerusalem black and blue, covered in blood and very sorry for herself indeed. The only woman I've ever met to survive a stoning.'

'They stoned you!' Rizpah could not believe it.

'They stoned me,' I said. 'I wasn't even an adulteress! Still, it was a long time ago and it's nonsense to say it broke the community.'

'It had a big effect,' said Joseph. 'About half the outer settlement said they were going to leave. Perhaps they did; I don't know. The core of believers is certainly still there.'

We walked on, telling more of the story but there was one aspect that still confused Rizpah.

'I thought you were Judah's wife,' she said.

'Yes I was.'

'But they said you were Yeshua's wife.'

'Well, we lived together in the same house but I was never his wife.'

'You could have been,' said Rizpah. 'You're only his cousin. Why didn't you marry him? You were of the same mind.'

'Because he wasn't going to marry anyone,' I said and looked at Magdalene. She was the one who had loved Yeshua as a wife would have done. All the same, Rizpah's remarks made me feel uncomfortable.

All that summer and autumn, Joseph went down to the Essenes regularly. Sometimes Magdalene went with him, although she just visited the surrounding settlements. They learned little that was new to us and it seemed that none of the outer circle had any knowledge of the Tree of Life.

'I dropped a few hints but no one took me up on it,' said Magdalene. 'I think it's fair to let them know that there is some teaching available to them if they want it but I'm not going to push it down their throats.'

Joseph was treated courteously within Qumran itself but would come back with tales of the great severity of the way of life there.

'They live so harshly because they regard themselves as re-creating the Exodus from Egypt,' he explained to us. 'We used to think the same at Emmaus but not quite to that extent. These men believe Jerusalem to be so evil that it is the same as Egypt was in Moses' time. To purify themselves they have chosen to live as the Israelites of the Exodus did. They have cut themselves off from all possessions and their laws of cleanliness are even more extreme than those I have encountered at other settlements.'

I wondered out loud if he missed the Essene way of life but he laughed. 'It was right at the time to be one of them,' he said. 'But these are even harsher than they were in the old days. They are so involved with looking for perfection and the Anointed that they missed one when he was under their very noses. I don't think I need to go back to that way of life having seen what I saw and learnt what I learned with Yeshua.'

We had settled in very happily to our new home. Joseph, Magdalene and Rizpah did much of the work, tidying up and putting things to rights while I concentrated on the house or roamed afield to find delicious herbs and roots to complement our first, rather meagre, rations. Each night we lit tallow candles and talked and prayed and laughed and, on the Shabbat Eve, we performed the ceremony of light, wine, water and bread that unify the Four Worlds of creation.

Occasionally we received a visit from those neighbours who could find us and we grew quite friendly with a few of the Essene followers nearby but we found the lack of spiritual kindness and joy in their lives depressing. Even the acolytes of the Qumran settlement had a kind of ascetic bent and they were far 'holier' than we. They, in turn, found us strange and unpredictable folk, rather prone to over-eating and merriment and, as time passed, they mostly left us to ourselves.

The evenings when the four of us were together were like an oasis in themselves and, in my mind's eye, I can still see our little group haloed in the light of the candles and the fire, talking, discussing, arguing and laughing. We each retold our life-story from the very beginning and caught up, in detail, with what we had done in Yeshua's last days while we had been apart. At last I could tell them the story of Judah's and my wedding in Cana and the miracle of the wine which never ceased to flow. I told, too, of Miriam's incredible story of Gabriel's visit; of Yeshua's birth and the portents around it. Sometimes, as I spoke, Rizpah made notes on tree bark. She said it helped her to learn and understand and perhaps, one day, it would help others too. 'Imagine,' she said. 'Long after we are dead others might come across these notes and it might encourage them to search for the Teaching as well. That is, if it does not spread the whole world over before we die.' We laughed at her enthusiasm, at the thought that all the world might come to believe in what we had been taught. 'But it's not so silly really,' said Magdalene. 'All things are possible with God. Look at what is happening in Jerusalem. It's a great centre of trade and for all we know the knowledge might spread. We can only do our bit.' From then on she too made notes on some papyrus she bought from the village.

Our stories went on all that year. One of the most touching was Joseph's account of his role in the days after Yeshua's death. He had succeeded in persuading the authorities to let Yeshua's body down from the cross before the Sabbath began so that it could be tended to and placed in a cave Joseph had managed to rent for that purpose. 'Again, it was taken care of for me, as all these necessary things are,' he said. 'It had only just occurred to me that we needed a special place to lay our beloved teacher when I met up with some people who had owned a space for many years. I bespoke it for a month for a very small price and they had no objections.

'For a month!' We were amazed and spoke as one. 'Did you know he would rise as he did?'

'No,' said Joseph. 'I didn't know. I just thought it was the right thing to do. Had his body remained there I would have made other arrangements later but, as you know, it did not. What happened to it in the end is irrelevant really for we know that he himself has risen and whether the Lord chose to take his physical body up into the Heavens with him or disperse it here on Earth so none could defile it, I do not know. All I do know is that the Laws of the Heavens are stronger and more flexible than the Laws of the Earth and what I did turned out to be the right thing.'

As he spoke I was aware, yet again, what a man we had as a friend. So loyal and true to God's word, master of himself and servant of Yeshua in one. As I thought those things, the air around me seemed to shiver and I saw a light shining down on Joseph's face. In that face I could see revelation, wisdom, kindness, discipline and beauty and, with a shock that ran through me like liquid fire, I found myself wondering if it were Joseph who were the new Anointed. Was he one who would hold the mantle of light for the Lord? Not James, but Joseph? The one the disciples had turned down in their blindness, choosing instead an untried youth. If so, oh the irony of it! No one had realised, including myself.

Joseph had finished his account and, in the companionable silence while the others reflected, he looked up and met my gaze. Yes, it was there, that unmistakable look in his eyes of the finger of God. I had to put my hand to my mouth to stop myself from crying out. Almost imperceptibly he shook his head, as if to tell me not to speak. Between us there passed such a look of friendship and understanding as would be enough for a whole lifetime. I knew that Joseph's job would be nothing like Yeshua's. He was not to be in the public eye or to reveal to the masses the mantle he carried. He was to work quietly behind the scenes, unrecognised, as he helped Yeshua's word to spread.

That was the most important teaching of the Tradition that Yeshua had taught – that there is always an Anointed alive in the world; someone closer to the Holy One than all others; someone to carry the light. Some become known, others do not. At the end of days we will all be one with God and the great Anointed, Adam Kadmon himself, will come. Until then, to seek for one man or woman to fulfil the Law for all eternity is to misunderstand the whole.

A hundred questions seemed to form in my head and when I looked up again, Joseph was smiling at me. If there was anything I needed to know, I would be told. For the moment, I was to be silent.

The story of that night had brought up one more matter for me which I found hard to lay to rest and one that I did need to confide to the others, no matter how hard it might be.

Both Rizpah and I had heard Philip and Stephen say that Judah had died, here, on this land. Where then was his body? Had it been buried or was it lost somewhere around us? I stammered when I first mentioned it for no one likes the idea of a dead body lying on their land, no matter how dear the person might have been.

The others were silent when I had finished and it was Magdalene who spoke first. 'If he is here, then we must find him,' she said. 'Not Deborah – that would be too hard. Not Rizpah, she is too young.' She looked at Joseph. 'It is up to you and me.'

They searched every possible place, high and low. I could not work out whether I wanted them to find him or not but, each time one of them returned to the house, my heart was in my mouth.

At last, Joseph found what he thought might be a grave. It was outside the boundaries of the land itself and it was just a patch of earth where it was obvious that the growth was new. What proved it to us was that someone had tied together two pieces of wood in the form of the cross of crucifixion and placed it in the ground.

Who could it have been? Maybe we would never know.

We spent that evening at the site of Judah's grave, saying kaddish and telling stories of his life. All four of us wept and it felt at last as though the story were complete. At that point I had still not told Joseph and Rizpah of my child – but I told Judah.

The storytelling in the evenings continued. After Joseph's, we heard Magdalene's account of Yeshua's life and death. Some of this I had heard before but it was wonderful to hear again of her love

for him and his for her. She told us how, after his death, she found
the grave laid wide open with someone there – she still did not
know who – telling her that Yeshua was gone. And then, later,
seeing someone she took for the gardener until he spoke her name.

'I've often wondered if I was just blinded by stupidity and grief,'
she said. 'I wasted so much time when I could have been talking
to him, knowing who he was. Such silly things haunt you afterwards when you try to remember.'

Then Rizpah told of how she heard of Yeshua's crucifixion the
day after he came to her in the well. 'Even if the dream were not
enough, I knew as soon as I heard the news that I must leave,' she
said. 'It was as though I had no choice. It was not a thought but
a compulsion. Even if I had not been married and divorced I
would have had to have left then, so all that happened helped me
to come to you, though it did not seem so at the time!

'What was so strange was how everything went so well for me
when I did leave,' she continued and, at that point, we all smiled
for we knew very well how the path would be smoothed by Grace
if a momentous decision had been taken. For Rizpah the blessings
did not stop when she arrived in Jerusalem for, within a day, she
had fallen in with Joseph and Magdalene, meeting them as if by
chance in the street.

'And that was our cue to come and find you, Deborah,' said
Joseph. 'We had planned, as you know, to stay there but there was
so much confusion – anger as well as joy – that it felt better to leave.'

On the Sabbath days and in the evenings when we had no stories to tell, each of us in turn taught Rizpah and each other.
Going over everything we had understood from Yeshua clarified so
many things in our minds and there were many lively discussions
on our different understanding on many points. What I had forgotten, Magdalene recalled; what we could not remember, Joseph
knew and understood. His extra knowledge, from years of study,
filled in many gaps and, in the secrecy of our little home, we drew
out the lightning flash of creation, the paths of the Tree of Life,
just as so many people had done for centuries before us, and studied it in depth. That one diagram supplied the principles on
which all Jewish Law and Yeshua's teaching were based and, as we
worked with it, the drawing carved into the floor began to take on

a life of its own. None of us would walk on it and we treated it as though it were an altar. We were not making a graven image of it nor worshipping it, we were using it as a tool to understand the nature of both God and man. It, in itself, meant nothing; it was what the knowledge within it taught us that we respected.

The house too was sanctified by its presence and we felt protected from all harm. In fact we were so happy that both Joseph and Magdalene forgot to return to Jerusalem at all that summer even though they had fully intended to visit.

Dear Joseph had been appalled when he realised that I was pregnant. Rizpah, of course, was delighted, only seeing the romance of a child coming to replace a much-loved husband. She remembered Judah with fondness from his time of teaching her and Chloe, her sister, in Tiberias. Although he had been a demanding teacher and Chloe had tried his patience sorely, Rizpah had responded to him and made him smile with her questions and enthusiasm.

I had worried whether I should tell them both that this might not be Judah's baby but where that would have reassured Joseph, who quite saw the gravity of the situation if the child were Judah's, it would have upset Rizpah who did not need to know.

There was another added complication in that I worried that my fertility must give Magdalene pain. She, a natural mother, had had no child and I, the spiky, independent one who had never craved offspring, was to be the one to give birth.

When I talked to her about that she laughed. 'Well, it is the unexpected we are always to expect,' she said. 'That you are pregnant at all is a miracle; it should not be possible with your history. Maybe it is Yeshua's last gift to you? At least you were married when you conceived – whether or not Judah is the father. If I were pregnant, I would have no excuses. There would be no covering story should the worst be true and the child is Roman. Anyway, I expect you will be a dreadful mother. You are far too independent and you have very little patience. I shall have at least as much of this baby as you, so I can have all the joys of motherhood without the physical pain or problems. I shall enjoy that!'

She was right that I was not a natural mother. I had found the sickness and lethargy upsetting and, once that had abated, my growing size irritated me. After the first delight at the little jerks

inside me, signifying life, I grew heartily to dislike being interrupted so regularly. I sometimes had imaginary conversations
with the soul, telling it to get its body to behave and it felt as
though it was laughing at me, merrily. 'You wait,' I told it. 'You're
going to be feeling a lot more trapped than I am once you are
born. At least I can leave you on the ground and walk away. You
won't be able to move freely for years!'

At night I was not so complacent. I went through what I am
sure are all the usual fears of death in childbirth both for myself
and the baby. I worried too about whether I would be able to see
in its face who the father was and, if it were one of the soldiers,
whether that would affect my love for the child. I worried about
how to explain to it who its father was. It is one thing to have had
a vision and a celestial knowledge of your child, it is another to
keep on remembering that all is well in the upper Heavens and all
is happening just as it should. On Earth, life can seem very frightening. I would comfort myself with the idea that whoever this
soul was, it was someone I already loved and had known before I
was formed in this body. I would recognise it as soon as the baby
was born; I was certain of that.

As the days and weeks wore on and summer swelled into
autumn, I became more and more aware of the soul's own person-
ality. Occasionally I felt it watching me as I searched for herbs or
roots or sat, meditating, in the sunshine. Often I felt its presence
during the evenings when we prayed or talked but at other times I
knew it was not there. Why should it be? It was preparing for its
new life and, although the development of the temple that would
contain it might be of interest, it knew all was well and the everyday growth of the foetus was not its primary concern. At times
when it tried out its new body I could sense mixed feelings of
delight at what was happening and frustration at the limitations it
would have to take on board by coming back into the World. No
wonder babies would cry and become furious so easily!

Magdalene and I spent hours trying to work out how far this
pregnancy had advanced in order to work out who the father
might be. My irregular cycle was no help for I could go for
months without a sign of blood. We both knew the baby was
more likely to be a result of my night in the jail, for surely Judah's

child would have been more developed than this, but neither of us wanted to face that fact.

'After all, you have been through much unhappiness,' said Magdalene. 'That can affect a baby's growth – slow it down, stop it developing. It is possible that Judah is the father, Deborah. I think it can only help you to believe that.'

It comforted me too to think that, even if Judah were not the one, it could be Vintillius, the youngest of the men, the one who had looked at me in Pilate's courtroom and who had given me a cloak and some hot ale the day after the assault as a kind of penance for what he regretted doing.

When I fretted too much I thought of Gabriel's visit and tried to remember that it was the soul's presence which counted, not who its father might be. No one would be its Earthly father and that was the only truth that really counted. I would have to do all I could for my child without the help of a husband.

More than anyone, I talked to Judah as I sat by his grave and wove braids of flowers and fern to decorate both our home and this tiny plot of land.

Joseph left to fetch Imma as soon as the winter season began. He was planning to travel first to Jerusalem and then, if she was not there, he would still have enough time to find her in Galilee. We three women missed him and, although we continued life as it had been, we looked forward to his return as much as I did to Imma's arrival.

She came just in time. The first pangs of labour had begun and I was beginning to be afraid. I was not ready to stop being just Deborah; I was not ready to be a mother. I was too old to be a mother; far too old. I could never manage. I could not give birth! Imma's presence was like a salve on a wound. It was not that I did not trust Magdalene but my own mother's capable hands and sensible words were doubly calming. As was her example. She had raised four of us and still been her own self. I felt soothed and comforted.

Then the pain began in earnest.

They told me afterwards that they thought they had lost me time and time again over the four days before my child was born. I, too, thought I would die, not from the pulsing, desperate agony but from the delirium which spun me back through my life to my own first years and my parents' death. I remembered the first time I heard of a Zealot being crucified and how I had stuck a stone into my hand to try and imagine the pain. Now I was experiencing it in every sinew of my body and my comfortable imaginings of what that man, any man, including my brother, would have felt were ripped apart with the unimaginable truth. At times I could hear ghostly voices in the background and the sound of someone screaming as though they were being tortured below. I swam upwards towards the light and begged to be allowed through, to safety, to somewhere I could rest and be released from the rest of my life. I begged and pleaded not to be returned to the frantic, helpless body below. 'Please,' I said. 'Please. I have done all I can. I can do no more.'

'One more try,' said an angel who looked like Magdalene. 'A life for a life. It has been agreed. Just once more.' I screamed and screamed with fury and pain and my son was born.

He was fed on diluted goat's milk and cuddled and nursed by my mother and by Magdalene and Rizpah. I did not recover consciousness for some time and, for more than a week, fever made me incapable even of looking at him clearly. My breasts remained empty of milk.

They asked me for a name but in my semi-conscious haze no coherent thought could run through my head. I had thought I wanted it to be Boaz for a boy and Ruth for a girl but neither would come to mind once the child was born.

Joseph circumcised him on the eighth day calling him Abraham, after the father of Israel, for he had to have a Hebrew name. Abraham was the name always given to a man who converted to Judaism but its appropriateness was not clear to me until the baby was nearly two weeks old and I was able to take him into my arms and look into his eyes myself.

It was a blue-eyed stranger who looked back.

During the long weeks of my slow recovery, Imma and I finally had the time together that we had wanted for so long. At first it was all mother and baby information and stern warnings of what I must and must not do. Firstly Imma told me bluntly that there could and must be no more children; the damage to me had been too serious. I told her with some irony that I had no plans whatsoever for another but she took that with her usual steadfastness. 'You never know,' she said. 'There is plenty of life in you yet. I've seen many women die from less than you suffered so I suspect the Lord has other jobs for you.'

As I grew stronger, Imma told me stories of Yeshua's first months and I listened entranced as she rocked my baby in her arms and wove a trail of magic as she spoke. I heard how all three had travelled to Egypt and lived there and how they had returned to Nazara. I heard, in full, about the astrologers – Zoroastrian priests – who had visited them and told her of Yeshua's destiny.

In return I told her of Gabriel's visit and coming of the soul of this baby. Now I could believe her own story far more easily, for I saw how all things were possible with God. Imma cautiously suggested that my baby's birth was similar to Yeshua's, for she knew from the dates how unlikely Judah was to have been the father, but I could not let her live with that illusion. It was time to tell her of the soldiers in the jail and, by then, it was far enough away for me to be able to talk of it without emotion. Imma was still angry for me and with me for not telling her and the others before. Reluctantly she agreed to keep the secret although she thought I would be safer if the world knew the truth. The baby at least would not be threatened by any fervent and uneducated follower of the disciples. I reminded her that although it had been the Sanhedrin who wanted to get rid of Yeshua, it was the Romans who had condemned him. The child might be safe but I would not be if I said he had a Roman father. What if I was thought to be a Roman sympathiser or collaborator, a loose woman who would sleep with the enemy? No, it was too risky, I said. I had tried being stoned once and that was enough for anyone!

Eight weeks after a boy baby's birth it was the custom to present him to the Lord in the Temple. At the same time the mother was blessed and cleansed by water and spirit so she could return to the life of a wife – normally to conceive again very swiftly.

Of course I would have preferred Yeshua to baptise and bless the both of us but I was content for my son to be taken to the Temple. It was his right as a Jew and he should not be denied that.

For the others, too, it would be a welcome chance to catch up with the news in Jerusalem. They had been such a support to me that I was glad to be able to offer a reason for the journey.

We agreed that all should be well as long as I stayed in a lodging house outside the city, with the exception of the Temple visit, and kept myself to myself. After all, we did not know that the hatred against Judah had escalated. Magdalene argued that they might have seen sense and the disciples might have decided that we were welcome again. I smiled but I had my doubts.

Two days before we left I took my son to Judah's grave to show him to the man I hoped to be his father. Then I carried the child down to the stream and baptised him myself. His Hebrew name did not appeal to me but none of the names I thought of in its stead seemed at all suitable for this enigmatic little boy. In the end, I asked the Lord to name him in His own time, invoking the name of God and the Four Worlds that Yeshua had taught me. I asked that the child's life be blessed and that he should be protected and guided. I did not ask that I should love him because he had more than enough mothers to dote on him. He was a jolly, trouble-free baby but he was far happier with Magdalene, Rizpah or Imma than he was with me and would hold out his arms to them, gurgling with delight. With me, he was still and pensive but I did not mind that. All my life I had held secrets, so the fact that we did not love each other as people would have expected us to was no harder than any of the others. Perhaps love would come of its own accord later when he was able to communicate with me but, for now, like my breasts, my heart was strangely empty when I looked at him. Sometimes I could still catch his soul with my mind and there was friendship and a recognition of like minds but the baby itself meant nothing. I did not even connect him with the stabbing soreness inside me or the bleeding which kept me so weak.

The only person I tried to say something about this to was Imma but she forestalled me. 'You did not have time to bond with him at his birth,' she said. 'It can take months. Don't worry. Just act as though it is true and it will become so.'

Even though we had planned to be gone from our peaceful home for less than a month, it was strangely sad to pack up and leave the secret area which had sheltered us so carefully. I walked around its boundaries before we left, cherishing every tree and flower as though there was some need to fix them in my memory.

We let the goats roam free as we left, knowing they would stay in the general area from habit – and probably move back into the house the moment we were gone! – and began the weary journey back to Jerusalem. I sat cautiously and painfully on the little donkey, my son wrapped inside my cloak and, as we left my land behind us, I felt a sudden tug of knowledge. I was not coming back here for a very, very long time.

I stopped the donkey and told the others what I felt. Imma chided me gently saying that I was still prone to fancies after childbirth and should not assume that all I felt was true. I looked at her, surprised, as she did not often contradict others, and saw a warning in her eyes. I did not understand it but I obeyed. Later on the journey Magdalene spoke to me quietly.

'I agree with you,' she said. 'I won't be going back again either.'

That was not what I had said.

We arrived in Jerusalem on a fine, early spring evening and found ourselves a small lodging house outside the city. Joseph went ahead to find out what news there was and was gone so long that we were asleep in bed before he returned. The story he had to tell us in the morning was upsetting. As far as he could tell no one we knew was in Jerusalem. The disciples and most of their true followers had left after a series of incidents of stoning and riots. No one was dead, from what Joseph could work out, but he could not be entirely sure. Peter and John had been arrested again and flogged and, worst of all, the majority of people who had been so enthusiastic about the new world had now turned their backs on it. The impulse had died and everyday life had reclaimed their attention. Confused and disheartened, even if only temporarily, the disciples had dispersed to teach elsewhere.

What we had not suspected, and which shook us to our very core, was that Saul of Tarsus was leading an authorised campaign against Yeshua's followers and having anyone who spoke in his name arrested and beaten. Rizpah squirmed when she heard this and, upset as we were, we felt compassion for her.

'We must all be very careful,' said Joseph. 'And not only because of Saul. There is a general air of unrest in the city. Herod

Antipas is in residence and there has been some more trouble just recently – hotheads throwing stones, you know the kind of thing. It could die down easily enough, or it could get out of hand.'

Later that morning we took the baby to the Temple together with a lamb for sacrifice. I still had to grit my teeth over that but I knew it was my son's right to have a formal entry into his faith; he could make his own decisions later. I was glad to have Joseph with me taking the place of a husband for, without him, there would have been no one to carry the boy through into the Court of Israel for the rites to be completed. I also thought that no child could be more blessed than to be presented to the Holy One by such a good and honest man.

The riot broke out after we left the Temple. Imma, Rizpah and Joseph had gone in one direction to try and find someone who could escort Imma back to Galilee and Magdalene and I went to do some shopping. We were buying a copper-bottomed pot from a Syrian merchant when a great noise erupted from around the corner. Before we could catch our breath or move, a group of about 50 young men came racing down the street. They were hotly pursued by Roman soldiers who caught up with them at the edge of the market square where we stood. Suddenly, all was pandemonium with screams and shouts and men fighting with swords and sticks, hitting out at anything or anyone who might be in the way.

'Stand still,' I hissed. Magdalene froze and we both prayed under our breath.

It would have worked. They didn't see us. All was chaos around us but as long as we withdrew our presence, we would be safe. But you cannot tell a baby that. He had been asleep in my arms but he woke and began making questing noises as he heard the cries of pain and the clashing of metal. If the attack had only been by foot soldiers we might still have been safe but five soldiers on horseback came racing down the street. They were passing us to chase the fleeing Jews but one horse, going too fast, slipped on the cobbled street and almost fell. The presence of a huge beast, only feet away with hooves flailing, was too much. Magdalene and I flinched with fear and the baby burst into screams of protest. The horseman saw us as his mount regained its balance. He turned and struck out just as Magdalene threw herself in front of me. She took the full force of his sword and fell like a stone.

I stood mesmerised, clutching my son to my breast, my mouth open and a sigh of terror in my throat. The man's horse reared so that he missed me as he cut backwards with the same stroke, the sword coming so close that it rent my veil and sent some hair flying, golden-red into the air. I tried to move back but the city wall stopped me. No escape, no defence, no chance.

'Halt,' said a voice, loud and authoritative. The solder ignored it. Just as he thrust for me again, his body tensed and jerked and I saw a second rider strike him hard with the flat of his sword. Slowly the man toppled from his horse's back, falling on top of us. The baby and I were pinned against the wall, gasping for breath. The soldier's unconscious body cushioned us against the horse's panicked kicks but I could only just protect my son from the weight. I tried to curl into a protective ball around him but there was so little that I could do. This must be the end.

A small, rational thought slipped into my mind. 'No. Not yet. It is not over yet. We are saved. I know we are saved,' and slowly, above us, I became aware of a group of Roman soldiers shouting at each other. The horse was scrabbling up onto its feet and, as it moved away, one man seemed to be standing in front of us, protecting us from the actions of the others. I could not hear what he said and I did not care for, whatever he was doing, the violence seemed to have stopped and I could start to push my way out from the weight above me. Desperately I crawled, behind the man and along the cobbled stones to where Magdalene lay, her body broken in pieces, but her face serene and her eyes wide open. They were bright and they could still see. Holding my baby in one arm and choking with fear and shock, I reached out for her.

'Magdalene,' I said, still gasping for air of my own. 'Oh my love, my friend.'

She turned her head to me and smiled and, in what should have been an agonising mess of blood and pain, I knew she was happier than she had ever been. Suddenly Yeshua's words came back to me.

'Yeshua told me,' I said. 'You will be with him very soon.'

'I already am,' she whispered with the echo of a smile. 'Can't you see him? It is all done. All is paid. A life for a life. It was agreed. He has come to fetch me and I am free.'

She said one more word before she died, moving her hand clumsily to touch my son's face. 'Luke' she said, so naming one who would make her immortal.

Five

Time does strange things in moments of crisis. It seemed as though I had been holding Magdalene's body forever when the soldier bent over me and spoke. Mercifully all the noise and chaos seemed to have stopped and I could hear what he was saying.

'Can you get up?' he asked in Koine. 'You are quite safe. I am so sorry about your friend, I really am sorry. Let me help you.'

As I looked up at him through a haze of shock and disbelief, it registered somewhere within that I knew him and, on another level, that he was a soldier of rank.

'I don't want to get up,' I said stupidly. 'I want to stay with her.'

'There is nothing you can do,' he said. 'Believe me. It would be best if you came with me. There is still trouble a few streets away. Anything could happen. Please come with me.'

'Why? Why should I? Are you arresting me?'

'No,' he said. 'No, I'm trying to help. I want you and the baby to be safe.'

'Why?'

He shook his head. 'Later. Just come with me now, please. Tertius!' he barked, so suddenly that I winced. 'Give the horses to Lucius and carry that woman to my quarters. The woman lying here. Now!'

Another soldier hurried up and lifted Magdalene's body carefully. I tried to clamber up, holding Luke in my arms, but the effort was too much for me. The man stopped me with a gesture.

'Put the child down,' he said. 'I will help you up and carry him for you.' I nodded and, still dazed and completely incapable of rational thought, allowed him to take my hand and lift me. Then I watched this half-remembered stranger bend over and pick up my son, noticing that he held the child with the greatest of care – and that he seemed to be looking for something in Luke's face.

'He doesn't look like me,' I said stupidly as I stood, shakily, on feet which felt as though they did not belong to me. As I tried to walk it was too much and I lost my footing on the cobbled street.

The soldier caught me one-handed and, placing Luke back in my arms, he lifted us both, just as the other had lifted Magdalene. He carried me down the street where cowed and frightened people halted in their efforts to clear up, watching the strange and incomprehensible sight of soldiers carrying women they had been attacking only minutes before. My control lost, I clung onto my baby and to this unexpected pillar of strength, sobbing into the soldier's neck, for Magdalene, for everything, and because I was so scared.

We were left in the care of servants at what I took to be the soldier's quarters, one of a cluster of individual dwellings linked by a courtyard with a fountain and marble walls. The soldier placed me in a chair by the entrance and Magdalene's body was laid in a side room.

'My name is Apollonius,' he said. 'This is where I live. I have work to do and I will return this evening. My staff are finding women to tend you. You will be well looked after and you may send for anyone you need – the lady's family or your own. You will have arrangements to make. All I ask is that you do not leave here – you or the child.'

'If I try to leave will I be allowed to?'

He sighed. 'I need to talk to you and it will be harder to do that if I do not keep you here now. I do have the power to make you stay but I don't want to use it. Please stay.'

'I have little family,' I said. 'Magdalene has none but myself and three other friends. I need to let those three know we are safe.' I began to cry again. We were all safe, even Magdalene. I just did not want my safety to have meant her death. The officer stood looking helpless but fierce nonetheless, waiting for me to make my decision.

'I will stay,' I said. 'I owe you my life and my son's, so I promise I will stay. Only do not set a guard on me. I have enough to bear.'

He bowed, turned and left.

Servants took care of us while Imma, Joseph and Rizpah were sent for. I still did not want to believe that Magdalene was dead but it was so obvious from looking at the body laid out on the white covers that all the vitality and strength of life were gone. I wondered how anyone could doubt another dimension after looking at the difference between a living and a dead body. What was there was beautiful but it was not Magdalene. Even so, I touched her forehead and thanked her for her gift of my life. It seemed so inadequate just to say those simple words but there was nothing more I could do. Her soul had left for the Heavens with Yeshua at the moment she had died and she would probably not even hear me. Perhaps she was the lucky one, not I.

I was so tired and shocked that it was easy to allow the servants to take care of Luke and to prepare a bath for me too. They asked me his name and I spoke it as though he had never been anything other than Luke. The name fitted so well.

It was better to do something than just to sit, half-paralysed with shock and wait with my body and clothes splattered with blood and dirt. I was not used to being attended in the bath but I felt so numb that it did not matter that strange women saw me naked. It was not so very different from preparations for the Mikvah even if no one here believed in the one God. Part of me noticed the sweet scents and oils which were added to the water to calm and caress me and part of me cried as the water ran pink as the women rinsed Magdalene's blood from my hair. The rest of me acted with an unconscious dignity, accepting the situation, even allowing them to robe me in a Roman stola and to dress my hair when I was dry. Politely, they did not ask me any questions about what had happened to me or to Magdalene, although they were more than willing to talk about who they were and about the man who had rescued me. Listening to them was a welcome distraction although it was an effort to concentrate on what they were saying. None of them knew the strange soldier well but they told me that his name was Apollonius Sextus and that he was a Primus Pilus, the highest honour available to a centurion. It was a position which could be held for only one year and Apollonius's tour of duty was just over. There was gossip that he was leaving the army but that was almost unheard-of for a centurion – they usually died in service. They looked at me, wondering how this strange, silent Jewish woman and her dead friend fitted into this unconventional pattern. I said nothing for I had no more knowledge than they.

I was offered fruit and cheese and a poppy-seed medicine for relaxation but I declined. I was too anxious to eat and I knew I needed my wits about me. Luke, however, did need feeding but I did not even have to tell anyone that I could not suckle him myself for no one here expected me to. A woman with milk in her breasts appeared from nowhere and was ready to feed my son as soon as I approved her. That, too, seemed strange but I did not have the energy to comment. This was obviously how it was done in a Roman home and I was glad that, for once in his short life, Luke had the chance to be suckled as he ought to be. Abraham would be his second name, Luke ben Abraham; the father of all Israel for the father he did not have.

Imma, Rizpah and Joseph had still not come by late afternoon and I was growing more and more upset. Were they all right? Who knew how widespread the riot had been? – it could have been two streets or twenty. And who knew the cause? Was it a reaction against the Messianic Jews or a completely separate incident?

One thing I knew; Magdalene's body must be buried, and swiftly, with the appropriate prayers and rites. If Joseph could not come, then who was there to carry out such a service? I would if it were necessary but, not only was it unheard of for a woman to do such a thing, I felt too weak and tearful to do it well. Magdalene herself might be safe in Beriah, the World of spirit, but her body deserved respect.

They came together, my Roman saviour, my mother and my friends, just as dusk was falling.

The soldier waited until we four had embraced and I had taken Imma, Joseph and Rizpah to see our sister, lying so regally in the beautiful marble room, her hair now washed and arranged ornately and her body attired in white. I was touched that the servants had cared for her body as lovingly as they had nurtured me. Joseph asked Apollonius's permission to organise her burial and left, shaking his head in sorrow. Imma, too, was silent but Rizpah's grief was more vocal and, as we comforted her, Apollonius walked up and down the courtyard looking uncomfortable. I noticed that he had a slight limp, almost as though his hip were twisted the way mine once had been.

Searching for memory, I watched him curiously. Then, like a sigh, a picture slid into my mind. I saw the soldier and myself, on horseback, riding back to Jerusalem to see Pilate. This was the man who fetched me back from the road to Qumran. On that day he had spoken hardly a word to me; it was his men who had killed my friend but now he was acting as the kindest of comrades. Since living and working with Yeshua I did not believe in coincidences; I believed in miracles. What this one was for, I did not yet know.

'This house is yours for the night,' was all Apollonius had said to the four of us together and I pondered his kindness as we managed to persuade Rizpah to lie down, gave her the sleeping baby to hold for comfort and encouraged her to drink some hot, sweetened cow's milk with a little of the calming poppy-seed mixture. Shocked and upset though she was, it helped her fall asleep quite quickly with Luke resting peacefully in her arms with the innocence of the very young.

The next task was to make our own preparations for Magdalene's burial. By the time Imma and I returned to her someone had sprinkled dried rose petals, red and pink, all around the still form. I wanted to say kaddish for her myself, as I had for Judah, as my way of blessing her spirit and wishing her peace and happiness in the higher Worlds. Imma listened as I recited the age-old prayer of joy and praise. Some would think it a strange hymn to death but its intent, perhaps, is to show that death is not an evil thing but part of God's creation.

Then I told Imma what Yeshua had told me in the Temple; that he would come to fetch her soon. And I repeated Magdalene's words as she died.

'What other epitaph could do as well?' asked Imma, wiping her eyes as I finished my story. 'She knew she was leaving us; she told me after Luke was born.'

'Was she ill?'

'Oh no!' Imma smiled at me. 'She was never healthier. She had a longing, though, a wish to go home. It crept up on her while you were at En Gedi. She said she worried about it a little, wondering if it were a denial of life or part of the grieving for Yeshua. But it was everlasting life that she was feeling drawn to. She had a feeling that once your baby was born, she had done all she needed to do. You know she wanted nothing more than to be with Yeshua.' Imma sighed. 'She loved him as much as we did.'

'More perhaps,' I said, my head swimming with this news. Imma smiled. 'As a wife would have done, you mean? Perhaps so, in a way, but she had a greater need to learn how to love a man without the physical side and it was that blessing she was the most grateful for.'

'I wish she had told me.' I was having to fight with the feeling that my best friend had chosen not to confide in me. I felt I had let her down.

'You had enough to deal with,' said Imma. 'She loved you very much and she told me all about how she came to join you and how grateful she was that you asked her to come when she had nursed you after the stoning. She told me that you had argued and quarrelled without stopping for seven days and, at the end of it, she knew that she must come with you to meet this man you spoke of with such love. Without you, she might never have found her salvation. She gave me this, to keep for her and to give to you when the time was right. She said you would know what to do with it.' From her cloak, Imma drew a small, rolled parchment criss-crossed with tiny writing. I recognised it – it was Magdalene's story written down so painstakingly during the summer months.

'She wanted her memories recorded because it is so easy to remember wrongly. You can keep it in Yeshua's chest perhaps?' said Imma, holding out the precious manuscript.

I took the testament, silently and reverently. Then, together, we wrapped Magdalene's body in the white shroud laid by for us by the servants. As we finished I drew the lightning flash of the Tree of Life over her and, as I did so, I felt such a rush of joy and completion shining down on me that I could not doubt that her calling home had been perfection. The tears I shed were more in recognition of her happiness than for my loss or for the manner of her dying.

At last Joseph and the other nine men he had found to say the traditional prayers for her burial returned to take her body and complete the rites. Before they started he asked me if I had any money left from the silver coins Judah had left me. I did and I handed it to him without question. Somehow I knew what he was going to buy. This time he would purchase, in full, the cave where Yeshua's body had laid so that his dearest of disciples could lie forever where her Salvation had risen from the dead.

In the group of men waiting to begin the funeral service I saw Nathaniel, Andrew and Philip but not one of them acknowledged me. That no longer concerned me; I did not need their approval or their understanding.

As they left Imma went too. 'I would like to be with her until the very end,' she said. 'You have business to complete here, Deborah, and you must stay with your children.' One of the wonderful things about Imma was her way of accepting every situation. She regarded Rizpah as my daughter without question and she had no fear of leaving me in the home of a Roman man. 'The Lord will protect you,' she would say, in any situation where there might be any doubt, and her total belief that He would do so inspired confidence even if previously there had been none.

Apollonius was waiting with a meal and, although I was so tired, I knew that I should eat. There was obviously something that he had to say to me and I would need strength to concentrate. I said a prayer for courage as we lay on couches, as the Romans and the wealthier Jews always did, and were served hot meats, fish and pastries, the like of which I had never seen nor tasted before.

In the silence, as the servants poured wine the colour of rubies and made sure we had all we needed, I looked at this intriguing man. He was not young, perhaps ten years older than I, with a tanned skin and dark hair turning to silver. His eyes were a dark grey and his face, in repose, looked stern and forbidding. When he smiled he was transformed but you could see that he had not had many occasions to smile.

He dismissed the servants and, once we were alone, he offered me food and took some himself. I ate, just able to appreciate the unaccustomed explosion of tastes in my mouth but tired and nervous enough to find it hard to swallow. It took him some time to speak.

'I knew it was you when your veil fell back and I saw your hair,' he said.

I waited.

'Do you remember me?' he asked. I nodded.

'Did you see me in the courtroom? I was there.' I shook my head.

'I am Vintillius's father,' he said.

Heat flooded through me as I remembered the boy who give me ale to drink and wrapped me in a cloak. 'If you need help, my father is a centurion in Bethlehem,' he had said, so long ago. It seemed so very long ago.

'I must keep my wits about me,' I thought, and, 'How hard for him to have to fetch me back to testify against his son.'

I voiced the second thought. He shrugged. 'It was my duty.'

There was silence. Apollonius sighed. 'No, it was more than that,' he said. 'I knew your brother.'

'Yeshua?'

'The healer, yes.'

'Where?'

'In Kfar-Nahum. I was billeted there for some months. I like the place. I got on with most of the people there and I had heard of your brother and the amazing things he could do.

'Vintillius was with me there. He had fallen ill of a fever. We had done all we could but he was dying. I went to your brother to ask him for help.'

I knew this story from Cephas and John but I shook my head in amazement at how our different lives had woven themselves together.

'I heard about this,' I said. 'You told Yeshua that he did not have to come himself but just to give the order and your son would recover. Yeshua said he had not come across such faith in all of Galilee.'

Apollonius smiled. 'I don't know about that,' he said. 'It just seemed to me that if your brother was as amazing as they said he was, the powers of life and death would obey him, just as my soldiers obeyed me. If you Jews are right and people are made in the image of one Creator then the Heavens must be ordered in a similar way as the Earth.'

'But why come and fetch me after Yeshua died?' I asked. 'You could have sent anyone.'

'I was going to ask you to be merciful,' said Apollonius. 'I thought you might have the same powers as your brother. He had already saved my son once and I wanted to ask you to do the same. You have something, I don't know what, but something because when I saw you, I knew I didn't have to ask.' He stopped and turned his head away for a moment. Tactfully I averted my gaze. We ate in silence until he was ready to speak again.

'There was more,' he said. 'You see, when I saw you I thought that he deserved to die anyway, whether or not you had mercy. He had received an incredible blessing – he was given his life back – and yet he had done this to the sister of the man who had saved him. I have seen what can be done to a woman...' He stopped, searching for words. 'Even if you had not been his sister... you are not the kind who is usually...' He stopped again. Then went on. 'There are some... I don't know how to say it... sometimes you can understand it. But not with a woman like you.'

We were silent. Servants brought in another course; spiced parcels of fruit. Apollonius served me again before taking a large portion for himself. He ate without speaking and I could see he was upset.

Eventually I asked, in a small voice, 'What happened to your son?'

'He was demoted and sent to Gaul.'

'Oh, I am glad he didn't die.' It burst out of me before I could think.

'Why?' asked Apollonius, sitting up and looking at me intently. 'Why are you glad? Why did you not condemn him? What is it about your family? What made you not speak? Any other Jewess would have condemned all of them with fury. Vintillius had humiliated you along with all the others. I've seen what soldiers can do. I've seen women die from what they do. I know he was young and easily led but what you did doesn't make sense to me. You could have been executed for defying Pilate. How did you get such courage?' I shook my head. It was impossible to start explaining here. Perhaps I did not need to speak. It was Apollonius who wanted to talk.

'Pilate sent them all to Gaul in disgrace,' he said. 'In some families Vintillius would have been made outcast. It's not that other soldiers haven't done the same, Mars knows they do, but they don't get caught. When they are caught, they have to pay. What would have happened to him in Gaul, I don't know. I was ashamed of my son too. A soldier needs to obey orders and one who will not is worth nothing.'

He stopped and sighed. I waited.

'In the end it was all one,' he continued. 'The boat was wrecked in a storm and Vintillius died all the same. My only son; my only child. And I can have no other.' He was silent for a moment, fiddling with his glass of wine. With a strange synchronicity we both raised our glasses together to drink. Apollonius looked straight into my eyes, held them for a moment, then we both looked away.

'I shouldn't have been in Jerusalem today,' he said. 'My army career is over. I'm leaving for Alexandria next week. But I happened to be riding back from Bethlehem with some of my men when the riot broke out.

'I saw your hair,' he said. 'Then I saw you had a child. I didn't think until it was all over, but at the time it all seemed very clear.'

'What seemed very clear?'

He looked me in the eyes again and there was an entreaty there.

'I think your child could be my grandson,' he said.

I closed my eyes, seeing again the Pargod, the great tapestry of lives in the Heavens showing how each and every soul is woven into a great pattern, meeting and parting over centuries, giving and receiving in equal measure over different lifetimes. Everything was paid for; every experience, no matter how joyous or how painful, equally valid.

Apollonius was still speaking.

'The other soldiers saw me pick him up,' he said. 'That may mean nothing to you but it is our custom when a man acknowledges responsibility for a life. When a child is born, it is placed at the father's feet. If he agrees to raise it as his own, he will pick it up to show the world. All the people there today saw me pick up your son. Jews and Romans saw. I have claimed him for my own.'

'And me?' Oddly, I was not horrified; I did not feel threatened, more intrigued at the Lord's way of mingling lives in His service.

'If the boy is to be a Roman citizen, you must become my wife,' he said awkwardly. 'You don't have to worry. It would only be in name. You wouldn't even have to come with me if you did not want to. It's just that citizenship is important to us and if you don't marry me, the child will not have that right.

'I have no wife living and technically I have had no legal wife at all. Soldiers are not permitted to marry while they are in service. We take partners, of course, but we cannot marry them and we cannot give citizenship to our children unless the woman we choose is a Roman citizen in her own right. The woman I loved, Vintillius's mother, was a Roman and she gave up her comfortable life to be with me. She died...' Apollonius stopped and I concentrated on my food so he would not know that I had seen his distress nor see how agitated I was feeling. We were silent for a few moments and when he spoke again he sounded tired.

'I had been wounded,' he said. 'Anyway, I did not care to take another... well, there was no point. Until now...' He stopped again. This time I looked up at him and our eyes met. In his there seemed to be a kind of embarrassment and an entreaty.

'I am leaving the army so I may now marry legally,' he said. 'It is an unusual situation. Centurions usually die in service. But my family...' he sighed. 'I had better tell you everything for if you decide to be my wife you will have a right to know. I was the eldest son of an old Roman family. We are not of equestrian status but our blood is ancient and the family is proud.

'I left when I was a young man because I would not marry the woman my father chose for me. If I had, the family could have been raised to the status it desired. In our society a father has the right of life or death over his children and I was lucky that I was permitted exile and not killed. I could have been a Tribune but I was in love and I enlisted in the ranks instead. I took Drusilla with me. We had a good life. She was very brave and put up with all the hardships.' He was silent again for a moment before going on.

'My father has died and I am now head of the family. The others live in Alexandria and Rome. My family has decided to forgive me and I now have the money and the opportunity to resign from the army and live and work in Alexandria.

'I wasn't going to take it,' he said, looking at me over his cup of wine. 'There didn't seem much point. I might just as well have gone on taking different army positions until I died or was killed. And I am too proud to want to be beholden to my family. But something told me I should accept the offer. And today I saw you and I thought perhaps I could have a family again; make a new start. Learn to live again.'

Automatically, I took another piece of food then, realising that my plate was still full from food I was unable to eat, I began to twist my hands together. I had to do something with them.

'If you come with me you would be taken care of, I promise you that,' said Apollonius but his words were like echoes in my ears.

Could this really be happening? What was I supposed to say or do? The two of us sat silently for some time. Apollonius was fiddling with some crumbs and looking everywhere but at me. I lay almost motionless trying to calm the clamour within. I could feel my heart pounding at the chance of a new life but other thoughts clamped down like ice. One in particular repeated itself continually inside my head. It was forbidden for a Jewish woman to marry the father of a man with whom she had lain. The law was explicit. As a Jewess I could not possibly take up this offer even if I wanted to.

Probably only a few moments passed but it seemed like a lifetime as I battled with my fears. The childhood memory of Abigail, a Nazarene girl who had died in pregnancy for fear of having broken the law, came back to me with a jolt. Thoughts circled in my head in confusion, making it throb and ache. 'The law...' I stuttered. 'It forbids.' Then I stopped. I did not know what to do or what to say.

'Think it over,' said Apollonius, kindly. 'If you hate the idea then I will not press you. I am quite aware that Luke may well not be my blood-line at all but I would be willing to adopt him even so. I don't know your law but I do know that your brother did not let Earthly laws hold him back when he saved my son. It is up to you but there is one thing which I think might help you decide. Your brother once told me that he did not believe in coincidences; he believed in miracles. There is a coincidence which you might like to consider. You will have been told that my name is Apollonius Sextus. It is not. That is the name I took when I ran away. My true name is Apollonius Lucius Alexis and, until I left home, I was always known as Luke.'

Sleep came with great difficulty that night. I thought of asking for some of the poppy mixture but I knew it might confuse my mind even more. The wet nurse was staying and there was no need for me to be with Luke when he woke. I was grateful for I needed time alone to think. Think and pray. Yeshua had taught us to watch for the signs and patterns in life which showed us which way to go and to check our reactions to every situation to ensure we were not living life without thinking; relying on other people's opinions instead of choosing what to do. It was called living in the Sun or the Moon. Living in the Sun meant you could look at a situation from a point of detachment and work out what was best for all sides. Living in the Moon meant being ruled by feelings and habits and family beliefs. To make it even more difficult, you needed to honour your intuition as well; that tiny voice which showed you the right way whether you liked it or not. When that opposed the law then the choice was difficult indeed. I knew what my heart wanted, but I did not think that I dared to do it.

Over and over again that night I saw the weaving of the pattern of Apollonius's life and mine together and I heard Yeshua's voice saying, 'Walk the untrodden path.' I remembered the times when he, I and the other disciples had broken the food laws and the laws of purity. I remembered when we had been chided by Pharisees for both healing and picking food on the Sabbath. I could recall my brother's teaching that the laws were there for those who could not have direct experience of God or their own powers of discernment and that sometimes an Earthly law could be broken for the sake of a higher duty, such as the preservation of life. The Law of the Ten Commandments was inviolable but the social, everyday laws were only necessary because we did not understand or obey the greater ones.

I wondered how safe Luke could be in a world which would always see him as the son of a betrayer and I shuddered at the thought of the vengeance which might be wrought against him. I saw a life of strength and circumstance for him in the Roman world but I feared wrong-doing, condemnation by God, loneliness and exile for myself. I remembered that, no matter what I knew of higher Worlds, I was still a Jewess who had never lived anywhere but her homeland and who had only ever broken laws through the grace of the Anointed. Now I was alone and I did not have the courage to throw aside my heritage or a law that had been made to protect the Jewish blood line. That I had not been married to Vintillius did not matter; that I had not consented to be his lover was irrelevant; that nobody alive but Imma and myself even knew that there was a link between us was no help. If I was not strong enough to say 'Unfair!' and stand up for what I wanted then I was not strong enough to marry a stranger. In Alexandria I would still be alone for all of Apollonius's kindness. It seemed obvious that Luke's destiny was laid out before him – but not mine. I must let my son go anyway; persuade Apollonius to adopt him without marrying me. I must give him up to a better life. I would go back to my own plot of land with Rizpah and live out my days there.

But what a waste when Alexandria was beckoning! Yeshua had told me of Alexandria; of a city where people of all religions could meet and talk. A city where the Tree of Life was understood by the Jewish intelligentsia. Where Joseph Barsabbas had grown up. A place of tolerance and wisdom. I would love to visit Alexandria – but could I face turning my back on my faith and leaving for good with a man I hardly knew, of a different religion and of a race all Jews were taught to hate?

Even more, if I chose to go against the law, could I bear to marry again? Judah's memory was still so precious but as his widow I had no rights, no name.

At last I gave up. I scrambled up to the window where I could see the stars twinkling in the midnight sky and handed my decision over to God. 'Lord,' I said, 'My will is to have the strength to leave; to go to a new life. But on my own I am not strong enough and I am afraid. I know that it is not my will which is ultimately important except in enforcing Yours. If it is right for me to break the law of my people and go, then show me clearly that it is Your will and give me the strength to carry it out. But if this is temptation and I must stay, then strengthen me in that resolve and give me a sign that I am meant to be here. Thy will be done, as in Heaven, so on Earth.'

Then I slept.

I awoke before dawn, knowing that I had to go to the Temple. It only took moments to dress in the simple white stola I had been given to wear with the gauze Roman pella for my hair. I opened the shutters and slid out of the window, wary of any guards who might try and stop me, and ran as fast as I could, barefoot, through the city streets. I needed to be told my fate or at least to make my decision in the place where I had last seen and sensed Yeshua's presence.

Just as I reached the outer walls a man appeared. He held up his hand to stop me and enquired my business so early in the morning.

'I am going into the Temple, Sir,' I said. 'As soon as the doors are opened.'

The man looked at me curiously and I recognised him with a sickening feeling in my stomach. This was Saul of Tarsus, the very last man I wanted to meet just then.

'I know you don't I?' he said. 'Why are you alone? It is not proper for a woman to come to the Temple alone at this hour.'

I had no answer for him but he needed none. 'I warn you,' he said. 'We've had more than enough trouble from your sect of heretics. I know you are one of the insurgents, the so-called Jews who think the Messiah has come. I am on the lookout for you and if I find you doing anything that is questionable I will have you whipped, do you understand me? You are not welcome here. You are an evil creature. May the angels of the Lord protect me against you.'

'I am not evil,' I said sturdily. 'If you think I am then you have much to learn. The Lord God is my God too. I do His work in my own way but it is still His work.'

'Get out of here,' said Saul with contempt in his voice. 'Get out before I have you arrested and stoned for your arrogance.'

I turned and walked away with what dignity I could muster, the sinking feeling that comes after bravery settling in my stomach. Was this the sign that I was to leave my city and country? No, there was still something more. As I turned the corner, away from Saul's piercing gaze, I shivered to think what it might be.

I wandered aimlessly for a while, thinking and trying to let go of the fear. Then, as I crossed a street where market-sellers were beginning to set up their stalls, a group of men approached from another road. Among them were faces I recognised as followers of the Messianic Way. Philip was there too and I moved forward to talk to him; to warn him about Saul's presence at the Temple. There would be trouble if they went there now. He saw me and stopped. They all did. They obviously knew who I was. I opened my mouth to speak but as I did one of them, a stranger, spat in my face.

'Whore,' he said. 'Roman whore. First the wife of a traitor and now the whore of the enemy. How dare you walk the streets of a Holy city!'

I stood, petrified, as the men gathered around me menacingly. 'Betrayer!' they said. 'Diseased mother of a traitor's spawn! Where's your filthy brat, whore?' Another man spat at me and I put my hands to my face. They knew about Luke! Terror and then relief flooded through me when I realised that they could not get to him. They might tear me apart but Luke would be safe with Apollonius. A tear trickled down my cheek as the men started to push and buffet at my already bruised body. It would only be a matter of time before one of them found a stone. There was nothing I could do but await my fate and then Philip spoke. 'Give her a chance,' he said. 'She may not be as guilty as you think. Let her go and then give chase. If the Lord is protecting her, she will go free. If she is guilty then she will die.'

I opened my eyes and looked at him. 'Run!' his eyes were saying. 'Run and take your chance, for the sake of the love we once all felt when Yeshua was with us.'

The group fell back slightly, considering, and I took that chance, diving through the gap and running as fast as I could. I had a moment's grace before the pursuit began and I raced down a side street, twisting and turning in and out of the market stalls where the traders were beginning to display their wares. To my panic-stricken mind the sounds of pursuit were everywhere but I was given the strength from somewhere to outpace the men long enough to weave my way through the city until I could hide behind the walls of a Synagogue. Curled up and trying desperately to quieten my panic-stricken breathing, I heard the men run past, still shouting threats and insults. Time passed but I did not move for fear that they might return and see me. Only when I was certain that they had gone their way did I allow myself to cry, releasing the horror and fear of the morning and hugging myself for comfort. I wished with all my heart that Judah were still here with me. I missed his strength and kindness so. I missed his sternness and trustworthiness. I missed his loving arms around me. As I thought of him, his dear, lined face with its heavy forelock of hair seemed to appear before me and I reached out towards it. 'Oh Judah,' I said. 'Come back. Protect me. Give me strength.'

The vision shimmered and changed and a celestial light took its place. In an instant I saw myself far away, in the last moments of a glorious sunset, standing by a great shimmering sea on a distant shore containing a great monument. I was older and wiser and standing with my arm in that of a man. At first I thought it was Judah and the yearning swelled within me but, just before the image faded, I saw the woman that was me turn towards her companion and speak. The man looked back with love and it was not Judah, it was Apollonius.

The decision was made and, as I accepted that, I understood that it had been made long ago; before the day I heard the crowd listening to the story of Judah's betrayal; before our marriage even; perhaps before my birth. But its fulfilment had had to wait until my child was born and my dearest friend was dead. Gabriel had told me but I had not listened. Only now, rejected by both sides within my own people, could I have the courage to leave. The beautiful plot of land where I had lived in peace had only been an oasis in my life. More was wanted and my future was not in the land of my birth.

I said a prayer for courage and forgiveness and accepted my task.

Apollonius was waiting for me when I returned. His face was anxious and he leapt up from his desk when they announced my return. I walked up to him confidently for, whatever the outcome, my decision was made.

'I will marry you,' I said. 'Then you will truly become Luke's father.'

His face changed and for a moment I thought he might take me in his arms. Then he pulled himself together.

'I cannot be a true husband, he said.'

'And I cannot be a wife,' I said. 'Maybe that is how the law will be fulfilled. That is the least of our problems. I am a Jewess, you are a Roman. You have many gods, I have one. You are an aristocrat, I am a Galilean. It is impossible, quite impossible. But it must be done.'

'You cannot be a wife?' he asked, ignoring every other thing I had said.

'I was told so when Luke was born. To bear another child would kill me.'

We stared at each other. The situation was so strange I could not think clearly. All I knew was that this was the untrodden path and the route I must take.

Apollonius reached out and pushed back the pella so that my head was bare. He touched my hair. 'You are beautiful, Deborah,' he said in Latin.

'And you are handsome,' I replied, in the same tongue.

He kissed me, just briefly, on the lips and then we looked at each other long and hard.

'It will work,' he said. 'By the gods, I don't know why, but it will.'

Six

It is one thing to make such a momentous decision. It is another to face other people's reactions to it.

I started with Imma when she came to see me the next day. We sat in the atrium of the house, sipping delicious fresh orange juice and sharing our sadness and memories. Mingling with my sorrow for the loss of Magdalene was the thought that this might also be the last time that Imma and I would sit and talk. Such an enormous step was before me that I could hardly think it to be real.

Imma opened the subject herself. 'What are you going to do now?' she said simply.

'I don't know how to tell you,' I replied and Imma laughed. 'At least you have a plan!' she said. 'I thought you would have. You usually do.

'Remember what I used to say to you when you were a little girl?' she added with a twinkle in her eye. 'You start at the beginning, go on until the end and then you stop!'

I heaved a big sigh and started to tell her about Apollonius's proposal, of my experiences in the city and of the vision of the future. As the story unfolded and I came to the issue of marrying a man whose son had already lain with me, I began to stammer. Imma leaned over to touch my shoulder briefly with a comforting hand. She listened to my fears about the law, sitting quietly and neither chastening nor condemning me, despite her quiet and profound observance of all she had been raised to believe. When I had finished, she linked her hands together in her lap, closed her eyes and thought. I waited impatiently but I knew that she would reply only when she was ready.

After what seemed like a very long time, Imma sighed. She opened her eyes, smiled at me and started to speak.

'The law,' she said. 'Ah, the law!' Then she laughed and took my hands in hers.

'Deborah, it was against what we believed to be the law for you to receive the vision of the Merkabah when you were a girl in Nazara,' she said. 'Those who are prophets have always walked on the edge of the law and it seems that the Lord Himself created them to do so. You were named for the Prophetess Deborah and it would appear that you are of the same spiritual line. You, too, are a Prophetess and, although that does not mean that you are above the law, it does mean that you must follow the word of God over the beliefs of man. If you had only followed your own heart and your own vision in this matter, you would not have needed the terror of the persecution of the others at the Temple. It is time that you sang your own song and no one here has the right to hold you back. I have no doubt that you and your child will be happy in Alexandria.'

For a while we sat in silence as I tried to take in all that she had said. It was not easy to acknowledge it openly but I did know that I had the power to see some of God's plan for me. To deny it would be to deny His wishes – no matter how inadequate I felt in taking up such responsibility. Suddenly I realised that I had not even thanked Imma for her kindness and understanding. As I began to stumble over words of gratitude I noticed a familiar look in her eye, one that I recognised from when I had been particularly unobservant or stupid in my childhood.

'What are you looking like that for?' I said.

'You haven't even noticed the far more obvious law you are planning to break, have you?' asked Imma. 'You have been worrying so much about marrying a man whose son has lain with you even to consider the law that says that Jews should only marry Jews.'

My mouth dropped open in realisation and then we both burst into spontaneous laughter. I had not thought of it for a moment – not even when the Messianic followers had called me a Roman whore!

'That one obviously doesn't bother you in the slightest,' said Imma. 'Do you remember telling the family back in Nazara that a Jewess should marry the Roman Emperor to make us safe, as Esther did when she married Ahasuerus? Perhaps that is what you are doing.'

'I hardly think so,' I said, still laughing.

'You never know,' said Imma. 'Stranger things have happened.'

'Come with us to Alexandria,' I said, on impulse. Imma shook her head with a smile. 'You are a changeling, Deborah,' she said. 'Not my child nor anyone else's. You have to stand up for yourself from now on and learn your own lessons. You would only rely on me if I came with you and, anyway, that is not where my heart wants to be. Until now your life has been guided by Joseph and me; by Yeshua, by Judah, by your child's coming. Now it is time for you to stand alone and make your own choices. Whether they are right or wrong, they must be your decisions and yours alone.' She kissed me and we wept a little for she knew as well as I did that we might never meet again in this world.

Telling Rizpah was the next task. In reality she had little choice but to come to Alexandria. She had left home and family to be with me and the only alternatives for her were returning to Tiberius in disgrace, staying with the disciples and trusting to charity or asking Saul to take her back.

I told her, as gently as I could, that I was not going back to En Gedi; that it had been made very clear to me by the disciples I had met in the city that my life was forfeit. I warned her, too, that she might well be tarnished by association. Staying in a Roman house overnight was an unforgivable crime for a Jewess. Once she had taken that in, I went on to say that Apollonius had known Yeshua and that he had offered to adopt Luke as his son – and to marry me.

Obviously it was a terrible shock for her. Rizpah had not thought of anything beyond the grief of Magdalene's death. To her, staying in a Roman house had been just a part of the strangeness of her new life but when she realised that I was suggesting a future for the three of us in Roman society it broke every taboo she knew. She had not been studying the Teaching for long enough to realise that the Romans were just human beings like the rest of us and not necessarily the cruel oppressors we liked to think they were. Her opposition to the idea of leaving was loud and outraged. How could I even consider marrying a Roman! How could I betray my own nation? How could I consort with the enemy?

I let her say what she wanted and listened patiently. None of it was considered; it was all learnt responses from society and her adopted parents but it was entirely understandable. I thanked God she did not know of any more with which to condemn me. When she had finished and had subsided in tears, I began to speak.

'No one likes to be a conquered nation,' I told her. 'And there certainly are Romans who are cruel and unthinking. But generally they have treated us and our religion with great respect.'

'What?' said Rizpah, outraged. 'They have just killed one of us – your dearest friend – and the Lord alone knows how many others died that day. How can you defend them, let alone marry one?'

I sighed. 'Because I truly believe it is God's plan for me,' I said. 'I have been left no alternative but to live an outcast in Judaea or be stoned as a heretic by either side and neither option is fair on me or you or Luke.'

'Surely we could go back to En Gedi and stay there,' said Rizpah. 'We could be safe. And anyway, how could God want you to marry an enemy?'

'He isn't my enemy,' I said. 'At the moment, my kinsfolk are my enemy. If your fate had been to be born a Roman, you would probably hate the Jews. It is tribal law to hate people who are different. The whole point of studying this Merkabah tradition of the Tree of Life is to rise above tribal differences and see each person as an individual capable of strength and love.

'Apollonius saved my life. Magdalene's life was completed. It had finished. She had lived and taught with Yeshua and truly wanted nothing else. The extra time she had with us being such a friend and an inspiration was a gift for us. Oh, Rizpah! She was so happy when she died! So joyful in her death! It wasn't so terrible for her, no matter how it felt to you and to me. I don't believe for a moment she would be willing to return to us now.

Why should she? What is there here for her now? I will miss her more than I can say but that doesn't mean I should try to hold her back.'

Rizpah sat, silently, taking in what I was saying. I could see how hard it was for her even to realise that she could change deep-seated beliefs and start to think of alternative opinions.

'You are grieving deeply,' I said. 'Of course you are. But think of Magdalene herself. Can you imagine her reaction to anyone who had been shown the way so clearly and who refused to take up the challenge? If I allowed racial hatred to get in the way of God's plan? Because it is God's plan for me, Rizpah, I do know that. Whatever happens, this is the way I must go. Where you go is up to you but I love you and I would value your friendship and your company in my new life more than you can possibly imagine.

'If it helps you,' I went on, 'I have enough experience to know that nothing is wasted. People are placed where they are needed most. There is a new branch of Judaism beginning in Jerusalem. It may spread throughout the Jewish world. If so, it will need protection. As you say, Jews and Romans often hate each other. And where could we help most but within a powerful Roman family? We may well have an important job to do and I, for one, am willing to do it.'

I left her to herself for a while for she had much to think about. I, too, was overburdened with emotions and welcomed the time to go and sit alone in my room and weep for my own grief and uncertainty.

Rizpah came to find me after an hour or so. She hugged me rather doubtfully and we cried a little more together. I knew then that she would come and I was grateful for I would need her support. I had to prepare for a future as the wife of a man who was a complete stranger to me even though I knew, secretly and almost guiltily, that I was destined to love him.

'Judah, do you mind?' I asked, wishing with all my heart that I could have him near me again. But what would it matter if he did? He could not help me any more and he would surely tell me to follow my destiny and not look back as Lot's wife had done.

I did not see Imma again before we left, though we sent mes-

sages to each other via Joseph. Yeshua had asked John to take care
of her and he had decided that they, too, should embark on their
journey North. John was going to Ephesus to spread the word
there and Imma and Joanna were to go with him. There had been
such a clamour within the group of disciples, when they heard
that Magdalene had been killed and I had gone with the killers
and stayed with them, that even my brave and sensible mother did
not wish to challenge the others by insisting on coming to see me
again.

Joseph was our strength in those last days in Jerusalem. He was
fascinated by my news and did not waste a moment on doubts.
He came to see us as soon as he could and told us how Magdalene
had, indeed, been laid in Yeshua's tomb which Judah's silver had
been able to buy. We spent a while together praying for
Magdalene's soul and remembering her beauty and spirit and then
we sat and talked for half the afternoon about Alexandria and the
new life ahead. He talked of the great library and the groups of
people studying the Teaching from all over the world but neither
of us touched on whether a woman would be permitted to join
those groups – or even whether her husband would permit her to.

I had had moments of wondering whether it would have been
easier to stay with him and ask him to take care of us in a society
we knew and understood but it was banished by his certainty that
the signs I had received were correct.

'What about you?' I asked, aware that he had spent nearly a year
of his life taking care of me and now I was going away. 'I always
hoped that you and Magdalene might marry and continue the
teaching together.'

'Really?' Joseph was amazed and I wondered whether the affection I had thought I had seen between them was more my wishful thinking than based on fact. 'I never thought of it,' he said.
'I'm a celibate. I don't think I could change my ways now!'

'You never know,' I replied with a smile. 'It would have been a
neat solution to our plans.'

'Maybe,' said Joseph but I knew he was not really interested in
the subject. 'I shall travel,' he said. 'Antioch, Ephesus, maybe
Cyprus. I do have some family there on my father's side and I
have often meant to visit them

'There is no doubt that Yeshua's life and death will lead to great things for the world,' he continued. 'Sometimes I wonder if I am imagining things but, despite the fact that so few of the people who came to believe last year have remained believers, there is a strong and steady core of people seeing the law in a new light. There is such a general air of expectancy and change that I know this movement will grow and grow. I cannot see the future but I do know that nothing will ever be quite the same again. I want to go out and teach now. That year of consolidating what I knew, with you and the others, was very helpful but I was getting restless – you know I was.'

In the end it was decided that we should meet again in Alexandria at Hanukkah. I told Joseph that our home in En Gedi was in his hands and that it could be used as a refuge for the disciples if they needed it and he was pleased.

'I will never be one of the inner circle of the disciples,' he said. 'You can often achieve more on the edge of a group than from within it. You can see things more clearly and do and say subtle things which are effective and which do not give offence. Yeshua proved that at Emmaus and it was his example which helped me overcome the form of the Teaching which was entrapping us there.'

He gave me some names and addresses in Alexandria where I could go to meet up with other Jews. 'They are a bit out of date,' he said. 'But through these you should find the kind of people who will accept that you know the Teaching. But be careful, Deborah. Yeshua was unique and others may not yet understand that women can have this knowledge, let alone teach it.'

The days from then on blur into a haze of plans and preparations. In fact, until the day before our wedding, Apollonius and I were not sure if we would be allowed to hold a ceremony at all. A Roman citizen had to get a kind of permission called a *conubium* from Pilate to be able to marry a foreigner and that could take time – or even be refused. Apollonius explained that most non-army staff did not bother; if they wanted to live with someone who was not a citizen they just moved her into their house without ceremony. However, legally any children would still be of the wife's nationality and would have no rights as Romans.

'If we are going to do it, we are going to do it properly,' he said. 'You will be a Roman citizen and Luke will be my legally adopted son. Even if we should divorce you will remain a citizen, but Luke would remain with me.'

That law was no different from our own – I knew that if a woman was divorced or re-married her children belonged to her husband. In fact, by the time Pilate had given his permission I had worked myself up into quite a state of nerves. Was the Lord going to stop me from breaking the law after all? Had I made the wrong decision? It was so hard to tell. There was a bustle of packing to be done and I threw myself into that as a distraction. Rizpah and I thought we had nothing to take but my precious olive-wood box but we were wrong. Apollonius had ordered clothes for us both and, for the first time in our lives, we were to own dresses we had not made ourselves. They were of fine linen woven by skilled craftsmen and with them came shawls, stoles, shoes, sandals, boots, nightclothes, underclothes and formal dresses. We were alternately delighted and appalled at the luxury that had come to us.

Permission for the wedding came through at last and it felt like a great weight lifted from my heart. Apollonius and I were married in the atrium of the house surrounded by garlands of flowers and plants. A traditional Roman wedding dress – white with an orange wedding stola – had been made for me of pure linen and flowers were woven into my hair and dress by the 'wives' of the other officers. My husband was kind enough to allow Joseph to conduct a Jewish wedding for us too, with a canopy of white and prayers in Hebrew.

Apollonius gave me a necklace of amber with matching earrings which I could not wear for my ears were not pierced. His perplexity when he found there was nowhere to hang the jewels gave us the first shared laughter of our married life together and banished the threatening tears which pricked behind my eyes when I remembered my first wedding at Cana, where Yeshua had performed his first miracle for Judah and for me.

There was a small wedding feast given for a group of ten people, none of whom I knew. These were colleagues of Apollonius's and their wives, all of whom were courteous and pleasant and brought gifts of wine or food. I never knew what any of them thought of our marriage or of Luke, who lay in his new father's arms for most of the day, for I had already discovered that Romans had different manners from Jews. Such a wedding in our society would have been unheard of – questions would be asked and all the family secrets discovered long before the event itself – and such a marriage ripped apart and debated for months. The Romans, however, seemed to accept strangers quite naturally. After all, they ruled the world and most of its peoples and they were used to all nationalities, shapes, sizes, colours and religions. There was nothing strange to them in a fellow countryman marrying a local girl, especially if they already had a child.

Apollonius spoke for me most of the time, seeing that I felt shy, and I was glad to let him do so. All I had to do was smile and receive gifts with thanks and remember not to show too much surprise or uncertainty. One woman said how pleased she was to see a Jewish wedding for she had often wondered what they were like. She assumed the Lord was just another of the multitude of gods and I managed to have the manners not to contradict her.

Rizpah was assumed to be my daughter and complimented on her looks. For the first time, as I stood with my husband to say goodbye to our guests, I took note of her prettiness and I wondered what would happen to her in our new life. Would she also find a Roman husband who did not mind her past? Divorce was not such a stigma on a Roman woman as it was to a Jewish girl. Once she was used to the strange customs and less uncertain of herself, perhaps she would be a sought-after bride with her striking looks – deep brown, dark-lashed eyes and thick, straight black hair.

At last, my husband and I were alone. Rizpah had gone to bed and Joseph, the only other friend who had attended, was the last to leave. His gift to me was the little book of the Torah that he had brought from Alexandria.

'It's time it went home again,' he said, kindly, as I gasped with surprise and pleasure but tried to insist that he needed it more than I did.

We watched him walk away into the lamp-speckled darkness of the Jerusalem night and turned to each other, tired and slightly nervous. Apollonius had said he could not be a husband to me but I did not know exactly what that meant. Technically I was now his property and if there was anything he required of me, I would have had no choice but to obey. I still shuddered if I thought of the way the Roman soldiers had laid hands on me and, even though I already liked and respected my husband, I did not know the rules of these strangers.

But I had nothing to fear. Apollonius kissed me twice, on the forehead and the lips, and thanked me for the gift of my life and my son. With twinkling eyes he suggested I might like to have my ears pierced so that I could wear his wedding gift and then he led me to my own room, bade me goodnight and left me alone. Part of me wanted him to stay and part of me was glad. I was quite alone for the serving girls who had attended me had gone to their beds. A couple on their wedding night would want no attention from others. In fact, although I was relieved, it was strangely lonely. I thought of going to sleep with Rizpah and Luke but that might have been an inappropriate thing to do. Instead, I spent much of my wedding night praying that I might be a good wife and remain true to myself. I asked for strength to do whatever tasks the Lord had set for me and for guidance whenever I was in doubt. As I prayed I felt the unmistakable sensation of angels gathering around me. Their presence, as always, seemed to be a rippling silk of silver water and, with them, came a vision. This time I saw Apollonius and myself more clearly, standing by a huge harbour with that great, tall building at its edge. It was dusk and fires burnt at the top of the tower, illuminating the dark sea. I knew this must be Alexandria and that it would be my home for many years to come. I saw the great city itself and a kind of light shining from another building near the harbour. It shimmered and drew itself into the shape of the menorah and from that, again, into the Tree of Life. As the vision faded I slept, knowing that the years ahead would be some of the happiest of my life.

I still felt a lump in my throat when our ship left the harbour at Joppa and my homeland faded into the distance behind me. But there was no turning back. Like Joseph, the son of Jacob, I had to go down into Egypt; like Joseph, I had no idea whether I would ever return.

We were two weeks at sea with a fair run – or so the sailors told us. For Rizpah and I, who thought we were used to rough waters on the Sea of Galilee, the difference between a lake and a real sea was enough to make us very poor sailors for several days. Once we could think straight, eat and look around us we still had to cope with the phenomenon of having no land in sight whatsoever. This ship was truly at the mercy of the waters with nowhere to run should a storm pursue us. I knew I had to trust that all would be well but it was hard not to repeat prayers for safety again and again, so showing my lack of faith. Apollonius laughed at the two of us but he admired us, too, for we did not moan and groan but swallowed hard and held our heads high. It was our great fortune that Luke was an excellent sailor. Had he felt as queasy as we did we would have been a very miserable little group.

On the second day, when Rizpah and I were both still feeling dull and nauseous with the rhythmic rolling of the ship, Apollonius distracted us by suggesting we looked out for dolphins.

'What are they?' I asked, concerned at the idea of anything big which might live in this vast, unfriendly, watery desert.

'They look like fish but they are not,' he said. 'Some people believe them to be half human, magical beings. All I know is that they love to swim with ships and to jump up out of the water as they ride the bow wave. Some people say they will swim with you if you fall overboard and take you safely down to Neptune's kingdom if you drown. Sailors say they are creatures of good omen and to see them means the god has accepted prayers for a safe crossing.'

Superstition, we knew, was a crutch to deal with fear but, all the same, Rizpah and I looked out for these strange creatures for much of that day.

'They don't eat people, do they?' asked Rizpah nervously.

'I don't think so,' said Apollonius gravely. 'But if they did, they would certainly fancy a lovely young girl for dinner. I should keep your face veiled, Rizpah, for fear they report your prettiness to the sea god. You never know, he might come to see for himself.'

Rizpah yelped and hid behind me until she realised he was joking. The trouble was that we could not be sure of anything in this new world! 'It's almost as though we are outside the Lord's dominions,' said Rizpah after Apollonius had left us. 'I know that is blasphemy but there is so much new and different here that it is as though there truly are other gods. It's hard to remember that the Holy One made all this as well as our home.'

I knew what she meant. We Jews were so busy believing ourselves to be the only chosen people that the rest of the world did not seem real to us. That there might be strange animals and birds and perhaps even colours and scents which we had never heard of was an uncomfortable feeling. And the idea of living in a land where other gods ruled and not our own Lord was very frightening. We knew that the Holy One was Lord of all but we were used to living with others who thought the same – even if they did spend much of their time arguing about how He should be worshipped. It all felt very odd and it was very tempting to believe that I had made the wrong decision after all.

When we did see the dolphins they seemed like a sign from the strange god of this strange sea that all was well. They were lithe, grey dancing things with mouths curled in a perpetual smile and small dark eyes which seemed to look at us humorously as we hung over the side of the ship, exclaiming and pointing at them. A group of dolphins raced with the ship just before sunset, the late afternoon light reflecting from the water thrown up around them by their leaping and diving.

'In the dark of the night when there is no Moon they bring their own light in the water,' Apollonius told us over supper. 'We call it phosphorescence. It's a cold green light but it is real light and, on a late watch or if you can't sleep, it's a comforting sight. It means that you are not alone when there is nothing else but blackness around you.'

'They are sea angels then!' said Rizpah and the idea stuck. In fact it became a teaching tool for me to show her the difference between the Four Worlds of Earth, Water, Air and Fire.

If you watched the dolphins closely you could see that they were just as fleet within the water as out of it but they had to come up to the top at regular intervals.

'I think they are breathing,' said Rizpah and Apollonius agreed

with her. 'If you look carefully, you can see that they have a
breathing hole on the tops of their heads,' he said. 'It opens when
they are out of the water. One of my soldiers told me he found
one on the sea shore one day and it was obviously able to breathe.
It died, but not from suffocation. They seem to need both air and
water to survive.'

'They are like us,' I told Rizpah. 'They have physical bodies
but they live in the World of water which, to us, is the World of
the psyche with its changing moods and feelings. One minute all
is calm and happy and the next there is a storm and we are weeping or angry. We get buffeted back and forwards by the rough
water but they are at home in it whatever it does.'

'Why are we similar then?' she asked.

'Because they understand the water and its nature. We can be
safe and happy in the psychological World as long as we know that
it is not all there is and that most of the angers and fears we feel
are illusions. If we know that we can reach into the spiritual
World where our true essence is then we are safe and storms will
not buffet us. And we are attracted to the spiritual World by the
light of God which is the World of fire.'

'So if we look up to God we are drawn up to spirit where we
can breathe clearly and that makes us safe in the rough waters?'
said Rizpah.

'Yes.'

'And the dolphins are called up to the air they need to breathe
by the light which shines down into the water?'

'Yes. Each of the Worlds interweaves with the others like the
threads of a cloth. The Kingdom or base of each World is the centre of the World below it and the crown of the World below that.
Look.' I sketched the map of the Tree of Life with my finger on
the wooden floor of the boat, trying to show how each of the four
images merged with the others as the Worlds above and below us
also did. Rizpah tried to understand and Apollonius looked on
with what seemed to be interest. Then, abruptly, he turned and
walked away.

'Oh dear,' said Rizpah and my heart sank too. Until now he
had been so helpful and supportive but I feared that I had offended him by teaching my own faith. I hoped against hope that he

would not be angry with us for long. However, it was just a lesson in not jumping to conclusions for Apollonius returned swiftly with a slate and some chalk.

'Draw that diagram properly,' he said. 'Then perhaps I'll be able to understand what you are saying.'

I laughed out loud at that and had to explain that one of the Jewish laws forbade anyone to make pictures or diagrams which were viewed as 'graven images.' Apollonius laughed too – but he was laughing at a restriction which seemed limiting and even stupid to him.

So, in this strange new World, still the creation of the One God but so different that it felt right to adapt the old laws to new customs, I drew out the Tree of Life on the slate together with a second picture showing how it interleaved with the three other Worlds. It took some time to match each part of the diagram for I had only seen it briefly as Yeshua had drawn it in the ground to make a particular point and I had learnt the names of each of the circles, or sephirot, by heart instead of seeing them written.

'It looks like a kind of boat,' said Apollonius, looking at the Tree itself. 'And that's a Temple,' pointing at the Four Worlds. 'Or is it a ladder?' he asked peering at the rather wobbly drawing.

'It's called Jacob's Ladder,' I said. 'Because it is a picture of what Jacob, one of our ancestors, saw in a dream. He saw angels going up and down between the Worlds carrying messages to and from God.'

'How extraordinary,' said Apollonius excitedly. 'Do our gods fit onto it too? They must do if what your brother said is true.'

'I expect so,' I said, throwing a hasty look at Rizpah who was about to deny the possibility of Roman gods being valid in any way whatsoever. 'I don't know how yet but that's the wonder of a tradition of oral teaching. With this diagram you can work out practically anything. I know the planets fit onto it, which is how astrologers work, and some of your gods are associated with the planets aren't they? Do you have one who is Queen of the Earth itself?'

'Yes, there's Ceres who is Mother Earth – or Juno, Queen of the Gods perhaps?'

'Well Malkhut means Kingdom but it represents the feminine

aspect of God too. Malkha means Queen so it might be Juno. Then
there's the Moon,' I indicated the second Sephira from the bottom.
  'That's Diana, goddess of the Moon. You would probably
know her as Artemis.'
  'I know!' burst in Rizpah. 'She's the one with the Temple in
Ephesus where John and Miriam have gone.'
  'And Hod, that's this one,' I said, indicating the bottom left cir-
cle. 'That's associated with the planet Mercury.'
  'The messenger of the gods,' said Apollonius.
  'Yes, Hod is all about communication, about thinking and
sometimes about being tricky or a scoundrel in a clever kind of
way.'
  'Yes, that fits. Go on.'
  'Well, Mercury is balanced by Venus, here on the right. That's
Netzach. It's the impulse which starts things off or the principle
of attraction. You know how a beautiful woman can set in motion
a whole chain of events just by walking down the street.
  'Then there's the Sun,' I said. 'Right here in the centre of the
picture. That represents our true self. Yeshua called it the
Kingdom of Heaven.'
  'That's Apollo. I was named for him.' Apollonius sounded
pleased. 'Or it could be Helios who is the Sun god himself.
Apollo is the god of the light of the Sun.'
  'That's interesting. Why two of them?'
  'Never mind that,' said Rizpah impatiently. 'We can work that
out later. What else is there.' I laughed at her wish for more
knowledge without taking in all the details she already had. I had
been like that once too.
  'Just a couple more then,' I said. 'After that, I will have to think
because we run out of planets. But there's Mars on the left above
Hod. That's Gevurah, the place of discernment, discipline and
judgement and the true soldier who watches and waits before
striking at the perfect time so that he may save his men. Balancing
him on the right-hand side, above Venus, is Jupiter, or Hesed,
which is loving kindness, mercy and expansion.
  Apollonius was intrigued. 'But Jupiter is the King of the gods,'
he said. 'Surely he should be in the circle at the very top.'
  'No,' I said. 'Higher than Jupiter means going into the spiri-

tual World. That is where the psychological gods make way for spirit. Above these are archetypes and principles and archangels where below there were angels. I don't think I can explain any more without starting from the beginning but I think that's why we Jews refer to the one God and you refer to many. The Highest of all is the Holy One and all the others, even Jupiter, are below him. "No other Gods before Me." '

For a moment, I thought I had gone too far. Apollonius was frowning but it was more through trying to understand than from irritation.

'Well, we won't have to worry about what we talk about in the winter evenings, will we?' he said at last with a twinkle in his eye. 'We will have to go through all this properly.'

We did not mention the Teaching again for the rest of the voyage but I was content. A little at a time was all that was needed and there was more than enough to learn about everyday life to fill every waking hour. That had to be my priority for the sooner I was comfortable with Roman life, the sooner I could be free to search for other people who knew of the Higher Worlds.

There were about twenty others travelling to Alexandria on our ship; all of them Roman citizens and many connected with the army. It made me feel very sober to realise that, only a week before, most of them would have regarded Rizpah, Luke and me as expendable.

We took care of ourselves and served Apollonius as we were used to serving the men in Judaea. Those small duties might have been routine for us but I could see that they touched him. For many years he had fended for himself.

Many of the travellers shared a kind of dormitory but there were cabins and the four of us shared one of them with a curtain for privacy. To start with Rizpah, Luke and I lay together on one rough mattress of horse hair with Apollonius sleeping separately. There was not much room for three of us on one side and one on the other but on the evening after the day we saw the dolphins Apollonius held his hand out to me and I had little choice but to follow him to his bed. That night and those which followed he held me close to him before we slept and I realised that I had to learn again the art of sleeping with the presence of a man's body next to mine. Had we been lovers it would have been easier for sleep comes more naturally then. Sometimes Apollonius would stroke my hair and I would nestle into his arms but there was no more than that. I grew used to the scent of his body and would raise my face willingly to be kissed goodnight. I began to wonder how bad his injury had been and whether it might ever be resolved.

We spent much of the days talking and finding out more about each other's life and times although Apollonius would not talk about Drusilla, Vintillius's mother, and I respected that, although I was curious to know how old she was when she died and how she met her death.

The post he was travelling to had formerly been held by one of his cousins. With the death of Apollonius's father it seemed that the whole family had moved up a notch, all changing positions and moving homes. 'That's the way it is in a Roman family,' said my husband. 'I didn't want any part in it when I was young; I could see all of the corruption and nepotism. But you cannot do anything about it if you just run away. Sooner or later I must have been destined to come back into the fold. Mind you,' he added, looking fierce, 'I will do my work honestly and I will not press for promotions. The work should suit me; centurions have a great deal to do with local traders and I enjoyed that, particularly as Primus Pilus. I shall like being involved in such a busy and influential harbour-business as Alexandria's.'

'What are your family going to think about me?' I asked shyly, for Apollonius still had family living in the city. They had not seen him for more than 20 years but it was over his choice of a wife that he had been outcast. An unknown Jewish girl would not be thought of as an improvement.

'I don't care,' said my husband, putting his great arms around me and giving me a bear hug which squeezed the breath out of me. 'Oh, don't worry. They won't be hostile. Really they won't. Times have changed in 20 years and it was my father's deathbed wish that the family should be reconciled with me no matter who my wife might be.'

Despite his reassuring words I preferred not to think of the inquiring gazes and curious people we would soon be meeting and I put it to the back of my mind. There was enough to take in and learn just on board ship without worrying about the future.

In a way, the journey was similar to one that Yeshua, Judah, Joseph, Magdalene and I had made from the banks of the Jordan to Cana after we left Emmaus; a time of peace and getting to know each other before meeting the rest of the world. Had we been thrown into the hurly burly of life in Alexandria without time to be together, it would have been much, much harder.

Alexandria! Surely the most incredible city in the world. Built on islands and promontories out into the sea as well as on the shore of Egypt itself. First, and unmistakeable, the great light-house itself on the peninsula of Pharos. We watched in awe as it appeared over the horizon. Four storeys of marble, reddish-purple granite and limestone ('The four Worlds!' whispered Rizpah). Four hundred feet of magnificence, windows everywhere and the powerful lantern at the very top. The light it threw was beyond the natural, enhanced by science; a great, silvered, mirrored lens that could multiply both flame and man's vision in ways that most could never understand.

The largest building I had ever seen before was the Temple of Jerusalem but this made the Temple look like a toy. Although its dimensions were just as I had seen them in my vision, nothing had prepared me for its size and grandeur in reality.

Beyond Pharos were yet more wonders and Rizpah and I must have sat with our mouths wide open with astonishment. The city was vast. Bigger than we could take in at first and the view from the sea was merciless in its clarity. We saw the Greek-Roman centre with its main street of colonnades up to 200 feet high, the great Temple of Neptune, the theatres and gymnasia, the Emporium of exchange, the great market areas and the Caesareum with its two tall obelisks marked with Egyptian hieroglyphics. To the North-East, the royal palaces and behind them the thriving Jewish Quarter. To the West, Rhacotis where the Egyptian population lived. Everything shone; everything bustled. It was terrifying; like being a child again with the first sighting of Jerusalem, breathtaking and terrible and beautiful in one. Then I had thought Jerusalem magnificent but, as Alexandria proudly showed us her towers and spires glittering in the midday Sun, my own city seemed nothing but a village.

Again I thought of Joseph's descent into Egypt. It was hard to understand that it was good to live there when all your training told of the importance of the Exodus, of leaving to search for the promised land. 'I will not forget you,' I promised Yeshua as we stepped down the gangplank into such a hugely different world. 'I will spread your teaching here, if that is God's will.'

Rizpah and I waited on the docks while Apollonius spoke with officials. His new responsibility, as an aide to the Governor, would be in the customs office and he went directly there to introduce himself. Much of the grain which fed the Roman world was channelled out of Egypt via Alexandria and this was an important position to hold.

We felt very small and insecure as we waited for him, even though we knew that everything necessary would be taken care of for us. 'It's so big and so noisy!' said Rizpah, staring around her in dismay. 'How are we going to manage in a place like this. How will we find our way around?'

'We'll be fine.' I put my arm around her, calming my own trepidation. 'Let's say the Shemah together. That will help.'

Quietly we began to recite. 'Hear O Israel, the Lord our God, the Lord is One. Blessed is His glorious Kingdom for ever and ever.'

'And it shall be that you will love the Lord your God with all your heart and all your soul and with all your might,' another voice continued behind us. We turned and a young man smiled at us as he carried a bag of grain down to the harbour's edge. A ripple of relief washed over me. It was illogical for the young man would probably have turned from us in disgust if he knew I was married to a Roman or a teacher of the inner wisdom but tribal links can be very comforting at times and that was exactly what I needed to still our fears at that moment.

Fortunately, we were to live in a villa on the outskirts of the city and, although the carriage ride to our new home was breathtakingly colourful, frightening and fascinating, Rizpah and I were relieved when the horse-drawn cart which had been waiting to take us and our worryingly large pile of possessions took a road out of town, away from the noise and the smells.

'How can people live in there?' asked Rizpah naively. 'I couldn't breathe.'

Apollonius laughed. 'You get used to it,' he said. 'Soldiers have to get used to all kinds of different cities. Alexandria is much more peaceful than Jerusalem and there are people of all nations here. People find the part which reminds them most of home and then they are comfortable. You will find a mini-Jerusalem down on the East side if you look and there you would not find things so very strange. You are free to go there, of course, but take care if you do and do not go alone. The Jewish people, as you know, can be very hot-headed and they might take against you now you are connected to me. They would be foolish to do so of course, but I know you would not wish to cause trouble.

'If you want to study, the best place to go is to the library. There you will find the intelligentsia but, even so, you will have to find someone who will sponsor you first to get you in. I can't help you there. I'm not an intellectual. I'm not even sure if women are allowed.'

'Someone will turn up if we are meant to go there,' I said, as much to ease my own sense of strangeness as to reassure Rizpah. It would take some time to feel as confident about everything here as I was about all I knew and understood in Judaea. I was hopeful though – not only did I have a good friend in my husband but time and perhaps the sea journey had done their work well in me. The pains and bleeding from Luke's birth had ceased and I felt physically stronger than I had for more than a year. Even so, I wished that there were someone in my life who could lead me with a greater spiritual knowledge and understanding. Despite my gratitude for both Apollonius and Rizpah I missed Yeshua, Judah and Joseph more deeply with each passing day. I missed Magdalene's strength as well. She would have made me laugh and shared the sense of responsibility I felt for the two young people in my care. It was all very well to teach and adapt but who would make sure that I, too, continued to learn and balance myself? Who would tell me if I were going wrong? Who would help me be a good mother to Luke as well as a seeker after the truth for myself?

'God will,' I thought bravely. 'If I make mistakes He will correct me through my life as He always has done. Oh well, we aren't given any more than we can handle.' But I still wished for someone to rest on and to turn to in the physical World. Perhaps, if I found my way to the library that would come.

The villa was beautiful. To us it seemed enormous and both cool and airy, although Apollonius laughed at us for being impressed. We had our own quarters although cousins of the family lived on the other side of the courtyard. Many of the men who worked in administrative buildings in the city also rented apartments and villas in the same complex and it was like a village of its own with tradesmen and pedlars calling regularly. The men also took rooms in the city itself for the times when they needed to stay over for business and, in the evenings when the men were away, the women could gather together either in the atrium, the bathing area or the dining rooms.

Slaves belonging to the villa were already there to meet us and, to them as to the others living there, I was just another Roman woman with two children. They did not know I was a Jew or newly married. All they knew was that I was their new mistress. Suddenly I realised that it would be far harder for me to get used to them than for them to adapt to me.

Of course I should have realised but the circumstances around my first days in a Roman home were so eventful that I had not considered the nature of the servants who had taken care of us. They had been respectful and kind and nothing like I had ever imagined slaves to be. The only times I had come across slaves before had been in the market-places where they moaned and groaned about their lives. Until I was fully grown, I had automatically assumed that they were unhappy and ill-treated. When Judah and I had first met so many years before our salute to each other had been 'Death to all Romans' and I had said it with feeling for I loathed the idea of slavery. Just as Rizpah had to change all her opinions about the Romans, I now had to look at mine about slaves. As Apollonius's wife I was the mistress of slaves and by law I had the power of life or death over other human beings.

Life with Yeshua taught us that nothing could be taken for granted, including the assumption that something was 'bad' or 'good.' Things that seemed 'bad' often taught us important lessons and encouraged us to move on and to change our minds. Things that were 'good' might lead to laziness or arrogance or might bring unhappiness to others. He taught me, specifically, that true slavery was a state of mind where you refused to take responsibility for life. It was easier for a group like us to understand that because we knew that each one of us would experience many different lives. As was so often the case, we Jews had never cared to examine that slaves could often work to win their freedom or that a lot of slaves were better off than many a poverty-stricken freeman. In what was called the free world a man, woman or child might be trapped forever in a way of life which did not suit them. Yes, there were terrible cases of abuse and cruelty in the world of slavery – but were they any greater than the disposal of a wife into prostitution or beggary for the crime of infertility or the stoning to death for falling in love with someone who wasn't their husband?

Even so, it was incredibly hard to come to terms with the idea of being a householder with slaves. Again I was blessed, for Apollonius was a strong and kind man and his slaves were all taken care of just as the most valuable of servants. They were well housed and each was given their freedom with land and money when they reached 45 years of age. Most of those who served us in Alexandria had duties which were not onerous and I found out later that many of them had other part-time jobs as well, so they were not even prevented from earning money – as long as it did not detract from their main work. Some of them even bought slaves of their own and often they treated them far worse than they were treated themselves.

It would be a long process to come to terms with and it was difficult for me to learn to command others. It was tempting to be over-kind but even such a novice as I knew that doing that would soon lead to a lack of respect – and that would make things worse for both sides. I made myself accept the situation for it was part of the whole and part of my destiny but it was not easy. I vowed, however, to encourage everyone who worked for me to be strong within themselves and aware that they did have greater possibilities in their lives – if they wanted to hear about them of course! I knew too well that many people did not wish to set themselves free, preferring to moan and grumble and blame others for their plight and slaves were no different from the rest of us in that respect.

There were times, too, when I was angry at the slaves' disregard for the abundance that surrounded them. Much of my life before had been so much more basic than theirs and I was amazed at the riches I could now command. That brought its own guilt, too, but it was the blind fury that I felt when I saw people picking the best parts out of good food and leaving the rest to be thrown away that was my biggest problem. Our slaves did it too; they could pick and choose what food they ate. They had no idea how lucky they were.

Those first weeks in Alexandria were a constant battle against fear and depression. I missed my home-land so much and wanted to talk about it all the time. If Magdalene had been here I would have had someone to turn to and there were many nights that I wept bitter tears for her.

Rizpah and Luke both took to Alexandrian life like ducks to water. My son, who had always had quite enough to eat or to play with and had been a peaceful, contented baby, was now surrounded by abundance and grew bored and fractious far more easily. He respected me but already it was Apollonius he turned to for love. That hurt, too, but I had to admit it was perfectly natural. I'd never been the most maternal of women. Rizpah gloried in her new clothes, the wonderful food and all the exciting shops and markets which I found intimidating and excessive for weeks. She lost the thinness that was her last block to a bloom of complete beauty and she glowed. I learned to keep quiet and enjoy her happiness; it would have been much worse if she had been pining too.

I tried to hide my discomfort from my husband but I'm not very good at suppressing my fiery temper so Apollonius knew exactly what was going on. He laughed at me which, at first, fuelled my indignation but I could see that he also understood the reasons for my anger. 'I've lived in places where food was scarce,' he said. 'I've felt the gnaw of hunger. I know what you are feeling. Waste is common here and we must live as others do as much as we can or we will be marked down as difficult. But you are right that the people of Alexandria are spoilt. They are lucky. But now it is our turn to be lucky too; let's not ruin the blessing of abundance by anger at what is being given to us.'

I felt shamed then. How come this man who had none of my background or training understood the ways of the Lord better than I did? Yeshua was always telling me that goodness and abundance was humanity's natural inheritance and that it was us who pushed them away by our resistance. 'It's not fair,' I said childishly and, even to my own ears, foolishly. 'You shouldn't know so much.'

Apollonius laughed. He had a deep, belling laugh that reminded me of my father, Joseph. 'You silly little wife!' he said. 'You're a fish out of water; you're faced with a world you never knew existed and you have lost everything and nearly everyone who was familiar to you, including your very best friend; I know you have no one to confide in here. You are doing very well, you know! One day, you may confide a little more in me and I will look forward to that.'

I shed a tear then and he gave me one of the brisk, bone-squeezing hugs that were so characteristic of him. At supper he gave me some sparkling blue topaz earrings and laughed at my contorted face as I struggled with pleasure, gratitude and guilt at the idea of owning so much beauty when so many had so little.

Even so, he gave orders to the kitchen that food should not be wasted and, if any were left over, it was to be used for animal feed or given to beggars. I know the staff thought that was excessively stern and it irritated them because it gave them more work to do but it had another good effect, too. It made them realise that Apollonius respected his wife and her whims were to be obeyed. I was accorded more authority from then on; I just had to learn how to use it.

There would be so much I needed to learn but Apollonius was the best of teachers. During the very first week in Alexandria he took me into the atrium, the central garden, and began my Roman education by explaining the two main gods of the household.

'Deborah, you know that you can practise as a Jew, honour your own festivals and worship your own God in your own way,' he said. 'You know too that I shall be delighted to find out more about your faith by watching you and learning more of your ways. But you will need to honour the Roman ideas of worship in public if you want to fit in with the society we have to mix in.

'I'm sure we can find a synthesis which will enable us to worship together. Your Tree of Life will certainly help once I've understood it! I have my own favourites among my own gods and I remember your brother telling me that my choices told me all he needed to know about my character and my life.'

'Mars?' I said, naming the god of war who stood at Gevurah, the place of the warrior.

'And Apollo too, of course,' he said smiling. 'And Jupiter. But it should be the goddesses who are your domain in the home, publicly at least. Do you know of our goddess Vesta and what she represents?'

I had heard of the Vestal Virgins, priestesses who worshipped Vesta and who were highly honoured and even given the same authority as men for the duration of their time of priesthood. More than that I did not know but I felt excitement within me, for one of my first disciplines in Alexandria could be to discover all I could of where each aspect of these foreign gods fitted into the whole. Again I thanked God for this blessing of a marriage. Apollonius was a spiritual man who had respected Yeshua and I knew we would be able to study and worship together.

He told me about the two household gods acknowledged in nearly every home. Janus, the doorkeeper and Vesta, keeper of the hearth. The head of the household – the father of the family – was responsible for the worship of Janus, the guardian of the house and the one who protected inhabitants from dangerous energies from outside and who strengthened them when they left the home to deal with everyday life outside. The woman's role was to worship Vesta as goddess of the household. The Temple of Vesta, where the famous virgins lived and worked, was the place of the sacred flame, fire, brought down from the Heavens. That was similar enough to the Jewish woman's task of lighting the sacred lights of the Sabbath and the festivals to show that here, too, there was a link between the religions. Woman was the one to receive and nurture the fire of the Lord, whether in her body as the mother of the next generation or in her spirit as the receiver of His wisdom. Apollonius taught me the rituals necessary for the worship of Vesta and those he undertook for Janus. 'But you, yourself are Vesta within the house and I am Janus,' he said. 'If you are anything like your brother, you can worship your own Lord through these rituals instead of seeing them as blocks against faith.

'It is very similar to the idea of God the Father and God the Mother which I learnt with the Essenes,' I said. 'So it is the same but with different names. I shall have no trouble with Vesta or Janus.'

We smiled at each other. 'Good,' he said. 'I knew you were an exceptional woman. I shall look forward to learning more from you.'

As the weeks passed I began to teach Rizpah the links of sacred womanhood so she, too, would understand fully that the Roman gods were not evil or to be despised. They were her one objection to her exciting new life. 'They have statues of naked women everywhere!' she said. 'And some of the priestesses are hardly clothed either! Have you seen them, Deborah? It's disgraceful!'

She missed the Jewish rituals, wanting to go and find a synagogue and announce our coming to the Jewish people, and it took some time to persuade her not only that it would be tactless to Apollonius's family but also that we simply might not be welcome.

'It's romantic to think they will welcome Jews from the Holy Land and that they will all be followers of the Teaching,' I said. 'But I am sure they will not. We will send discreetly to the places Joseph Barsabbas told me of, and then we must wait for them to contact us.'

Rizpah capitulated reluctantly and agreed to study what Apollonius had told me. Her natural intelligence made her swift to learn and she discovered that she enjoyed worshipping the feminine in the Lord openly instead of always referring to all aspects of God as 'He.' She even went into the initially despised temples to find out more. Together we showed the women slaves two tiny variations I wished to have made to the rituals honoured in our home in order to bring them in line with our own worship. They accepted them easily, assuming that we were just adding a regional difference. Transforming Vesta into the Shekhinah, the Holy

Spirit or the feminine aspect of God was simple if you knew the Teaching and both Rizpah and I were comforted amid all the strangeness. It was a sound foundation on which to begin learning the life of Roman women.

Seven

All the other wives who lived in our buildings came to visit in the first week of our life in Alexandria. Three of them, Livia, Claudia and Estella were now relations of mine and were eager to investigate this new phenomenon of a long-lost brother and a Jewish wife. But even before they arrived we had another visitor, a foreigner like ourselves; Constanzia, who was the wife of an assistant to the governor and who lived almost next door. I took to Constanzia immediately for she was as helpful as she could be in assisting us to settle in – without letting on that she knew that I was uncertain of so much.

'Sometimes real people are angels,' I said to Rizpah after Constanzia had quietly let me know the origins and family links of each of our neighbours and family members; who had quarrelled with whom and which topics it was unwise to address, not to mention all she knew about the slaves in the villa. She spoke without malice or self-interest and I knew that all her knowledge would help me immensely – if it were accurate. It was; all the information turned out to be both shrewd and well-observed. It was Constanzia who told me, too, from her own experience, that it was all too easy to upset people when you came from another tribal background. Although slaves were bound to obey, they could make life unpleasant if they had been offended. A good and thoughtful mistress was valued, whatever others who preferred an iron hand might say.

Religion was the most difficult aspect, she said. Some of the people who came from the countryside might see the gods in a different light from those who had always lived in the town. Different aspects were worshipped in different places. Rizpah and I exchanged looks. We had got away with our changes so far but there was so much more to discover! I wondered what Spanish Constanzia's own chosen religion was, but I suspected I would have to wait to find that out.

At first we were all but smothered by relatives. Apollonius, Rizpah and I found the amount of people and the repetition of questions and answers exhausting and increasingly tedious. It was hard to know when to let the assumptions go unquestioned and when to correct them – and how to do that without seeming rude. Most people assumed that both Luke and Rizpah were Apollonius's own children and that was complicated for, although we were happy for them to think that about Luke, Rizpah wanted to be known for who she was. This, of course, led to confusion and muddles and explanations and I heard stories that Rizpah was my sister, my daughter; Drusilla's sister, Drusilla's daughter; the daughter of another woman completely, Apollonius's mistress – and all kinds of other things. Constanzia, who seemed to hear and know everything that was going on, put me on my guard tactfully but there were a few people us who actually enjoyed letting me know what was being thought. My pride came to my rescue there for, although I was angry, I was not going to let anyone know that I regarded their opinions as being of any value whatsoever. Apollonius and Rizpah remained in merciful ignorance of most of the gossip and both of them had enough natural charm and openness to win over even the harshest of critics in time. Those people learned not to bait me either. I found that I had a way of looking which could quell people without giving open offence and I learned to use it, perhaps a little more than I should have done. Even so, these people were my husband's family and I was careful never to say anything against anyone's character. My greatest relief was that Apollonius found them as tiring and almost as irritating as I did and was perfectly willing to talk about it.

'They'll calm down,' he said. 'We are just the latest fashion. Once they discover that we are not at all interesting they will leave us in peace.' I hoped he was right but, even so, we were still constantly pressed to see more of the family than we really wanted to. We got used to it and made excuses where we could. 'Thank the Heavens we both feel the same,' said Apollonius as we both made faces over yet another invitation to an event which we knew would bore us to bits and we laughed. In that respect we were like co-conspirators in this strange new country. It was even a little like the relationship I had had with Yeshua when we had wanted to stay away from the meaningless chatter and inanities of the social life in Nazara.

Apollonius, at least, had work to go to. Like Constanzia's husband, he was an assistant to the governor and he was out of the house six days a week, mostly down at the harbour offices. Without him I felt very vulnerable but, again, Constanzia came to my rescue. She adopted both Rizpah and me and showed us around the areas of the city that a Roman wife and her daughter would need to know. When we protested that we took up too much of her time, she laughed. 'Time?' she said. 'My life is filled with time. I have more time than anyone of my acquaintance. Why should I not use some of my time to be amused and to see this city through new eyes? Mars knows it has bored my own sight for many years.'

Under Constanzia's lazy, patient eye, I had my first experience of being carried in a litter; found out where to shop, where to go for beauty treatments and for hairdressing. I swallowed my embarrassment and learnt how to appear as a respectable, middle-class Roman wife with my fingernails polished and my eyelids tattooed and painted. I chose coloured materials to be made into dresses for Rizpah and for me. I visited the appropriate women in the city and took Luke to visit their children.

'How can you bear it?' Rizpah would ask.

'How can you?' was my reply.

'That's easy,' she said. 'I love luxury; I am not a holy woman. You are teaching me to read and to write and you've taught me to worship the One God through different aspects and that's enough for me. I want to learn from you but I am still involved in this physical World and I love all this beauty. It must be harder for you.'

And yet it was beguiling too. I could see the ease and danger of sinking down within the everyday life of idleness and opulence.

When I was a little more settled, Apollonius took me to the races and the plays and the games which were held throughout the city. For all he was of a serious bent (and so was I) we agreed that we must be seen to do what normal Romans did. It was important for him to be seen to go to public events and wives were expected to go too.

He was kind enough to appreciate that I could not face any activity where humans or animals were killed for the bloodlust of the audience – but it was challenge enough to watch the combats of strength and the chariot races, for death occurred there too. 'In a way this is good for you, Deborah,' said my husband kindly as he held my hand while I gasped at the life or death tragedy being acted out before me after two chariots collided. 'It makes you stronger. For all your knowledge, you must become more detached and see the wider picture. That is the theory that you tell me each day; but you have never had your beliefs tested so much. If they hold it will only make you stronger.'

'It's Yesod that's the problem,' I said to Rizpah. 'The ego consciousness, the everyday World and how you react to things. I can be squeamish and "Holier than Thou" which is my gut reaction, or I can learn to view things from a distance. What I cannot change I must endure or embrace. Otherwise I make myself more visible; I draw hostility or attention where it is not necessary. Hard though it may seem, this is not my business. These lives are not my concern. If they were brought in front of me and I had power in the situation that would be one matter but when they are pageants of another's life then I must allow them to be and walk on when I can.'

'It's hard, though,' said Rizpah, who was as squeamish as I but who had a greater choice in where she could go and what she could see.

That I could not deny.

We went to the zoo where wild animals had been caged for the curiosity of humans. Such a strange idea! We could not decide whether we were thrilled to see so many strange and incredible animals or whether we were just sorry for them. 'You are like me,' I whispered to a couple of great striped cats called tigers. 'In a strange land, fed strange foods and expected to perform for strange people. Good luck to you!'

I went to see those beasts often for they seemed like a talisman to me. In the years that I lived in Alexandria many of the animals in the zoo faded away, pining for their home-land, their freedom and their own kind but the tigers stayed strong, glossy-coated and proud. They gave birth to three little cubs and with each year that passed their roar was still as fierce and as frightening as it was on the day I first saw them. They had adapted to their new surroundings and accepted their life and I took that as a good sign.

Rizpah and I also settled down and adapted to this busy, bustling world. Once the first resistance was over, part of me enjoyed myself very much for everyday life was so much easier than it had been in Judaea. Even so, living in Alexandria felt as though it were some kind of illusion – as if the real Deborah was resting inside me, waiting for her turn to come forward again.

Apollonius's work at the harbour meant that we had to entertain many foreign visitors and other officials. To my amazement I found it fairly easy to be a successful hostess. I was so curious for a start; I wanted to know everything and I was not afraid to ask. I did not have to talk very much, just prompt a few questions and then I could just watch and listen for people loved to talk about themselves. My ignorance was profound but I learned not to make a fool of myself with stupid queries. I would question Apollonius later when we were alone and he would answer with patience and humour at my inaccurate assumptions and my insatiable curiosity.

The years of living and travelling with Yeshua had taught me the valuable lesson of how to listen to what people had to say. In those days, when a woman had come to me with a terrible problem, I had often felt helpless. But if I listened, fully and patiently, even if I had nothing to say to her, the woman still felt helped and loved and the time was not wasted. Often she found the answer for herself just by being allowed the luxury of speaking the truth without fearing judgement. My ability to listen and say little helped me to fit in for those first strange months in Alexandria for it meant I was not trying to make a place for myself at the cost of anyone else. Once the first jostling for position was over and I had made it clear that I was friendly and willing but not a weak vessel to be taken advantage of, I was content for the other women to teach me, making a mental note to review everything later on to see whether their suggestions would serve me or not. When Apollonius was home and we entertained others, I was happy to let him do most of the talking and to watch and listen to him to make sure I adopted the correct customs. Each time I opened my mouth I was bound to be different enough without breaching etiquette through thoughtlessness too.

The Greeks did not have the respect for women that my own race conferred upon us and I could see that, had I lived in Alexandria when I was younger, that would have angered me greatly. As it was I felt strong enough inside and in the respect of my husband that I did not react to the general male opinion of women. I could see, anyway, that the opinion belonged only to men of our own particular class; the sons and brothers of women who were frustrated and bored with their lives. Such men would draw to them wives who would either agree with them that women were stupid or feeble – or give them a very hard time! The true aristocrats, one level above us, the merchants one level below and the slaves all worked as equals.

Once again, it was not my problem; not a factor which existed within my marriage. And I gave daily thanks for that.

One of the things which amazed me most was that I was considered beautiful in Alexandria. My youthful freckles had long gone and the pale skin of a natural red-head was much prized in Graeco-Roman society. Women of our class and above even wore a kind of white paint on their dark skins and dyed their black hair yellow, brown or red according to the vagaries of fashion. I, who had not cared about such things was, ironically, everything they sought to be. Once my pale lashes had been dyed and eyeliner tattooed onto my skin, my face had much more character. My height and thinness made the Roman dresses look elegant and the parochial, Galilean accent so despised in Jerusalem was thought exotic and attractive. Slowly I began to grow in confidence and dared to speak out and test the waters. To my amazement, once I admitted my origins, I discovered that non-orthodox Jews were quite fashionable in Roman society and nowhere more so than in Alexandria. Many people who were tired of all the different Roman gods were fascinated by the idea of one Lord who took care of everything instead of dozens who demanded different prices for their favours. Instead of thinking me strange and igno- rant, as I had feared, men and women began to ask my opinion at dinner parties and listened to what I had to say. Alexandria was a cosmopolitan city with many different races and so many gods and goddesses that a foreign woman's views on religion were lis- tened to, if not accepted.

It was a stunning lesson in how open Roman society was to dif- ferent races and religions. These rulers of the world were thought to be cruel and savage (and often they were) but they were also far more tolerant of strangers than their 'subjects' including the orthodox Jews, who kept themselves rigorously separate from oth- ers and complained continually of being oppressed.

I'm sure I was lucky but no one even had any problem with my refusal to eat pork or shellfish or my wish to keep the god Saturn's day as the Sabbath. Apollonius did not enjoy shellfish himself so we never served it at home. Pork I could avoid easily enough and, if ever there were a meal where I accidentally ate some (or some rabbit or a meat which had been sacrificed to one of the gods, making it ritually impure to a Jew), I was able to remember Yeshua's teaching that nothing can defile the body if the spirit is cleansed. It took some time but, eventually, I even instigated the idea of a Sabbath day for everyone in our house, not just for Rizpah and me. For practicality's sake, the slaves were given time off in rotation and often they chose not to take it – many of them just took another part time job to earn some money. I did remind everyone that rest was important and that they should take care of themselves to encourage good health and happiness but, once I had fulfilled my part of my bargain with the Lord, it was not up to me to impose my belief on those who refused to accept it. Plenty abused the system and that caused resentment among the others but I kept to my principles and weathered those storms as just another aspect of the life of a Roman wife.

As the weeks and months went by I had nothing but confirmation that Apollonius was the best of men. Every day I would thank God for another example of his thoughtfulness. He always made sure I understood what my duties were and who we were going to meet, so that I could be fully informed and give the welcome that was required, but he did not do it in a condescending way; rather he treated me like a foreign princess who had never before had to deal with everyday matters. Sometimes I would burst into laughter and tell him he should have seen me chasing chickens or cursing and covered in ash as I tried to light a reluctant fire at home in Cana or Nazara before he spoke to me with such respect. Then he would laugh too and kiss me on the forehead and cheeks. 'You are the sister of a prince,' he said once. 'So you have to be a princess. Now, then, don't cry! You silly, sweet girl. Are you so homesick? Is it so very hard?'

That was not why I cried. It could easily have been so different – a less sensitive man would not have cared about the fate of a Jewess and her illegitimate son; but then, a less sensitive man would never have asked a strange, wandering prophet to heal one of his soldiers either.

Apollonius's adoration of Luke was obvious to everyone who saw them together. Apollonius knew, as well as I did, that it was entirely possible that the child was the son of any one of the soldiers who had raped me or even, as I hoped, of Judah but, even if that were true, the bond between the two of them was more than that of blood. Luke knew that Apollonius was his true father from the first day they were brought together and, if he were home, the child would not be content until he could sit in his father's arms or play at his feet. Luke never acted towards me as though I were his mother; for comfort he wanted Rizpah, his nursemaid or his father. However, he would sit or play quietly with me for hours as long as I was teaching Rizpah, reading or praying and the first words he spoke were Hebrew, picked up from my repetition of prayers or my reading aloud.

Often, as we sat in the beautiful atrium with its gloriously-scented lilies, Apollonius would ask me about Yeshua and I would tell stories of our travels and the miracles I had witnessed. I talked too of my childhood and how Yeshua had helped me turn from a stubborn, crippled little girl who hated the Lord of Israel into a woman with a faith almost as strong as his. I told stories, too, such as the one where Yeshua stayed behind at the Temple when he was twelve and how we had to turn back to find him. There was a kind Samaritan on the way back who took pity on the little lame girl who was struggling so much and who gave her a donkey when everyone else was angry. That was the inspiration for one of Yeshua's favourite parables.

'You are taking it all in, aren't you?' I would say to Luke as he sat on his father's lap and his wise little face would light up with a smile. It might just have been indigestion, of course, but I was not likely to believe that. Unnatural mother or not, I still thought my son was the most intelligent of children; an old soul who would achieve much.

I was waiting until the day Apollonius asked to know more of the Tree of Life and Jacob's Ladder before I taught him more, just as Yeshua had waited for me to ask, so many years before, when we lived in Emmaus. To offer information before it was asked for was often a mistake. One day, however, I drew the Tree of Life again, this time in the earth in the atrium, to illustrate one of the stories and Luke clambered down and crawled across to look at the picture. 'Pretty,' he said and tried to copy it with his unsteady baby hands. At such moments I would have died for Luke and he for me but at those times we were two souls who understood each other completely. As others held Luke or played the normal child-hood games with him, I would stand by and watch and wonder who he was and what he had come to Earth to do.

Time passed and we heard nothing from Joseph Barsabbas. We half hoped he would still come for the first Hanukkah but, although we posted watchers at the harbour in case he arrived without writing to us first, there was no sign of him. I had no idea how to contact him and, although Apollonius asked colleagues visiting Judaea to look out for him, there was silence as to his whereabouts. At night sometimes I would stand silently staring up at the stars, trying to reach him with my mind. I knew he was still alive – though I could not explain how I knew. I just wanted to know how he was and what was happening in my homeland. It often felt as though Yeshua, Judah and Joseph were one entity in my mind, one being whose presence I missed above all things. Yeshua was watching over us, I was sure, from the place of the Great Ones in the Heavens. Sometimes I felt an echo of Judah as well. I could still cry at his memory even though, in this World, I was so blessed.

Apollonius and I looked the model of a happily married couple but, behind closed doors, we lived separately. No one but us would have known, for the aspiring upper-middle classes and the aristocracy always had separate apartments for husband and wife. My room was next to Luke's and Rizpah's was next to mine. Apollonius slept on the other side of the courtyard with its pool filled with golden and silver fish, its fountain and the beds of bright, colourful flowers. He would always come to find me to say goodnight if he had been out until late or kiss me on the forehead, cheeks and lips when we had spent an evening together, playing draughts or chess or talking but he did not offer more. The nights on the ship receded into distant memory but, as I grew fonder of him and the loss of Judah receded within me, I began to wonder whether there was anything my knowledge of herbs and oils could do for him – and for our married life together.

I could see from my visits to the markets that the Alexandrian herbal medicines available without consulting an apothecary were often not of good quality and the ignorance with which I heard them prescribed was quite horrifying. So far I had been able to deal with all Luke's childhood problems with the herbs and potions I had brought with me from Judaea in the little olive box that Yeshua had made for me more than 15 years before. But I knew that soon I would either have to start growing my own medicines or find an apothecary I could trust.

Apollonius raised no objections when I asked to have a small section of our land for my own garden. He was content to let me do whatever I wished and whatever help or transport I needed were always available. Over our first two years in Alexandria I slowly created a garden filled with herbs and medicinal plants and, as my childhood teacher Rosa had taught me, I taught Rizpah. We grew hyssop and golden rod for burns, henbane for muscle spasms and sleeplessness, lavender and jasmine to soothe rough emotions and poppies for pain relief. I smiled when I remembered Rosa and her herbs and salves and her secret plants for the private visitors whom I was never meant to see. Now of course I understood the problems of women; in those days they were a complete mystery to me.

Constanzia helped me, too, once she could bestir herself from her sofa. This gentle, lazy foreigner was bored to tears with her life and my digging and planting revitalised memories of her own childhood in Spain. At least two afternoons a week she would rest under an awning in the garden, nibbling her favourite almond biscuits and telling me new ideas from her country of birth. Mixing that knowledge with what Magdalene had taught me of the secrets of her trade before she followed Yeshua, I finally understood how to make the women's secret tinctures and oils from Rosa's secret plants. I, too, grew strangleweed which could be used as a poultice for stings and bites but also as a contraceptive for any woman who might wish to enquire for one. I grew chrysanthemums and tansy and grafted mistletoe to the little apple tree for women in more serious trouble and, as word spread about my little garden both through the slaves I treated for minor ailments and the other officials' wives, I began to receive occasional visits from local women whose hearts were heavy or whose burden was becoming too much. There were plenty of midwives in Alexandria who knew their trade well but there were fewer who had the time or the inclination to listen to those who had fears and doubts about their life.

Constanzia was a natural helper of others though she was wonderfully lazy and relaxed about life. The only time she would exert herself was to help someone else and even then she did not worry about their problems once they had gone away. In that way she was an inspiration to me for I was constantly tempted to do too much. 'Why bother?' Constanzia would say. 'They won't appreciate it if you break your back for them. If someone really wants to see you, they can come at a time which is convenient to you. You don't have to rush around and fuss and make life hard for yourself.' What she said was true but it was hard to carry out in practice. What Constanzia believed was completely in line with Yeshua's view of life, although he never gave the impression of laziness as she did. He said – and I knew he was right – that the best help was given from Tiferet, the place of stillness and detachment within. It did not stop you caring for the person who needed you but it made sure you were not drained by their pain or needed their gratitude to help you feel good.

There was one thing which Constanzia envied me. She could not comprehend what she called my 'secret ingredient' which was the simplest of all things. If anyone came for help, I prayed for them and laid my hands upon their shoulders as Yeshua had taught us to do in Galilee. Never once did as much power flow through me as had through him but there were little miracles here and there. Sometimes it felt as though Yeshua himself were in the garden with me and, at those times, I could relax completely for I knew that the ailment or trouble being explained before me was being understood and resolved in a higher place than I could ever reach. For all her loving kindness Constanzia could not touch that extra healing power for she was too self-involved to step back and allow it to flow through her. I did, eventually, ask her about her beliefs but she had none, just went to the appropriate temple at the appropriate time. 'The gods are a figment of our imagination,' she said. 'We invented them. They don't bother me and I don't bother them.'

I was busy and, for the most part, contented but I was still waiting for the opportunity to find the heart of Alexandria; the place and the people Joseph Barsabbas had told me of, the ones who studied the Tree of Life. I had contacted all the addresses that Joseph had given me but to no avail. His information was either out of date or those who received my notes did not wish to answer them. The Essene group that he had belonged to appeared to have moved on or hidden itself more thoroughly although there was still a fairly similar group known as the 'Therapeutae.' When I first heard of them I was certain that this was the answer for these were groups of men and women, mostly Jews or proselytes, who lived apart from others and worshipped the One God. One commune in particular was within half a day's travel from Alexandria and Apollonius was perfectly willing for us to visit them.

'Let me find out a little more about them first,' he said. 'We don't want to make a wasted trip.'

There was not much that was known except that the men and women lived totally celibate lives apart from each other. It was thought that they learned the same things, fasted regularly and never ate before sundown. Part of me was discouraged by that but, even so, I was still keen to visit them. What was more commonly whispered abroad was that they were a sanctuary for wives who had run away from their husbands and embraced a life of celibacy, hidden away where they could not be found. Certainly no ordinary husband would have been willing to take his wife voluntarily to see such a dangerous group of people, particularly in Alexandria where Greek customs were very much the fashion – meaning far less freedom for women than Roman law allowed.

But Apollonius was an exceptional man as well as a confident one. He knew full well that even if I loved the life of the Therapeutae, I would not leave him or Luke. Perhaps a small part of me was affronted by that very confidence but I also knew that we had struck a bargain and that I would not go back on that.

We hired a carriage and Apollonius drove me to the commune himself. The River Nile had just finished its annual flood and the marshy land around the city was damp and steaming in the harsh sunlight. I kept a watch out for crocodiles because they lived in this kind of terrain and I was half-fascinated and half-fearful at the idea of seeing one but they were busy elsewhere that day. The road itself was not in good condition once we were out of the cluster of villages which surrounded Alexandria. The Therapeutae did not encourage outsiders to visit and they rarely came into town so there was no need for a good track.

Rather to our surprise the land where the community lived was dry and cool, high enough to catch the sea breezes and with no sign of marshes at all. But, even from a distance, the settlement itself looked very sparse and, to my Essene-trained eye, there seemed little sign of a good water system for bathing – apart from the sea itself.

'Are you really sure you want to go on?' asked Apollonius, watching me eat lunch with my usual good appetite. We had set out early and taken our own food (and we were eating it before we got there so as not to offend anyone). 'I can't see you taking to this type of life even part of the time and you know perfectly well that I'm not going to let you go and live with them anyway.'

There was such an irony there for we were both celibate and we could easily have joined in with a community which simply did not allow sex between partners. One which segregated them all the time and demanded that its adherents lived totally within the walls of the commune might have been a different matter. 'No, I

want to go on,' I said. 'Just to see. If they have the same knowledge as I do there will be something we can do together. If not,
then at least I'll know.'

The visit was a failure. The men would not speak to me and
the women would not talk to Apollonius. With a wry look at each
other we consented to be separated and both went off to talk to
our respective groups. I stayed for longer than my husband, but
only out of politeness, and we were soon on our way back to
Alexandria, rather silent at first for we each did not know how the
other would react.

Apollonius broke the silence. 'You actually lived like that?' he
asked, referring to my time at the Essenes in Emmaus.

'Oh no,' I said swiftly. 'I lived in a mixed community. Nothing
like that at all. And we had our own rooms, not dormitories.'

'Well?' said my husband. 'Does it appeal?'

Thinking over the sparse living arrangements, the meagre diet,
the almost slavish attention to ritual and the complete lack of
involvement of the women in any of the services, I started to say
that it did not. Then I noticed that my husband's shoulders were
quivering and he had turned his face away.

'Are you laughing?' I said, my sensibilities outraged that he
should be amused at such a holy community.

'It's just the thought of you living there!' said Apollonius. 'The
idea that you could give up all the luxuries you have been learning
to enjoy so much in Alexandria.' He was laughing openly now.
'I'm sorry, I can't help it. If you had seen them when you first
came you might have been tempted; you hated the excesses of
Alexandria so much. But now I just can't see you there. Don't
even think of asking me if I would go and live with such a crowd
of humourless, self-centred, intolerant bores!'

My mouth dropped at his irreverence and then, before I could
stop it, a wave of giggles threatened to engulf me too. 'Stop it, it's
not fair!' I said helplessly. 'They're very holy. They're following
their own deep beliefs. You have to respect that.'

Apollonius said a rude Alexandrian-Egyptian word which both
summed up his opinion and commented on the agricultural fer-
tiliser used by the Therapeutae. It was a word I had never heard
him use before although I heard it often enough in the markets of

the city. I hardly knew whether to be insulted or to be pleased that he felt intimate enough with me to drop his guard so much.

'And don't try looking so outraged at me either, Deborah!' said my husband, putting his arm around me. 'I'm quite sure you think they are all a load of idiots just as much as I do; you're just too polite to say it. Would it help if I forbade you ever to go there again because, believe me, I'll do it. I'm not having the joy in you squeezed out by that self-righteous bunch of miseries.'

I have to say that I felt a rush of relief at his words. Part of me had been willing to fall into the trap of thinking I 'ought' to want to be with the Therapeutae even if I were not willing to follow their ways. One thing they certainly did not seem to do was laugh and I thought laughter was vital to life – and to worshipping God!

'They didn't seem to know about the Tree of Life anyway,' I said, still trying to keep my dignity and then, like my husband, I began to laugh helplessly. 'No,' I said when I had recovered a little. 'I couldn't live like that and I can't see how it would make God happy if I did. Surely He enjoys a little fun and laughter as well as all the worship! Not even the Essenes at Qumran were as bad as that.'

We drove home together comfortably, talking about everyday matters. That night I thought long and deep about the Therapeutae and about my life and I realised that, even if I had wanted to, going to them would have been like going back in time. Yeshua had freed me from such a community and taken me to teach with him in Galilee. Surely my place was in the outside world, not shut away in a place where the women did not read or learn on their own account.

But I still did not give up my search. I went to the great library many times and was able to join the section which would lend you books to take home. But although I would hang around and ask questions, the hallowed halls of the great scholars remained closed to me. You could make appointments with those who maintained the library but a woman enquiring tentatively about the Merkabah Tradition of the Jews seemed to have as many doors slammed in her face there as she would have expected in Jerusalem.

It was wonderful to be teaching Rizpah (and in a small way to be teaching Apollonius) but I wanted to learn more myself. I had copy scrolls of the Torah to read and study and Joseph Barsabbas's precious book but I wanted so much more.

I wanted to find a group of people with a teacher who could instruct me. Apollonius kindly invited some Jewish families to dinner for, even though he was sometimes amused by my fervour, he knew that the search was important to me. But the only Jews who would come were on the fringes of the community and were not observant or interested in anything more within their own faith. I learnt much from them but it was mostly about Greek thinking and philosophy and not the inner secrets of Judaism. Their leader was the great Alabarch of the city, Alexander Lysimachus, who dealt with all the Jewish people's taxes and liaised between them and the government but he was such a cosmopolitan man that neither Apollonius nor I found him worth approaching for details of faith.

Once we knew that we were accepted within our own circle of society, Rizpah and I did go down into the Jewish quarter to sit in on Synagogue services and to talk to the men and women afterwards, in case that would prove to be the way, but no one encouraged me to visit their homes or meet their menfolk and many were openly contemptuous of a woman in a mixed marriage. Once or twice Rizpah was invited to visit on her own but she refused to go without me. We had quite an argument about that; I thought she should take the opportunity to go and get to know some people so she could find out more and maybe meet up with some Jewish men who might give her a clue as to what our next step should be. She, in turn, was adamant that it would do no good; that she would be stuck in the role of unmarried female helper and not allowed anywhere near the men's teaching.

Some of the intelligentsia among the orthodox Jews visited us when they had business with Apollonius and they were unfailingly courteous to me but none of them appeared to be open to the idea of further study or the mystical knowledge.

At last I lost my temper with the Lord, ranting and scolding Him and even throwing a pair of shoes at the Shabbat candlesticks I kept in my room. As I stood shaking my fist and venting my fury, I felt the air around me shimmering again and clear as a bell I heard the sound of laughter. The angels and the Lord Himself were laughing at me and my lack of patience. Almost against my will I began to chuckle too and, by the time Apollonius came to find out what all the noise was about, I was sitting, giggling, on the floor, holding my shoes and the candlesticks on my lap.

I could not explain to him exactly why I laughed so much but as I sat there and the images of my life and its miracles seemed to flow in the air around me I could hardly believe that I could still lack the faith to know that the Lord would find me a way in to the Inner Teaching here, exactly when and where it was appropriate. I was not in Alexandria by accident; there would be work for me to do. The test, as always, was to be patient and to wait.

In the end it was nearly three years before the door opened. Time for me to become stronger and surer of myself and to give time to my new life, my son and my adopted sister-daughter. Luke was raised with Yeshua's teachings for his bedtime stories; Rizpah learned to understand the Teaching as well as I did and to read and write in Greek and Hebrew. We both studied Latin and she far outshone me as a scholar. Apollonius and I came to know and appreciate each other more, though there was still no sexual relationship between us. He was interested in my garden pharmacy but he never asked for anything for himself and I never quite dared to ask if there was anything I could do for him.

I continued to study the Roman and Greek religions as well as the cult of Mithras (as much as I could for it was closed to women). I spoke to priests and priestesses of all faiths, comparing their knowledge with mine and pondering long and deeply, in the winter evenings, how everything fitted together in the Higher Worlds. The more I learnt the more I saw that it was so.

I even spoke with a follower of an Indian teacher Yeshua had spoken about, called the Buddha. Apollonius met him in the market place and invited him to eat with us for he knew that I would want to find out more of his strange faith. It truly was fascinating for it did not involve a god at all. All enlightenment came from within without the need to look for a higher being. This man and I talked into the early hours, long after Apollonius and Rizpah had

gone sleepily to their beds and the slaves watching over us had fall-
en asleep at their posts.

I drank in what I could as we spoke for this man carried a light
as strong as any I had seen around Joseph Barsabbas. A worried
thought at the back of my mind wondered how there could be
two such men at once until I remembered Yeshua's speaking of
the thirty-six righteous men who existed in the world at all times
to be the inspiration to us all. The Buddhist was surely one of
them.

What amazed us both as we talked was that for all the difference in our attitudes we had no points for disagreement in practice. When he left, continuing his journey to the Western
lands, we bowed deeply to each other and smiled, knowing we
would never meet again in this life but that we had a friend in
each other forever. I never knew his name but for many years I
would think of him sometimes and feel strength flowing into
me. It was a privilege to understand that one of the great, righteous ones of the world was not of the race known as 'God's
Chosen People' for it proved to me that all religions lead to the
Lord in their own way and that He knew and understood that
too.

One day, when I had begun to notice the first signs of silver weaving their way through the mass of my ever-rebellious copper hair,
Apollonius brought me a present from one of the Jewish markets
in the city. It was a book. A small, bound copy of the Prophets
in Hebrew and, to my great delight, it included the story of
Queen Esther. At Emmaus I had never been able to read the story
for myself for the Essenes had thought Esther unimportant and no
copies of her story had been kept at the community. Maybe I was
just contrary but that had both angered and intrigued me and I
had always believed that the story would contain a message for me
and, perhaps, for all women.

I took the book, almost speechless with delight, hugging the
precious document to my breast and thanking my husband with
such enthusiasm that he laughed at me anew. By then I had long
stopped being offended at his amusement over things I said and
did because I knew it was born from affection.

It was late that night before I had the first opportunity to read the story and I thanked the Lord again for the prosperity which meant I could call for lamps and curl up in comfort, uninterrupted, in my own room.

I read voraciously and learned anew.

Esther, I already knew, was a Jewess who married the King of Persia when our people were in exile. She saved the Jews by interceding on their behalf when one of her husband's henchmen, Haman, an Amelekite – sworn enemies of the Jewish people – planned a massacre of the Jews throughout Persia. When I was a child and heard the story in the Synagogue I had asked why no Jewess in our day had married the Emperor in Rome to free our people and was told to be quiet for my pains. Perhaps, even then, some part of me had known that I too would be married to a gentile, just as Esther was.

As I read the story, shivers ran up and down my spine and I saw why the book was not used by the orthodox for the Lord was never mentioned once. Esther had to make her journey alone, relying on her own knowledge and trust in herself. She was separated from her people and all conventional links to her God. She had nothing to help her but herself and the inner link to the Holy One that all humans have, whether they know or believe it or not.

This was the antidote indeed to the stories of Lilith and Eve who, according to the Torah and the oral tradition, took the wrong steps and plunged womanhood into confusion. Lilith, Adam's first wife, was too proud and too greedy, trying to take Adam's power and refusing to see her own. She flew away and became the consort of demons – and a stick to be used to threaten any woman seen to be above her station. Eve, created later to be Adam's consort, also 'failed' in that she believed the word of another over herself and lacked the strength to follow her own belief.

Yeshua, of course, had seen another side of both stories. He said that Lilith should be an inspiration for women to understand their own power and strength; then they would have no need to steal from others. And, when he talked of Adam and Eve, he said they were children in Eden. Anyone knew what would happen if you forbade a child to try an exotic new fruit when just one from so much abundance would never be missed.

'Do you think the Lord didn't know what would happen?' he would say. 'Do you think it was not part of the plan? What if Adam and Eve had stayed in paradise? How would they have grown towards the Lord? How would they have grown or learnt? To use Free Will can be painful but it is the only way to learn the great truths of the Universe. We make mistakes; that's how we learn.'

I had Yeshua to teach me. Esther, abandoned and confused, stood alone and worked out the answer for herself. As Queen of Persia, no one knew her Jewishness. She had to learn to bow to her enemy, Haman, in public for he was in favour with the King when she was not. Lilith would not have done it; but Esther understood that to bow was not a dishonour, it was an action required of one who knew the greater Truth and who could see into the pure heart of anyone, however evil they might appear. She knew that all men and women were equal no matter what the social mores taught.

Esther had to face death to approach her husband with a request to see him in private. The Emperor of all the Persians could not be seen without permission; even a Queen did not have official access to the King. Reading between the lines I saw that Esther and her husband had quarrelled for, had they been sharing a bed, she could surely have used some influence with her husband then.

Esther could have been killed as she went before him unannounced but to be willing to face that probability was an even greater death. It represented the death of her ego, the death of the need to be proud and not to bow to the higher will of God. If she didn't do it, her people would perish.

As I read, I began to see how Esther's story would fit onto the Tree of Life and into the Four Worlds. Hastily, I scrawled out her journey through the psyche on one of the pieces of parchment I kept by my bed. It fitted perfectly! What was more, Esther finished up in the place known as the Kingdom of God. The place of the Messiah.

I slumped back on the bed. This story was everything a woman needed to hear to understand her own Divinity and it was there, in the book of the Prophets, hidden and ignored. The story of Esther even had its own festival, Purim, but that was only seen by the orthodox as celebrating the physical saving of the Jews and revenge on Haman. No one saw it for what it was; woman's public understanding of her greatness and her return into the realms of God. Yeshua and the Teaching had always said that Messiahs came and went; some great, some hidden, some failed. What no one had ever said was that once, at least, there was a woman who had reached the place of the Messiah.

I burst into tears. What was I to do with this knowledge? Oh, if only Yeshua had been here to listen to me, to tell me that I was right. To advise me what to do next.

'But you would never have found this answer if he were still here because you would not have looked,' said a shimmering voice in my head and the room was bathed in glowing, flickering light until it vanished. I was in the Heavens themselves, supported by the wings of invisible angels.

'Gabriel?' I said, tentatively, not recognising the echo of voices which surrounded me but knowing I was being lifted into the higher realms. 'Raphael, Haniel?'

A whisper of song from the Seraphim and then, golden and fierce, terrifying and awesome, one word: 'Michael.'

The Archangel Michael, guardian of the Kingdom of God, the place of the Messiah; gatekeeper of the World of Azilut, the way through to God Itself, past the limitations of male and female and the World of form and image. No other words came. Instead, I felt a deep silence around me, resonant and glorious and then I saw the celestial dome of the highest Heavens as though I were standing at the gateway to its inner courts. Yeshua was there and others even greater than he; Metatron, the greatest, the incredible brightest star who was also Enoch, Melchizedek and a thousand other beings of light simultaneously.

And Esther.

She came forward to me, crowned in golden light, robed in colours I could barely see. Her hands reached out to hold mine as we looked into each other's eyes. I saw the soul of Imma, my mother, inside her and my own soul too. Esther. Esther, who stood alone and risked all. The only known Messiah who was born a woman. Our sister, our mother, our self.

When I woke, it was morning. Late, for the Sun was high in the sky and my handmaiden, Dorcas, was calling my name as she stood anxiously by the bed.

'Madam,' she said. 'Madam, are you well? We let you sleep but now there is someone to see you. You must wake up, Madam, please. Here, I have brought you fresh orange juice.'

I shook my head, dizzily trying to see in this strange, dim, Earthly light. A feeling of heaviness and depression settled on me that I was still in this harsh, challenging World and not free in the Heavens with those who loved me and wished to lift me to the higher understanding.

'I'm all right,' I said, taking the juice with a shaking hand. 'Just a very deep sleep. I will be fine.'

'There is a man to see you,' said Dorcas. 'A Jew. He says he has come to see you about a book the Master bought. He is very insistent and he has been waiting for some time. Will you see him?'

'What is his name?' I asked to buy time. This must be about my precious volume of the Prophets. Did some Alexandrian Jew object to my having it? The thought brought a flare of anger.

'I do not know his name,' said Dorcas 'Just that he is a scholar and a fellow of the library of Alexandria. I would not have bothered you if he were just a merchant but he is a respectable man.'

I leaped up. The library! Perhaps this was the way in at last!

'Tell him I will see him,' I said. 'Ask him to wait a little longer and give him refreshment. The best, Dorcas, the very best. Oh! I am so glad he has come. Go! Go now and see to it. Don't worry about me. I can dress myself.'

I washed hastily, dressed and pinned my hair as well as I could. There was no time to call another slave to help me and anyway, my hair would be covered by my pella. Appearance did not matter in itself, it would be how I spoke with this man which would tell. Would he let me into the library; into the inner Jewish teaching?

I recited Yeshua's favourite prayer to bring calmness before I left the room. Dear Lord! Let this day's daily bread be my chance! Then, picking up my new and precious volume of the Prophets, I almost ran down the corridor to the entrance hall where the man would be waiting.

He was small and neatly dressed; balding, freckled and with a round face which belied his stern expression. The Jew bowed to the Roman lady he saw in front of him and began to state his case.

'My name is Philo,' he said. 'I regret to inform you that your husband bought a book yesterday which should not have been sold to him. It had been stolen from the library and we had been searching for it. It is a holy book and it should be returned to us at once if you would be so kind.'

'Here is the book,' I said. 'If it is yours, you may, of course have it back. That is, if you do not feel that a Roman has defiled it by touching it.'

'I do not think so,' he said with a bow. 'The book has been handled by many in its time and a book, as you may know, is never ritually pure to an orthodox Jew.'

'Then you are not orthodox but you are learned?'

'I would hope a little,' he bowed again.

'Then I ask one favour of you.' I said. 'I wish to copy out the Book of Esther for myself. I can read and write in Hebrew but I will need access to a place where I can do this work. As a woman I am not allowed access to the inner areas of the library and without this book I will have no access to the story. Will you help me?'

Philo stepped back in surprise. I could see that he thought me presumptuous.

'Hear, O Israel, the Lord our God, the Lord is One' I said softly in Hebrew and he jumped again. This time, he looked up at me and peered into my face as if seeking evidence of what I was implying. I could see his mind working, saying, 'a pious Jewess? In a Roman soldier's home? What?'

'I seek the Tree of Life,' I continued, gently, still in Hebrew. 'I seek the four Worlds of Azilut, Beriah, Yetzirah and Assiyah.'

There was silence.

'Who are you, child?' asked Philo, speaking even softer than I.

'My name is Deborah bat Joseph of Nazara in Galilee, lately of the Essene community of Emmaus,' I said. 'I am the sister of Yeshua of Nazara who came and studied the Merkabah Tradition with the inner core of Alexandria ten years ago. He taught me all he knew and I have been hoping to meet with you. I believe the book has been an instrument to bring us together and I humbly ask you to help me find the place where I can continue my studies here in Alexandria. Will you do so?'

To my surprise, the old man began to cry. The tears trickled down his cheeks and he stood, shaking as though he would fall.

I reached out to offer him my hand, hesitating in case he would consider himself bound by the laws of purity, but I did not have to fear. Philo took my arm and leaned against me.

'Thank the Lord,' he said. 'His sister. At last. I have been waiting for you, my dear, for so long.'

Eight

'Your brother,' said Philo, as we walked together through the streets of Alexandria, 'was recognised by many of us as the Axis of the Age.'

'The what?'

'Ah! I beg your pardon. It is an Eastern term for the Messiah. There are many other words from many different religions. We, being blessed with communication between the faiths, tend to mix our words. In everyday life, of course, we take care not to but then, these topics are rarely discussed in everyday life!

'Are you sure you are comfortable walking?' he continued, changing the subject from the sacred to the mundane with the greatest of ease. 'Roman ladies, you know, are always carried by litter.'

'I'm perfectly happy to walk.'

As we made our way through the streets of the city, dodging between carriages, shoppers and merchants, I told Philo how his friend's sister came to be in Alexandria and married to a Roman. The little man listened with his head on one side, enjoying the story and guiding me skilfully up this street and down that avenue. Now and again he pointed out some shop or building of particular interest, interrupting my words but so good-humouredly that it was impossible to take offence. He seemed to have the mind of a bird, jumping from one thing to another but treating all with equal interest, whether it was a Jewish woman's breaking the law or a pretty pair of slippers on a market stall which he said would suit me well.

'And are you happy?' he asked when I had finished my story.

'Yes,' I said. 'But I have been searching and searching for the inner Alexandria. Now you have found me I will be happier still.'

'Yes, yes, but you mustn't make the mistake of thinking everyone of the intelligentsia here is tolerant,' said Philo as we made our way down the city's main business street with its great colonnades. 'We have our fair share of bigots in Alexandria, too. In fact there are probably only about 30 or so of us who truly believe in the equality of faiths and even we, secretly, know our own faith is the only one.' At that he chuckled and I liked him even more.

'You remind me a little of another friend from Judaea who was raised here,' I said. 'Do you know of a man named Joseph Barsabbas?'

'Indeed I do. You know he spent some time with the Essene group who used to live to the East of the city?' I nodded. That was one of the addresses Joseph had given me but the community there had moved on.

'I'm fairly sure he came to some meetings I attended when I was younger,' Philo continued. 'It must have been twenty years or so ago, now. In fact I heard of him again only recently. I gather that he has cast his lot in with a man named Paul at the moment. There is a possibility that they may even come here sometime in the next few years as they travel, spreading the news.'

'Oh, I am glad to hear of him! What news do you mean?'

'Of your brother of course! That the Four Worlds have come together in a new Messiah. That the Teaching has been shown to the gentiles and the Holy One is spreading his Word throughout the world. Though to be honest, my dear, I suspect it will be corrupted until it becomes merely the beginning of another religion.'

Philo's cynicism made me smile. Most people would have regarded the founding of a new religion as an amazing thing but, as he and I both knew, there was nothing new in what Yeshua had taught.

However, it appeared that the impulse of faith in Jerusalem was still spreading slowly and steadily throughout Judaea, Syria and even to the northern provinces of the Roman Empire. This was a shouting in the streets that the Messiah had come – with all its attendant miracles and persecutions. Perhaps it had already reached Alexandria but I had not realised? The thoroughfares around us were busy with people and I had plenty of time to think as Philo and I continued on our way – time, too, to deal with my resentment that it was all happening without me and probably without the other women as well.

I consoled my ever-hasty ego by reminding it of what I had seen during the night. The women's teaching existed too; I did not need to fret. My job was in the world behind the scenes, not shouting from the hilltops. It was far more important to me that I was about to realise my ambition of discovering the heart of the two great buildings which housed most of the written information in the whole world. That was truly worth savouring. Let the others convert the world!

As we continued to walk, Philo told me about his own family and where they lived. I gave a snort of exasperation at myself when he revealed that he was the brother of Alexander, the Jewish Alabarch, whom I had decided not to visit or to ask about the inner Jewish world because I had assumed that he would not be interested in such things. All the time I had been only a few steps away from achieving my goal but I had missed it through my own bad judgement and unwillingness to try just one more time.

'Such is life!' said Philo when I told him and then began on a long and complicated story of how he had almost missed meeting someone for the same reason. As I got to know this charming little man I learned that stories were part of his reason for living; Yeshua had taught parables but Philo was a master of the art.

We were entering the scholar's door of the larger of Alexandria's great libraries in the Bruchaem before he returned to the subject of the Messianic movement. 'There is both good and not so good in these new developments,' he said, waving an airy hand at the door attendant who obviously recognised him and swung the doors open for us without a word. He went on speaking, diverting me from trying to take in every detail of the beautiful hallway with its stone pillars and coloured, carved ceiling and leading. I almost bounced beside him; I was so excited.

Philo led me down a dark corridor into a private antechamber. There, we were surrounded by tables and chairs scattered around both for study and for entertaining. Light streamed in through

tall, arched windows but it was cool and restful. 'I will be pleased
to hear your views on it all,' he went on. 'But I must tell you that
the followers of the Way here are a little doubtful about some
aspects. But first, you must have some refreshment, a maté perhaps? There are servants here who will gladly make some for us.'

I agreed and Philo clapped his hands. A young Egyptian man
stepped out of a side room and bowed to us both. Despite his
lower status, he and Philo were obviously friends of long standing
and spent some moments exchanging greetings and enquiries.

'Some maté and some titbits for myself and the lady,' said Philo
eventually. 'This is a very special visit so we will have Jewish titbits if you please, Achmed, none of that Egyptian rubbish you like
so much.'

The young man bowed again. 'But Madam might like to try
some local cakes,' he said persuasively. 'She will, surely, not be a
prejudiced as you! I will bring you a selection of both and then
she can decide for herself.'

'Servant or slave?' I asked with interest after Achmed had gone
and Philo had invited me to sit in one of the ornate chairs ranged
around the room. 'You said servant but surely there are no servants in Alexandria?'

'Oh yes there are,' said Philo, sitting himself and pulling up a
small table for our drinks. 'The way you live is all in the mind,
you know. I would go as far as to say that most of the free men I
have met in this city are just as much slaves as those who take care
of them. Slaves to their beliefs and emotions and to their careers.

'But here, at the library, we purchase slaves who were scribes, or
those who have an interest in learning, give them their freedom
and pay them a wage to take care of the books and look after the
visitors. It would all be thought of as very irregular, of course, if
anybody else knew about it but they don't because we don't tell
them. We have enough benefactors to have the money and it
works very well.'

'You are telling me about it.'

'Ah, but you are trained in the Way. You know how to keep a
secret.'

'You seem to know a lot about me.' I was increasingly intrigued
by this fascinating little man.

He scratched his balding, freckled head. 'I suppose I don't really,' he admitted. 'I just liked your brother immensely and I certainly remember his talking about you. He was very fond of you, you know. And proud of you too.'

I blushed but could not prevent a broad smile from spreading across my face like sunlight. It was such a delight to hear about Yeshua and from someone who might have fresh things to tell me.

'He did not tell me you were pretty, though,' said Philo. 'Nor that you have dimples when you smile. Now, should I have said that to a Roman lady or not? I can never remember the etiquette of these things. I think I shall regard you as a nice Jewish girl unless you correct me. That's probably the best thing.'

I laughed out loud as he spoke; this little man was doing me so much good. But he had important things to say as well as his old-fashioned flattery.

'Ah yes,' he said as I reminded him that we were talking about Yeshua. 'What I do recall more than anything else was one particular thing that he said and, I'm afraid, I've been rather hanging my hopes on it.

'You see,' he said, leaning forwards with a rather touching eagerness. 'We, in Alexandria, have got rather out of date with the outside world. We know the Teaching has to develop and Yeshua ben Joseph was a breath of fresh air in here. I told him that at one time and he said, "You wait until you see my sister. She will turn your beliefs upside down and, if you will just believe in her, she will one day save our people with her knowledge of the Shekhinah." It was a prophecy, you see, and I've been waiting all this time in the hope that you would come and fulfil it.'

I was speechless with surprise. Fortunately Achmed returned to the room at that moment with a strange glazed terracotta pot and two tiny, matching drinking bowls and two plates of sweetmeats. One batch of pastry was soaked in honey and the other frosted with cinnamon and toasted nuts. The friendly banter between Achmed and Philo went on for some time, giving me a chance to recover some of my composure.

'You see why I'm such a hypocrite?' said Philo cheerfully as he waited until the servant had bowed and turned away before choosing a cinnamon biscuit and popping it into his mouth. 'I spend my life writing and teaching the importance of detaching from the fleeting attractions of the physical World and I cannot resist a sweetmeat. Very good, Achmed,' he called to the still-open door. 'Almost good enough to be Jewish.'

Once Philo had helped me to a bowl of the steaming, thick bitter-sweet liquid and pressed me to try a biscuit, he went on talking. I was relieved that, so far, I had nothing to do but listen. There was certainly nothing I could say.

'My whole philosophy is based on the idea of taking the Torah to the gentiles,' Philo continued. 'I've spent much of my life studying Greek philosophy – do you know of it?'

I shook my head. 'Only a little. I have studied some since I've been here but it has only been the kind that is readily available to anyone.'

'Plato! Said Philo. Wonderful stuff! It's basically the same as Mosaic law but then, of course, everything is when it comes down to it.'

I smiled. I could agree with that, from what Yeshua had taught me and from my own studies of other faiths.

'And this idea of a mission to the gentiles with your brother's teaching – forgive me but we refer to him as Jesus, not Yeshua; I hope you can bear with us on that?'

'Yes, of course.'

'Anyway, there's nothing wrong with the idea of taking the Torah out to the world and having a Messiah to do it with is ideal. I'm quite sure that's the idea in the World of Spirit but what does worry us is two particular aspects. One is that the Teaching is following the line of popular thinking, that there is only one Messiah and that he has come in the form of your brother. There is probably no harm in that, the masses have believed in one saviour for as long as they have believed in the Lord. After all, we do not want to reveal all the inner teaching to everyone, do we? There would be nothing for the seeker to look for if it were all laid out in the open. It would be sadly misused as well, of course. So, we are not so very worried about that aspect although it seems to be gathering a certain amount of belief that the last days are coming. The great Messiah is supposed to come to herald the end of the world and that is what is expected. Of course, it is not at all in line with any of the Torah; and anyone with a brain in their head would see that the great plan is nowhere near fruition but if it makes people think a little, I suppose there's not too much harm in it.

'The other issue is a more subtle one,' said Philo, hesitating over whether he would have another biscuit and offering me the plate. 'It appears to originate with this man Paul who is a kind of pro-tégé of your friend Joseph.'

'Yes?' I took a biscuit, enjoying all the different levels of this conversation. My senses were alert for the name 'Paul' was stirring something in my memory.

'Well, this Paul is obviously a gifted teacher. However, from what we have heard, he appears to be saying that Jesus actually is God.'

Recollection flashed through my mind of Yeshua's spirit in the Temple. 'Tell Paul I am not God,' he had said. At last, it was beginning to make sense.'

'It is always difficult to work out whether messages on the grapevine are accurate,' I said carefully. 'People often misinter-pret, especially when there are different languages involved. Just what exactly is this Paul saying? Is it that Yeshua... Jesus... is God or that he is Lord?'

'Exactly!' said Philo triumphantly, leaning back in his chair and regarding me with great approval. 'He is (I hope) saying that Jesus is Lord but, to the gentiles (and, I'm afraid to say, most of the Jews) there isn't any difference, you see. You, dear lady, obviously know and understand the ten Divine principles of the Tree of Life and how each aspect on its own is not God, just a principle of Divinity in the abyss. God, the Holy One, the Beloved, the aspect of wonderment which is so vast and unthinkable that we have no words even to approach explaining It, let alone understanding It, is way beyond Messiah-hood – and I'm certain your brother would be the first to say so.'

'Yes, he would.'

'It's fine to explain to those who understand something of the principles that the place of Adonai, the Lord, on the Divine Tree of Life is part of the Azilutic World which reflects the Holy One. It is without a doubt the pathway through to the Divine, so what Paul is saying is true in one respect, in that we all (one glorious day) will go through that place to merge with the great and holy souls who are already there and move on to the Higher Realms; but implying that that part of the journey is all that there is, that Jesus of Nazara – oh, that's what we call your home town, my dear; I expect you pronounce it differently?

'Nazara,' I said, my head spinning with Philo's words.

'Yes, well, I'm sure you are accustomed to nationalistic changes by now. Your Greek by the way is excellent...'

I suppressed a smile for I had had little chance, nor wish, to say very much at all.

'Well, anyway,' said Philo. 'It would appear that this Paul of Tarsus is implying...'

'Paul of Tarsus?'

'Yes, it's a Syrian city...'

'Yes, I know,' I interrupted him hastily. 'Are you sure it's Paul not Saul?'

'Oh, do you know him?'

My heart jumped and sank simultaneously and I must have looked bemused for Philo launched into the story, pausing only to sip his maté and pop another biscuit into his mouth as he spoke.

It seemed that Saul, that hater of Messianic Jews who had threatened me in Jerusalem, had devoted his whole life to persecuting Yeshua's disciples and their followers. To some extent, he was succeeding. I bowed my head in sorrow when Philo told me that charismatic Stephen had been stoned to death.

'Not surprising really,' said Philo. 'I gather that he had lectured the priests themselves, telling them he saw Jesus at God's right hand and that they should listen to him for enlightenment. Not entirely unexpected that the priests and their supporters turned on him. It's the lack of tact, you see. Never a good idea.'

Stephen had been taken outside the city walls and stoned to death. Peter and John, too, had been arrested again but they had managed to escape Stephen's fate, being flogged and released with another warning.

'How do you know all this?' I asked.

'Oh, there is a network of communication going backwards and forwards from this library to every place where there is knowledge,' said Philo. 'We hear most things eventually.'

He continued with his story. It seemed that Paul had been travelling to Damascus to seek out and persecute a pocket of believers. On the way he had had some kind of experience, a vision of
Yeshua which blinded him and converted him to our way of
thinking. He had been taken, blind, to a Jew who believed in
Yeshua's teaching in Damascus. This man had restored his sight
through a miracle and, since then, Paul had thrown as much
enthusiasm into discovering all about Yeshua's teaching and his
work as he had to condemning it.

'These converts are always controversial,' said Philo as I listened, aghast. 'They don't have the steadiness that a basic, long-
term belief instils in you. They have to leap up and convert others and, although they do much good in encouraging people to
seek the truth behind what they say, unfortunately most of those
who listen are too lazy to do anything to check it out or, worse,
too inaccurate in their memory of what was actually said to pass
on anything which makes any sense.' He sighed and poured us
both another bowl of maté. 'Teaching gentiles the Torah is one
thing,' he said. 'Throwing it like pearls before swine is another.'

'Surely it's not that bad,' I said. I had to say something to cover
my confusion that Saul, Rizpah's former husband, was teaching
Yeshua's work.

'Well, I don't know,' said Philo. 'It's just something we have
become aware of. If he is implying that Jesus is God, not simply
standing to the gateway of the Divine World as Messiah, then we
may have a problem. However, as we think he will be coming to
Alexandria...'

'He's coming here?'

'Oh yes, didn't I say? Yes, he and your friend, Joseph
Barsabbas, and possibly a couple of others. Not yet, of course.
They are planning to travel around all over the place. Mostly in
the East at the moment – I have my spies you know! They won't
be arriving here for a couple of years or so if the schedule we
have heard about is not altered but one never knows and they
could turn up tomorrow. That's why it is so wonderful that you
are here; because you lived and worked with the Jesus that Paul
now seems to regard as his own. So when he does come (and he
will get a good audience in Alexandria, you know!), if he is out

of balance, you can put him right.   It really is a miracle that I have found you!'

'If Joseph is with Paul then all will be well,' I said firmly. 'Joseph knows far more than I do and he would never tolerate a companion who was so misled or one who was wilfully misrepresenting what and who Yeshua – Jesus – was. You can be sure of that.'

Philo looked sceptical. 'Can I?' he said. 'I trust your opinion, of course, but time passes and memory dims. And Joseph, if I'm not mistaken, was an Essene and a teacher at that. Old habits die hard and although there is much good in the Essene teachings they do tend towards the fanatical.'

I laughed a little bitterly for I had experienced the fervour of Essene beliefs first hand, although I knew full well that different sects had different levels of belief. The Emmaus group, where I had lived, was less strict than those at Qumran but even so they had so objected to my teaching the other women that I had just escaped with my life. The Qumran group did believe that the end of days was imminent and obviously their opinions were influencing the Messianic Jews in some way. I was glad to tell Philo a little more of my story, including how sensible, kind, loyal and reliable both in principle and practice I had always found Joseph Barsabbas to be. 'And he's strong too,' I said. 'He knows when to speak and when to be silent but I'm sure that he would not be silent if Saul – Paul – were to be misrepresenting the Teaching.' I said nothing of who I believed Joseph to be – Yeshua's natural successor in the Messianic line – but I managed to reassure Philo to the extent that he was happy to discuss other matters, even to answer many of the questions I was aching to ask about the library, the museum and the people who met here in private to talk, to meditate and to pray.

We must have talked for most of the day and my hunger for an equal to discuss things with instead of just teaching others made me blind to the time that passed. After Achmed had brought us some rice and vegetables for a midday meal, Philo showed me around the known library from end to end Then he took me further in, to the hidden places where only the initiates worked.

'This is what you really want to see,' he said, opening the door to what I found later was his own private quarters. It was a large, oval room with furniture around the sides and wall-hangings and paintings of perhaps a dozen different interpretations of the Tree of Life and the Four Worlds. Mostly they were based on the menorah but one or two showed similarities to the lightning flash I had seen in a vision as a child.

Before I could exclaim and run up to them to look closer, Philo drew my attention to the floor. The central part was empty and now I could see why. Carved and stained in different colours was the most exquisite image of the four Worlds with the Sephirot, the triads of experience and goals, the pathways between aspects and the names of every angel, planet and archangel which ruled each holy place.

'Look' said Philo as I stood, amazed. 'You can play on it. You can meditate on it. You can walk it. You can really experience it. What do you say to that, eh?'

'It's wonderful,' I breathed, stepping as daintily as I could onto the bottom Sephira and beginning to work my way up, step by step. 'We drew one a little like this in En Gedi but we had to look at all the Four Worlds in One. We did not have them all displayed like this. And of course we had no colour. Oh! It's just wonderful!'

Philo was pleased by my enthusiasm. Quickly he showed me two games he had developed using the diagram which involved throwing coins or hopping between the Sephirot or the triads.

'You see?' he said. 'You lose your balance in the areas which show that there is work to be done and stand steady where you are strongest.'

'It could be co-incidence,' I said doubtfully as I had stumbled on the triad representing fear and passive emotion and I did not like to think that I had any more work to do there.

'Don't be silly!' said Philo cheerfully. 'You know that just to make this structure imbues it with holiness. But if you like, you can do the dance again. If you stumble at the same place, will you believe it then?'

'Yes,' I said but I did not try again.

Instead we talked about the triads themselves. They had been the hardest part of the structure to grasp when Yeshua had been teaching us but being able to walk up the ladder of the Four

Worlds did help to make it much clearer. Each one represented a part of you, as did the Sephirot and the paths or lines between them. The bottom three, enclosing the place of the ego, or every-day life, represented 'thinking,' 'feeling' and 'action' and with Philo's help I could see far more clearly how important it is to balance all three in your life.

'All of us lean towards one or another of them, of course,' said Philo. 'The constant student who does nothing real, the person who is always either crying or laughing and the man or woman who always has to be doing something. Extreme examples of course but worth looking at. Without the balance you just can't get to your true self at Tiferet.'

'I can see how this structure would show how you are out of balance but how do you use it to re-balance yourself?' I asked curiously.

'Well, it's very simple,' said Philo. I find the triad that is out of balance and I sit in it to meditate. There are other techniques, of course, but I usually find that works. The simplest things are the best, after all.

'Of course, the real secret is to be honest enough with yourself to investigate which parts of you are strong and which are weak. But that's the whole task of life isn't it?'

Time was moving on so, reluctantly, we left the beautiful room and Philo took me to see the wonderful books and scrolls preserved in the heart of the museum for the use of scholars only.

'Every book, every piece of literature, every map, every plan which arrives in this city is brought here and copied,' he said. 'We are meticulous in making sure that no alterations are made but now we have a repository of the world's greatest knowledge. It is not available to everyone of course but, as you have found for yourself, those who need to get here will get here.'

'How did the book that brought us together get stolen?' I asked.

'Ah, well that was on loan to a Jewish student who foolishly left his study-room window open,' said Philo. 'Most people would say that a common thief took it but the wonderful thing about knowing that higher Worlds exist and that everything is for a purpose means that it might just as well have been "borrowed" by an angel so that you could find your way here.

'That's a bit pretentious!' I said with a laugh but Philo would have none of it. 'Don't mock it!' he said sternly. 'Surely you can't tell me that you have never had miracles in your life?'

'No, no I can't possibly say that.'

'Well then. A miracle is only one World being affected by an action in a higher World. A thief may have been used to do the job – or not. We will never know. It's very simple for the Lord and His angels. It's no different from any human being letting an insect or a mouse out of a container where it has got trapped. To them that is an intervention of a higher World. To us it's just getting rid of an inconvenience with a little mercy!'

We talked on and on as the day sped past until, even to us, it became obvious that it was time to leave.

As I made my way slowly back to the villa, my head was reeling with the events of the day. Philo had insisted on ordering a litter and sent Achmed ahead to explain why I would be so late home. For it certainly was late and dusk had already fallen.

Before we parted Philo returned to the subject of the Messianic teaching. He was still full of ideas of how Paul and I could work together when he and Joseph arrived in the city. In vain I said that Paul did not like me and would not listen to any philosophy of mine. Philo discounted that as the prejudice of a non-believer and, remembering the strange way that Saul had looked at me in the Temple, I thought he was probably right. It was my own mixed feelings towards this man that I had to deal with; that and the knowledge that I would have to tell Rizpah that he was coming to the city.

If all this were not enough, my head was buzzing with information and excitement from all I had learnt and seen that day. Philo had issued me with a pass to all parts of the two libraries so I could go whenever I wanted and could make my own copies of whatever I wished. I could pay a scribe to do it for me, he said, but I knew that I wanted to do the writing myself.

I found myself telling him about Magdalene's record of our time with Yeshua and he was keen to read her account for himself – and to copy it for the library. 'That should never have got through without our knowledge!' he said, shaking his head.

He also invited me – and Apollonius and Rizpah, once I had

explained our relationship – to supper at his home to meet his family and some friends. 'You would be most welcome on Shabbat Eve,' he said. 'Any time, although you must leave it for a few weeks for I am going South for a short while. I'll send you a message when I am back and you must come. Just let us know beforehand so we can make sure there is enough food.'

I thanked him enthusiastically. I was not sure if Apollonius would come nor, despite his great kindness, how he would feel about eating in a Jewish home. It might not be appropriate for him to do so but he would surely allow me to go.

However, my uncertainty was compounded when I got home. I arrived, tired, dusty and full of news to find that everyone was waiting for me and, to my horror, that Apollonius had brought unexpected guests and extremely important ones as well. Aulus Avillius Flaccus, Prefect of Alexandria and several of his henchmen, as well as three Tribunes. Not only had I not been there as hostess to greet them but I had given no orders to the kitchen for any meal at all, let alone a banquet. In truth, I need not have feared on that account for Rizpah had been quite capable of organising the household and standing in for me. When she received notice that Apollonius and his colleagues were on their way she had done a wonderful job, finding time to decorate the room with flowers and silks and inspire the cooks into creating a meal which was a miracle of contrivance but, as Apollonius made it clear, that was not the point. I was his wife; I should have been there to greet them. Even worse, here I was, arriving late, in my day clothes, with my hair only simply plaited and no jewellery to show off my rank

I was permitted a few moments to change and re-pin my hair. Dorcas, my handmaiden, had put clothes ready and she washed the grime of the city from my skin as I hastily brushed and re-plaited my hair. That Dorcas and I had become friends as well as master and servant showed in her speed and kindness. She had picked orange lilies to place on my breast and in my hair once the light evening veil was attached and I kissed her in gratitude. She made sure that, as I met Apollonius's guests, I looked as well as I possibly could – maybe better for being dressed more simply than was now my custom. It did not seem to help Apollonius's mood

but he was too polite to let anyone else but me know how angry
he was. I knew he was furious with me. For the very first time I
saw the fire of anger in that strong face directed only at me and I
quailed before it. He had always been so kind that I had never had
to consider him as the soldier or the merciless side of a Roman
man which could end a life, a contract, a relationship at a stroke.
Now I could see what made him an officer to fear as well as
respect. I had crossed him and, later, when our guests had gone,
I would know of it.

We put up a good front for our visitors; it was only manners to
keep our private issues separate from the everyday task of entertaining. Even so, it was not the easiest of evenings. Flaccus, himself, was no trouble for I soon realised that he was only interested
in talking about himself and all which was required was a willing
pair of ears and an admiring smile. I could provide those and still
keep an eye on the other guests to see if there was anything needed.

One of them, a lanky, pale young man who was introduced as
Tiberius Capricus Norvanus, was unnerving. He seemed very
intelligent and curious about everything but it was not the kind of
interest which made people comfortable. Some of his remarks,
though admittedly very clever, were a little too close to the bone
and almost insulting to some of our guests. I avoided his eye
whenever I could but, as the pastries were served, he looked me
straight in the face. As he opened his mouth to speak, the Worlds
shifted and, like ice in my mind, I knew who he was. This was
the Roman Emperor's nephew and (the knowledge was certain),
the man who would succeed him. His real name was Gaius but
that would not be the name by which he would become known by
future generations. In that swift moment I saw him in Imperial
robes and I saw the mania which would overtake him in the years
to come. For now, it was dormant; he was just an arrogant young-
ster, let loose from his shackles and having a joke on strangers who
had not been told who he was. However, any Imperial prankster
was dangerous. 'What do I do?' I asked in my head and the
answer came. 'Remember Lilith. Bow.'

Lilith's lack of belief in her own strength and power had led her
to refuse to bow to her husband. She believed that to bow showed

her to be inferior and she rebelled and ran away. Had she not
done so, Eve would never have been created and the whole of
mankind's history might have been different. As it was, Lilith was
too eager to be slighted and to grow angry to realise that Divinity
is within us all and to bow to another is to bow to yourself – and
to God.

So distracted was I by this thought that I missed hearing what
the young man said to me. It was something about music but
luckily our chief server, Corin, had heard and he answered for me.
Our regular musicians were indisposed, he said, but he had
arranged alternatives who were standing by, should I approve
them. I had to get up and go to speak with him about them and
this gave me the chance to pass Gaius as he lay on the couch,
slightly apart from the others. He was still looking at me and, as
I passed, I made obeisance to him solemnly and whole-heartedly.
Whatever his state of mind or what I truly thought of him, this
was what was required of me and I knew that it had something to
do with the day's events, with Philo and with the Teaching. What
it was would reveal itself in its own good time.

I was able to answer the young man on my return saying that
we had an excellent lyre player waiting to perform. I need hardly
have bothered, for he was so obviously taken aback by my action
that he had quite forgotten his request and he showed no sign of
listening to the lyre player when he began to play. Instead, I had
the impression that he watched me suspiciously for some time
but, as I did not look in his direction again, busying myself with
my other guests, I could not be sure. I had to play my part carefully for any good I might have done by recognising and acknowledging this strange young man could be banished in an instant by
spoiling his fun and giving away his secret.

In spite of that distraction and the nervousness from wondering how Apollonius would express his anger with me, I was still
able to notice that one of the officers, a young man named Lucius
Norbanus, seemed very taken with Rizpah and she with him. I
could see that her position as a stand-in hostess and her providing
of such a good meal with little advance warning would have done
her great good in his eyes. 'Isn't he handsome!' she whispered to
me, round-eyed, while the other men's attention was taken up

with business talk. The young man was watching her out of the corner of his eye and I saw her blush each time their eyes met. For all Rizpah's studiousness, I knew she wanted a proper husband and a family and Apollonius had often brought home young men whom we hoped might be suitable for her. One, Tobias, had seemed perfect. He was the son of a Jewish mother and a Greek father and he believed in the one God but was interested in other faiths, too. He, I knew, was very taken with Rizpah and only waiting for a sign from her before he asked Apollonius for her hand in marriage. I wished she could have loved him but she said that she found him a bore.

Rizpah was a creature of deep passions and her animal soul wanted excitement and flair in a partner, not reliability and strength. She might know the theory of the Tree of Life and how our life's task was to rise above the vegetable and animal levels, where our senses ruled us, into the realm of consciousness and greater purpose but she was young and headstrong. And who could blame her? The passions of youth are all-embracing and it is almost impossible to see the wisdom of choosing a partner who would be likely to remain a friend for life rather than an ardent lover.

Apollonius, as her legal guardian, could easily have insisted on Rizpah's marriage to Tobias for his parents were more than willing for the match. But he remembered his own rebellion against his family's insistence that he should marry someone he could not love and he would not impose the same on Rizpah. Until now I had relied on the fact that Tobias was kind and would have made a good husband and I had continued to hope that Rizpah would come to love him. Looking at the handsome but feckless face of Lucius Norbanus I now knew that would never happen.

It was late when everyone left. Flaccus was fulsome in his praise of the meal and our hospitality but could not resist throwing a slight farewell jibe at my late homecoming and the independence of foreign wives. I smiled and ignored the thrust, my mind half distracted by the furtive whispers which were going on between Rizpah and Lucius in a corner but, to my surprise, Tiberius decided to make an issue of Flaccus's remark. He drew attention to me, pointedly and in a way which embarrassed everyone there, by declaring that I looked like his mother and therefore, by default, must have the most beautiful face in all of Alexandria. I did not have time to respond to this strange compliment before he began kissing my hands and my face passionately and demanding that Flaccus should agree with him and regard me as the perfect hostess. The kisses were unpleasant but I managed to stop myself recoiling. Had I not been so surprised I might even have enjoyed Flaccus's discomfiture. He obviously knew who the young man was and was bound to keep the secret. Outranked by this ill-mannered boy, he had no choice but to obey him.

He agreed that my beauty was outstanding and bowed to me but I knew that I had made an enemy. Tiberius would have that ability, I sensed, of putting people at odds with each other for his own amusement. However, in the run of things, perhaps it was best to have the favour of a man who would be Emperor rather than that of a state governor. I had done what I could and the rest was with the Heavens.

Nine

Once the guests had gone, I felt exhausted. It was all I felt I could do to crawl into my bed to sleep but, before I could even think of resting, I had Apollonius to deal with. As soon as all the others had retired, he allowed his simmering anger to burn into a fire.

I had let down his trust, he said. I had not been here when he really needed me. I had gone out without saying where I was going. I had not sent messages back to say I was safe. I could have been killed or kidnapped or anything.

I let him vent his fury without interruption thanking God, again, for Yeshua's teaching of standing back from a situation and seeing it for what it really was. Reacting would have been so easy. I wanted to hurt him as his harsh words were hurting me. I managed to breathe deeply and back away mentally, accepting his anger as an expression of his feelings rather than as a personal attack on me. For at the root of Apollonius's rage was genuine concern for my safety and possibly even a flame of jealousy. The servants had told him that Philo was a Jew and it was obvious to him that I had finally found my kinsfolk. Perhaps this great, powerful man was afraid that I would leave him. On top of that, Gaius had kissed me in a way that Apollonius never did. I was both sorry to have hurt my husband and touched that he cared enough to be so angry.

'You are right; I was thoughtless,' I said when he had finished. 'And I am truly sorry to have upset you. Believe me, I would never do that consciously. I was excited at the idea of discovering the library and I did not keep track of time. But I have so much to tell you and I need your help and advice so, when you are less angry with me, I would greatly appreciate the chance to tell you about it all.'

It was not enough. Apollonius was not trained in detachment and he needed a fight. He began his complaint again and I could see that my passivity was only firing him to believe that I did not care. I knew he could not listen to reason but I did not want to join in with his anger. It was very tempting for he was beginning to use words which could not be easily unsaid. The word 'divorce' loomed, so far unspoken but close enough to be a real threat. But more than that, his anger stirred a deep realisation within me that losing this man would mean much more than losing security and safety. I genuinely loved him and it was that which would be both my strength and my weakness. Somehow I had to get through the layers of anger and disbelief to reassure him that I did care; that I had not just used him until I could find my own kind again. My mind raced, searching for remedies. If I were right and jealousy were the root cause, I knew what the instinctive answer would be – but in our case it was not possible. Or was it? It would be taking a huge gamble if I followed that path and I could end up in a genuinely irreversible situation. On top of that, I was risking much for myself. The last time I had lain with a man I had been taken by force and this, if it worked, might be no different. Could I bear the same again? The stakes were high but, if I loved him, I had to gamble them on one throw.

There was silence. Apollonius had finished what he wanted to say and was waiting for my reaction.

I made my decision. However, the first thing I had to do was distract him so that he would have time to recollect himself. That was easy enough. 'The young man with Flaccus was Gaius, nephew of the Emperor,' I said. 'Whatever I have done the two of us have, at least, pleased him tonight.'

Apollonius's mouth fell open in shock. 'How do you know that?' he said. 'Who told you? How could you possibly know that?'

'I was told,' I said. 'While we were eating. An angel if you like.

You know I can hear things sometimes. But you do not have to believe me; you could easily find out for yourself.'

Apollonius was instantly diverted by this information and I thanked God for the insight which had helped to create this distraction from his anger. 'It could be so,' he said. 'He arrived in the city in a very comfortable carriage with more slaves than you would expect of just a Tribune.'

'Is that what Flaccus told you he was?'

'Yes, but it didn't ring true. Flaccus was far too deferential to him. I was puzzled at the time...' he stopped, looking half angry and half confused. This was not what was meant to happen in an argument.

'He kissed you,' he said accusingly.

'I wish you would,' I replied, swiftly, before he could say any more. I pushed back my pella so that it fell down my back. Then, looking Apollonius in the eyes, I began to unbraid my hair.

'I did not want him to kiss me,' I said. 'It is you I want to kiss me, not some arrogant stranger. I love you. You are my husband and my greatest friend. The kisses of an ill-mannered young man are not pleasant to me, whoever he might be. Those of a dear and beloved husband would be all that is delightful. They might also help heal any ills between us.'

I knew my hair was beautiful for the Roman oils and unguents had made its curls smooth and silky where once they had been wild and harsh to the touch. When it was loosened the hair cascaded down to my waist and made it less frightening for me to begin to slip out of the silken robe. As I did, I began to tremble at what the outcome of my action might be and I found myself twisting the material, unable to let it fall in one neat movement and ruining the effect of what I had hoped to do.

As I fumbled, I knew that if Apollonius was truly crippled I could have lost not only the battle but also the war. I would have humiliated him on top of his anger. But if I was right and it was only his belief that he might be impotent or that he would be scorned for his scars that had kept him away from a woman for so long, then perhaps we could both win. For a long moment he watched me as I grew more and more embarrassed. Finally I stopped helplessly, still clothed and with tears of frustration forming in my eyes. We looked at each other and my husband began to laugh. Laughter had always been his most attractive trait to me and I began laughing too.

Suddenly the air around us seemed to crackle with light and heat. The Heavens were there between us, as they always had been when Yeshua was giving healing, re-creating the true image of man or woman. I felt dizzy from the intensity of the air. Then, just as swiftly as it appeared, the light was gone and Apollonius stepped forward. 'Let me help you,' he said and in one swift movement he released the dress and took me in his arms.

What followed was rough and raw; he took me on the couch, there and then, so that I gasped with shock and had to fight to breathe as his mouth and body bore down on mine. It was exhilarating and poignant and passionate and everything that the time in Pilate's jail had not been. Through that broken barrier (and there was physical pain for both of us) we, at last, began to forge a bond which meant that we were truly married on all levels despite the anger and fear held over from the past and unleashed in the present. And, afterwards, there was release, relief, tenderness and forgiveness.

I slept that night in his arms and, as dawn slipped into the room, Apollonius made love to me, gently and carefully, letting me touch and understand him for the first time as he began to understand me. We kissed and sighed and spoke and laughed and held each other tightly and, afterwards, I was able to see where fire had ravaged and twisted his lower body.

He told me how, 16 years before, he had tried to save his beloved Drusilla and their children from a blaze begun by Gauls who attacked the garrison town where he was posted; how he had snatched Drusilla and five-year-old Vintillius from the flames but was overcome himself as he returned for their younger son and daughter. Falling and choking on the smoke and buried by burning wood he, in turn, was dragged out after Vintillius raised the alarm. The boy, miraculously, had remained virtually unharmed but the two younger children were dead and Drusilla was too badly burnt to survive for long. Her heart was as broken as her body and she had no strength to fight her way back to life. Apollonius himself could not walk for six months; he could not lie or sit in comfort and everyday ablutions were agony. He spent nearly two years recovering – more through his own willpower than anything else.

No one expected him to return to the army, let alone to active service, but he found the only solace he could in hard work and more hard work. He nurtured Vintillius through the ranks and taught himself to ride a horse, which was painful and difficult but meant he did not have to walk too far. He was an infantryman but officers could be mounted and he was experienced enough to be given command of a Century in an unregarded, peaceful province when he could prove he was fit enough.

'I spent some years in the backwoods getting my strength back,' he said. 'Then I was posted to Kfar-Nahum. I did not think of finding myself anyone else to live with me; I loved Drusilla and I still had a son alive. You have seen the damage now, Deborah. Then, it was far worse. I could not ride without pain and walking was still agony. I never let on to the other soldiers but I tried every god there was, hoping for healing. I made sacrifices, I gave money, I tried strange and evil-smelling 'cures.' I even gave funds to build the Synagogue in the Kfar-Nahum, hoping against hope that the Jewish God would help, but nothing did. I had given up by the time I met your brother.'

I listened peacefully, my head on his shoulder, fascinated by the comparison with my own life and its years of covering up lameness and pain.

Apollonius continued his story. 'I didn't ask Yeshua for help for me; at that moment it never occurred to me.' he said. 'I was terrified that Vintillius was dying and I thought only of asking for his sake. But, as he recovered, I seemed to get better too. The pain left almost completely and I could walk with less of a limp. The other part I could live with. Or I thought I could and now you, blessed girl, have done the rest!'

'I hardly think it's a miracle alongside Yeshua's,' I said but I remembered the crackling of light from the Heavens and sent up a fervent prayer of thanks.

'Well, I don't care if it is or it isn't,' said Apollonius. 'It is to me. You do love me. I always hoped that you would and now I know. You, a Jewess, from a proud and unassimilable people, genuinely love a Roman. You and your brother have brought such blessings to me that as far as I'm concerned, from now on, your people shall be my people and your God my God – what is it my love?' For with his words, spoken to me as Ruth had spoken to Naomi, I burst into great, gulping tears of relief and happiness that I should so taken care of and so blessed.

We were not the only ones who were growing closer together. Rizpah's love affair flourished and she and Lucius were married as soon as they possibly could be. Apollonius and I did not object but I was slightly worried for it seemed to us that Lucius took liberties with Rizpah, taking her to places where she would not have wished to go without him and, I am sure, becoming her lover before he obtained Apollonius's consent for their marriage. This was commonplace in Alexandria but to a parochial Judaean like me, it was still shocking.

We could see how much in love they both were but some inner, insecure aspect of Rizpah's character made her think that we opposed the match and that caused some friction between us. When somebody wants you to have a problem about something it is incredibly hard to resist them. No matter what I said, she would twist it so that it sounded as though I was critical of her lover and when I was silent that, too, was seen as opposition. The young have a tendency to rebellion and they need to find something to rebel against.

The situation was not helped by the fact that that I felt very sorry for Tobias, particularly as Rizpah would not tell him herself of her betrothal but left us to carry out this delicate task for her. Tobias, of course, was very upset and for a while it was awkward to keep in touch with him while Rizpah was so obviously glowing with excitement and passion for someone else.

Lucius was a civilian brought in as a Tribune, as so often happened, so there was no restriction on his getting married. His family was of a higher rank than ours but they were happy enough with the match and, as they and their family lived locally, there was no need to hold back the wedding for travellers.

Neither Lucius nor his family had raised any objection to Rizpah's being Jewish or divorced – Romans were accustomed to meeting women of all races and creeds. It was enough for her lover that my adopted daughter was beautiful and wise and, to start with at least, he was happy for her to continue to worship as she wanted. He, himself, worshipped Mithras and, as I had studied what I could of that faith, I knew there was much good in it even though it excluded women completely. I thought it a great shame that they could not worship together but Rizpah did not mind. She had fallen in love as she did all things, thoroughly and decidedly and she said that they could talk philosophy and they had the same inner belief. However, she stopped her studies with me and no longer came to celebrate the Shabbat Eve with us, preferring to go out to dine with Lucius and his friends instead.

She made a shining, blissful bride in the traditional orange and white and everyone celebrated for a full week with all possible festivities.

'It's like a second marriage for us too,' said Apollonius as he watched me rearranging flowers in the atrium. 'Perhaps love is wasted on the young! I loved you from the moment I saw you on that dusty road from Jerusalem but I could not admit it to anyone, let alone to you. You were so dignified and silent.'

'I was terrified,' I said. 'Not only of you or of Pilate but that I would fall out of the chariot – let alone what would happen on the back of that horse!'

'But you held on,' said Apollonius. 'You rode as if you had always ridden.'

'I loved it,' I said, putting down the flowers and remembering. 'I had no idea how beautiful it felt to ride so swiftly. How still it is in the centre of all that speed.'

My husband took my hand and kissed it. 'When this is over I will take you away, inland, to a place where you can ride horses to your heart's content,' he said.

Such a series of events in such a short time had exhausted me and I was glad to take the holiday Apollonius was offering. We went South for two months, renting a villa on the fertile Nile. For the first and only time we left Luke behind with his tutor and his adoring nursemaid, knowing he would be thoroughly pampered and spoilt without his mother's restraining influence.

Alexandria itself is bordered by marshy, unhealthy lands but further East and to the South, forests and lush, fertile lands abound and it was a joy to be completely away from the city and all its activities. I allowed myself to be looked after and cherished as though I, too, were a brand-new bride and those weeks were times of great contentment and peace for both of us. Apollonius and I talked and talked and, at last, he asked to learn the principles of the Tree of Life and the Four Worlds in detail. We would sit for hours in the shade of cypress trees discussing everything I had learnt and drawing pictures in the earth. His interest and ability to question the very heart of all my knowledge was both testing and inspiring. In return, he taught me how to ride a horse properly and we spent as many days riding in the hills and valleys as we did talking and thinking. I never forgot those times of freedom when we shared the strength and speed of our horses and explored the beautiful lands around our holiday home. To gallop on an eager horse brought bubbles of glorious emotion and laughter to my throat so that I would shout out aloud in encouragement and race my husband's steed with all my might. We would stop, our horses blowing and steaming but still catching at the bit, as fervent as we were at the mood of the moment. As the animals sidled and pranced we would try to hold hands, laughing breathlessly with delight.

One thing I did worry about and that had taken me to Constanzia before we left. I was fairly confident that neither Apollonius nor I could create another child but I needed to be sure. I did not want to confide in anyone about the change in our marriage but I did need advice on what best to do. Much as another child would have been welcomed by both of us, I believed Imma when she said I could not bear another and live.

I need not have worried; Constanzia said that it was perfectly obvious from the glow I carried with me that something new had happened between us and she did not need to know the details. What we did discuss was my menstrual cycle and my mental and emotional attributes – for all these were as important as the others in deciding which herbs or potions would suit best – and we made up a potion for me to take regularly once a month. Once my body had adapted to it, I found that it suited me well. In fact my menstrual cycle regularised itself more than it ever had done and I stopped having the painful cramps and intermittent bleeding which had plagued me since Luke's birth. I took supplementary herbs, too, for each medicine has its own side effects and I could say, with hand on heart, that for the first time in years I felt as well as I had when Yeshua was alive.

The love that Apollonius and I felt for each other continued to deepen and with that came confidence. He was happy enough to let me travel to the library whenever I wanted without feeling threatened. He was pleased to invite Philo to visit us on our return from the South and he even accepted our new friend's invitations to dine with his family on Shabbat Eve and to dine with the Alabarch himself. It was soon obvious that very few of that family were interested in the inner teaching (and the women even less so than the men) but they were all delightful company and made us feel very much at home.

Philo, himself, had sent a beautiful Jewish embroidered picture as a gift for Rizpah's wedding. In Hellenic-Roman society men often embroidered far more than women and the Jewish pictures particularly, with their Hebrew and religious images, were very beautiful to me. In Judaea, of course, they would have been forbidden, being seen as graven images but here they were accepted. I envied Rizpah for I would have loved such a picture myself but perhaps it was not meant for her, for she left it behind when she left and I had the benefit of it, after all.

I missed Rizpah's presence around the villa but it was an even greater wrench to lose touch with her soul. For the moment at least she was, physically, not far away. Lucius continued to be charming, interesting and amusing and it was obvious that he had good prospects. We all knew that he had no immediate intention of staying in Alexandria beyond this and that they would both soon be leaving for Rome. I wondered if it was the Holy One's intention to move Rizpah away from Alexandria before Paul arrived but, even if it was not, now that she was safely married I certainly felt less concerned about how his arrival might affect her. Whatever Paul's own marital state might be by now, it was important that whatever had happened between the two of them should be forgotten. I knew Rizpah was eager to hear news from home and we both hoped that Paul would arrive in time to be able to give her that. Letters to her family in Tiberias had, from the very beginning, gone unanswered and, although letters were rare in Judaea and neither her mother nor her sister could read or write, Jairus certainly could. Not all of them could have failed to get through, especially as Apollonius sent them via troop ships and with express instructions for their delivery. However, it was not surprising that we heard nothing. That Rizpah's communications came through the hated Roman enemy must have combined with her rebellion to produce an insurmountable reaction against any possibility of forgiving her. Her family must have expunged her from their lives and, if they had had a moment's doubt about their actions, it would certainly be dispelled once they received the news that she had actually married one of the enemy.

'Remember how angry you were at the thought of my marrying a Roman!' I teased her as Luke and I visited her new married quarters. Rizpah and Lucius lived within the city itself but still in a house with its own atrium and with enough room for Rizpah not to feel too claustrophobic from the noise and bustle of Alexandria's busy streets.

'Remember how you thought you would never get used to living here!' she replied, reaching out to hold Luke, now a strong and sturdy boy who certainly did not need to be carried. I had gone with a specific invitation for her and for Lucius to join us at Philo's for Shabbat that Friday night. She would have loved to go, said Rizpah, but they had had family party to attend.

Apollonius and I often travelled into the Jewish Quarter together that Autumn and watched, listened and joined in as Philo and his wife brought in Shabbat surrounded by their three sons, two daughters and innumerable grandchildren. After the noisy, squabbly, friendly evening meal was finished we would go with Philo and his eldest son to the wonderful oval room in the library where twelve other Jewish men greeted us courteously and invited us to join them in discussing the wisdom of the Four Worlds. Towards the end of the evening, Philo would lead an exercise from the Merkabah tradition of Ezekiel where we all closed our eyes and listened to his voice taking us on an inner journey up through the Worlds until we were given the opportunity of a glimpse of the World of Azilut through the Kingdom of God. For me this was often a bitter-sweet experience, taking me back in time to those precious evenings with Yeshua and Judah and the other disciples. But during the questions and the talking time after the exercise, I found it touching to see how interested the men were in hearing about Yeshua's teaching and our travels and how willing they were to listen to me, a woman, answering them.

They told me, too, more about my brother's time in Alexandria and it was good to hear new stories of his life. I thanked them for their strength and love of the Truth in allowing a woman to come to their meetings which made three of them confess that, had it not been Jesus of Nazara's sister who had wanted to come, they would not have agreed at all!

'It will take a long time, I think, for that prejudice to go,' said Philo. 'With respect, many women do not help their case. Most are not interested in the Work or will not make the effort it requires. They say they have too much to do with everyday life – and of course they are right. But they do not see that everyday life is easier with the Lord's help. Those who are interested usually wish to steal what we have learned instead of finding their own path.' Remembering Lilith I was able to agree for that was just what Yeshua had taught us – and I believed him to be right. It was up to us to worship as women rather than try to use services invented by men for men and I knew that the legend of Lilith was meant to be an inspiration to us of how we could be instead of how we often were, not the insult it was, so often, purported to be. However, I still argued for, by then, I had read some of Philo's essays and his written opinion of women was very Greek – or very Jewish! They should stay in their homes and take care of their men and not worry their pretty little heads about religion or learn-ing.

'Yes, of course I wrote that,' he said airily when I challenged him. 'Just as I say that most men should also just get on with their work and leave philosophy to others. You can call me an elitist as much as you like, my dear, but I know full well that what I say is accurate for the vast majority of people. Those who disagree and who want to change their lives will find a sympathetic listener in me – or at least a good argument. If they don't even have the spir-it to fight what I say, then why should I waste any of my time or the precious knowledge I have amassed on them? You are here arguing with me and I love you. I adore our discussions. You are more than a daughter to me. But you are rare, Deborah, and rare ones find their own way. Encourage everyone and you will debase the knowledge. You know that.'

I repeated Philo's words to Rizpah later but she bristled, more, I think, from the feeling that a barb had been aimed at her (which it was not). I tried to clarify what my friend had meant but she was not willing to listen. Yeshua had once said the same; 'Don't throw pearls before swine' and, although it was perfectly true, it was never easy to explain to people.

After a while I learned not to talk to Rizpah about the meetings. However many times she said that she was going to come with us, there was always a reason at the last minute why she could not. We never criticised her for it, accepting her reasons and saying nothing but I, particularly, was already in the trap of being thought to disapprove and although I could – sometimes – detach myself from it, Rizpah could not. From her childhood there was a need to rebel and to be thought different or wrong. Now she had to rebel in her own way and we had to let her get on with it.

I continued to go to the meetings and Apollonius came when he was free to do so. It was best that he was not always there for he had many questions which I could see were distracting for the more experienced men who wanted to debate and study in earnest. When he did come we used the time to recap on what we knew and to teach, often finding disagreements between us in the meantime which needed discussing and resolving. As time passed, the situation resolved itself automatically.

I taught the men how Yeshua had used the Shabbat and Festival Eve service to encompass all Four Worlds and we developed our own weekly ritual with light, wine, water and bread which encompassed all the Sephirot on the Tree of Life. This service we could hold together or alone, wherever we were, not only on a special evenings. Apollonius and I once held the service for Rizpah and Lucius at our house and she, I know, enjoyed it greatly. Lucius was polite and interested and said he would like to come to the meetings with us sometime. He said that again each time we met and we always said the same. 'That would be lovely. You just have

to talk to Philo first, for they are his meetings, not ours.' He did
not do so, and Lucius and Rizpah continued not to come.

The following Spring Lucius was promoted to the prestigious
Praetorian Guard, the Emperor's own elite corps in Rome. He
and Rizpah, pregnant with their second child, were to leave immediately. Ironically, the partial estrangement between us made her
departure easier for us both. However, we still wept and held each
other tightly at the moment of goodbyes for we had never stopped
loving each other, just moved in slightly different directions.

'It may not be forever,' she said bravely. 'It is a terrible wrench,
not just leaving you but Alexandria too.'

'Remember the Teaching,' I said, knowing immediately that,
yet again, I had said the wrong thing. She smiled. 'I do remember it,' she said. 'It is always in my mind. When I have time I will
study more but with one baby already and another on the way and
so much to take in and to do; now is not the time.'

'There is never not a time,' I said, with difficulty. 'In times of
new challenges it is even more important to remember.' I knew I
sounded stiff and stilted and Rizpah made an exasperated face at
me. 'It's all right for you,' she said. 'You don't know what it's like
to have an ambitious husband, a small baby and be to pregnant
again and all the pressures of moving. I don't have time to learn.
It's easy for you. How can you understand what it's like for me?'

I did not let her see how much that hurt. I did not say that she
could have spaced the birth of her children just by asking for help.
I did not say that she knew perfectly well that I had had my own
share of difficulties. Perhaps I should have but I did not know
how to. There was a wall between us, invisible but insurmountable. I did not know how she had built it or how I had helped her
to do so.

I missed her but no more than I had been missing her already.

Paul and Joseph did not arrive. No letters came either and Philo
heard nothing more on the grapevine. Meanwhile, Apollonius
and I grew in knowledge and strength, happy and fulfilled in the
little community of the library. Through Philo's contacts we met
Hellenic Jews, proselytes, the teachers of the inner wisdom of the

Arabic gods and philosophers of all races and creeds. Apollonius grew fascinated by the study of the stars. He learned all he could from the astronomers associated with the library and loved to work with them in calculating answers to questions based on the positions of the planets. As a golden time it was comparable to the years I spent with Yeshua and Judah but I was careful not to make the mistakes of my youth in setting myself above the others. I taught when it was appropriate but I listened to other points of view as well, whether I agreed with them or not. In all that time I never met another woman who studied the inner teaching, though there were a few who wanted to learn, so I started a beginners study group of my own with Tobias and the three women, Sarah, Maria and Lucilla. We made progress slowly and it was as much a group for finding out about all philosophies as one which studied the Tree of Life. I, myself, studied in the library and learnt more of the world's languages.

Philo and I grew as close as father and daughter and together we researched and studied the Tree of Life down the ages, from the Archangel Raziel who gave the teaching to Adam and Eve to Moses and Samuel and Solomon. Magdalene's scroll was copied and preserved in the library too – though the battered original seemed to have become Luke's personal property, as was demonstrated by his furious grief when he found it missing. I had to take him down to the library to fetch the original back and from then on Luke became the scholars' and servants' darling. If I ever wanted to take him with me there were always more than enough people to take care of him.

My son grew and thrived and developed such charm that he was cosseted by all who knew him. He was a serious little boy with dark, straight hair, slender and brown-eyed. He understood his Jewish heritage as well as the stories of the Roman gods and he was equally at home in both worlds. He learned to read in Aramaic as well as Hebrew and Latin and, whenever he wanted a bedtime story from me, it was always his wish to hear about the old days in Judaea. He had plenty of battle stories from his father to balance mine and was as keen with a wooden sword as any boy his age.

That year Tiberius, the Roman Emperor, died and news came

through that both Gaius, his nephew and Gemellus, his grandson, were to succeed him together.

A feeling of tension spread throughout the city. Two men to govern! Knowing Roman history, little good could come of that! Every street corner was filled with gossip and speculation and I was uneasy too. None of my visions or 'knowings' had ever been wrong and I had been given no knowledge of a man called Gemellus. I could not help wondering how long he would live for I suspected already just how dangerous a man Gaius could be.

He acted fast. First he overturned his great uncle Tiberius's will and declared the former Emperor insane. This disinherited Gemellus. Apollonius told me that it was well known how Tiberius had favoured Gemellus over Gaius but that when he was deciding on a successor, he had asked for a sign as to which of the two it should be. Gaius had been clearly indicated but Tiberius never forgot his love for Gemellus, hence the dual succession. The word in Alexandria was that another year of Tiberius's life would have seen Gaius disinherited completely and then who knows how Gemellus would have turned out as Emperor? As it happened (and to no one's great surprise) he died, conveniently and swiftly, leaving Gaius as the sole heir.

So, we had a new Emperor. A young man who immediately began to court the affections of the Roman people with the traditional lures of festivities, gifts and fun.

The people in the streets were delighted; the officials and the army waited to see what kind of man this 'Caligula' would turn out to be.

'Why are the army calling him Caligula?' I asked Apollonius. 'That means boots doesn't it? Is that his nickname?'

'Little boots, yes,' said Apollonius. 'It was what he was called when he was a child and his parents took him with them in the fight against Gaul. He wore soldier's uniform even though he was only a baby. I don't know whether he got the name because he was liked or whether he was too big for his boots. We will have to wait and see. He was certainly no friend of his uncle's policies so there will be some changes. I don't know of any serious harm in him but he is unpredictable – we at least have met him and even we noticed that!'

'Great good came from his actions when he was here,' I said, smiling and my husband gave a rueful grin.

'How can I deny it?' he said. 'But when it comes to affairs of state, I'm not so sure. Things were not easy with Flaccus after that dinner, although it did not matter to me. I think that perhaps now is the time to retire. We are rich enough and I am certainly old enough. I am tired of dealing with people who have no understanding of truth, justice or mercy. I would like to spend the rest of my days studying, not having to cope with new rules and regulations or turnarounds on policy for the sake of change itself.'

Strong words from one who had been a committed soldier and who had expected to die in service but, just as everyone who devoted their life to the Inner Teaching changed within, so had Apollonius.

As he suspected, Caligula's succession did spark some changes almost as soon as the excitement had died down. Although the intelligentsia of Alexandria all lived together peaceably there were often scuffles on the streets between races and religions. Never more so than between the Greeks and the Jews who seemed to have a particular dislike for each other. For us, living in the paradise of a multi-cultural home outside the city centre and with the protection of Rome all around us, these little uprisings and troubles had meant very little. It was no different from Jerusalem where riots such as the one which killed Magdalene had sprung up at regular intervals. But now it seemed as though Isidorus, the leader of the Greek section of the city, was actively looking for trouble and targeting the Jews. A race which regarded all others as heathens and lived apart was easy prey, especially when it was a nation of volatile people constantly on the lookout for persecution.

However, until now Flaccus and his army officers had always held these disturbances in check. The Greek contingent saw a new Emperor as an excuse to persecute their old enemies, probably because the fashion was to deify any dead Emperor and, of course, the Jews would have none of that. Suggesting that they should was like waving a piece of raw meat at a hungry lion. For a while we avoided the city itself, expecting the haphazard outbreaks of violence to die down but it was these riots which finalised Apollonius's decision to retire. Many Jews and Greeks worked at the harbour side and those who did came under his jurisdiction. 'They are behaving like children,' he said. 'Both sides are as bad as each other. I want to bang their stupid heads together and tell them to grow up and learn from their cultures that there are more important things than picking quarrels.'

I questioned him carefully on his decision and we worried a little but, in the time-honoured manner, we did not really think anything much would happen – not to us at least. But Caligula had other ideas.

Ten

Gaius Caligula was so reviled within a very few years of his death that it is often easy to forget his initial popularity. That he must always have been a schemer and a megalomaniac was nothing new in a Roman Emperor. A King lived a life apart from the people and, having the instant power of life and death, could easily take on the role of tyrant.

The people generally do not care about such matters. What they want is a leader with charisma who removes taxes, praises and loves them and puts on good entertainment and, for the first year or so, that was exactly what they got. Although Gaius had been to Alexandria and many other cities, the majority of the last six or seven years of his life had been spent in virtual captivity on Tiberius's home island of Capri, so it was an almost unknown young man with a pretty young wife and an adored and beautiful sister who came to power. He overturned as many of Tiberius's unpopular dictates as he could and, of course, the people loved it. The nickname Caligula became far better known than Gaius as it was the people's way of taking the new young King to their hearts. Instead of some far distant, old and out-of-date Emperor they believed that they had a man of the people. How wrong they were!

With hindsight, it was easy to see that something catastrophic was brewing for the Jewish people from the very beginning of Caligula's reign. All nations under Rome took great care to pass formal resolutions honouring the accession of a new Emperor and the Jews of Alexandria were no exception. The trouble was that

Flaccus, the Prefect, somehow omitted to send these good wishes to Rome. This was not a good start although, to be fair, Flaccus did make it clear, once the omission had been noticed, that it was not the Jews' fault. However, by then there was enough civil unrest in Alexandria for the Jews easily to be judged at fault for many other matters. To those on the margins, like us, it seemed that the fighting was not purely sporadic – almost as though there was an organising mind behind it all.

Philo, who always gave his fellow Jews the benefit of the doubt, suspected the nominal leader of the Greek faction, Isidorus.

'It's all tribal,' he would say wryly. 'One man starts something and everyone else follows like sheep. The Greeks on the streets are half barbarian, not worthy of their heritage. I may admire their philosophy but Isidorus doesn't know a single ounce of his country's own great knowledge and even the lowliest of Jews knows some of his own heritage.'

'Then perhaps he should know better than to react to goading from the ignorant,' I said. 'If we Jews are the chosen people then with that comes its own responsibility. We need to be greater in heart than all others.'

'Agreed,' said Philo. 'But we are much sinned against and much provoked.'

'I'm not surprised,' I said. 'The misunderstood are always disliked and if we will not bow to others' customs or explain their differences with a humble heart we are asking for trouble. You know as well as I do that we think we are a cut above the rest.'

'I can't deny that,' said Philo. 'But it is still worrying to see just how much unrest there is on the streets.'

It was worrying but I did not take as much notice as perhaps I should have for we had much to consider ourselves.

The next event made it look as though Rome might be our destination as well. News came through that Caligula was concerned at the lack of ancient 'good' blood in the Senate and had decided to elevate a large group of Roman families to the equestrian rank – so making them eligible to become Senators. Apollonius's family were agog at the news and every minute of every day was filled with anticipation and desire for their family to be one of those so honoured.

I'm afraid to say that my heart sank at the news and not only from concern for my husband. If my life's destiny was to have to move and change my life every time I felt happy and content, then I must accept it – but I didn't have to like it. If Apollonius, as head of his family, was selected I was fully prepared to rail against the angels and the Holy One in my usual manner.

It is one thing to say you don't want a position before it is offered to you and another to have status and responsibility handed to you without warning. The Alexis family was raised to equestrian status and Apollonius was called to the Senate to Rome. There was not a great deal of choice about it; to refuse such an honour would be seen as an insult to the Emperor.

'But I wish it hadn't happened,' he said. 'Under Tiberius's rule and before I knew what we have been learning here these last years I would have taken it without a thought but, despite the great honour he does me, I am uneasy about this young man. The worship he inspires from the people would be enough to turn any man's head and, from what I have heard of him, Caligula is not stable. Even if he were, how can one be an honest Senator? The Senate is a place of intrigue and bribery and bias and even of death for those who don't play their part. It's full of very rich men and although we are wealthy by most standards we couldn't compare with them. I don't think I would fit in very well. Am I a coward for saying so? I feel that I must be.'

I shook my head and took his hand to give reassurance. 'There is a phrase which I learned many years ago,' I said. 'Those who study as we do are referred to as being "in the World but not of it." It is very hard to live in the everyday world with knowledge of truth and justice and mercy as the average man and woman does not even wish to comprehend. If you refuse to be dishonest or to see things their way, you evoke hostility because they assume you are taking sides against them. You have found it difficult enough these last years here in Alexandria and you have had no friend in Flaccus who, despite being Prefect, is an ordinary man. You are extraordinary by most people's standards and that rarely makes people popular. As for Rome itself, well, the only question you really have to answer is whether you want to go. What does your intuition tell you?'

'The easy answer to that is no,' said Apollonius. 'But I have been away for 25 years and it seems that family responsibilities have caught up with me. If I refuse, we will be disgraced and I don't think I could do that to the family. I have deserted them once before and they are so excited about this elevation.'

'Could you not accept the elevation but recommend a cousin for the Senate?' I asked.

'No, Caligula has named me, for the work I have done here,' said Apollonius. 'If I refuse, then the whole family will suffer.

'We could visit Rome for a few months so that I could take up the place and see how the land lies. After all, I can leave later on if I want to – it's easy enough to get yourself un-elected! I have to think about the future for Luke as well. He should have the right contacts and education to start his career as a Tribune and the best place for that is Rome.'

'Does that matter if he does not wish to be a Tribune?' I asked. Luke was a scholarly boy and, although he played happily for hours with his toy sword and shield, I was doubtful that he would be army material. Part of that might have been my natural wish for him to be safe and secure – I felt the age-old conflict of what I wanted for my child and what he might want.

Apollonius looked surprised. He had never thought of Luke's doing anything else but Luke had blood other than a soldier's in his veins. Whether he were the son of Vintillius or any of the other soldiers he was my son, too, and had the blood of fishermen and carpenters and holy men within him in equal measure. Over the years, of course, I had watched him anxiously to see what hereditary signs he showed. I wished above all that he were Vintillius's son and, as time passed, I did think I saw signs of Apollonius in him. He had the usual Roman or Jewish dark colouring but nothing else distinguished him yet. I often thought I could catch a glimpse of the elfin-like movements Yeshua had as a child of that age but that could easily have been wishful thinking. The thought of this exquisite child becoming a Roman soldier horrified me but, if that was truly what he wanted, then I must not stand in his way.

'Of course Luke wants to be a Tribune,' said Apollonius. 'It's in the family. Besides, he's always playing soldiers with his friends.

I've never considered anything else for him. What else could he possibly want to be? It's ridiculous to think he wouldn't want to be a Tribune. How else would he get on in life?'

'Well, you managed!' I couldn't help smiling at my husband's all-too-common incomprehension that a child should be allowed to choose for himself. Conveniently he ignored the fact that he had run away rather than face the course mapped out for his career and he was acting like any normal, self-respecting Roman – or Jewish – father. I remembered Abba's upset and anger when Yeshua chose not to marry and become a carpenter but to go to learn from the Essenes and how Imma's intervention had been needed to dissolve the argument. Luke was only seven but, even so, he might have more idea of his true destiny than we had.

I explained this to my husband but I could see that Apollonius had a great battle to fight with his deep inner conditioning before he could even consider any alternative but the higher ranks of the army. We let the subject go for several days while he thought it through and, with his constant and extraordinary willingness to try and understand different points of view, he decided at last that he was, at least, prepared to speak to Luke and see if he had any particular wishes. 'All he knows about being grown up comes from my stories of war,' he said. 'Everyone expects him to be the same as I am. I do! But I will, at least, ask him if he has any other ideas.'

We sent for Luke, who was with his tutor. He shared a teacher with five other boys, sons of other officials, many of whom were destined for the army. The slender, dark-haired little boy came running to us, glad to be set free from the tyranny of adding and subtracting and always glad to be called to see his father. They embraced and then he bowed and smiled to me. To a boy of his age it was essential to seem very grown up and it was traditional not to cuddle mothers once you had a tutor. As neither of us was naturally demonstrative towards the other, this did not bother me at all.

As a child myself I had hated being expected to kiss and hug others. I would do it when I wanted to and enjoy it but to be obliged to do it was purgatory.

'Son,' said Apollonius. 'Your mother and I would like to know if you have any particular wishes as to what you would like to be when you grow up. I know you probably want to be a soldier like me but it is time to be serious now and tell us if that is what you really do wish.'

I looked at my husband with love. How many other Roman fathers would treat their son with such respect and kindness especially when such an alien concept as giving the child a choice was involved? I had seen enough of Roman life to know that a child's lot was not always a happy one, especially when great things were expected of them. Luke looked up at his father with great interest.

'You want me to choose now what I am going to do?' he said. We both nodded. 'If you know,' said Apollonius.

'Oh that's easy,' said Luke. 'I want to be a doctor like Mother.' He turned to smile at me then looked back at Apollonius. 'Except that I would prefer to be able to treat people openly and wherever I go instead of having to keep it quiet like she does.'

I sat, amazed. I had no idea that Luke knew exactly what I was doing when I met with women in my garden. He had often played there and, of course, he was as old as I had been when I first began to work at Rosa's so he was old enough to understand. I had never thought he was the slightest bit interested. Even more than that, I was overcome by the name my son had given me. For the first time ever, Luke had called me 'Imma,' not 'Mater' preferring the Judaean over the Latin word.

Apollonius was as amazed as I – and not pleased. Neither apothecaries nor surgeons were our social equals even before we were elevated to Equestrian status and it would be considered most odd for a child of the aristocracy to train in medicine. He questioned Luke again and I watched them as they spoke. Young as he was, Luke was perfectly aware of what he was saying. He understood what he was expected to do and to be and that his chosen career would be unacceptable to the father he adored. Suddenly I saw Yeshua in him, plain as the day; that implacable belief in life's pathway combined with the will and the wish to honour those whom he loved. But Luke was not as strong as Yeshua and without my help he might crumble under the expectations of others. Apollonius, too, was at a loss, torn between anger, amazement and a wish to have the situation resolved.

'Luke,' I said, quietly, the name falling into the silence between husband and son like the petal of a flower. Imma's presence engulfed me as I spoke, for her words had smoothed the path for my brother to go to the Essenes while honouring her husband's position in his home and family. Perhaps I could do the same.

'Luke, you must do what you truly wish to do but for the moment it is too early for you to do nothing but to learn to heal,' I said. 'If you would be satisfied to be educated and brought up as a Tribune should be brought up but you were willing to study even harder, going to extra classes in medicine, then you could have both options. Perhaps you can bring medicine into the higher ranks where it deserves to be.

'Tribunes, as you know, do not have to go to war or serve in the army itself. They are organisers, communicators, vital links between armies, governments and people. Perhaps that would be a suitable goal for you? If you have watched me healing and talking with people you will know that it is their minds and emotions that need help as much as their bodies do. In fact, their bodies often fail as a last resort to make them listen to their feelings.' As I spoke my son, Yeshua's nephew, looked at me and we both knew that he would never be a Tribune. He turned to his father.

'May I study medicine too, when I am old enough?' he said. 'I will be raised as a Tribune should be but I would wish to study more.'

Apollonius looked at me and to my amazement there was a twinkle in his eye. He was trying to be angry, trying to be stern and he knew that he was failing. 'Wretched woman!' he said. 'So be it. Luke, you will train as a Tribune would. You may study whatever you like in your spare time but if I find that you are neglecting your conventional studies for this fancy of yours then I will punish you severely. Do you understand me?'

'Yes Sir!' said Luke.

'Very well,' said his father. 'You may go now.'

We both watched as Luke walked back through the courtyard to his friends and his tutor. At the door, he turned and waved to us with a smile. As he did so, a lock of dark hair fell over his forehead and he flicked it back with his other hand in a manner so familiar that time spun backwards over more than twenty years.

My heart stood still and I had to put a hand out to one of the pillars to stop myself from falling.

Apollonius questioned me anxiously as I sat down with my head swimming but what could I say? It could easily have been an illusion, a coincidence. Never before to my knowledge had Luke made that particular gesture. Maybe memories of my childhood had turned my subconscious thoughts back to Rosa's garden where I had first seen Judah and he had made exactly the same gesture with both hand and hair.

I accepted a glass of water and, somewhat feebly, excused my shock as reaction to the whole of Luke's extraordinary decision. That was quite sufficient for Apollonius was keen to go over and over the whole interview with his son. Half of him was outraged and the other half fascinated. A doctor! Well, there were doctors who were respectable but there had never been one in his family. Perhaps Luke would be a great physician – or perhaps it was a childish fantasy and we should give him more time to decide. If Luke really wanted to be a doctor then he could train here in Alexandria but there would probably be better schools in Rome; he did not know, he would have to look into it.

'I thought he was going to be a Tribune,' I said innocently. Apollonius stopped. 'He is!' he said gruffly. 'Of course. It's just interesting, that's all. Maybe he will combine the two. He has the brains.

'Oh! Deborah! I should be furious! With you particularly! Why am I not? Why am I laughing? I don't understand.'

'Destiny,' I said. 'When you see it in a child there is nothing you can do. Fighting it only ruins life for everyone. He will do better with the best education and it will strengthen him to have to fight for his goals a little but we will never stop him. After all, did your father stop you? And all you wanted was to marry an unsuitable woman!'

In the end it was decided that we would all travel to Rome. Apollonius's family were beside themselves with delight, not only because of their new status but because they would be going to the great capital of the world and seeing long-lost relatives who already lived there. And it was the looked-down-upon

Alexandrian contingent which was bringing the fame and glory to the family, not the cosmopolitan Roman side.

It was impossible to resist the family impulse once it was in full flood. Everyone's career would benefit from the move; excitement swept through the whole clan and the chatter about Rome, glorious, beautiful, cosmopolitan Rome, was never ending. Alexandria was nothing in comparison to Rome! Oh! the joy of leaving this backwater and living in real society with people of rank and style! Apollonius and Luke were swept up in this enthusiasm. I shed a tear quietly behind closed doors. I was the only one who seemed to be losing anything – but what a loss it would be.

In leaving, we were giving up our tenure on the villas in Alexandria and we had to decide what to take with us, what to sell or give to friends and (in our case) what to put into storage for our possible return. Whatever happened, whether we came back swiftly or not, we were leaving this particular house and this land and, yet again, a beautiful garden. My tears were public over that for, in the six years we had lived in Alexandria, I had nurtured and loved the herbs and plants which made our house so fragrant and beautiful and helped those who needed aid. In return they had thrived, blossomed and fruited. My one consolation was that Constanzia and her husband were moving into our apartment and she, at least, was happy to continue our work. Maybe, one day, perhaps, I would be able to return and take cuttings of the plants and flowers and start yet another garden.

The real pain was leaving Philo, his family and the wonderful library. My friend was as deeply saddened as I was when I told him that we were leaving, although his fervent belief in the ways of the Lord convinced him that the move must be right. He promised to ask his brother for helpful contacts in Rome for me and to see if he could win me any introductions into the esoteric life of the city. One thing Philo did know – that there was a group of Messianic believers there. Cephas (whom he called Peter) had certainly been there already and perhaps Paul and Joseph as well. That gave me hope for surely these Romans would have some of the inner knowledge and it would be a help in my new life to have people of similar beliefs around, even if they were not scholars or adherents to the Merkabah Tradition itself.

For some reason I did not fret that I might never see Philo again. The strange inner knowledge which I had from time to time was certain that this was not the end of our relationship on this Earth. I told him so and he snorted – Philo had little time for visions – but he was pleased all the same, even if he did put my feelings down as a woman's intuition. We parted fairly calmly, both trusting that the Lord and His angels knew what they were doing.

The sea journey was uneventful, although I was a little seasick. I thought it was grief for leaving Alexandria and it did give me an excuse to mope and keep away from the excited family and other passengers. Apollonius and Luke were enthusiastic, too, although my low spirits affected them.

It had been claustrophobic enough meeting Apollonius's family in Alexandria but they were as nothing compared with the welcome we received in Rome. A hoard of people embraced us as though we had been lost at the end of the world. We were all to live in an apartment block above Apollonius's two half-sisters, their husbands and their families and numerous cousins right in the city itself and it felt just as constricting as my arrival in Nazara so many years before. Again there were people constantly thinking that they owned you and that they had every right to your time and interest whenever they wanted it.

The air of Rome seemed so thick, yellow and polluted that it made me physically sick for three days. There were so many people in what seemed to be so little space, so much manufacturing which relied on fire day and night and, of course, sacrifices to the myriad gods in a thousand temples. We had a small atrium which we shared with all the others but no garden and no space around us to help me breathe or see the sky. The lights of the city never went out and the noise and the bustle were never-ending. In addition to the family duties, we were inundated by visitors, invitations and events which it seemed we 'had' to go to almost from the moment of our arrival.

I found myself surrounded by family quarrels and expected to follow their lifestyle in all things. The relatives who had come with us threw themselves into the idea with delight, casting off their parochial Alexandrian attitudes but I stood back, half-shy, half-dis-

gusted by the excesses, the waste, the pointlessness of life and the
continual round of purchases, amusements, pampering and gossip.

The Roman women 'took me in hand,' regarding me as a complete foreigner and, before I knew it, my wardrobe was transformed yet again and my face, nails, body, hands and feet mas-
saged, lotioned and cajoled into looking appropriately smooth
and idle.   I had thought I was pampered in Alexandria with
Dorcas's loving care and all the facilities available to me there but,
in Rome, women were expected to have a massage every day; to
rearrange their hair twice a day; to go to Temples several times a
week; to visit circuses and fairs and plays and to gossip, gossip,
gossip.

I hated it.   I hated the superficiality of the people, the lack of
privacy, the dirt in the streets and the 'clients' – people who sought
favour from aristocrats and who hung around their houses, hanging on to their every word and doing favours for them in return
for basking in their fame or getting better deals for themselves
because of their connection with them.   I could give a wry smile
when I remembered how busy and dirty and noisy I had thought
Alexandria when we first moved there but it was hard to keep a
sense of humour or perspective when every minute of the day
seemed to be crowded with people.   I found the pressure on me
stifling.   Compared with Rome, Alexandria was a village.   The
great city took you over, swallowed you up and, within days, you
were subject to its seductive belief that it was the only place in the
world which mattered. Alexandria? Pretty, of course, but so back-
ward and parochial. Jerusalem? My dear, how amusing! Those
funny people with the fearsome god who cause so much trouble
and do not know when they are well off. So you are a Jewess are
you, dear? Well, you can forget that; you're in the big city now
and we'll take care of you and let you know what you need to
know. What do you mean, you don't present sacrifices to the gods!
How droll! You do now, dear! Believe me, if you know what's
good for you and your husband, you do!

And I did.   I who thought I was strong and committed, wise
and experienced enough to evade all that I did not wish to do,
found myself helpless in their hands.   I tried to keep my perspective; tried to see the Tree of Life in all the Temples I visited and to

work out the sacred roots of each preposterous service or piece of ego-ridden priest-craft. I saw oracles and soothsayers (such fun – so fashionable!) and I was so worn down by it all that I began to develop headaches and even to limp a little, just as I had so many years before.

I barely saw Apollonius for he was out all the time; either at the Senate or at some function he and the other men had to attend.

I could not really blame him for being pushed along by the pressure all around him when the same was happening to me. The only way to do well in Rome was to rise as fast as you could. But I did blame him, for all that; for coming to Rome in the first place, for not being able to resist the temptations and the pressures, for not helping me; for having such a ghastly family. I succumbed to much of the other women's wishes because there was no defence and resistance took up so much time and energy. Being 'bookish' was scorned and one of Apollonius's sisters had deliberately thrown away one of my precious scrolls to discourage me from trying to be an intellectual. What she must have thought of me for exploding with anger and then going, personally, to the place where refuse from our building was dumped to try and find my manuscript, I never cared to ask. I did find it but it was damaged beyond repair and parts of it were missing. I made a fair copy but had to leave gaps where my memory failed me. Philo, bless him, wrote with the quotations I needed but that took months to come through and I made sure that I never again allowed anyone but myself to see any of my work.

There actually were places for a woman to study in the libraries and museums in Rome but they were not the places that I hoped they would be. Greek philosophy was debated and studied by women and some of the Roman religions. It was thought rather provocative and very modern to be a poetess of Greek thought and syntax as opposed to the old Roman manner and some of the meetings I went to did have some limited appeal. They were as contemptuous of what I had to offer as I (secretly) was of what I saw as their limited perspective. Jewish people and their beliefs were not popular in Rome and without the linking of the different systems and faiths I did not find anything to satisfy me at the women's 'courts.'

I followed up Philo's Jewish contacts but the results were no different from when I first arrived in Alexandria. The men I spoke to swiftly made it clear that although I was welcome to attend synagogue or visit the women, it was only on Philo's recommendation. Foreign women who had married 'out' were not favoured and a woman with pretensions of studying Judaism was heartily disliked. There seemed to be no inner circle where I might go and, even if there was, it was as tightly closed as the inner group of the Essenes at Emmaus and no one was going to speak to me about it. I tried to find the Messianic Jews or 'Christians' too but my questions met such a barrage of hostility within the family – including accusations of child-eating and devil-worship – that I was shocked into giving up, for the moment at least.

At home, too, I was expected to conform to the Roman ways of worship and my own faith was relegated by the others to being an anachronistic hobby. The intelligentsia here were predominantly Hellenic and the disturbances and discord the Jews had been feeling in Alexandria were also echoed in Rome and made my race even less acceptable. At least in Alexandria, Jewish knowledge was appreciated. Here it was not. My lifeline was long letters to and from Philo who, try as he might, could not discover anyone who could help me in exile.

My last hope was Rizpah. She was in Rome but too far away on the other side of the city for easy contact, although I pressed and pressed to see her and, after a while, we sometimes walked together in the parks and talked. I asked if she had any contacts but Rizpah, it seemed, had not even tried to find anyone with whom to continue her studies. She had every excuse; her second child had died very soon after the birth and she had been, understandably, devastated. Now she was pregnant again and totally involved with motherhood. She, like me, was living with other families so her time was filled with children and chatter. I tried hard not to begrudge her that pleasure; as she said, again, it was an important stage in her life and she could return to studying later. I also managed to say that it was only my beliefs and my learning which had taught me to deal with bereavement. I would have thought she would have turned for help at such a dreadful time. But then, there would have been no one to turn to here.

She could cope but, for me, it was different. I felt that without both my studying and my garden, I was cast adrift. I prayed, of course, and kept the festivals quietly, when I could, and I understood that I had been incredibly lucky in all things up until now. I knew that our stay in Rome would only be a fraction of my life and that there would be a reason why I was here. But I was still upset and homesick and I found it very hard.

One evening I broke down into hysterical tears while I was out with some of the women of the family. It was an over-reaction to some fragrance or incense or whatever, in some Temple to which I had been taken 'for some fun' which had spun me into a twilight world and which frightened me so that I could not control myself. Once I had returned to sanity, I found the courage to walk out and make my own way home in the dark without the others. As I wove my way in and out of the people in the busy streets I began to realise that I had to do something. I had to pull myself together or I would be destroyed.

Apollonius was sympathetic to my plight but he was enjoying himself. Backed by Roman society, he did not encourage me to find other literary outlets. I could take a rest, he said. Enjoy being purely feminine for a while, being pampered and taken care of. For the first time in our marriage there was cause for genuine discord and I often found myself crying in the night after he had gone to sleep. I was worried too about our life together; Apollonius was out or away so often and I was so rarely amenable or feeling well enough to encourage him to be my lover. At the back of my mind was also the thought that I had limited supplies of my herbs for contraception and I had not had the time or the energy to find any alternative. Our love for each other seemed to be fading into the background after only a few months in Rome. Something had to be done.

In desperation I tried again to find the Messianic people – the 'Christians'. After working my way through another barrage of hostility I did, finally, discover an address where they were said to meet and found myself knocking, tentatively, on their door one Friday night.

It was not easy to gain admittance; many suspicious questions were asked of me before I was allowed in. Some instinct told me not to mention who I was; I just said that I had lived in Jerusalem and had met Yeshua of Nazara and that I had come to Rome with my husband. At that, I was welcomed in with open arms.

To my surprise, the meeting was in a large hall, filled with people, all of whom were welcoming and friendly. They were about to listen to a speaker, they said, and they looked forward to talking with me afterwards. I looked around cautiously; there were no Jewish people here as far as I could see — although who would think me to be a Jew? The people looked reasonable and I met many smiles as I caught an eye here and there.

Then the show began.

The speaker talked of Paul and I listened in fascination. He mentioned Joseph too and 'Peter.' Then he began to talk of 'Jesus' and his ministry. It was extraordinary. I knew most of the stories – but I did not know them. I had been there but now I felt like a stranger. Nothing quite added up. What was more, the man who was speaking began to prophesy in a strange voice, claiming it was Jesus who was speaking through him. As he did so, another man stood up and began to speak in a strange language and, before I knew it, many were on their feet, speaking in tongues.

I sat, silent and small, trying to take it all in. This was so very unreal to me. No stranger, certainly, than all the places of worship I had visited in Rome but this was a religion founded on Yeshua! Not on a faith extended and expanded by him and used to enhance the love of God but a faith which worshipped him himself, as though he were a god! I couldn't work out what I made of it at all. I was used to prophecy – in Rome there were prophets on every street corner – but people saying that 'Jesus' was speaking though them? Was he? Would I know? Would I not?

Before I could make my mind up, one man began to sway and moan and declaim in Hebrew. He tore his clothes and lamented and threw himself onto the floor before the speaker, begging his forgiveness. The crowd roared in fury at him and I could hardly hear the words behind the shouting, weeping and lamenting. When I finally realised what was happening I felt bile rise in my mouth and I had to turn and run out of the building before I was violently and ashamedly sick. Somebody followed me – a kind woman, babbling some rubbish about how affected she had been

the first time that demon in human form, Judas the betrayer, had
appeared before them begging forgiveness for his sin. 'His soul is
locked in hell,' she said. 'He knows now the enormity of what he
did. He knows he betrayed the Messiah, not the fake he thought
he had exposed. Yes, he burns in hell. He knows what he did.'

As she spoke I looked at her beaming, complacent face in wonderment. Was I dreaming this? I tried to stop her from saying
any more but she went on and on, her face lighting up at the
glory of Jesus the Christ and the iniquity of that despicable
Jewish traitor.

I hit her. I slapped her across the face with all the strength of
my hand and began to scream at her like a street woman. I must
have pulled out some of her hair and scratched her for I can still
see her shocked and horrified face with blood trickling down it.
Poor woman. How could she know whom she was dealing with?
She had come outside to help me and found a vixen spitting fury
and yelling what she knew to be devilish heresies.

It was lucky for me that the Christians needed to worship in
secret. Before a crowd could gather around us, the woman was
enfolded into the arms of her community and taken back inside.
To their credit, the men who came out spoke softly to me and
used no violence. They simply sent me on my way, assuming me
to be a mad woman and forbade me ever to enter their portals
again.

I crept home miserably, filled with guilt and despair. The diseased story of Judah's 'betrayal' had spread even to Rome. There
was no hope now of stopping it becoming the 'truth' especially if
those kind, gullible people believed the words they spoke as either
their own inner personalities misled them or mischievous spirits
possessed them.

Apollonius was there when I arrived and his face set into the
now habitual mask of irritation when he saw that I had been crying again. Something in me snapped.

'Give me some money,' I said. 'Enough to buy my passage
home. I won't stay here any longer. I am a burden to you and to
myself. I cannot live in this city.'

To this day I have wondered what would have happened if I had
been married to a lesser man. He could so easily have bundled me

off to Alexandria, divorced me and married a more amenable woman. As it was, he looked at me very sadly and said. 'Deborah, I think we need to talk.'

We sat up in the early hours and tried to make some sense of the whole situation. 'What I can't understand is what has happened to us,' said Apollonius. 'It seems to me that you don't want to know me any more and that your hatred of Rome has rubbed off on everything else. I don't understand why you don't want to hear about the things I am learning; I wanted to hear about your knowledge in Alexandria.'

Despite my unhappiness and anger, I bowed my head. I knew that it was jealousy that would not let me listen to his knowledge. Apollonius was continuing his studies in Rome easily enough, though from a more Hellenic point of view than he had encountered through Philo's friends. He had met with several men interested in the science of the stars (although astrology itself was officially disapproved of in Rome) and he was learning steadily. I had pointedly not been interested for it seemed such a lesser knowledge than my own and my jealousy resented it.

'Isn't it worth trying to sort this out?' asked Apollonius.

'But I've asked you for help for weeks now and you've ignored me!'

My husband put his arm around me. 'I don't think you would have taken any help for all that,' he said. 'The problem had become too precious to you.'

I tried to shrug his arm off because I did not want to face what he was saying.

'I don't like Rome as much as Alexandria,' said Apollonius. 'But I didn't like Alexandria as much as I liked being in the army. I had to adapt.'

'Well so did I.'

'Yes. And we are having to adapt again.'

'But there's no time for us!' I burst out. 'We have no Sabbath. We have no privacy. We are surrounded by people who think differently and we are starting to think like them. I feel like a light inside me is going out. I feel like I'm dying.'

'All right,' said Apollonius. 'I admit that I have not found enough time to be with you. I know it has been easier for me but then you are not a traditional woman, are you? Let's work out what we can do to make it better for both of us.'

By the time we had formulated a plan, the Sun was rising over Rome. I managed to sleep a little, still fighting the resentment that whatever we might plan to do, Apollonius was the winner, not I. I said a prayer for help, rather sulkily and with the rather shame-faced realisation that I had stopped talking to the Lord as I had become more depressed. No matter what the opposition, I must find time for being quiet and meditating, I told myself as I dropped off to sleep.

We did improve our life although, at first, I still found it hard to listen to Apollonius's accounts of where he had been and what he had learned while I had been doing nothing of interest. However, once I was prepared to try, his customary kindness and generosity wore down my anger and pride. He informed his family that one night a week at least he and I wished to be alone, with no interruptions. Everyone thought that strange but it was accepted especially once it was discovered that my sulkiness and temper abated as soon as we were given that small time of privacy. Apollonius was glad to share his new-found knowledge with me and, once I had accepted how things were and conquered my devilish pride again, those evenings sitting together and talking were like oases in a desert. I would trace the information he taught me onto the diagrams of the Tree of Life to help us both understand the workings of God's Universe. Everything fitted, of course! I knew the Essenes at Qumran studied the stars and that the science was an ancient and honourable one used by the priests for centuries and, despite myself and my prejudices, I began to be genuinely interested. After all, did the Lord not say of the planets and the Sun in the Torah: 'And these shall be signs for you'? On that level my knowledge was enhanced and my pride took yet another lesson as my husband, whom I had taught for seven years, began to teach me.

He also bought me a lyre, the most beautiful instrument made from tortoiseshell, mother-of-pearl and mahogany. As he placed it in my hands one evening I gasped and almost dropped it. I was about to say 'I'm not musical! I can't play!' but, by accident, my fingers crossed the strings, drawing a pure, thrilling sound, and music entered my heart. Apollonius wisely said nothing, just left me to fall in love with the instrument and the way it could sing.

His idea that music would help me to find the beauty that I had lost in my life showed how much better he knew me than I knew myself and, of course, a senator could attract the best of teachers for his wife. I began the lessons with misgivings but once I found that I had a natural ability I came to love the music that I made almost as much as I loved the lyre itself. Given the life of leisure of a Roman matron, I could have lessons every day and almost at once I felt myself walking taller and the smile returned to my lips.

My tutor, Paulinus, was kind but firm and insisted that I learnt theory as well as practice so music became another discipline to be absorbed as well as a joy. Like the oral tradition it was the spaces between the notes which made the melody and the fact that I could understand that made playing easy.

Luke took time to settle down too. He went to school with other senators' sons but he suffered from being in a family recently elevated to Senatorial status. Whatever our ancestry, we were provincials according to the others and he was teased extensively. I questioned him anxiously but was relieved to find that the rough treatment by the others did not extend to actual bullying. It might have done if Luke had not been tougher than he looked and I had to turn a blind eye to a few bumps and bruises which showed that he was giving as good as he got.

We had found a place which gave evening classes in medicine for young men and boys and we were pleased to find that the college itself was becoming quite well thought of – although the idea of the son and heir of a family studying science was much less acceptable. Luke might have held his own at school but at home he became a quieter and slightly clingy child which was as annoying as it was understandable. I was better able to deal with an unhappy child when I was happy but I realised that it was probably my lack of contentment which had been spreading to him. There were other children in our apartment block but none of his age and most of them were girls – and if there was one thing Luke had learned from school, it was that playing with girls was not acceptable.

I would sit down with him whenever there was a quiet moment

away from all the other relatives and ask him about his life and tell him about mine. I had always been totally honest with Luke and spoke to him as I would to another adult, so he probably knew more about how I felt than was comfortable for him. However, I also knew that if I did not talk to him he would still be able to pick up my feelings with his senses and my lack of communication with him might make things even harder for us both.

Luke was too old for cuddles and petting according to Roman and even Jewish traditions but now – if we were alone – he would lean against me so that I could put my arm around him and sometimes he would even climb onto my lap. All those years when he was more affectionate towards others seemed to have been overturned but I knew it was more through the lack of a more motherly figure than anything else. Luke's life, like mine, had been a series of movements and changes and I was the only constant in it. Even his beloved father was usually away or busy or expected him to be very grown up nowadays.

Our favourite times were still the telling of the old stories of Yeshua and the disciples and the years in Judaea. It was like a fairyland to Luke, a place of miracles and magic and he never tired of my telling him of the glories of the Temple and of the beautiful Sea of Galilee or of the strange and stern Essenes. I had told him that Judah was my husband before his father but he never made any connection between his life as a Roman and my life as another man's wife. That was just a fantasy to him. I was careful to explain how he was born in Judaea before I met Apollonius but that we regarded him as God's gift to me and to Apollonius and, so far, he was happy with that.

One day, when he had had a bad time at school, I told him yet again of the birth of Yeshua and the great star which called people for miles around to witness this great event. He liked to hear of the priests but he preferred me to tell him about the shepherds who had also come to see the baby. 'The Zoroastrians were holy men,' he said. 'They were like Papa; they studied the stars so they could see how great Yeshua was. The shepherds didn't know anything but they came because they wanted to. Their faith was bigger than the priests.' I had never seen it like that and, to be honest, I had only thrown the shepherds in because I was trying to make the story last longer! It was true that Miriam and Joseph had been visited by shepherds but I had assumed that it was because they were just passing the inn. Women and children had come to see the new arrival as well and Miriam had been everlastingly grateful to them for their gentle advice and help in her recovery after the birth. Luke, however, was not interested in that. He was convinced that the shepherds were told to come by angels and, as that was as likely as anything else, I did not correct him.

I still had Magdalene's manuscript, written in her own hand and Luke still loved it better than any other toy. We kept it secret in Yeshua's chest for Luke, too, had learnt that it was unwise to appear too scholarly to the family. I would take it out and tell him about Magdalene and how much she had loved him and how Yeshua had helped her to grow strong and beautiful after a hard and troublesome life. He did not understand why the two of them had not married and to that I could only say that it was something he might come to understand when he grew up.

Eleven

Living in Rome did not automatically mean meeting the Emperor or the Imperial family, even if you were a Senator's wife. We did have to go to many of the games or gladiatorial contests which were attended by the Emperor and which, together with theatre, formed the staple entertainment for the Roman people but, apart from seeing Caligula and his entourage there, we had no contact with them.

I made as many excuses as I could not to go to such events. Apollonius had to attend as part of his duties (though it was more a social obligation than any other) but, so far, I had managed to avoid too many such invitations. Seeing humans and animals pitted against each other still made me feel the same way as animal sacrifice had done when I was a child and the amount of invitations fell away when people realised that a guest who was threatening to be sick most of the time was not the ideal companion! Jewish people were not very popular in Rome and what was seen as our stand-offish and holier-than-thou attitude towards entertainments in general was one of the reasons. At least I had reasons of race to fall back on but I was not popular – and I can understand why.

I could not objectively understand how people could be so cruel, although I could feel the excitement and rawness of the mood around these events and it was true that there was a strange seductiveness to them which was tempting even to me. It would be much easier to release the anger I felt about the restrictions on my life by shouting and yelling and getting involved in the tribal mood but I had an inner feeling – and I don't know what it was exactly – holding me back. Trying to explain that I thought the fights 'wrong' was also a waste of time. Perhaps they were not 'wrong' and it was only my perception. I ate meat, so was I not as 'wrong' as those who actually enjoyed watching killing? Should I not cheer when an animal got its revenge by killing a human? Yes, I had often thought of giving up meat altogether but making your own vegetarian diet when you lived in fertile Galilee and did your own cooking and trying to do it in a city was another matter. But these are all excuses. If you truly want to do something you can do it whatever the opposition. Ascetics gave up eating meat – and I had met a few of them on my travels – but they were not filled with love either so it did not seem to do them much good!

Since leaving Judaea I had also learnt that the sacrifices at the Temple in Jerusalem were probably among the kindest of ways to kill animals for food. In Alexandria and Rome there were animal sacrifices aplenty but they were not always as humane as the Jewish way of killing. It was an ironic thought that, as soon as I found that one thing which had horrified me was, perhaps, not so bad after all, another situation would appear to give me just as much to cope with.

I discovered that it was best to keep off the streets before and after any big event or festival for thousands of people would throng the roads and avenues, often drunk or carousing. The atmosphere could feel quite dangerous, especially for a woman, and there was plenty of wild talk and not a little violence. I knew I was a spoil-sport; even Luke did not mind the events and he went to many in my place. It was hard to walk the line between being true to yourself and being overly precious and I would have liked to have done it better.

Once the family had discovered how uninteresting I was and that Apollonius was almost as bad, interest in us died down some-what. We lived as quietly as we could but we heard the gossip on the streets as much as anyone else. Rumours abounded about who in the Imperial family or the higher ranks of officials was sleeping with whom and who was unkind to their wife or husband – and even who was rumoured to have poisoned their partner – but they were just names to me and meant nothing.

One evening, however, when Lucius and Rizpah came on a rare visit, we got closer to a rumour than we liked. Lucius was full of the news that that the leader of the Praetorian Guard, one Cassius Cherea, was growing increasingly angry at Caligula and his behaviour.

'Though I have to admit that some of Cherea's dislike is personal,' he said. 'The Emperor thinks Cherea is effeminate – that he wears women's clothing or that he goes with boys or something like that! It's quite hysterical really. I don't know exactly what's going on but it's raising some hackles, that's for sure. Caligula makes sure that the official password they have to exchange whenever Cherea is on duty is one which presses the point and the Emperor laughs like a child when he sees how much he offends.'

'But Cherea is a sensible man,' said Apollonius. 'Surely he can ignore it?'

'Well, no he can't,' said Lucius. 'In fact he's getting pretty dangerous about it. Word is even going about that he's looking for others who feel the same way he does and who would be prepared to do something about it.'

'That's dangerous talk, Lucius.' Apollonius was suspicious and uncomfortable. 'The further away you can get from that the better. It's not safe even to speak of it.'

'Don't worry,' said Lucius. 'I wouldn't if we weren't alone.'

'Well don't tell anyone else or you'll be in desperate trouble.'

'Oh, relax! It's all just loose talk at the moment,' said Lucius. 'I'm not saying it's not serious but it wouldn't happen yet anyway. The biggest problem at the moment is who would succeed if Caligula did die, for whatever reason. Claudius is the only possible successor and Caligula hates him so, therefore, Claudius is out of favour with everyone. Without a designated heir, the Senate would probably vote for a return to a republic and then we'd be in a huge mess. Maybe even civil war. So, if anything were to be done, it would need to wait until Claudius was back in favour so that he could take over swiftly and knock any rebellion on the head at once.'

'Are you implying that Claudius is at the heart of this?' Apollonius had met the Emperor's uncle and found him an unassuming and even a pleasant man. Apparently he was well-read and of a higher understanding than was usual for a member of the royal family but he had not been generally admired even before Caligula's dislike became so obvious – probably because he was a very unprepossessing man with a stammer. Some even thought him retarded.

'No,' said Lucius. 'He wouldn't dare. He'd be horrified anyway and probably blow the whole plan by sneaking it to Caligula. Claudius hates violence. He doesn't even go to the games if he can help it. He'd far rather have his nose in a book.'

I could see that Apollonius was disturbed by the conversation and I tactfully tried to change the subject. Both he and Rizpah followed my lead and Lucius took the hint that we had heard enough. That night however, before we slept, my husband and I talked it over in whispers.

'Do you really think it is a plot to assassinate the Emperor?' I could hardly believe it possible. Apollonius shrugged. 'It might be,' he said. 'Talk is cheap, of course, and Lucius might just have been showing off but, then again, he might not.'

'So is Lucius is involved in this?' I asked. Apollonius sighed. 'I'm afraid so,' he said. 'He wouldn't know so much about it if he weren't. I know Cassius Cherea well enough to know that if he has a genuine grudge he might well act on it.'

'What do we do?'

'Nothing. It's just speculation as far as we are concerned. Anyone with any sense would just ignore it. It will probably just die down.'

We put it out of our minds – not least because we were soon assured that Lucius and Rizpah were safely away from any plots which might be in the wind. The young Tribune was posted overseas to Espania – Constanzia's home – and, although we never found out the reason for this apparent demotion, it was a relief to know that they were away from any intrigue. It was as well that our minds were at rest for it was only weeks later that we, ourselves, came directly into contact with the Imperial family.

To those in the far reaches of the Empire the supreme ruler was just an image, a seal or a signature on a piece of paper if you were in authority. His wishes were imposed through the Prefect or

Governor and it was he who was the one in charge for most of the time. In Rome, once the Emperor took notice of you, there was no escape. Those in the Senate were often marked men and, as Apollonius had feared, they were judged entirely on whose side they took. Their wives and families stood or fell with their menfolk. There might have been a couple of hundred Senators but that was still too small a number to hide in if you happened to have been noticed. It took quite a few months but in the end we were spotted. Perhaps Caligula was just bored with everyone else; perhaps Apollonius spoke out for honesty and truth in a debate and was shouted down. Whatever it was, Caligula noticed. What's more, he realised that he had met this particular Senator before in Alexandria and that he happened to have a wife who had acknowledged his majesty before he acceded. For a man with an ego as large as Caligula's who had been threatened by Tiberius's will, naming Gemellus as his equal, that was a story to be remembered. Once she had been identified, that woman was in danger of becoming a potential favourite and, in Caligula's world, that was a very dangerous situation to hold.

We were invited to an Imperial banquet. Even I was quite interested in seeing one of those! Apollonius's family were delighted at the honour and I had a hard time resisting being dragged off for even more clothes and make-up. One of the half-sisters, Livia, even suggested I dye my hair blonde but, fortunately, Apollonius overheard her and burst into guffaws of laughter. Although my objections were unimportant to her, his meant that the idea was dropped immediately. I was beginning to understand at last why women became so manipulative. It seemed that they had no confidence in themselves or in other women's opinions but if they could only persuade their husband to agree to something they could ensure that it would be done. It was a shame they had to operate in that way because it became a self-defeating system. They, too, ended up teaching their own sons and daughters that women had no power or importance except in relation to men.

We set out for the banquet rather nervously. Apollonius wore the traditional purple-striped toga, sign of the Senator, and I wore the simplest of white dresses I could get away with in the welter of advice surrounding me, together with the customary pella over the natural curls which seemed to be the envy of all Roman women who spent half the day crimping their own hair into ringlets. My jewellery was a very simple matching set of gold and turquoise – collar, earrings, bracelets and anklets but, even so, for a moment before we left I remembered that little Jewish girl who had sat, amazed, in the streets of Jerusalem watching the Roman women there and wondering what it would be like to wear trinkets of any jewellery at all.

We took a litter to the Imperial palace and, once inside, milled around with all the other guests for an hour or so waiting for the Emperor and other important people to turn up. Then we took our places on great couches ranged throughout the largest room I had ever seen. At such a time I still felt very provincial and was hard-pressed not to gawp at this awe-inspiring magnificence, let alone to wonder how many beggars and poor folk could have been set up in business by the cost of just painting such a huge area.

The food at the banquet was not particularly special though I was painfully aware that not only was I eating meat sacrificed to pagan gods but also meats which were considered unclean by my own race. 'Well, I've broken worse Jewish laws!' I thought and tried a portion of shellfish when it became apparent that to refuse to do so, yet again, would cause offence. It was not very nice with an odd, rather chewy texture and I was quite happy from that moment on to refuse any more on the excellent grounds that I simply did not like them! That was an acceptable answer in Rome; religious bigotry was not.

Caligula was seated at the far end of the room together with his wife, Paulina. There was an empty space at this top table, marking the recent death of the Emperor's favourite sister Drusilla. There were rumours that he had killed her himself and even that they had committed incest – which just goes to show the kind of gossip there was in Rome! Caligula seemed listless and unwilling to enjoy himself. Of course, it might just have been boredom at yet another tedious evening but what little I knew of Caligula did not dispose me to think he would even bother to turn up if he had not wanted to.

It was after the meal when the so-called lucky ones might get the chance to say their goodbyes and thanks to the Emperor per-

sonally, hoping for a moment's favour which they could use for
their political advancement, that we were brought forward from
the crowd. We were singled out by one of the Praetorian Guard
who were always present wherever the Emperor went and told to
present ourselves as Caligula wished to make our re-acquaintance.
Apollonius could not help but be pleased with this singular honour and I walked at his side with eyes downcast, hoping my
demeanour would be taken for modesty and not fear.

We were thanked very courteously for our hospitality in
Alexandria and Caligula complimented me on the simplicity of
my gown as opposed to all the other 'overdressed matrons.' I
bowed and smiled and said nothing but I was not to escape that
easily. Standing next to Caligula was a very dark and swarthy-
looking man of about his own age. The two were obviously very
good friends and it was with shock mingled with disbelief that I
found myself being introduced to him. 'This is Herod Agrippa,'
said the Emperor. 'You know who he is, don't you? He's a Jew like
you! Tell me, Agrippa, what is the protocol here? This Jewish
woman is your subject because she comes from Judaea and you, of
course, are King of Judaea. Should she bow to you or to me?
What do you think?' The young Emperor's face took on a kind of
glee as he asked the question. Oh, yes! Caligula enjoyed putting
people in difficult situations. But he would punish those who did
not respond as he wanted them to.

'She should bow to you of course, Sire,' said Agrippa swiftly but
that was not the answer Caligula wanted. He had obviously been
drinking and was feeling potentially quarrelsome. I felt a fleeting
sympathy for anyone who was his friend. Agrippa might be a king
but he was a puppet, too, and could be disinherited at a whim.
And here was I caught between these two men who had life and
death in their grasp. The truth of it was that they were still just
men without any command of themselves, swayed by their emotions and thoughts but I could not exactly say that! Kings, I
thought, should be taught spiritual disciplines with their mother's
milk. How else could they not be driven insane or have their egos
shattered by their position? Yeshua had been far more a king than
either of these. But I had to be here for a reason and it was my
task, as Yeshua's disciple, to bring light wherever I could. Here, yet

again, was a chance to bow before the Divinity within man. Everyone bowed to the Emperor but he knew inside that they did it because they must, not because they saw any greatness in him. The inner knowledge of respect given falsely would be enough to destroy a weak man. I hesitated momentarily and then spoke. 'Sire,' I said. 'Perhaps I should bow to Agrippa and then, perhaps, we should bow to you together, King Agrippa the once and myself twice. That would honour those you have raised to high places with the esteem with which they are due but show that you are Emperor of us both.' Agrippa looked at me long and hard and waited for Caligula's reaction before he himself responded. I had done the right thing and the Emperor smiled. 'I told you about this woman,' he said to his friend. 'She reminds me of my mother, Agrippina.'

The smile on my face froze slightly. The last thing I needed was such praise but worse was to come. Caligula raised his voice and hushed the assembled crowd then, holding my hand up to identify me, he told the story of how I had bowed to him as though he was already Emperor when I had met him in my own home. I had seen the greatness within him long before anyone else who should have done had had the wit to do so.

I was publicly invited to visit him, his wife and sisters at the palace and my hand was kissed with great ardour. As I bowed again and was complimented on my modesty, the Emperor's mood swung once more. 'Don't be so maidenly,' he said suddenly. 'Let me see your face'.

With his hand he took hold of my chin and raised my head so that our eyes met. I looked with curiosity as well as fear to see who this person was and why our destiny seemed so tied up with him. They were intelligent eyes but there was a shattered foundation behind them. A childhood of being spoilt and adored, alternating with great periods of fear and hatred as those he loved were removed from him or died, had made its mark on a naturally self-centred ego. This man was truly dangerous and, if I could have, I would have run all the way to the port and boarded the first ship to anywhere but Rome to escape him.

It was a Roman joke of long standing that an Emperor's disfavour was a terrible thing to have but not much worse than his favour. Favourites who disappointed were far more likely to lose their lives than those who were cordially disliked or ignored and who got on with their own particular business. For the moment, Caligula had decided that he liked me – though that did not automatically mean that he would like Apollonius on my account. As we went home that evening my husband and I were unusually silent. There was nothing we dared say in the open street for it could easily be misconstrued. To speak lightly or disparagingly of the Emperor when you did not know him was one thing; to say anything open to misinterpretation when he had singled you out for attention was another.

At home, in the privacy of our room, we talked long and quietly. Both of us could see how dangerous the situation could become. And yet both of us knew that if we had been brought before Caligula's attention it must be the work of the Higher Worlds.

'You, or maybe both of us, have some part to play in his destiny or the destiny of your people,' said Apollonius. 'Did you ever imagine when you started travelling with your brother what he was starting? Or that you would one day be in a far distant country representing him and all he stood for?' I shook my head with a smile. 'Sometimes it's much better not to know,' I said.

That night as Apollonius slept, I prayed with all my heart to see and understand God's will; to know if I were deluding myself or whether I truly was meant to do some act that affected the world. I could not marry the Emperor even if we were both unmarried – and a sweat of fear came to the surface of my skin at that thought for Caligula had the power of life and death in his hands – I was too old for him and, despite the envy my hair evoked, not beautiful as so many of the Roman women were beautiful.

At first light I fell into a light, dream-filled sleep and woke feeling better. I reminded myself that my life had constantly been blessed and, no matter what calamities befell me, there was always good behind them if I remembered to look for it. Nevertheless I was more loving towards my husband for the fear that Caligula inspired had made me realise how easy it is to take for granted the ones who meant so much to me.

As was traditional for those singled out for attention, we sent gifts to Caligula the next day. To forget such a formality would have been deeply unwise although in our case we did not wish the recipient of our gifts to remember us and continue to offer us his favour. I waited, nervously, for a summons to the palace but my anxiety was unfounded. The next we heard was that Caligula was out of the city, visiting other parts of the country. What a relief that was! He was away for some weeks and, even on his return, I heard nothing and I began to relax. Expectations of being summoned to the palace or being 'adopted' by Caligula's sisters faded away, too, and the Emperor's fancy showed exactly how fickle it was. I was almost amused when I realised how chagrined my relatives were that so much glory had slipped from the family's fingers on the changing whim of a Prince. They had been holding on to the reflected glory with the greatest of hope and they were devastated when nothing happened.

I almost forgot the whole incident, but I should have known better. The Holy One never wastes an opportunity.

It was Herod Agrippa who sent for me in the end. Caligula had returned to Rome and contracted some fever. He was not responding to his doctor's medicines and had started raving and calling for his mother. Agrippa thought of me and my apparent similarity to the dead woman and wondered if my presence might soothe the Emperor. The summons was nearly the end of me in itself! To find members of the Praetorian Guard banging on your door in the early hours of the morning is not a pleasant experience, to say the least. Apollonius's brother-in-law, Decimus, answered and hurriedly came to fetch us both. We went down, hastily attired and were met by three soldiers. 'It's your wife we want, Sir,' they said to Apollonius. 'His Eminence Herod Agrippa says she should attend the Emperor immediately and we have come to escort her.' Apollonius and I looked at each other. This was almost a copy of the time he had come to fetch me from the road to Qumran on Pilate's orders. My husband squeezed my hand. 'You will be fine,' he said. 'I'll pray for you and keep vigil until you return.'

The soldiers had brought slaves with a litter and, as I was carried through the streets of Rome towards the Royal palace, I found myself mouthing over and over again words from a prayer that Yeshua had taught me; 'Deliver us from evil; deliver us from evil.'

More than anything, I was confused. What could I do for an ailing King? Most of the salves or herbs I might have had in Alexandria were used up and unavailable to me now. Anyway, the Emperor's doctors had far greater knowledge than I. I did know and understand some techniques of healing and light could, on occasion, come through me – but for Caligula? And then, again, why not? If, as Lucius had said, Caligula's death could lead to rebellion, then perhaps it was for the highest good that he should be saved.

Agrippa met me at the door. His face was pale and anxious and although I bowed automatically he seemed eager to treat me like an equal. He apologised for disturbing me but said Caligula's comments on my likeness to his mother had made him think that my presence would calm him. He might assume that I actually was Agrippina and then I could persuade him to take some medicine. Until now he had refused everything the doctors suggested and they, on pain of execution, had not dared to insist.

With that strange feeling of unreality which makes you question whether the circumstances around you can possibly be happening, I let the King of Judaea hurry me down the corridors.

I could hear the sick man screaming with rage and frustration long before we reached him. Half of me recoiled from such fury and the other half was filled with compassion for such a wounded psyche. There could be few of the poorest of the poor who were more afflicted in heart and mind than this, the most powerful man in the world.

He had been poisoned. That much was obvious from first sight but not poisoned with anything which had been intended to kill him. It looked more to me as though it was an overdose of some stimulant – such as an aphrodisiac. There were only two possible answers to it without recourse to any medicines and they were either to dilute the substance, whatever it was, or to make him vomit it up. The doctors were huddled around the doorway as the poor, deranged creature in the bed rolled around in his bed, screeching and foaming at the mouth. I hesitated but Agrippa pushed me forwards. 'Go to the bed,' he said. 'I will protect you, I promise.'

Fine words to hear! I walked forward and took a deep, deep

breath. 'Gaius,' I said. 'Gaius, what have you taken? What did you eat or drink?'

For a moment he stared at me lividly and then something in him relaxed. 'Mother!' he said faintly. 'It's Mother! Oh Mother, you came! Oh Jupiter, am I dead?'

I leant over the sick man stroking his forehead. 'No you are not dead,' I said. 'You are not even dying. I have just come to help you get well. Gaius, can you tell me what it was that you have taken? Do you know?'

'No,' he said. 'I don't and I'm afraid.' Now he was a little boy looking for comfort. I smiled at him. 'It's a nasty attack but it won't kill you,' I said. 'Is it fire in your stomach or is it an ache? I need to know so that I can use the right cure. You will get better, Gaius, but please tell me.'

'Fire,' he said but I could see that he was beginning to relax already. It was as much temper and fear as indigestion which was troubling him. He reached out for my hand and put it to his lips. 'Mother,' he said again.

I put my other arm around him and spoke to Agrippa. 'Water,' I said. 'Lots of it. Some clear and some heavily salted. Now!'

'It's already here,' said one of the doctors, venturing forward. I gave him a quick sign which acknowledged his words and that I knew that he had obviously already made a good diagnosis but also told him to stay out of sight. It was Agrippa who brought forward the flasks of water and two beautiful goblets.

'Now Gaius,' I said. 'You must choose which of these you want to drink from. You know which will do you the most good. Just reach out your hand and take one. I will drink from it too so that you know that it is safe. No one will hurt you.'

It was a big risk, but I did not know what the poison was so I did not know which of the two to give him. I sent up a prayer for him to make the right choice – whatever that choice might mean. 'Into your hands, Lord,' I said. 'Life if life is appropriate but not if it is not.'

Gaius gestured towards the cup in my left hand. Carefully I took a sip. It was slightly saline but also contained herbs which I could not identify but which tasted like something which would stimulate the stomach into cleansing itself. I gave the cup to

Gaius and he drank deeply. Almost immediately he was violently sick. The vomiting lasted for some time, during which I held him and spoke to him and comforted him. At last he was purged, exhausted and pale but out of danger. He managed to drink some wine mixed with water and allowed me to cleanse and dry him. Almost invisible hands provided new clothing and bedding and soothing camomile-scented oils. When all was finished this strange young man drifted off into a natural sleep and I stood back, trembling a little from the after-effects of such an experience.

'There is a bath and attendants waiting for you,' said Agrippa, appearing quietly at my side. 'Thank you, from the bottom of my heart. He is a difficult man but I am very fond of him and I would not have him die. He has been good to me. If there is ever anything I can do for you in return, know that I will do it. If you have family and friends in Judaea I will see that they are honoured.'

I remember thanking him and saying there was nothing that I wanted other than letting Apollonius know that all was well and being free to go home as soon as I could. Then I allowed myself to be led off and bathed by attentive slaves in a place of unbelievable luxury. My own soiled clothes were taken away and new ones brought in their place. Once I was dressed my only desire was to leave but one more ordeal stood before me this incredible night. Caligula's wife, the Empress Paulina, appeared, her eyes big and frightened in her pretty, weak face. 'Please help me,' she said, taking both my hands. 'I heard what you did. It was me. I poisoned him. I didn't mean to; it was meant to make him look kindly upon me but the dose must have been wrong. What can I do? He'll kill me if he knows – and he will know, someone will tell him.'

In all the teaching I had received, truth was revered above almost anything else. But Yeshua had always taught me that truth needed to be applied equally with discernment and loving kindness. In the oral teaching it is clear that loving kindness is greater even than truth. 'Then tell no one,' I said. 'Go to Agrippa and say that Deborah wishes him to inform the Emperor that no one wished him ill; it was not a poison, just a summer fever. No one should be punished, including the kitchen staff or the servants. He asked me if I wanted a favour so please tell him that this is what I ask. He will fulfil it. Then destroy whatever it was you used and never try the same thing again.'

Paulina kissed my hands and ran away. I shook my head in amazement and wondered if I had done right. I must have done for she had given me the chance to ensure that the slaves and food-tasters surrounding the Emperor would not be killed for a crime they had not committed. Looking back in future years on the fate of that poor, unhappy girl, I am glad I was able to offer her some kindness. Her drug did not work and Caligula divorced her within months to marry his mistress, Caesonia, who was already pregnant with his child. Poor Paulina's infertility destroyed her for her life spiralled downward from that moment and within a year or two I heard that she was dead.

However, I did not feel so charitable towards her at that time for there was no doubt that the change in Caligula dated from her ill-thought out action. All Emperors of the Romans were thought to be Divine and each of them enjoyed the power of that reputation but, probably, they did not entirely believe it. Caligula, on the other hand, began to act as if it were true. He started experimenting with the idea that he actually was a god and he took to dressing up as Mercury or Mars or Jupiter. Even more oddly, he would dress as the female gods which surprised and horrified many a visitor. He demanded that he be addressed as an equal to the gods and no one ever knew when they were summoned to see him whom he might be pretending to be. One man saved his life when Caligula's strange appearance left him speechless with amazement, by explaining that he could not possibly have spoken for only a god could address a god.

He did not remember that I had been there during his illness and I don't think he ever thought of me again but I often wondered whether his vision of his mother coming to save him had fuelled his wish to be Divine. That was a heavy burden of guilt to carry, although Apollonius dismissed it.

'It might have been a tiny factor,' he said. 'But it would have happened anyway. With a more balanced man he would have realised either that it was a dream or Agrippa would have told him the truth when he was well. Maybe he did tell him! Maybe you had nothing to do with it at all!'

I was grateful for his sensible thoughts and took comfort.

Since the end of the Republic, all the Roman peoples had paid lip service to the idea of the Emperor being a divine being and both Tiberius and Caligula followed the custom of making ritual sacrifices to Augustus at special events. As Caligula's megalomania became more pronounced and he demanded sacrifices to himself as a god in all the Temples and places of worship, the Jewish people sensed trouble and went quietly to ground. A few hot-heads held demonstrations and spoke out against the Emperor but they were speedily removed, either by the Praetorian Guard (who would have executed them) or possibly by their own people. Those who drew attention to the Jews at such a time were a danger to themselves. We knew in our hearts that this Emperor could be the most dangerous opponent we had faced yet and even the non-orthodox kept quiet about their beliefs. Herod Agrippa and his family went on a visit to Judaea with admirable timing and everyone whispered prayers to the Lord for protection. Nevertheless, it soon became clear to Caligula that there was one strand of his Empire which was not acknowledging his correct status. This strange nation which believed in only one God who did everything would not acknowledge any other. It would not do. He decreed that his statue, in gold, was to be set up in the Holy of Holies in the Temple of Jerusalem and that all the Jews were to sacrifice to it and pay homage to it as the Lord's equal. From that moment on, no Jew was safe in any place throughout the Roman Empire.

Apollonius came home from the Senate early that day and before he even spoke I knew from his shaken expression how serious the news must be. When I heard, I was speechless with horror. The consequences of such a decree were too terrible to contemplate and I retreated into prayer, tearing my clothes and wailing just like an old orthodox woman who had lost her sons to the enemy. It was the only thing to do to release the fear and the anger and the sheer terror of what must happen next. The riots, the massacres, the anger and the revolts in my homeland up to now would be as nothing to the slaughter and destruction that this edict must bring.

Apollonius comforted me as much as he could but, for my own safety, he had to order me to stop – and when I tried and failed, he held me closely so I could hardly breathe and put his hand over my mouth. 'You must be quiet, Deborah,' he said. 'You must! We will be in even greater danger if you go on like this. Please be brave. Please be quiet. I couldn't bear it if anyone reported you.'

I struggled and choked down my anguish, knowing only too well how right he was. Walls had ears and even though we knew our own small group of house slaves, those belonging to the rest of the family could easily report him. One of Caligula's most popular new laws was that slaves could report any indiscretion of their masters or mistresses, even to the point of getting them imprisoned or executed. The monetary rewards of betrayal were tempting enough apart from the revenge of a slave with a grudge. We knew of several respectable men or women who had suffered because a careless word had been reported – as well as some who richly deserved to be exposed.

'There must be something we can do. There must be,' I said when I had recovered enough to speak coherently.

'I wish I could believe that,' said my husband sadly. 'I wish we had never come. I wish I had not allowed my ambition to get the better of me or allowed my family to sway me. We were all happier in Alexandria – even Luke. Perhaps we could find our way out of this maze. We can, at least, go away during the summer heat and think.'

'Can't you do anything about the statue?' I asked, in a small voice. He was a Senator after all.

'I could try,' he said. 'But it is known that my wife is Jewish. They might assume I was siding with the Jewish people and that I, too, did not wish to worship Caligula as a god. That would be more than enough to throw me into jail and then what would happen to you?'

'I don't know. I don't know.'

We held each other close and I tried to be calm and reasonable. If God wanted something done about the statue, He would do it. If He needed us, we would know soon enough. There was nothing I could do on my own, worry and fret as I did over possible plans and ideas, all of which good sense showed me to be futile or worse.

It was late June and the Senate was due to adjourn at the beginning of the following month when Caligula moved to his summer residence. We, too, could take the opportunity to get out of the city and breathe untainted air.

We found a small villa near to the sea, surrounded by cypress trees and shaded from the fiery summer Sun. It was only a few minutes from a tiny, sandy cove where we could bathe or watch the fish in rock pools and make pictures in the sand. Luke adored it and we spent hours drawing animals and angels together and gilding them with stones, shells and seaweed. Luke had no Jewish inhibitions about making images of animal or beast – everywhere you looked in Alexandria or Rome there were statues and paintings of one kind or another and one of his favourite games was to draw. He still drew the Tree of Life sometimes but since he had come to Rome he had stopped asking about it. I expected he wanted to fit in more with the other boys and they had different religious disciplines. At the villa he was like any other Roman boy, running around, playing with the local children and growing brown as a berry.

Luke and I walked together in the cool woods above the coastline in the late afternoons while Apollonius worked and he loved spotting herbs and medicinal plants and chattering away about how they could be used. I was constantly amazed at how quickly he learned and understood the properties of each leaf, root or flower. He knew quite a few indigenous plants that I did not, having learnt from his tutors and from watching his friends' mothers.

In the evenings the three of us would often sit outside in the dusk, the wind from the sea fanning us as we talked or I played my lyre. It was easy to believe in the Roman gods at such a time because I could feel the spirits of the land, the trees and the sea all around us. They came for the music and we were surrounded by their song and dance. After Luke had gone to bed and the music stopped, they vanished into the dark and Apollonius and I would discuss again and again what Caligula's edict would mean and what, if anything, could be done to stop it.

One day, when we had been at the villa for nearly a month, a note arrived by horseman. To our complete amazement it was a letter from Philo. Completely unknown to us, he and a special delegation had arrived in Rome to appeal to the Emperor over the ill-treatment of the Jews in Alexandria. Now they had to try to stop the statue as well. The letter had been written in haste from near Caligula's summer palace where delegations were received and business went on as usual, even in the hottest months.

We read the note in silence. It was wonderful to think that we might see my old friend again, but not in circumstances such as these. Things must already have been desperate with the Jews if Philo had come all the way to Rome and it was so often the messenger who would take the brunt of any anger. 'What can we do?' I said anxiously.

'Nothing,' said Apollonius.

But before we even had time seriously to wonder what was going to happen, Philo himself had arrived at our door.

Our delighted but confused greetings were mixed up with his profuse apologies for arriving unannounced and, what was worse, in bad favour with the Emperor. After we had all spoken over each other's voices, interrupted each other, hugged and disentangled ourselves from the general chaos of such an unexpected meeting, we were all able to sit down and take stock of the situation. Philo said he had time to stay only for this one night and I had the servants set to at once to prepare a larger supper than we had planned.

Firstly we needed to hear about the delegation; its reason for coming and its chances of success. Those, at first sight, seemed unpromising to say the least. Caligula had greeted the men and dismissed them almost immediately. Their only hope was to stay in the vicinity for the rest of the summer and then go into Rome itself after that, if necessary, in the hope that he would give them an audience.

Philo could not help himself from being downcast and apprehensive. 'I wonder sometimes how we manage to get into such a mess,' he said. 'It's not only the Jews, though our situation is critical – believe me, there will be deaths beyond counting if this statue is erected.'

'You mean it hasn't been done yet?' I leaned forward hopefully. 'I had assumed it was already in Jerusalem.'

'No,' said Philo. 'And we have a friend in the new Prefect, Petronius, although not many are willing to see how very accommodating he is being. He is taking as much time as he can in talking to the people in Judaea and getting their point of view before he implements the command. Of course I am assuming that there is no more news than that. He knows we are coming here so I am sure he will succeed in delaying the erection of the statue until our mission is finished.'

Once we had eaten and shared what other news we had, Apollonius realised that Philo and I would want time to talk together and drew Luke away. My old friend and I talked philosophy for some time, each of us drawing strength from our common interest and knowledge. For me it was like manna from Heaven.

At last we fell silent.

'What hope do you have?' I asked gently.

'None whatsoever of this delegation,' said Philo. 'I am just going through the motions, if you like, although those who are with me are committed to getting the Emperor to change his mind. I wish them luck, for a more unbalanced young man I have yet to meet. But the Lord may yet save us in his own way. No, I am really here to see you, Deborah.'

'Me?' I was pleased but also suspicious.

'Yes, you.' Philo leaned forward in his characteristic way, pulling at his little beard with one hand and staring intently into my eyes. I waited. He seemed to be searching for words. When he spoke it was slowly and deliberately.

'You remember the day we met?' he said.

'I do.'

'And how I spoke of your brother, Yeshua, and his words about you.'

'Yes, I remember.'

Philo stood up and began to pace up and down the veranda of the little house. Behind him bats were flying above the cypress trees and I could see the first stars beginning to shine as the cloud layer dispersed.

'This is the time,' said Philo. 'I truly believe that this is the time your brother spoke of. He said you would save the Jews with your knowledge. Deborah, it is up to you to do what you can. You can no longer hold back. If you have contacts at the palace you must use them. If you have powers greater than the human, you must use them.'

I closed my eyes, a feeling of helplessness running through me and an anger, too, that I should be expected to do something, at great risk to myself, for a people who would happily condemn me as a heretic and a betrayer. What chance had I got?

'None of yourself but, with God's help, every chance,' said a voice in my head. It was quite clear and so present that I opened my eyes in surprise expecting to see another human being there. Philo was standing, looking out over the grassy slope which led down towards the sea but, apart from him, I was, physically, quite alone.

Not once since I came to Rome had I listened for the angels. I had only moaned and groaned about not being able to find people to help me and about having to be in Rome at all. Even when I heard the news about the statue I had assumed I could do nothing and had allowed Apollonius to reassure me that I was right. Now it seemed that there was a task I had to do, even if it meant losing my own life. I shivered, for life was precious. But if mine was treasured, what about all the others? What was the cost of one when so many Jewish men, women and children would almost certainly die if I did nothing? For the first time I truly thought it through. My own blood-sister, Salome, and my nephews and nieces were in physical danger from Caligula's edict. Imma, Cephas, Thomas, James, Joanna; all those I had almost forgotten apart from so many thousands I had never met. How could I abandon them now? I had seen enough miracles to know that nothing was impossible. With God's help, with Yeshua's help, there must be something I could do, otherwise I would not be alive now; nor be in Rome; nor have the knowledge I had.

Words from the Book of Esther floated into my mind as though the characters were speaking them directly. Philo, standing in front of me, giving me time to reflect, was now Mordecai speaking to his niece.

'Who knoweth whether thou art come into the Kingdom for such a time as this?' Was this my destiny then? Without a doubt. And must I, like Yeshua, die so that the people might be saved?

No! How would my death help now? This was a physical problem, not the spreading of a great and holy knowledge which had to be available to the world.

'And which you have not taught,' said my own mind. But 'Not true!' came the answer. 'Not true. That is not your job. Teaching in public is not your job. But this is.'

I must have made some slight sound, perhaps a sharp exhalation of breath, for Philo turned and came back to me with his hands held out. He said nothing, just looked at me.

'So you are Mordecai and I must be Esther,' I said. 'The difference is that I am not the bride of the King.'

'No but you are the wife of a Senator. Perhaps it is through him that this will be done,' said Philo.

'Perhaps,' I said. 'But I suspect not. Will you leave me to think? I need some time alone.'

'Of course,' said my friend gravely. 'I shall retire to bed and see you in the morning. May the Lord bless and keep you – and may your brother advise you.' He kissed my hand and left and I was alone, the lamp beginning to gutter and a hundred stars dotting the sky above the cypress trees.

I walked down towards the sea. There was no Moon but it was not entirely dark and I knew the pathway well. Only when I was at the edge of the water did I stop and sit on the sand to allow my thoughts to rush forward, engulfing me as the sea itself would close over a stone. At the forefront was fear, followed by anger at the Jews' rejection of me and the fact that I was now needed to help. Behind that was ego, the feeling that I was important and powerful and could save the people; be a heroine; be remembered for good. Then bitterness. Even if I did this thing, I would not be remembered; my part would be glossed over or forgotten. 'Don't need to be loved,' Yeshua had said to me. But I did need it.

I let all the thoughts run through my mind, not checking nor judging them. By the time they were finished I was exhausted and the night was dark and deep. I continued to sit at the water's edge, still listening, waiting to feel the deep silence within beginning to spread. Then, and only then, I began to pray.

'Blessed art thou O Lord our God who has made me according to Thy will,' I said, my hands held out and my tear-stained face turned up to the thousand stars overhead. 'Please tell me, please show me what it that is you would have me do. Send me your angels to advise me or, if it is appropriate, your son, my brother, to comfort me and help me to take the better path. Of myself I am nothing; with You I am invincible. Make me the perfect tool for Thy work.'

Nothing happened, nothing changed. The sea lay, dark and restless, sighing and swelling along the shore at my feet. Within it fish, great and small, slept in its lullaby movements or roamed the deep for prey. Shellfish opened their beautiful multi-coloured shells to feed. Dolphins followed in the wake of boats out beyond the horizon as strangers, with their own troubles and joys, made their precarious, salty way to new or familiar destinations. A bat flew overhead, followed by another and another, questing for gnats and flies. Behind me the cypresses whispered eerily, their night-blackened fronds creaking in the circling, cooling wind. I could sense the Earth spirits within bending and bowing with the breeze, involved totally in the cycle of birth and death and rebirth.

The sky had turned from black to a deep, midnight blue, each star an angel's eye looking down at me and twinkling. As I idly looked for constellations that I could recognise, my eyes began to lose their focus and I found I could see beyond the visible stars to see yet more stars in clusters together, like families. Thousands of these groups spreading over the whole of space. In my mind's eye they began to form patterns, each one repeating in some kind of structure greater than imagination could perceive; but I kept looking. The colours expanded and the image grew deeper and more intense. Light was everywhere – and then darkness, a great whirling void which to enter would mean no return.

'I'm not afraid,' I said to the Tempter who stood by the entrance. 'Yeshua will be there.' But I was afraid; ice cold and terrified. I felt myself moving forward towards the darkness but an almost physical hand reached out to stop me. 'Not yet,' said a silver-blue voice. 'But be comforted. Go home now and listen.'

The images shifted slightly as my eyes began to focus of their own volition. I was staring at a handful of grains of sand, held before my face. Within them was the cosmos and they were of the cosmos.

Yeshua was holding the sand. He stood in front of me with the expression I knew so well from our years together. Whenever I had resisted or fought or struggled he would gaze at me with this mixture of compassion and sternness and wait until I came to my senses.

'Cyprus,' he said, looking deep into my eyes. 'Go to Cyprus. The answer is there.' And as I tried to take in the words his image faded into the mound of sand which was now held cupped in my own two hands. As I sat, staring at it, drops of liquid began to appear, soaking through and darkening the smoothness of the patterns. 'I must have cut myself,' I thought as the blood spread, making the sand feel heavy and sticky but I did not move, just sat and watched and was still.

Later, I climbed the pathway back to our summer home, undressed and washed. I bandaged my hands with cotton and lay down beside my sleeping husband. He half-woke, turned and put his arm around me and I nestled into his dear, warm, familiar body thanking God for this moment and this life.

Life can proceed for years without incident but it seems to me that when one great event begins to happen, others flood in on top of it before you have time to breathe. With hindsight, of course, it is easier to see them all as part of the whole but, that following morning, it appeared at first that life had been thrown completely into chaos. More than that, Apollonius and I had been set on opposite sides of the camp.

The clattering of horse's hooves in the outer courtyard woke us with a start just after dawn. Apollonius put his hand out to restrain me as I made to jump out of bed. Silently he pulled me to him and held me closely. We did not have to see the soldiers to know that it was the Imperial Guard. No one else was so co-ordinated, so efficient and no one else would have knocked on the door with such authority.

Such arrivals of soldiers in and around Rome always struck fear

into the heart of officials and their families. Arrests and deaths
came quickly and often the reason was never truly known. You
had favour with the Emperor or you did not. That was all there
was. This could be anything from promotion to disgrace and
death.

We waited a few more moments, holding the time as precious
drops of rose oil. Then, as Luke ran into our room to raise us we
pulled apart, dressed hastily and Apollonius went out to meet
them. On his insistence both Luke and I remained behind, the
boy trembling with fear and excitement at my side. We would be
able to hear perfectly clearly what was said and I held my son
tightly, reminding him to breathe deeply and calmly to relieve the
fear.

It was not bad news. At least, until the previous night, it would
have been wonderful news. Apollonius was posted back to
Alexandria with immediate effect. The Emperor was sick to death
of the fighting and squabbling between Egyptians, Jews and
Greeks and my husband was to head a task force group of men
sent to calm the territory. Failure would not be an available
option.

In effect this was a demotion. Alexandria was only a province
but it was news which would have gladdened Apollonius's heart.

'When do we leave?' I heard him ask.

'Tomorrow,' said the centurion. 'We will escort you and your
family back to Rome today and the ship departs at dawn tomorrow, weather permitting.'

'We will be ready by midday,' said Apollonius. 'Water and stable your horses and I will order food for your men.'

As he came back into the house, his face was alight with plea-
sure. We could go home! Luke ran forward to him laughing and
Apollonius flung him up into the air. 'We're going back!' he said.
'Isn't it wonderful?'

Of course he did not understand why I was not delighted at the
news. I, who had missed Alexandria even more than he, was
stony-faced and silent as I supervised the servants as they began to
pack. My heart was breaking; I so wanted to go home with them
both, but I could not.

'What is it?' he said, again and again but I shrugged him away.

'There isn't time now,' I said, indicating the servants. I could not speak in front of them. 'I'll tell you on the journey. We have to hurry.'

The truth was that I did not know how to tell him. He had his instructions from the Emperor, I had mine, via my brother, from God. I had to go to Cyprus. I could not disobey, even if I wanted to. If I did, my whole life had been wasted. All my training would be thrown away. I had work to do. What it was I did not know but I must do it or die.

But Apollonius was a persistent man. He would not let me wait and he would not take no for an answer. He took me out on the veranda out of earshot of slaves or soldiers and demanded that I tell him what was wrong.

I did not look at him as I recounted the story of my vision. Of the clarity of Yeshua's words and how I would not disobey them.

'But you are my wife,' he said, outraged. 'You come with me!'

'No,' I said. 'I'm going to Cyprus. I did so hope you would come with me but, if you can't, I must go alone.'

'Deborah, I forbid you! What about Luke? What about us?'

'I know, I know,' I wept. 'Can't you see how hard this is for me? Don't you think I want to go with you? Don't you think it's my heart's desire? But I am under discipline. Under God. I have to do what is necessary. We who know the teaching make that commitment. If I do not go, then my whole life is forfeit. I will die in spirit if not in body. Please trust me. Please let me go. I must.'

'But you can't go to Cyprus!' Apollonius took the most logical route to oppose me. 'I can't arrange for it; there isn't time! It's outrageous that you should even think of going alone.'

'I know. I know. I don't know what to do.' I said, my heart churning with the pain of losing this man I loved, perhaps forever. Unbearable thought! Unbearable! 'I have to go to Cyprus. I don't know why but I must.'

A soft cough behind us made us both turn sharply. Philo stood there apologetically. We had completely forgotten him in the disturbance.

'I didn't mean to interrupt you,' he said. 'But, as you don't seem to know, Cypres is the name of Herod Agrippa's wife.'

The journey back to Rome was not easy. Even with the answer to where I was to go Apollonius was still furiously angry, with me – and with God.

'How dare you!' he said, again and again and I was not certain whether he spoke to the Lord or to me. I rode, miserably, behind him while Philo tried to divert Luke who was alternately excited at the prospect of going home and upset that his parents were quarrelling.

'I can stop you, you know,' Apollonius said. 'I can make you come with me.'

'You would lose me if you did that,' I said. 'Not my body per-haps, but my soul.'

'Do you want to leave me?'

'Of course not! Of course not! How can you think such a thing?' For the first time I actually understood why Yeshua had chosen not to marry. When something is asked of you, you must go but the pain of parting from loved ones is unbearable. I did not know how I would survive without them – for Luke would go with his father, not with me. I could not bear it; I could not face it but I knew I had to do it.

Apollonius refused to sleep with me that night. The evening we spent at our villa in Rome was cold and angry and Luke was visibly upset. The pain and disbelief in his eyes when he realised that I was not going with them was more than I could bear. I ran out of the house and spent half the night walking the streets of Rome. There was nowhere I could truly go and be comforted but I went into the Temple of Jupiter – the place of Hesed, Loving Kindness on the Tree of Life – and sat there for some time, trying to contact the Lord and ask for help to solve this crisis. I needed the love of the Lord and I needed to feel love for my people in order to act for them. Jews do not kneel to pray but I knelt, imploring, begging for help in facing my task. I knew that if it had been given to me, I could do it. But the price was higher than I thought I could pay.

When I returned, Apollonius was sitting in the atrium, deci-phering a scroll by a pale, flickering lamp. I knew which one it was, not only from my own handwriting but instinctively. He did not see me, being intent on his reading. As he translated the words, he brushed aside the tears which were forming on his eye-lashes, blurring his vision. Around him I could see a strange light and I could recognise it as an echo of the celestials who must be standing there with him. I walked forwards with more confidence than I believed I could ever have felt again.

'Did they come and see you in the night, Beloved?' I asked softly and he looked up. I saw then, for the first time, how he had aged since we first met. He was still a fine, strong man but his hair was now mostly silver and the distinction of his features marked by etched-in laughter lines and the furrows on his brow. But I was no child either; my beautiful hair was far lighter than it had been, the silver and copper hairs mixing gently but inex-orably. I knelt at his feet and he put his hand on my head in blessing.

Apollonius sighed deeply. 'Something came.' he said. 'Something, someone. I don't know what. I would have said it was a god. It... They said I must go back to Alexandria without you. That I must set you free to fulfil your destiny here.

'You must go into service for Herod Agrippa so the Jews can be saved. I cannot do it – I did ask. And the wife of a Senator in Rome would not go into service. I must leave without you and I must leave you destitute for there is no other way you would need to throw yourself on their mercy.'

As he spoke, he loosened his grip on the manuscript and the Book of Esther fell from his lap to the floor. Neither of us took any notice. Apollonius had such an expression on his face as I imagine Abba must have had when the angel visited him before Yeshua's birth. He did not understand but he, too, now knew that he was under the discipline of the Lord and that the path was right.

'It's... hard,' he said. I nodded. 'To leave you with nothing...' I took his hand.

'I know,' I said, kissing it. 'I do know. But it is with my con-sent. And I will be taken care of.'

The next morning we stood together on the banks of the great River Tiber watching the loading of the beautiful Alexandrian ship bound for home. We were both exhausted. We could not let go of each other for every moment now was precious. Luke was helping the servants with our goods and sulking. I had tried to speak to him but now he wanted to be on his own.

'I pray with all my heart that you will return to me,' Apollonius said, kissing my hair. 'I have loved you like no other, Deborah, and learned more from these years together than I could ever have comprehended existed.

'I'm so afraid that we may not meet again in this life – even if your mission is successful it may take time. I am not young and sea voyages are dangerous – ' I put my hand to his lips to quiet him. 'We will be taken care of,' I said. 'We will meet again. We will be given an old age together, sometime soon, in Alexandria. I know it. I saw us once, standing together on the harbour side, older than we are now and still loving each other. These things are always true. Not one vision has ever failed me. You know now that they are true. We will live and love again together, one day.'

Somehow I said goodbye, to him and to Luke. My son would not kiss me, he could not understand. His face was cold and hard and, when I tried to embrace him, he turned and walked away.

Apollonius sighed. 'I will explain to him,' he said. 'It may take some time but I will do my best.

'God bless you, Deborah, in your task. Come home to me safely.'

Then he turned and boarded the ship and was gone from my sight.

Twelve

To the rest of Roman society, what happened to Apollonius and me would have seemed just like the break-up of any other marriage where the husband abandons his ageing wife and leaves her apparently destitute. A nine-days' wonder perhaps and food for all the gossips that mixed marriages did not work.

For all my faith, when Apollonius's and Luke's ship slipped out of sight down towards the estuary of the great River Tiber, I wept as though I truly had been abandoned. Then I walked slowly back to the apartment block we had shared with Apollonius's family. No one else was there for they, like the rest of aristocratic Rome, were away for the summer. Our furniture had already been packed up and transported and the place had a lost, sorrowful air.

I sat in the atrium and considered all my possessions in the world. I had Yeshua's chest with its precious scrolls and vials and some books hidden in a small bundle of clothes. My precious lyre was on its way to Alexandria with Apollonius – I could not afford to keep it with me and, anyway, women who played music in public were thought of in just the same way as actresses were. I had just enough money to take care of myself for a week or so while I learnt the art of being one of the previously despised 'clients.'

I knew that Herod Agrippa and his family were still in Rome, having returned quite recently from Judaea. I had thought I would wait a day or so before making my way to their magnificent palace but it was so lonely in that empty house that I could not bear to stay for long.

It was a fair walk to Agrippa's magnificent home and, even in the heat of summer, Rome was still crowded. There seemed to be more beggars than ever, sitting on doorsteps, on the bridges and in the Forum itself; their hands ever held out and their voices asking, wheedling, pleading. Apart from my books I was now little better off than they, for some of them could collect many sesterces in a week. And yet, ironically, I was probably the richest woman in Rome for I had a purpose and knowledge which was worth more than all the goods in the beautiful and expensive shops of the Regia Tusca and the Via Sacra together. At least, that was what I tried to tell myself as I made my way past those places of luxury and opulence. A very large part of me was not convinced.

The Forum was crowded with hawkers and performers. In the summer when the aristocracy left there were fewer shows and circuses and many of the shops were closed. The people of Rome looked to street entertainment instead and performers who would not usually be permitted in the great city flooded in to make some easy money. Often they brought disease with them, so it was wise not to go too close and to watch with a cloth filled with spices held to your nose and mouth to filter any foul air around them.

I dodged around the crowds keeping my eyes averted for to pass through the Forum unaccosted was difficult, particularly for a single woman, unattended and carrying baggage. To anyone there I would have looked like fair prey either for coercion or to be duped into some scheme or other. A few crude invitations and insults were levied at me as it was and I felt resentful tears behind my eyes. Why did I have to go through this? For what purpose? It was all very well being holier than thou, having visions and knowing about a higher purpose but all I could realistically feel was anger and grief.

I arrived at the King and Queen's door, swollen-eyed and increasingly nervous. I had no idea what to do or what to ask if I managed to catch their attention and I thought I had better sit with the other supplicants and clients and watch the etiquette of this strange new life until I could get the hang of it. There were plenty of people who swarmed around any powerful Roman and Herod Agrippa was no different. I noticed many Jews in the crowded courtyard, even some who were orthodox, by their dress. They usually thought that Agrippa had fallen further than Lucifer but, if help were needed, Jewish blood ties were stronger than anything else. I watched and waited and cringed with embarrassment at the fawning and flattering which went on around me. These people were beggars, just as much as those on the street. They were parasites, living off the largesse of another with only sycophancy offered in return.

One of the reasons Apollonius had not been considered a worthy member of the Senate was his dislike of such acolytes. We attracted a fair few, as did everyone, but only those who were interesting or useful in their own right were encouraged. The rest of the family were far easier prey and they would intercede for their clients with pleasure, feeling proud of their influence with Apollonius – and even with me.

As I sat watching, I wondered whether my intolerance with our clients would rebound on me here. As I had had no time for them, why should Herod Agrippa or Cypres have any time for me? I sighed; I had to trust that there was some service I could do for them, some reason why it was appropriate for me to be there.

It took three days. I went out to the baths and, for exercise, I walked around the streets but at night I slept on the floor of the entrance hall, my head resting on my roll of possessions and with Yeshua's casket in my arms. This was not rare; clients would hope to see their Lord and Lady at any time of the day or night in the hope of being given some commission or being of some use and I was not alone. People were called in just to listen to a new poem someone had written in the early hours of the morning. Clients, of course, would praise it to the skies and would be rewarded for their compliments and devotion either by money or recommendation to others.

I was propositioned by several men, including slaves of the household. They assumed I had fallen on even harder times than it appeared and seemed certain that I would do anything for a roof or some money. I refused them as politely as I could, for to offend staff in this house was to ensure that you never got near the Master and Mistress. I was insulted and barged across each time Agrippa or his wife came past by others who were pushier than I and knew far better what to say or to do, so much so that I despaired of speaking to either of them. Cypres I had never met and the idea of appealing to her seemed even more daunting than the chance of hoping that Agrippa would still recognise me. Cypres was dark and elegant and she passed through the atrium and the great hall with just the kind of expression that I expected I had worn as I made my way out of our home, past the irritating burr of unwelcome people.

By the second day I had my words rehearsed; that my husband had left Alexandria without me and I, a Roman citizen but a Jewess and their subject, was destitute. I was a herbalist and a scholar and I needed work in their household. That a respectable woman could have sunk so low was shameful but, eventually, they must give me work, otherwise all was lost. As I reminded myself, somewhat doubtfully, although humans may waste time or opportunities or send people on unnecessary errands or misunderstand instructions or requests, God does not. If I had interpreted my instructions correctly, I would be taken care of.

The introduction, when it came, could scarcely have been more dramatic or more appropriate. Cypres appeared, as usual, in the morning with her women and was weaving her way around the clients, ignoring everyone she could when something happened – it seemed to me as if someone tripped or fainted – but whatever it was, a scream went up from one of her attendants and all the crowds around fell back hurriedly. The falling sickness was prevalent in Rome and this might be someone infected by it. Where there had been a cluster of people, there was suddenly a space. I could see a young girl, lying huddled on the floor with Cypres leaning over and holding her.

The girl was moaning and breathing with difficulty. Spasms in her abdomen were causing her to twitch and groan and the slight mound under her stola told me all I needed to know. Miscarriage. And in someone so young! The girl's face was white and terrified. Someone was shouting for a doctor but I could see Cypres's expression. It was frozen with fear – but not just for the child's welfare, it spoke of fear of discovery and exposure – and she looked straight at me. Thanking God that I had just returned

from the bathing house, clad in clean clothing and with my hair
freshly arranged and that I looked respectable, I stepped forward.

'I am a Jew and a herbalist,' I said. 'I can help this child.'
Cypres looked up at me in surprise and hesitated. Then she made
a snap decision and nodded permission. I knelt beside the child.
'Madam, ask your attendants to clear the room.' I said. 'This may
be infectious.' As I spoke I looked at the Queen and told her with
my eyes that I knew full well that there was no danger of infection
but that I understood her need for secrecy.

In moments the great hall was emptied. Only three of the
Queen's women remained. Speaking calmly to the girl, who was
still conscious with eyes glazed with shock and fear, I checked to
see if the baby had come but there was no sign of it though blood
was now seeping through the terrified child's clothing. Although
I acted automatically, I was puzzled. My intuition told me that
there was no soul present, no life principle here. However, I could
be wrong. With hands shaking, I opened up Yeshua's chest and
found the little bottle which still contained a few drops of the precious herbs which, if they were appropriate, would stem the bleeding and give the pregnancy a second chance.

As I brought my hand out, the girl focused on me. Her face
was white and drawn and she tried to speak. 'It's all right,' I said
firmly and leaned down towards her but it was not until my ear
was right by her lips that she spoke in the most breathless of whispers.

'I don't want it,' she said. 'I mustn't have it. Please don't make
me have it.' Then she gasped and twisted as more blood rushed
out of her body.

The sixth commandment is 'Thou shall not commit murder'
but in the case of miscarriage the lines are rarely clear. I was certain that this girl's life was in danger and she must be the priority.
Without the mother the child cannot live and, even if a soul were
there, discarnate, it could have another chance to come later. I
realised that the girl might have taken something to dispose of the
pregnancy herself – if so, she had overdosed. She was killing herself as well as the child. I looked an urgent query at Cypres for
clarification but she lowered her deep brown eyes. The decision
was mine. 'Please help me make the right choice,' I prayed. As I

did so, my attention was drawn to the paleness of the girl's com-
plexion and a pinched look around her nose. Yes! Suddenly I
knew the tincture she had taken. To an observer my hand would
hardly have been seen to move as I dropped the one bottle and,
with a silent prayer for healing, took up the one next to it.

'Trust me,' I said very quietly, offering the draught. 'This will
not harm you and all will be well.'

She opened her mouth and allowed me to pour the herbal tincture down her slender little throat. Then I held her for the few
seconds it took her to relax and lose consciousness. As I did so, I
felt the tingling on the crown of my head which meant that the
healing power of the Divine was present. 'Talitha cumi,' I whispered as Yeshua had said to Rizpah's sister, Chloe, all those years
ago. A rush of power ran through me and into the child's sleeping soul and I sighed deeply. I had made the correct decision.

'Cover her up; she needs warmth,' I said to one of the attendants and a rug was placed over the girl's body and legs. I looked
up into Cypres's frightened and suspicious eyes and held them,
unafraid, for I knew the child would live. After a while the Queen
nodded again and, when she spoke, it was with sufficient warmth
for me to know that I was trusted.

'She is my daughter,' she said softly. 'Mariamne. She is just
twelve. Unmarried.' I indicated that I understood.

In my arms, the girl's body convulsed slightly as the unwanted
burden slipped gently away from her. I listened inside my head.
No, there was no soul. No child had never been intended to be
born. It was just a severe warning for a foolish little girl. No
more, no less.

I carried Mariamne to her room myself. She was a tiny little
thing and the fewer people who had the chance to see what had
happened the better. Cypres and the three attendants followed
me. 'They can be trusted,' said the Queen of Judaea as she closed
the door behind us. 'She will live, won't she?'

'Oh yes,' I said. 'She will live. She will need a little care and
advice however.' Again Cypres's eyes and mine met and she
dropped hers. Either she had been neglecting her daughter or hers
was the hand which had given her the dangerous herbal potion.

Swiftly I wrapped the pathetic non-evidence in a cloth. It was not formed and no sigh of spirit regret or acceptance accompanied it, so I needed to spare no thought or prayer for a soul's welfare. One of the attendants took the towel from me and the others moved in to wash and make comfortable the now-stirring girl. I gave instructions to give her camomile tea and a restorative and stood aside to give myself a moment to rest and give thanks.

When I opened my eyes a servant was waiting to offer me a bath and a change of clothing. I looked down at my creased and stained clothes and smiled. Cypres was a Jew and she knew me to be a Jew. She would do all that was correct and orthodox whether that was her personal practice or not. Her staff would be making arrangements for me, should I want to, to take the ritual Mikvah after being in touch with sickness and blood. It was many years since I had been to the ritual bath, relying instead on the cleansing of spirit through quietness and prayer, as Yeshua had taught me. Still, it would be good to experience the familiar old routine.

It seemed to me as I was escorted through the corridors that the luxury of Herod Agrippa's home was greater than that of the Emperor himself. However, it might just have been the style and the artefacts which reminded me of Judaea making me feel that way. The pre-Mikvah bath with scented oils and asses' milk was delicious and the towels used to dry me were softer than any I had ever experienced before. At the Mikvah itself my mind flew back to the Temple in Jerusalem and Imma's loving arms holding the child that was me as we jumped together into the holy water. Now I was older than she had been then. I jumped, a prayer for cleansing and guidance on my lips and my whole body shivered with the shock of the cold water after the steam and heat of the bathing room.

Fresh fruits, crushed with milk and honey, were brought for me to drink and a selection of plain but good-quality clothing offered for me to wear while mine were cleaned. I smiled to myself for Cypres was obviously careful of her rank and would not offer her own clothing to a mere medicine woman. Contrast that with Apollonius who had given me the very best in silk and linen and even Paulina, the former Empress, who had given me a dress of her own.

I chose a simple white dress which was a little too short – nearly all borrowed clothing was short for my height – and a blue pella. I plaited my hair myself using the combs provided, for mine also had gone to be ritually cleansed for me while I bathed. When I was ready, I was summoned to the Queen.

She was sitting in a long, airy room decorated with royal purple awnings and her manner was entirely regal. The moments when she had been an anxious mother were banished and instead the woman before me was every inch a Queen. Had I intended to question her about her daughter's pregnancy or what she had been given to induce a miscarriage I would have had to have been a very brave woman. As it was, I did not have to be impressed. After all, I was Yeshua's sister, I did not have to bow to anyone. That was what made it so easy to do so.

I made obeisance to her Majesty and waited. Part of me was amused at this charade of Queenliness after we had knelt together in the hallway nursing a critically ill child. However, I was watchful for I knew this was my chance to enter the household. The Holy One might set up the opportunities but it was up to the individual to prove a good or a bad tool.

Cypres thanked me gravely for my services that morning and I bowed again. Behind her, servants were laying a table for a midday meal and it was obvious that she wished to be rid of me before others joined her.

'You were with the other petitioners this morning and have been there before,' said the Queen. 'The very least I can do for you now is to hear your petition. Speak. If I can, I will grant it.'

It would have been so easy then to have said 'Madam, I beg you to ask your husband to persuade his friend the Emperor not to place his statue in the Temple in Jerusalem,' but that would have been too bold, too soon and too intimidating. Instead, following Queen Esther's lead, I played down my desire.

'Madam,' I said. 'My wish is to be of service to you and your family. I came in the hope that my medical and herbal knowledge would be of use to a royal family who knew and respected the Judaism of my birth and the knowledge that I gained there in my youth. That is my only petition.'

She was interested. Petitions were rarely for anything other than money or recommendations for higher posts and personal preferment. I had proved myself proficient and I appeared to be discreet.

'Well, you have, indeed been of great service,' she said. 'I would like to reward you for that.'

I bowed. 'Madam, to be of further service is all the reward I require.'

'Come now,' Cypres was half intrigued, half scornful. I could see that her own love of wealth and pretty things found it strange that I was not asking for physical reward. I wore combs in my hair and some, if not much, jewellery so I could not be some fanatical ascetic who eschewed the comforts of life. 'Do you not want money?' she asked. 'Do you not want a recommendation to the Emperor's family? I can do both those things for you.'

I smiled. 'Thank you Madam. I do not scorn money but I am not in need of it. I do not scorn helping anyone but I am most delighted to help my own King and Queen.'

I think she might have offered me a post within the household as a servant and, although it was many years since I had waited on anyone, I would have had to have been content with that, seeing it as the Lord's will. But at that moment we were interrupted. A palpable rush of energy preceded the men as they came into the room and Herod Agrippa strode in, flanked by acolytes and guards.

He greeted his wife with courtesy but, with a soldier's bluntness, came to the point immediately. 'Is she still here?' he said. 'I heard what the Rebbitzen did for Mariamne.' Cypres indicated me with one casual, almost languorous movement of her beautiful neck and stood back, handing the situation over to her husband as was the correct etiquette for an orthodox Greek, Roman or Jewish wife even if she were a Queen. There was a slight arrogance about her pose as if, for some reason, she thought it was right that her husband should be dealing with this very female incident. I assumed that she was just grateful to have the decision over me taken from her hands for she, definitely, had been most uncertain as to what she should do with me!

Herod Agrippa took both my hands as I dipped in the formal bow. 'Oh, but it's you!' he said in surprise and turned to his wife with a few words of explanation about Caligula's sickness and how I was the woman he had sent for then.

'But I thought you had gone to Alexandria with your husband!' he said to me, once he had spoken to Cypres.

'No, Sir,' I said. 'Apollonius and our son travelled alone. I hope to join them sometime soon but for the moment my place is in Rome.'

'What's this?' said the King. 'A wife's place not at her husband's side? Has the rascal left you?' In any other circumstances his tactlessness would have hurt deeply but I, at least, knew that Apollonius and I had not parted for lack of love.

'No sir,' I said gently, for I knew I had to be totally honest. 'Apollonius needs to be in Alexandria. You know how difficult matters are there between the different races, including our own. You know that he has been sent to try and help there. For the moment he thinks it better for me to stay here in safety.' I took a deep breath but Agrippa interrupted me.

'Come now,' he said. 'A Senator's wife left alone in Rome when her husband leaves? I don't think that rings true, my dear. You don't need to be so proud, you know. If he has left you, he should smart for it! And without a penny eh?'

'I have a little money,' I said, defensively.

'Hah!' said the King. 'A little money eh? Not a lot I should imagine. Well, we Jews are a proud race and I don't think any the worse of you for that.

'We will do what we can for you. Without you Mariamne might have died.'

Behind him, I saw Cypres stiffen. This was confusing! Did she or did she not want her husband to know about the matter? 'It was just a female incident, Sir,' I said hastily. 'Probably not life-threatening at all but frightening just the same. I think, perhaps, your daughter has not been eating well and her blood is not too strong.'

'Yes,' Cypres broke in. 'She has been pining, Sir, as you know. She has not taken care of herself.' She turned to me with a smile. 'Young girls take such stupid fancies sometimes and, in our liberal times, it is hard to explain to them when a connection is not suitable. In this case the man was not at all worthy of her.'

'And you don't like him, whoever he is,' I thought, closely followed by the impression that we were performing in a farce. Who
was lying to whom and why? But then, I was playing a part as
well. I kept my face impassive.

'Yes, yes,' said Agrippa, testily, now sounding as though he was
not interested in silly girls' problems where before he had been all
concern. He turned to me again. 'What exactly do you need?' he
asked.

'She wanted to offer her services to me and my women,' said
Cypress, hastily, glad to change the subject.

'Well, you would be welcome to join our court as one of my
wife's women, if that is what you wish,' said Agrippa. 'But I
would hardly think it suitable for a Senator's wife!'

If only he knew he was talking to a carpenter's daughter from
provincial Galilee! I bowed again and said I would be honoured
to be a part of the women's household.

'As you wish,' said Agrippa. 'But no nonsense about your place
with us please. You will not be a servant but a valued client. You
will eat with us and the others of our household who are our considered friends. I'm sure we can find somewhere for you to stay.
You must be hungry. Now, you must excuse me for I am wanted
by the Emperor's guard.' He bowed to his wife and kissed her and
swept out of the room together with his entourage.

I had the feeling that such intimacy was not what Cypres had
planned but with a lofty wave of her arm she invited me to join
the three other ladies who were reclined around a table. Once we
had joined them, servants brought plates of pastries, shellfish and
cold meats. The rather fixed mask of welcome on Cypres's face
vanished and she raised her arm, gesturing the meats away with
barely disguised fury.

'Your Majesty,' I said hastily. 'I thank you for your extreme
courtesy but I am happy to eat Roman meat.' Both Cypres and
the servant hesitated. 'A piece of chicken would be lovely,' I said
with a smile and, on his mistress's nod, the servant placed the plate
before me. All the other women waited until I had made my
selection of the food before they chose to eat exactly the same. So
they were all Jews but Jews in name only and they were terrified
that I might be more orthodox than they. I felt laughter bubble

up inside me. No Jew should eat of forbidden food and that included meats not sacrificed to the One God. Poor Cypres's servants had just demonstrated that neither she, her husband or their court followed the letter of the Law. It was obvious that I was not a hard-line Jew for I would never have come to their gate in the first place but, even so, I could have turned up my nose at their way of eating. Not for the first time, I realised how Yeshua's way was a pathway out of the prison we Jews often locked ourselves into so that we could not teach or learn from other people and other traditions. It was one thing to be a chosen people with great spiritual knowledge, it was another to regard those with different paths as being inferior.

I commented that I had no taste for shellfish myself having tried it – and the atmosphere relaxed almost at once. Several women reached out to take a prawn and a cheerful debate ensued on which shellfish was the tastiest. From then, the meal passed fairly easily and I answered their questions with politeness and good humour and managed not to say anything which could offend anyone. Once or twice I caught Cypres looking at me cautiously and I smiled at her but said nothing. When we had finished one of the women offered to take me back to see Mariamne and I agreed with relief. As I had, as yet, no idea what I was meant to do here, the best thing I could do would be to keep as low a profile as I could.

Mariamne was awake but sleepy. She was half-inclined to be afraid of me, especially when I sent all the slaves away and sat down beside her, asking her to tell me what had happened. She stammered and stuttered until I made it clear that I was not angry with her or judging her. Then, in her natural desire to talk about a loved one, she poured out the whole story of forbidden love, secret meetings and the terror on finding that she was with child. She did not name her lover and I wondered whether he were slave or freeborn. Few would be thought fit to mate with the daughter of a King and she might just have chosen badly.

'It's not that I wouldn't like to have a baby,' she said shyly. 'If I could have married him I would have had it happily but, you see, he's married already.'

I bit back the retort that he, whoever he was, had no business to be messing with a mere child but that would have alienated me immediately with the girl who was so desperately in love.

What I did say, as gently as I could, was that she must look after herself for some time and not allow him or anyone to love her physically for, although she would recover fully if she took the greatest of care, she would not get well if she repeated any of the actions which had made her pregnant.

'You were very lucky this time,' I said. 'The medicine you took was much too strong for you and it could have killed you along with the baby. If you ever took it again nobody could help you.'

She stared at me, wide-eyed, and then began to cry. I knew that her heart was breaking at the idea of not being able to be with her lover. I held back the traditional older person's impatience with youth's insistence that passion is all and comforted her as best I could. She snuggled into my arms and I dried her tears gently. 'It's not his fault they gave me too much. He wouldn't have wanted to hurt me,' she said, just before she slipped back into sleep.

I held her for a while, my mind running back over the morning's events, especially the scene with Herod Agrippa and his wife in the great hall. Something about it did not ring true. Suppositions, each as wild as the other began to crowd into my mind. Then the truth, sharp as a sword and twice as deadly, cut through them. The girl's lover was the Emperor himself – and both Herod Agrippa and his wife knew it.

I sat there, holding her as the afternoon shadows lengthened along the floor. Women whispered in and out of the room and I was told that a room had been made ready for me and that someone was available to fetch my clothes and personal effects. When I said I had none but what I had brought with me, I received several funny looks and there was plenty of muttering. I could see I might be rather a cuckoo in this nest.

As I sat, I thought and wondered. I realised that, if I needed to know which hand had been the one to give this child a near-fatal dose, I would be shown but I was human enough to look at all the possibilities for myself. Had the intention been to kill her? Was the Emperor tired of her already and was he truly capable of such a thing? I had heard rumours of his killing his sister and even slaughtering animals with his bare hands but had discounted them as just street gossip. Or had the dose been given to Mariamne by one of his servants – or by one or other of her parents to prevent shame falling on their family?

As dusk fell, the girl in my arms stirred again. She would be thirsty and there was a cup of water by her bed waiting for her to drink. Warily I dipped my finger into it and tasted a drop. It did seem a little bitter but it might just have been my own suspicions. Nevertheless I laid her down and walked to the well which bubbled up into the atrium and presumably into the Mikvah I had used earlier. There, the water was fresh and clear. I rinsed the cup and filled it and carried it back to the now fretful and wakeful girl. She was hungry which was a good sign and, as I gave her the water, I remembered Yeshua's command for Chloe, Rizpah's sister. 'Give her nourishment,' he had said, meaning physical food, psychological help and spiritual guidance. Would Mariamne be any more amenable to learning the secrets of life than Chloe had been? I sighed, for I doubted it, but I was willing to try.

As the days passed I checked and tasted Mariamne's food and found my fears on that score to be unfounded. She was a lonely child, orphaned and rather lost in a Roman palace among people who chased political favour rather than self-knowledge or comfort. She had brothers and sisters but now that she was, in her own eyes at least, a woman, she did not mix well with them. As no one really knew what to do with me I became her mentor and confidante and it took Mariamne less than a week to confide the identity of her lover. I was glad that I had known before, for the shock would certainly have shown in my face, whereas I was able to take the news calmly and speak to her only as though he were an ordinary man that she loved.

To my more experienced years it sounded like a simple, passing, act of lust from a man with no thought or care of a young virgin's feelings or her future. To Mariamne it was a wonderful experience, a fulfilment of dreams and she envisaged a love affair continuing as soon as Caligula returned to Rome. I tried, very gently, to introduce her to the idea that she must take care of herself but all she was really interested in was a method of contraception so that she could make love without fear of another pregnancy. Ironically, her memory of the sex act itself was not particularly pleasant. I had to stop myself from grimacing as she told me when and where and how it happened and I had a strong urge to give Caligula a resounding slap for his insensitivity. I knew I would be very surprised if he sought the girl out again or even if he cared whose daughter she was and what might have become of her.

It was Cypres who had given Mariamne the drug and I was soon convinced that the overdose was simply an accident. Agrippa had known of the pregnancy but whether he had been involved or not in its ending, I never knew; the King had a very clever way of hiding himself – which was why he had survived so long at Caligula's court.

The Queen was more reticent than her daughter but she, too, was lonely in her magnificent palace surrounded by sycophants. As the days and then weeks passed, she would send for me more and more often to talk about our homeland or so that we could sew together. She was a talented seamstress while I was hopeless but she taught me a little and her nimble fingers reminded me of Imma's. Cypres's own weakness, she admitted, was cookery and she missed many of the dishes of her homeland. She could not remember recipes (why should she when she had never had to cook?) and had never found a good Jewish cook to run her kitchens. Her talent was as a hostess and a glittering figure of fashion and taste. I took over some housekeeping duties as time went on as I did remember some recipes from home. From what little I saw in the kitchens their cooks obviously deceived their masters – or were lazy – for the food they served was often not of the standard expected in such an illustrious place. I found out that much was cooked outside the building and hurried in at the last minute. This was customary in Rome for many homes had no cooking facilities at all and whole families would rely on buying food from the thousands of stalls on the streets but, in the great private houses, that should not have been necessary.

I also became a kind of apothecary for the household, treating minor ailments and listening to problems. That did not trouble me and I was glad to be busy for it held back the continual ache I felt for the lack of Apollonius and Luke. My husband and son haunted my nights and I would pray for their health and happiness with every spare moment. I also prayed that I might do whatever was required of me as swiftly as possible in order to be reunited with my family. I was still convinced that we would meet again and that all would be well but, as each week passed, that goal seemed further and further away.

To comfort myself and, because it was meat and drink to me, I prayed and meditated, continued my studies and followed the Jewish festivals as best I could. Agrippa and Cypres only paid lip service to Judaism of any sort but their household did honour the festivals and I found it comforting to take part in the age-old rituals. The Queen enjoyed my lighting the candles on Shabbat Eve and would often encourage me to recite the prayers she remembered from childhood when we were alone together. I made several tentative mentions of there being further knowledge to have but they were totally ignored.

At last, the day came when I was alone with the King and Queen one afternoon. Mariamne was visiting friends and I was worried about her. Caligula was already back in Rome and I felt I would have to broach the subject. Fortunately Agrippa himself was the first to mention it and, for the most part, all I had to do was listen.

It took him some time to build up to the subject – what father would not find it hard to discuss with a virtual stranger? But he had Mariamne's welfare at heart and something needed to be done.

What could they do? he asked. Although Caligula was a friend, he would so easily turn into an enemy. If he showed more interest in Mariamne they were helpless.

'Then take her away,' I said.

Not possible, was the answer. Of course it was possible but I did not say that. I understood the resistances people felt and Agrippa's fear of Caligula was founded on good common sense.

'Then you must pray and trust in God that the Emperor's attention is distracted elsewhere,' I said. 'And, if possible, allow Mariamne to see aspects of him that she will not like which might affect the infatuation she feels.'

We talked a little more and I could see that just bringing the subject out in the open was alleviating their anxieties. They knew Caligula well enough to see that his fickle attention was unlikely to linger – in fact, he had already been back for more than a week and he had not even seen her, something which was already distressing Mariamne.

'She may try and see him,' I said, wryly.

'Well, we can do something about that,' said Cypres.

We sat in silence for a few moments and then Herod Agrippa began to speak again. It was not just the dishonour of his daughter which was at stake, he said. It was the whole Jewish situation.

Carefully I enquired as to the final outcome of Philo's mission.

'He left for Alexandria some weeks back,' said Agrippa. 'Nothing came of it. I was there a couple of times when the delegation met the Emperor but they did not handle it well. You know as well as I how arrogant the Jews can appear. Although Philo is a good man, even he was visibly annoyed by Caligula's rudeness and Caligula just reacts to that by being even ruder. That's all I can say. Walls have ears.'

'Would you be willing to intercede yourself?' I said cautiously. 'You know that raising the statue in the Temple would be a terrible calamity for our – your – people.'

'I would if I knew how,' said Agrippa. 'Caligula loves to be honoured and feted and – yes, even worshipped. He sees it as his due. If you play by the rules and, as long as you ask for things in public when he can't pretend that it didn't happen, he is the most generous of friends. In private he will forget what you asked for in seconds! Please him and he will offer you the Moon. Refuse to accede to him and you are in trouble. To tell him that some strange and foreign race won't bow to him just won't work. I can't think of an answer.'

I could. As he was speaking an idea formed itself inside my head. If I had Agrippa's support and we followed the story in the Book of Esther, perhaps we could prevail after all.

'I have an idea,' I said.

I reminded them of Esther's story. How she had won back her husband from his friendship with Haman the Jew-hater by asking the two of them to the best possible banquet. They had eaten and been entertained so well that the King promised to honour any request that Esther might have. Could Caligula be so flattered?

Perhaps he, too, would offer any request that Agrippa asked after such a banquet – and then the King could save his people by speaking out in public.

Nobody thought that my plan could possibly work and I had quite a battle with myself not to be impatient with them for their short-sightedness. But at least the discussion did seem to bear some fruit. After thinking it through, Agrippa decided, instead, to go to Caligula directly and talk to him. We all had doubts as to how successful even such a good friend of the Emperor could be, considering that he was a member of the very race which was defying Caligula's pretensions to be a god but I was glad that something, at least, was being done.

Both Cypres and I awaited Agrippa's return anxiously and we did well to be concerned, for the behaviour of the Emperor to his friend was so savage that Agrippa was brought home in a dead faint. Cypres became hysterical and the servants afraid. It was down to me to do the best I could with him.

The King was unconscious for more than a day. I never learned all of what happened in that fateful meeting but it left Agrippa weakened and mortally afraid. I nursed him with the greatest of care, not asking questions but fearing, as he did, that the Imperial Guard would come to claim him as a traitor at any moment.

It did not happen. Perhaps Caligula was capable of love and the appreciation of loyalty after all. But, even so, Agrippa's credit was lost unless he could do something – and soon – to regain the Emperor's favour.

Once he was strong enough to get up again, I reminded him, tentatively, of my idea. This time it did seem appropriate for it might heal the wounds between the two men. 'Very well,' said Agrippa. 'Do as you like. But you will have to do it yourself. I can do nothing. It is up to you.'

That night, I sat in my room almost paralysed with fear. So this was my destiny; to follow in the footsteps of the woman I most revered. There was another piece of Esther's story which I had hoped to set aside – the risking of her life to talk to her husband in his courtroom when she had not been summoned. But where Esther was married to Ahasuerus and he loved her, I was nothing to Caligula.

'Not quite nothing,' said a voice in my head. 'Physically, you remind him of the only woman he has ever truly loved.'

'But he's mad,' I whispered back. 'And I am a Jew and he hates the Jews.'

'Only because they will not bow to him,' said the voice in my head. 'You are a stiff-necked people. An unassimilable people. Your neck, Deborah, will bend like a willow tree.'

'And splinter,' I said, putting my hand to my throat, feeling its narrowness and how easily it could be broken.

'And if he kills me?' I asked.

'Then it is only one life, given in joy and gratitude to God,' was the answer.

'I can't do it.' I was emphatic.

'Others have.'

Then I jumped up, anger coursing through me. 'Yes,' I almost shouted. 'Holy men and women. Not ordinary people like me. You can't expect it of me! Not for a people who have despised and rejected me! Not for those who hate me! I'm not great; I'm not holy. I'm not good enough or strong enough. I can't. I can't. I can't!'

'You are right,' said the voice. 'You are not great, nor holy, nor good, nor strong. But you're all we have. Without you it is already lost.'

Both Cypres and Agrippa thought I was mad. I quite agreed with them but I knew that if I did not do it then I might as well lie down and die anyway. Yeshua once told me that there were three people at any one time who could do a particular job. Philo had tried – and failed. Agrippa had tried – and failed. There was only me left.

There was no point in sending to ask for an interview with Caligula. Such things just did not happen unless you were summoned into the presence. Waiting on the off-chance to see him was also impractical – and I did not have the courage to wait. It had to be as Esther had done – boldly and surely and in outright risk of my life. If Caligula did not choose to spare me, then I would die.

Cypres dressed me herself, in cloth of gold. She burnished my hair with henna and oils and teased and plaited it into the nearest style she could remember to that shown on Agrippina's statue in the palace. She rouged my cheeks and lips and painted my eyes with colour and let me take one, just one, disbelieving look at the extraordinary creature in the silver looking-glass.

It was good to see this moving statue, because she was not me and that, strangely, gave me comfort. Cypress offered me a drink before I left and, as soon as I put it to my lips, I knew that it contained the poppy syrup which I used to control pain or distress. Oh, what temptation! Drinking it would deaden my senses so that I would not care so much what happened to me. But it would dull them too and, if angelic voices needed to speak through me, they would not be able to get through.

I refused it but, as is so often the way, I took the next temptation. Cypres pressed a tiny silver box into my hand. 'It contains a poison,' she said. 'It will kill you in moments. Keep it to hand in case you need it. If the worst should happen, it would be the kindest way.'

I thanked her, my voice trembling, and slipped the little box into a pocket of my stola. Then, without saying or thinking more, I began the walk to Caligula's palace.

Agrippa had provided guards for me who would be able to ensure my entry to the palace itself as an official envoy. It would only be to the outside of the stateroom itself, where Caligula would be hearing petitions of law – from then on, I would be defenceless.

There is a great stillness in the mind when fear is so deep that you can taste it. I would like to say that I was praying, safe in the knowledge of God's protection, but I was not. The only coherent thought I had was that if the Jews of the city knew what I was going to do, they would probably kill me. And, even in those horrible moments, I could almost find that amusing.

It seemed to take an age to reach the throne room. I felt as though everyone was staring at me and it occurred to me, somewhere deep in the echoes of my mind, that it might help if I did play the part of a Queen; the Queen of Persia if not of Rome.

She came to my aid at the exact moment that I had walked forward, alone, and pushed open the doors of the throne room. For an infinitesimal moment I saw every face turned towards me and the guards moving, as if slowed down in time, with their daggers drawn. She helped me find Caligula and look straight into his shocked eyes with dignity. The Voice of the Daughter of God spoke through me: 'All Hail, Gaius Caligula the Divine,' she said and, slipping neatly beneath the guards, I prostrated myself on the floor.

There was no sound. I was aware that two men had their swords at my neck. I could do nothing but wait. No prayer came; nothing.

Silence.

'Let her up,' said a voice.

I must not cry. I must not cry. I must not give way now. I must get up with dignity. I must speak with dignity. I must act with dignity.

Caligula looked at me. He seemed confused.

'Mother?' he said. He had obviously forgotten that he had ever seen me before. But he did see a resemblance. There was hope.

'Lord,' I said. 'I am a Jewess from your city who sees in you Adam Kadmon, the Divine Man, the firstborn of the one Almighty God. You are his representative on Earth and I bow to you unreservedly.'

Caligula said nothing. His fingers drummed a rhythm on the side of his ornate, golden chair.

'I have come, on behalf of Agrippa, King of the Jews and of the Jewish people themselves, to invite you to a banquet which is to be held in honour of your Divinity,' I said, my voice sounding feeble and stupid to my ears.

Silence. Then Caligula's restless fingers stopped. He got up.

'My mother sent you!' he said. 'What fun! I knew you Jews would come to your senses. I shall come to your banquet. But you should go now because I don't like women in the courtroom. You'll be gone when I turn round again.' He turned his back on me and I backed away as fast as I could.

Then, I was outside the throne room again and, as soon as the doors were shut, doubled over and fighting for breath as nausea tore at my body.

The banquet we planned was the most magnificent that Rome had ever seen. Without Agrippa's generosity (and his ability to get himself cheerfully in debt and trust that all would be well) it would have been impossible. The Emperor let it be known publicly that he was pleased with the idea. Having had the Alexandrian delegation dogging his footsteps 'like half-dead mourners,' to use his words, and opposition to his statue being whispered in the wind all over the Empire, had angered him more than anything else. Now, a banquet which would honour him from the heart of the Jews was the succour which his great ego required.

I was sick and shaking for three days but, once I had recovered Cypres gave me free rein, especially in the kitchens and I hired cooks and pastry-makers by the dozen. With Herod Agrippa's own guard I scoured the Jewish quarter of the city and, with some persuasion and a great deal of opposition, I managed to find Jewish women who were prepared to help with recipes and ideas.

We decorated the banqueting hall with scarlet, blue, royal purple and white, painting Caligula's image and placing statues of him everywhere. We invited everyone we knew that he liked and hired in as many half-Jews and full-blooded Jews who were willing to help. We did not tell them everything but we let it be known, unofficially, that with sufficient backing we might be able to get the order overturned. Complete strangers began to turn up at the door offering their assistance or just their company as guests. The underground links of Judaism were doing their work well and we even found a metal-worker who was willing to re-create the menorah itself, as large as he could make it – out of copper rather than gold – but it was just what we wanted as a final touch.

We turned the entire hall into the image of the Temple with different courtyards (although the walls were very low so that everyone could see), flowers and fountains. We set up Caligula's own table in the court of Israel and left the Holy of Holies empty but for the white drapery and the menorah. The final act of our theatre would be carried out there and on it rested the fate of the nation.

On the evening itself I was exhausted from tension and work but I had done all that could be done. I had prayed for help and I had received help. I had blessed every glass and platter and sanctified everything I could think of. Together with the other women I wove the fragrance of flower oils through every piece of fabric and into the air itself.

When Caligula arrived we had a choir to sing for his entry. We had his favourite musicians, his favourite foods mixed among the Jewish delicacies (some more Arabian and some from even further afield but all exotic). He was entertained like the Emperor he was.

Then we staged the finale. It was a Friday night, the Eve of the Sabbath and the King and Queen, Mariamne and I each had our part to play. To the undiscerning eye we represented different stages of life. Mariamne, adorned in the most beautiful of blue dresses with fresh flowers in her hair and over her bodice, represented youth. I, with my resemblance to Caligula's mother, represented maturity. Agrippa and Cypres represented beauty and kingship. We invited Caligula into the space for the Holy of Holies and, remaining outside, we enacted the Sabbath Eve service before him, complete with the ritual prayers and song. I lit the candles, drawing down the Shekhinah, the feminine of God from the Divine World and blessed Caligula with my prayers. Agrippa sanctified the wine of the spirit and offered it to his Emperor. Cypress took the water and washed Caligula's hands and Mariamne offered him the bread of life.

Each of us was perfect for our role. Mariamne loved her Lord directly with the ardour of physical passion, as the young and beautiful do. Cypres honoured him from her psychological knowledge of what was due in order for her to maintain her position of social power and acceptance. Agrippa bowed to him as a King, to a King whom God had decreed should rule over him and his people. I looked into his eyes and, through the blessing and mercy of God, saw and honoured the divinity within even his divided and shattered soul. As we performed our sacred ritual, even the entertainment-sated Romans became quiet and watched. They did not know why this caught at their hearts but the time-honoured, ancient and sacred ritual did its work as it always will when done for the love of God.

At the end the four of us, the Four Worlds of Creation, bowed to our Emperor and we stood back to await his pleasure.

Silence filled the hall. My heart was racing.

Caligula was enchanted. He turned to Agrippa and thanked him with tears in his eyes. There had never been such a banquet in his honour, he said. No one had ever done him such reverence. If there was anything, anything he could do or give to Agrippa in return, it was his for the asking.

Agrippa thanked him, dismissing our efforts as was correct demeanour and saying that what we had done was merely the Emperor's due from his loving people. Caligula pressed him and, for a moment, I saw a flash of fear in Agrippa's eye.

My heart sank. The King was back in favour. Would he have the courage to put all that in jeopardy again?

He appeared to think. Every eye in the room was focussed on him. I held my breath.

'My Lord and Emperor,' he said, slowly. 'I do have one request of you. That you listen to this woman here, standing before you and that you grant her request, rather than mine.'

I stood, stock still and icy cold. Inside, a tiny, bitter voice began to berate me. 'Of course it wasn't going to be that easy,' it said. 'Of course he would lack courage at the final moment. Of course it would all be left up to you. And now, after all, you are going to fail. And you – and your people – are going to die.'

Caligula had burst out laughing and everyone around him was chuckling too. He pounded Agrippa on the back and said: 'Just like you! So I must now honour some woman's little request to spare some insignificant life or stop the carriages going down her street so late at night or pay for a doctor to see her child. Well, my friend, I will listen to her and, if I can, I will grant her request.'

A thousand pairs of eyes looked at me and my knees trembled. 'Come on, woman,' said Caligula kindly. 'I know you. You have had the courage to approach me in my throne room. You may speak. What is it to be? Do you wish me to come to another banquet?'

That was the answer! When the King had asked Queen Esther what she wanted after her banquet she had said only that they should meet again the next night and repeat their celebrations. That's what I should do! After all, this was just a repeat of the same situation. Then Agrippa could ask tomorrow.

'But you are not Queen Esther; you are Deborah,' I heard inside my head.

I closed my eyes for a second. What should I do? Everything depended on my making the right decision. There would be no second chance. There was a bitter taste in my throat and I feared that I might faint. I opened my eyes with some effort and looked at Caligula.

'My simple request is that you truly know in your heart that we, as representatives of the Jewish nation, honour and accept your Divinity – and that you have mercy upon us and honour our humble request for you to withdraw your order for your statue to stand in the Temple in Jerusalem,' I said.

The silence was long and, to me, seemed to crackle with tension. This was not what the Emperor had expected and his face was a mask of stone. For a moment he lifted his arm as if to condemn me there but he hesitated. He was aware that he had agreed to grant anything and there were a thousand witnesses.

'Very well,' he said curtly. 'I grant your request.' As he said it, for the very first time I did see some of the greatness of Kingship in him. He would honour his word. Something passed between our eyes and then it was gone and a different entity entirely was looking at me; something salacious and nasty and crude.

'And I think I deserve a reward for honouring such a serious request,' he said softly. 'Don't you?'

Around me the air appeared to flash with fire and I felt giddiness flood through me. The weight of fear took away the last of my strength and the only thing I remember was Mariamne holding on to me and guiding me to a seat before I fainted away.

When I came to myself I was lying on a couch in my own room. One of Agrippa's chamberlains was with me and two women, one of whom appeared to be washing my hair.

'What?' I exclaimed but the second woman put her finger to her lips urgently. 'Be quiet,' she said. 'Your life is in danger. We must work quickly.'

She continued her own work on my hands – using what looked like walnut juice to darken the skin half-way up my arms.

'We must get you on the next ship out of Rome,' said the Chamberlain. 'Everything is being arranged. You have no need to fear.'

No need to fear! What had Caligula decreed? What had happened in those few minutes since he had granted my request? My mind was blurred; I could not believe what I thought I had heard. The Chamberlain told me swiftly and succinctly that Caligula had ordered for me to be sent to his rooms to await his pleasure. It was only Cypres's request to allow me time to beautify myself which had bought these few precious moments.

I knew, as well as the chamberlain, the rumours of what happened to the women who were sent to Caligula's rooms. Nothing was ever confirmed for the women did not live to tell. And age was no barrier either. The Emperor's fancies were many and varied. If I had been summoned then it almost certainly meant my degradation and death.

'Can you save me?' I asked. The chamberlain smiled. 'It has never been done before,' he said. 'But if we are swift, it may be possible. The disguise we are painting on you is more for our benefit than yours. If it is found that we tried to help you, we will all die.'

He was a Jew, not orthodox but a Jew nonetheless and he knew how important this evening had been. He would help me to the best of his ability just as the two women, so swiftly working on changing my appearance, would do.

Less than an hour later I stood on board a small but swift boat and looked my last towards Rome. My hair was coiled in barely dry black ringlets and my skin tinted as dark as an Egyptian's. I carried money and the papers of Camilla of Tyre, the widow of a merchant, travelling to Sicilia where she would catch another ship home to her family in Alexandria. Who she was or if she ever existed, I know not.

I only had a few moments to tell the chamberlain of my heartfelt gratitude to him and to Agrippa, Cypres and the women for acting so swiftly. 'How will they explain my absence?' I asked.

'They will say that you were a goddess, his mother incarnate, come to visit but only briefly,' he said, with perfect composure and I tried not to laugh hysterically. Yes, Caligula might fall for that one! But only if the real woman had vanished completely, never to be seen again.

The one other thing I needed to hear was that the decree to Petronius, Governor of Judaea, that, if the statue had not already been raised, it was not to be so, was on the very same ship as I was.

Nothing could call that back once it had left the coasts of Italia and the Jews would be safe. The Tribune, and his men who were carrying it to its destination, ignored me and I kept as far from them as I could.

The boat slipped down the Tiber and I wrapped myself in the black wool cloak I had been given, watching anxiously for signs of pursuit on land. There was none. If anyone were searching for the red-headed woman who had caught Caligula's eye, they did not look for her on the river. All the same I worried, quietly and exhaustedly, until long after we had docked at the river mouth and I had found my way to the *Alessandrina,* a strong, swift ship bound for home. She did not sail for 24 hours and I lay exhaustedly in a shoreside boarding house all that time trying to sleep, to recover but starting at every sound, every footstep and every passing cry.

I did manage to eat a little and carried extra food onto the ship as we embarked, in the hope that I would be able to regain some strength. Huge relief flooded through me as the crew cast off, the oars began to lever us from the dock and the great ship began to sigh and creak her way towards the open sea.

Then the cavalcade of horsemen came racing down the cobbled road to the harbour. Soldiers mounted on strong little ponies, shouting and yelling. My heart constricted and I put my hands to my mouth in terror. And they rode straight past the *Alessandrina* and on towards some other ship with its own fugitives – and then we were more than an oar's length from the shore and the wind caught at each of the sails as they unfurled slowly and gracefully, obeying the commands of the sailors and the ropes.

'Thank you,' I said, bowing my head to the One God and his angels. 'Thank you for my life.'

It was neither an easy crossing nor a swift one. The *Alessandrina* had errands to fulfil on other islands and in other countries on her way to her home port.

I shared a cabin with five others, all mildly curious but satisfied with my brief alibi and my wish for solitude. But by the time we were nearing home there were golden roots showing in my dyed black hair and the dark skin on my arms, face and legs was beginning to peel away.

None of that mattered as soon as I saw the one thing I had been watching for, day after day. Rising from the sea ahead of us after weeks of rough seas, calm seas, high winds and driving rain I saw, once again, the tip of the great lighthouse on the island of Pharos at the gateway to Alexandria and I knew that, for the moment, my travels were nearly over. The fire in the top chamber was not yet lit but, as the tower rose over the horizon, the beautiful city behind it began to twinkle as though with the light of a thousand lamps and candles as glass and metal reflected back the rays of the late afternoon Sun.

No one ever knew when – or even if – any ship would arrive but there were always scores of boys waiting at the harbour's edge, ready to run with messages to family, business associates and friends, announcing a safe arrival. I disembarked with my small pile of luggage and, not knowing where Apollonius was living, sent a message to Philo's home. It would only take the boy a very short time to run that distance and he had the incentive of the second half of his money when he came back to tell me where I could find my husband.

I sat by the water's edge, half impatient, half contented, realising how much I loved this city and how grateful I was to be home. For it did feel like home. Judaea was so far away and that life seemed so distant now. Yet again I gave thanks for the direction that my life had taken and my safe delivery through all the journeys.

The boy took longer than I thought he would but the wait was worth it. Apollonius came himself. I saw his tall figure hurrying through the milling crowds of seamen and porters, as the boy who had fetched him pointed me out. Apollonius paid the messenger automatically, his eyes fixed on me in some puzzlement. Of course! My hair and colouring were wrong! Picking up my roll of possessions I ran forward to meet him, calling out his name. For a second he hesitated, then looked aghast and then swept me up into his arms with a roar of joy.

We wept. It is one thing to have faith that all will be well and another to see and feel the proof in front of you. Although we had much to say to each other we stood silently together on the harbour front and watched the last rays of the sunset together, too happy to speak, just absorbing the perfection of that moment. At last I turned and looked up at my husband and I knew that this was the moment I had seen in my vision so long ago, in Jerusalem, when I made up my mind to leave my country. It must be finished. I had done all I needed to do.

We smiled at each other just as I had seen us doing before in my dream. Then, as the Sun slipped over the horizon, it seemed to me that my husband's face changed. For a moment it was not Apollonius standing there but another man – and one whose face was strangely familiar. Saul of Tarsus, now called Paul, looked back at me with that piercing, mesmerising stare of his and I felt the strangest of feelings within me.

'I'm just tired,' I thought, shaking my head so that the image would go away. Then I heard the words 'Deborah, my love, my life. Now we will be together forever.' It must have been Apollonius who had spoken them and, slowly, his face came back into focus. I buried my face in his chest as he put his great arms around me. Whatever the future might hold it was now that was precious; now that was forever.

Hear, O Israel, the Lord our God, the Lord is One.

Deborah's story will be completed in *Leaves of The Tree*.

Visit www.treeofsapphires.com

Also by Maggy Whitehouse

The Book of Deborah

The first book in the 'Deborah' trilogy tells of the hidden link between Jesus of Nazara and Judas Iscariot. Her name is Deborah – Jesus' sister; Judas's wife.

Deborah is crippled and bitter after a childhood accident and filled with hatred for the Jewish God. But with the death of her parents she moves to Nazara, to the home of Joseph and Miriam and her new and rather unusual brother, Yeshua, becomes her greatest joy as he slowly teaches her how to view God differently and how to rebuild her own life.

Together, Deborah and Yeshua move to an Essene community in Emmaus, near Jerusalem, living and working together and studying the Jewish esoteric tradition until Yeshua begins his ministry around Galilee and Jerusalem.

Deborah and her husband, Judah, follow Yeshua and his disciples, teaching and working with the women. The story of the 'handing over' is seen through Deborah's and Judah's eyes, not those of succeeding generations.

The book ends, after the crucifixion, with Deborah's own revelation and her plans to continue teaching the hidden tradition to those who will hear.